WITHDRAWN Praise for
ANN TATLOCK and
Things We Once Held Dear

"Tenderness and fierce drama—these are the hallmarks of Ann Tatlock's *Things We Once Held Dear*. Tatlock spins wickedness and corruption into the same stew with holiness and grace. The paths her characters take are never easy or convenient. . . . [they] will renew your faith in the power of the novel, not only to entertain us, but to show us how to live."
    —Daniel Bachhuber, author of *Mozart's Carriage*

"*Things We Once Held Dear* takes us on a young widower's courageous journey back to his hometown and the unresolved past. Brillantly choreographed, Ann Tatlock's tightly woven tale holds us in its grip, only to release ~~ ~~~ ~~~~ wings. Savor

~~~ES and the

~~~ Her capti-
~~~ you join
~~~ ewal and
This is a
in your

a gentle
Ann Tat-

"*Things We Once Held Dear* is a beautiful story with moments of intrigue and pain and joy. Ann Tatlock's prose is lovely and her ability to layer story upon story superlative. A great read."

—Kathryn Mackel, author of *Outriders*

"Ann Tatlock takes us on an intriguing journey into the history that defines us. An excellent and well-written peek into our own personas."

—Kristin Billerbeck, author of *What a Girl Wants* and *She's All That*

"The family secrets and small town intrigue in Ann Tatlock's *Things We Once Held Dear* will keep you hooked from beginning to end."

—DeAnna Julie Dodson, author of *In Honor Bound* and *By Love Redeemed*

things we once held *dear*

ANN TATLOCK

BETHANY HOUSE PUBLISHERS

Minneapolis, Minnesota

Things We Once Held Dear
Copyright © 2006
Ann Tatlock

Cover design by Ann Gjeldum

Published by Bethany House Publishers
11400 Hampshire Avenue South
Bloomington, Minnesota 55438

Bethany House Publishers is a division of
Baker Publishing Group, Grand Rapids, Michigan.

Printed in the United States of America

Library of Congress Cataloging-in-Publication Data

Tatlock, Ann.
    Things we once held dear / Ann Tatlock.
       p.   cm.
    Summary: "Returning home to Mason, Ohio, Neil Sadler's past creeps up behind him and is mirrored in the present. Neil discovers the truth of a childhood love and his childhood faith"—Provided by publisher.
    ISBN 0-7642-0004-6 (pbk.)
    1. Mason (Ohio)—Fiction. 2. Ohio—Fiction. I. Title.

PS3570.A85T48   2006
    813'.54—dc22   2005028048

⟿ DEDICATION ⟾

This book is lovingly dedicated to
my first cousin once removed,
Virginia Erbeck,
who grew up in The House,
and to my second cousin, her son,
Bob Erbeck,
who introduced me to The House.

Books by Ann Tatlock

A Room of My Own

A Place Called Morning

All the Way Home

I'll Watch the Moon

Things We Once Held Dear

ANN TATLOCK, author of the Christy Award-winning novel *All the Way Home*, lives with her husband and daughter in North Carolina. She has won the Midwest Independent Publishers Association "Book of the Year" in fiction for both *All the Way Home* and *I'll Watch the Moon*.

⇻ AUTHOR'S NOTE ⇺

This is a work of fiction. The characters in this story and the events recorded here are all imaginary, with a few exceptions. These include Rebecca McClung and the account of her murder, the 1974 tornado that ripped through Main Street in Mason, Ohio, and the gist of the story behind the Widow's Bridge. It is also true that when radio station WLW was broadcasting at 500,000 watts in the 1930s, residents of Mason reported picking up its programming through their drain pipes, metal fence posts, and bedsprings, as well as in the fillings of their teeth. My descriptions of the town of Mason itself are essentially accurate, though for the sake of the story I resurrected the Dinner Bell restaurant on Main Street, which actually closed sometime in the 1970s.

The Sadler House, or the Gothic Horror, is based on an actual farmhouse. My father's first cousin, Virginia Erbeck, lived there as a child growing up in the 1920s and 1930s. The house, built in 1850, was just as it is described here: a farmhouse, with a ballroom and a tower room, that stood on 237 acres of land between Mason and Lebanon, Ohio. Virginia's father, my great-uncle Virgil, grew corn, wheat, and soybeans on the land. Uncle Virgil's twin brother, Algernon, raised dairy cattle there. When my father was a young boy, he and his sister Carolyn visited their cousins and played in the many rooms of the house, including the tower room, as well as outside in the fields and in the barn.

I am acquainted with the house only through photographs,

and then only the outside. No known photos of the inside of the house exist. I have based my descriptions on the memories of the people who lived in it or visited there. In 1945 the house was sold, and the new owner lived in it with his family until 1952, when they had it demolished. Its bricks were buried in what was once the basement. A modest ranch house was erected just in front of where the old house stood.

While doing research in Mason, Ohio, in October 2003, I visited the owners of the ranch house. They kindly invited me in to talk and to share their memories of the farmhouse. It was the woman's father who had bought the place from my great-uncle and tore it down because "it was too hard to heat."

The original barn, though, still stands and the property is still farmland. When I visited in late fall, the corn was just ready for harvesting. I stood on the spot where the house was buried, imagining the bricks in the dirt beneath my feet. I tried to imagine Dad and Virginia and all the young cousins playing in the very barn that stood there now, Uncle Algie milking the cows, and Uncle Virgil on his tractor out in the fields planting corn.

Many of those people are gone now, but life goes on. That's what this story is all about.

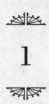

1

"AND NEIL—" SHE STOPPED, turning suddenly in the middle of the hall, as though she had missed an earlier cue—"I'm so sorry about Caroline."

He nodded thinly. He shut his eyes and opened them, buying a wink of time. He'd been expecting it, of course. Still, it always seemed to catch him off guard. He didn't like this place of apologies for something no one had done. But it was a place that wouldn't be avoided.

"Thank you, Grace."

He had said it dozens of times, maybe hundreds of times, punctuating the phrase with hundreds of names. Who were all those people he had thanked over all the wearisome months? It didn't matter. What mattered was that he had said it and that it seemed to be the right thing to say. The recipient had been satisfied every time, turning away from the business of condolences and going back to the business of living, while he went on living without Caroline.

Grace led him up the stairs. "Yours is the only room on the second floor that's ready," she said. "The rest of the guest rooms are a disaster." She finished her sentence with a laugh and a wave of her hand.

"Well," he replied, gripping his suitcases more tightly, "that's why I'm here."

No, that wasn't true. He hadn't come to remodel the house into a bed-and-breakfast. He had already decided to spend the summer months in Mason, Ohio, when he had learned of Grace's plans and offered to help.

They reached the second-floor landing, turned left down the long hallway, and walked to the bedroom in the northwest corner of the house, just above the front porch. Neil remembered it well. He used to come this way dragging a brown duffel bag that held his pajamas, a toothbrush and comb, a few days' worth of clean clothes. He and his brother and cousins had spent many summer days and nights in this house just north of Mason proper, over the Union County line. His father's cousin, Thomas Sadler, had owned it then. Uncle Tom, as Neil called him, was a man who loved the land, a man who spent his lifetime working the soil. He spent more time in the fields and in the barn than in the house, scarcely noticing the hordes of children that flocked there every summer to play in the country.

"Well, what do you think?" Grace stopped just inside the bedroom door and glanced about, her face registering her own approval.

Neil took in the room slowly, feeling the disappointment rise and settle in his chest. All had changed. Where was the water-stained floral wallpaper of faded yellows and greens, the old feather bed with the tarnished brass frame, the painted chest of drawers with the two missing handles? What had happened to that simple room of mismatched furniture, musty curtains, tattered shades? Now this same space was a carefully designed arrangement of coordinating colors and stately antique furniture. The wallpaper was of a blue and white fleur-de-lis pattern, the wainscoting a solid blue. The bed was a four-poster of dark maple, cozy under a thick comforter of royal blue and cream-colored octagons, the dust ruffle a matching solid blue. The drapes and valances over the room's four windows were of the same pattern as the comforter. Wooden blinds replaced the vinyl pull shades that had been drawn at night for years. The room's furnishings included a rolltop desk, a teakwood chest of drawers, a free-standing full-length mirror in a wicker frame, and a rocking chair with an embroidered seat.

"It's beautiful," Neil said. But not so beautiful as that other lost room. "I scarcely recognize it." That, at least, was true. The room was a canvas that someone had painted over, making it more pleasing to the eye while disregarding the soul. He wanted to scrape away at all that was new and get back to the original, no matter how seemingly unstylish and worn.

But that wouldn't be possible, of course. The room had needed to be changed. The whole house had to change. And that was the root of the problem, Neil thought. Time passed, and everything changed. He couldn't come back to this house as it had been when he was a boy and his cousin Grace was living here and his uncle Tom was farming the land. When Tom retired, no one had wanted to take up where he left off with the farm. Tom's two sons, Grace's older brothers, had both run from the prospect of owning an oversized house on 237 acres of crop farm in the late twentieth century. Grace wasn't interested in farming either, and even if she had been, she knew it was a precarious occupation at a time when so many midwestern farmers were falling into bankruptcy. But she desired to keep the house, not wanting to be the Sadler from whose fingers it slipped away.

And so, upon Tom Sadler's death, Grace and Dennis sold 225 acres of the original 237 to a neighboring farmer at a pretty price, leaving Grace with an even dozen and her branch of the Sadler family verdant with profit.

As Grace told it, when she and Dennis, their children grown, tried to fill up all the empty spaces in the house with just the two of them, they found the task impossible. Finally Dennis muttered, "This house needs people in it," and Grace replied, "I've been thinking of turning it into a bed-and-breakfast for years," and Dennis shot back, "Well, why didn't you tell me sooner?" and before that day was over, the fate of the house was sealed.

The land was gone—or most of it—and there would be no more farm families living and marrying and partying and dying in the Sadler home. Now the house would be a tourist attraction of sorts, a "Country Getaway for City Folk," as Grace described it. She and Dennis hoped to attract the business of the well-to-do but urban-weary souls of Cincinnati and Columbus.

It was a sign of the times, Neil thought. Even a house was entangled in time, like everything else.

"Well, there's an incredible amount of work to be done yet if we're going to start taking guests by September," Grace said.

"We'll get it done," he assured her, not sure at all himself it would get done.

She smiled. "I'm glad you're here, Neil."

He looked at his cousin and tried to return her smile. He hoped she didn't notice his consternation. Grace was more than a decade older than Neil, and though he had expected her to have changed in the intervening years, her appearance startled him. He was almost taken aback by the creases and colorlessness of age. She was still an attractive woman, and yet she was far from the image that Neil had carried with him to Mason, that image of a much younger person. When he had seen her last, her hair had been a smooth and healthy brown, her skin a firm sleek covering over cheekbones and jaw and neck. Now her hair, though pulled back youthfully into a loose ponytail, was an uncolored gray, her skin wrinkled and dotted with age spots that, at least at the moment, she took no pains to hide with makeup. Last he had seen her, she was a young married woman and the mother of a toddler. Now she was not only a mother but a grandmother as well.

How old must she be, Neil wondered? It would be impossible to calculate. He had two first cousins and fifty-two second cousins—Grace being one of the second cousins—and that was on his father's side alone. It was a formidable task to remember all their names and ages. It was challenge enough just to remember their names. When he figured in the first, second, and once-removed cousins on his mother's side as well, it was nearly impossible. While growing up, Neil had been only too aware that he was in one way or another related to a large percentage of the population of Mason, Ohio. In the 1960s and 1970s that added up to several hundred people in a town where the census peaked at something like six thousand. From there his family splintered into the surrounding towns of Lebanon, South Lebanon, Maineville, Kings Mills, Foster, and Morrow. There was a lot of Sadler blood right there in Warren County, no question about that.

Neil turned his eyes from his cousin's face, and Grace, watching him, followed his gaze to a painting on the wall above the desk.

"What's this?" he asked.

"Oh!" She laughed briefly and said, "I thought you'd like it in your room while you're here. I'll replace it later when we start taking guests. Take it back to New York with you if you'd like. After all, it's yours."

Neil moved to the wall where the painting hung. It was a child's painting, his own, of the house he stood in now. "You must have been on some sort of archeological dig to unearth this thing," he quipped.

Grace laughed again. "Actually, I was going through the boxes stored for eons in this room when I found it. Already framed. Mother must have framed it years ago. Do you remember it?"

He shook his head. "Vaguely."

"Not bad for—what would you have been? Nine or ten?"

"Something like that, I suppose."

"Of course you've come a long way since then."

Neil smiled. "I should hope so."

What he noticed first was that common trait of childish landscapes: one strip of blue across the top of the painting for the sky, another strip of green along the bottom for the ground. The lack of a horizon, as though there is no point at which sky meets earth. But other than that, the painting did show promise of the artist he was to become. The colors were right—mostly. The proportions of the house acceptable. The detail quite incredible for a young child. There was the obvious suggestion of brick; one could look at the painting and know that the house was not stucco or clapboard but a solid fortress of red brick, made right there from the clay of the land. There were the twin columns at varying distances along the broad front porch, the hood molds over the tall arched windows of the second and third floors, the ornate gingerbread trim along the eaves and gable edges, the steeply pitched roof culminating in the pinnacled tower room. He had even been careful to include the finials, five on the tower alone and one on the tip of each gable, the lancet-like ornaments that pointed skyward, the jewels on the crown of the house.

The Gothic Horror, his father had called it. "Wouldn't live in that thing for a million bucks. Too big, too costly to maintain, too much wasted space. Seventeen rooms!" Jim Sadler complained. "And a ballroom, for crying out loud! What kind of fool would put a ballroom in a farmhouse?"

But Neil had always loved the house, loved its spacious rooms, its creaking floors, its endless nooks and crannies perfect for exploring, hiding, imagining. He loved the feeling of never running out of space, of tall ceilings and bay windows, of open air and sunlight even on cloudy days. He loved the smell of aging furniture and spices in the kitchen and the lingering hint of a pungent aftershave in the upstairs bathroom.

Perhaps most of all he loved the history of the house. He could never enter its rooms without feeling connected to the people who had lived there for more than a hundred years, his own family, the line from which he had descended. People had been born here, died here, lived out their whole lives right here in this place. These rooms were full of stories, as real as the air, and what Neil didn't know about the people who had lived there before him he could sense instinctively, because they were a part of him and he of them. Without them he wouldn't exist. Without him and the others of his generation, their story wouldn't go on. It was good to take his place in the unfolding history of the house.

"You must be tired," he heard Grace say. "It's been a long trip."

From New York—a ten-hour drive. From his childhood—an eternity.

"Why don't you rest awhile? I'll call you when supper's ready."

"Thank you, Grace."

She turned to go, but reaching the door, she said again, "I'm really glad you're home, Neil."

Until recently, home was where Caroline was. Now he didn't know where to call home.

"I am too," he said.

She left, and he moved to the window. Well, here he was. How odd it seemed after all these years. He had stayed on for a year after graduating from high school in 1976, working at the Mason Lumber and Coal Company alongside his father, dreaming all the while of New York City. When he finally did escape Mason in the late summer of 1977, he was not just a small-town boy seeking his place in the art world of the nation's most important city, he was a disillusioned young man seeking to leave behind something too painful to stay and face.

Afterward, he returned to Mason only a handful of times, and then never again after 1979, when his parents moved away and he no longer felt obligated to visit.

He had shut the book on Mason then and placed it high up on the shelf. In a sense, after he left that final time, Mason, Ohio, ceased to exist for Neil. It had been real once, but by the spring of 2003 when he decided to come back, it seemed almost fanciful to think that he could. He felt as though he could no more return to Mason than he could step into the endless winter of Narnia or visit Tolkien's Middle-Earth.

As he looked out over the land, the fields of newly sprung corn, and Route 42—still a two-lane highway—slicing through the plowed acreage and rolling north toward Lebanon, he heard a curious voice in the back of his mind say, *Oh, so it is real after all.*

Neil Sadler had returned to his birthplace, the hometown of his childhood, and he wasn't even sure why. He stood there by the window with two suitcases at his feet, an ache in his chest, and a gnawing awareness of the ticking of the clock on the antique rolltop desk. He had heeded the call to come back. And he wondered what on earth he ought to do now.

2

THE HOUSE HAD BEEN STANDING on this plot of Ohio soil since 1850, built during the rush of Gothic Revival architecture that swept the country for much of the mid-nineteenth century. The surge had begun in England in 1749 to romanticize medieval styles but had later been brought to the States by the architect Alexander Jackson Davis.

Davis was a man of unusual taste. While studying the simple rural dwellings in America, he once lamented that it was "positively painful to witness here the wasteful and taste-less expenditure of money in building." To begin remedying this problem, he constructed the first American Gothic house in Baltimore in 1832. From there, the style's thumbprint became evident everywhere—in small timber cottages, country churches, and even stone castles like Lyndhurst in Tarry-town, New York.

Jedediah Sadler, Neil's great-great-great-grandfather, had been enamored of the style, and he very kindly sought to alleviate what he perceived to be his neighbors' pain by giving them something of beauty to gaze upon. He also thought that living in a house of some magnitude might make a fitting architectural statement concerning his financial success. Born in a log cabin to German immigrant parents, he had been reared on the land and would himself always be a farmer, but he had risen out of poverty through the art of persuasion.

While a young man working summers on the railroad in Cincinnati, he had managed to woo the only daughter and sole heir of a prosperous railroad magnate, winning her hand in marriage, much to the chagrin of her father. Jedediah swore true love, however, saying he would have married Annabelle Morrow whether she were wealthy or not. Everyone believed him, including Belle herself, and even his reluctant father-in-law was eventually won over by Jed Sadler's earthy charm and congenial nature.

The marriage lasted more than fifty years and produced eight children—six of whom survived infancy—so there was undoubtedly some truth to Jed's allegiance. Later generations enjoyed retelling the love story of Jedediah and Annabelle Sadler, though they generally tacked on the comment that a little bit of money never hurt a marriage either.

At the start of their life together the couple lived in a modest but comfortable home on the patch of farmland first settled by Jed's father, some thirty miles north of Belle's hometown of Cincinnati. But when Abelard Morrow met an untimely and ironic death in a railroad accident, Belle came into her inheritance and Jed made plans to further improve their lot. He bought out two neighboring farms to take on an additional 137 acres and started making floor plans for the dwelling that his neighbors would eventually dub the Castle of Warren County. Later generations of his own family called the place the Gothic Horror, an epithet that originated with Neil's father, Jim Sadler.

Neil remembered how, years ago, Grace was the only family member who took offense at the house being called the Gothic Horror. "That's Gothic Revival," she corrected Jim Sadler whenever he derisively referred to the house's style of architecture. "There's nothing horrible about this house, Uncle Jim."

While Jim Sadler only laughed in response, Neil noticed how Grace lifted her chin and seemed to bite at the inside of her cheek, as though she were trying not to say something she wanted to say. Neil knew what it was. He'd heard her say it any number of times behind Jim Sadler's back: "He's just jealous, you know. After all, this house is a far cry from that tiny bungalow of Uncle Jim's. Why, you can hardly turn around in that matchbox of a house without knocking your elbows on one wall or another."

It was true that Jim Sadler's family lived in a matchbox of a house, and that was probably why Neil felt so free, so ready to soar through the large rooms and open spaces of the farmhouse whenever he was there. He didn't care if the house was called the Gothic Horror. He didn't care what the place was called. He just wanted to be there.

As it happened, Neil's growing-up years coincided with the rise of the Gothic romance in popular literature, a companion to bored housewives who hadn't yet fallen into step with Betty Friedan and the feminists. Neil's own mother read them; she had stacks of them on her nightstand—paperbacks with cover illustrations of beautiful women running white-gowned and terrified from haunted castles or dastardly villains—with titles like *The Lady of Westminster Manor, Bride of Midnight, Murder on the Heath.* Whenever Elinor Sadler finished a pile, she'd pack them up in a brown paper sack and carry them over to Helen Syfert, who was practically bedridden and needed something to do. Neil knew that this gesture made his mother feel as though she were being helpful. But Neil's cousin Mary, Helen's daughter, complained about these offerings of pulp fiction. After all, Mary was the one who had to read the books aloud to her mother, whose eyesight was failing.

"They're just the same old story over and over," Mary had told Neil with a sigh of disgust. "Some ditsy blonde in a creepy old house who finds herself in trouble but who's saved in the end by some handsome hero who may or may not be a good guy—you don't really know—but he's obviously good enough for her. I'm tired of all this damsel-in-distress stuff. I wish Mom wanted to read Vonnegut or Salinger, but she doesn't."

Neil couldn't muster up much sympathy for Mary. What fascinated him was the way the books, even unread, spurred his brother, Jerry, to create what he called Jerry Sadler's Gothic Horror Stories. These were used on summer nights at the farm to whip the younger cousins into a frenzy of terror. Jerry spun these tales long after dark when the house was eerily quiet and the children were supposed to be asleep. Unlike the Gothic novels that promised a satisfying ending for the heroine, Jerry's version was meant to frighten. The damsel was never saved but was bludgeoned, stabbed, shot, or otherwise gruesomely murdered, her soul doomed to wander restlessly through the rooms of the Sadler house.

Whenever he reached the part about the restless spirit, Jerry would fall momentarily silent. The wordless gap was a dizzying vacuum, and the shadowy figures of half a dozen cousins would sit hugging their knees to their chests, stone cold with fear. Hardly anyone dared to breathe.

"If we're very quiet," Jerry would whisper, one finger to his lips, "we can hear her moving through the rooms. Listen! Do you hear those sighs? Can you hear her sighing?"

Sure enough, when they sat very still and listened, when they held their breath and strained to hear, the hundred-year-old sighs drifted through the passageways and open spaces of the house. At the time even Neil was certain he heard them. To quash the shivers running up and down his spine, he would snort and try to laugh.

"Quiet, Neil," his brother would scold. "You'll make the ghost mad, and then . . ." Jerry would end by drawing his finger across his throat while making a cutting sound.

It was usually about this time that one of the youngest cousins would jump up and exclaim, "But there's no such thing as ghosts!"

And that was just what Jerry was waiting for. He'd turn wide eyes to the frightened youngster, strike a pose of challenge, and say, "Oh yeah? Then what about . . ." and here he'd pause again, lean forward, narrow his eyes, and hiss, "Rebecca?"

Gasps would sound all around! Hands would clamp over mouths to stifle screams. The youngest child would beat a path down the hall and leap into bed between the slumbering Uncle Tom and Aunt Sarah.

Oh yes, Rebecca! Now there was a true story, an actual bit of history. Everyone knew about Rebecca McClung, Mason's only unsolved murder. Rebecca's body lay under the largest monument in Rose Hill Cemetery, but her soul was said to haunt the house where she had lived—and died—on Main Street.

As the story went, it was in the early hours of an April morning, 1901, that Rebecca was awakened by a stealthy tap of footfalls entering her room. She opened her eyes to the image of her killer bending over the bed, and that was the last thing she saw in this world. Her piercing screams awakened another resident of the house, a Mrs. Baysore, who lived in an apartment downstairs. Mrs. Baysore, terrified, dashed from the house in search of the constable. When the two returned, they found Rebecca dead in her room, her body bludgeoned horribly, her face pummeled beyond recognition. Two pieces of ash wood lay beside her, and a track of bloody footprints led from her body down to her husband, John, who was wandering aimlessly about the yard with blood on his shoes.

When in 1974 a tornado roared down Main Street in Mason and took the roof off the old McClung house, the locals blamed it on Rebecca. It was Rebecca, they said, and she was angry. Angry enough to tear the roof off of the house that was stained with her blood.

Never mind that the house had changed hands many times over, was no longer a house at all but had evolved from house to hotel to restaurant and speakeasy to antique shop and back again to restaurant, it was still the scene of the brutal slaying. Over the years the owners who came and went, the patrons who ate and slept and drank there, reported their experiences of doors slamming, windows flying open, screams in the night.

Jerry Sadler had had a heyday with the stories of Rebecca McClung, and for Neil, it was all great fun. Neil wanted to hear the Sadler house sigh and bump and scream the way the old McClung house did. He leaped at the chance to go up to the tower room alone on a dare. He gladly accompanied his brother on what they called "expeditions"—sneaking out of the house late at night to wander the fields in search of restless spirits. He half wished the stories were true and that there had been a murder in the house, just for the sake of excitement.

Yes, it was all great fun until that day in 1977 when there really was a murder in the family and a young woman was left in distress, and Neil, instead of acting as hero and saving her, left Mason without a backward glance and stayed away for the better part of three decades.

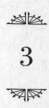

3

I WILL GO TO THE TOWER ROOM, Neil thought. *I will begin there.*

He had always favored the tower room over all the other rooms in the house. It was there he had been introduced to art and had fallen in love with it. The room had once been Evelyn Sadler's studio, and when Neil was growing up, her paintings had been stacked against the walls and her brushes, tubes of paint, and palettes still lay on the worktable, where she had last placed them before she died. The room was left undisturbed for years, and unused, except for when the children went there to play. It was in that room that Neil first smelled the pungent scent of pigment, first held a paintbrush, first ran his young fingers over the bumps and crevices of dried paint on canvas.

Neil moved away from the bedroom window and made his way up to the third floor of the house, where all the rooms were in various stages of disarray. When finished, this would be Grace and Dennis Weatherston's private living area, while the rooms on the second floor would be the guest bedrooms, and the rooms on the first floor—including the living room, dining room, library, and former ballroom—would, of course, be open to all the guests. The Weatherstons' son, Mike, and his wife, Valerie, were slated to help run the bed-and-breakfast; they and their two small children were already living in the former tenant house about three hundred yards from the main house. Both Mike and Valerie were involved in the renovations. Neil's first job, Grace had told him, would be helping Mike hang drywall in the guest rooms.

Neil walked through the long cluttered hallway of the third floor, stepping over paint cans, toolboxes, a couple of two-by-fours. At the end of the hall he came to the door that closed off the staircase to the tower room. When he reached for the handle and turned it, a small thrill ran through him. This was where he had found his place, himself—at the top of these stairs.

The door opened to a staircase that was a narrow and lightless upward tunnel. The steps, uncarpeted and worn smooth by long decades of footfalls, were scarcely more than shadows. The banister—the very one that Jedediah Sadler had installed, the one that Evelyn Sadler had used time and again when she climbed to her studio—was smooth and cool beneath the palm of Neil's hand. Neil started to climb, and as he did, he remembered with amusement how his cousin Jennifer had always been inspired to sing "Stairway to Heaven" whenever she came this way. In a sense, climbing these stairs *was* like climbing to heaven, because at the top one came out of the darkness and into the sudden tumble of light that streamed in through the tower's twelve tall windows.

As Neil climbed up, he wasn't sure what he expected to find at the top, but certainly not what he *did* find. To his surprise, the room was no longer a repository for Evelyn Sadler's paintings but rather was furnished with a bed and a side table, a rocking chair, a dresser, a bookcase, and an overstuffed chair under one of the windows. There was no bathroom, but oddly, a portable commode—the kind found in nursing homes—was tucked off to one side, not far from the bed. But perhaps the strangest thing of all was that there was a person stretched out on the bed, lying atop the covers, apparently asleep.

Neil took a few steps forward to see who it was, but he didn't recognize him. Whoever he was, he was a very old man, his eyes, cheeks, and chest little more than sunken pits, his arms and legs thin and angular, his hair a few wisps of gray moss. He looked so skeletal—so cadaverous, really—that Neil had to watch for a moment to be sure the man was breathing. For a fraction of a second, Neil felt certain the man was dead, that perhaps he had intended to nap but had instead drifted off into the Big Sleep. What would Jerry make of this—cousin Grace keeping a dead man in the tower room? A dead man fully clothed in slacks and cardigan, with dark-framed glasses on one end and a pair of new athletic shoes on the other.

But no, the frail chest rose, fell. Air was being sucked in through the open lipless mouth.

Neil stepped quietly to the bedside table, where a framed photograph sat among the clutter of prescription medicine bottles, plastic cups, and crumpled tissues. He picked up the photo, and with an odd mixture of amazement, horror, and profound sadness, he realized who the old man was.

It can't be, he thought.

The man on the bed was Bernard Sadler. Uncle Bernie, an older cousin to Neil's father. There was a time when Bernard Sadler might have become the owner of this house and all the land, had he wanted it, but he didn't, having been called to a religious vocation rather than to farming. He had persuaded his father, against all family tradition, to leave the farm to his younger brother Thomas, who wanted it, and who went on to work the land while Bernard went on to seminary.

In the Mason of Neil's childhood, Bernard Sadler had been variously referred to as Father Bernard, Uncle Bernie, the Padre, Chappie, St. Bernard, and simply, the Saint. Bernard had laughed at all the names, saying, "You can call me anything you want, just don't call me late for supper!"

Such a laugh. Such a man. Beloved, with not one enemy that anyone could point to. He had a whole passel of family and friends in Mason—around the country, really—who loved and trusted him. A chaplain in two wars, pastor of a local Episcopalian church for—what?—thirty years? Maybe longer. For as long as Neil could remember.

Neil looked from the photo to the old man and back again. And he wondered, *What does time do to people?* He didn't know how old Bernie was, but certainly he was old enough to look as though he belonged alongside his ancestors in Rose Hill Cemetery.

It was a wedding photo Neil held in his hand: Bernard in his Army chaplain's uniform, his wife, Rita, in a prim tailored suit, a spray of roses in her arms. Rita the war bride, plucked from the bomb-ravaged city of London and carried to the small midwestern town of Mason, Ohio, where she became distinguished for her accent and her scones. Everyone loved jolly old Rita as much as they loved the Saint. And nobody loved Bernard and Rita as much as they loved each other. Lovey, he called her, and Duckie. Chappie, she called him, and Dearest.

The only apparent heartache in their marriage was their childlessness. Like Neil and Caroline. Neil didn't know why that had been so—not for Bernie, not for himself. Not by choice, certainly. For a moment Neil's thoughts left the tower room and settled somewhere in New York years ago. He couldn't remember how the doctor had explained it, couldn't remember what he had concluded after all those tests. Perhaps Neil simply hadn't heard. What did it matter anyway, the reason? What mattered was that they couldn't have children. "We can adopt," he had suggested hopefully. She wasn't so sure. "It's not the same," she said, "as raising a child you've carried and borne." He tried to understand and hoped she'd come around, hoped she would decide she could love any child as well as her own. Instead, as the years passed and she didn't change her mind, he finally decided it was just as well. He was happy and satisfied, and life was good, as long as he had Caroline.

Neil replaced the photo on the table, intending to leave so as not to disturb Uncle Bernie. But suddenly, in a voice as rusty as weathered nails, the slumbering figure said, "I'm afraid the outer man is wasting away."

Neil felt a rush of tenderness at the sound of the old man's voice. He smiled down at Bernie kindly. The older man gazed up at him in return, his eyes shining with an unmistakable joy.

"Neil," Bernie sighed serenely, "you have come back."

"Yes."

Bernie lifted a hand and Neil clasped it. The aging flesh felt rough and bony and warm.

"I'm so glad," Bernie said, "so very glad."

Neil helped Bernie sit up against a mountain of pillows, then took a seat in the rocking chair beside the bed. "Uncle Bernie," he said gently, "what are you doing up here?"

The old man's eyes twinkled with a bit of mischief, the corners of his mouth turned up. "I am waiting to meet my Maker."

Neil shook his head, suppressing a smile. "He wouldn't be willing to meet you down on the ground floor?"

Bernie laughed loudly and heartily. "I was born in this room, and I intend to die in it. You can humor an old man in his final wish, can't you, Neil?"

Evelyn Sadler was Bernie's mother. Neil remembered now. She had had a daybed in her studio, where she had brought her three children into the world. She had insisted upon it. It was in this room that she had wanted them first to open their eyes and see light. And so they had.

"I understand completely, Uncle Bernie," Neil said. "I'm just . . . surprised. Grace didn't tell me you were here."

The smile remained. "I suppose she figured you'd stumble upon me sooner or later."

"But . . ." Neil paused and looked around the room.

"Grace takes good care of me, as do so many others—family members, my former parishioners, my friends. I am rarely alone."

"I see."

"And if I am"—Bernie nodded toward an intercom that Neil hadn't noticed earlier on the bedside table —"help is always the push of a button away."

Neil, nodding, said playfully, "So you want to go out where you came in, do you?"

"Yes. I always did like circular stories; they seem so neat and tidy."

Neil wondered how long Bernie had been up here and what he did all day. He didn't ask. He said, "This has always been my favorite room in the house."

"It's a good room," Bernie agreed. "Full of sun during the day, and at night I can see the stars."

34

It would be a good room, Neil thought, in which to meet your Maker, if you believed in that sort of thing. He looked around again and wondered what had become of Evelyn's paintings. He would have to ask Grace.

"So, Neil, you are really here at last. It's been a long time. I've missed you."

"I've missed you too, Uncle Bernie." Only as the words came from his mouth did he realize how true they were. He had missed this man, this house, his family. And yet he had stayed away, pushed the thought of them out of his mind, and had kept the lines of communication open with only the occasional letter, the annual Christmas card, a rare phone call to one person or another. "I should have come back long ago. I'm sorry."

Bernie lifted a hand and waved it slowly. "Never mind, Neil. You're here now. That's what matters." He looked at Neil directly, his eyes wide with compassion. "Though I am afraid you came because of Caroline. I know how terribly you must miss her."

Neil nodded. "Yes, I do."

Bernie would know, of course. He would understand. Rita had died suddenly at the age of fifty-two. That too, after all, was young. Not as young as Caroline, but still young enough to add an element of tragedy to her death.

Neil remembered when Rita died, that winter of 1977, the winter of the horrible snowstorm. She had chosen a bad year to die. The worst. Not because of the storm; what did snow matter, after all? It melted; it went away. It was the worst time because that was the year of the murder, the event that changed everything for Neil. And for others. Changed it all forever, no going back. Being dead, Rita had missed it, of course. *Perhaps,*

Neil thought bitterly, *she was the lucky one.*

Bernie had outlived Rita now by more than twenty-five years. Neil searched the old man's face, a webbed portrait of serenity. He wanted to ask Bernie if it got any better, if the ache ever diminished, if a day ever again felt ordinary. But he didn't dare. He was afraid of the answer.

"Is that why you came back, Neil?" Bernie asked.

Neil thought a moment while a line formed between his brows. "I suppose," he replied, "you might say I'm looking for a teapot in a tempest."

At that Bernie smiled and reached out to squeeze Neil's hand. That had been Rita's expression, a twist on the British phrase "tempest in a teapot." Whenever Rita felt harried or worried or overburdened, she called on God to give her a teapot in a tempest, a place of quiet where she could rest and retreat and—sometimes literally, sometimes figuratively—sip a cup of tea in the midst of the storm.

"You will find it here," Bernie assured him.

"If it's anywhere, yes, I'll find it here."

The two men fell quiet again for a moment. Finally Bernie asked, "When did you get here?"

"I've only just arrived."

"Did you drive?"

"Yes. I bought a car." Neil laughed suddenly at the thought. "The first I've owned since leaving Mason. I've never needed one, or wanted one, in New York. The subway takes me everywhere I want to go."

"It's a whole different world there."

"Yes."

"Mason will seem very dull."

Neil shook his head. "Mason will seem very quiet."

The smile again, small and brief. "You're right, of course," Bernie agreed. "You can't enjoy a cup of tea without the quiet." Another squeeze of the hand. "Well, Neil, you've had a long trip. Why don't you go rest awhile?"

"There is so much I want to know—about you, and everyone. . . ."

"There will be plenty of time for that."

"Yes, I suppose so. I think I could use a little lie-down, but—You'll be all right?"

"Of course. Mary will be here soon. She's coming to help this evening."

At the mention of her name, Neil felt something in his chest, in the pit of his stomach. "Mary?" he asked. "She's in Mason? I thought she and her husband lived in Cincinnati."

"They did, for many years. But she and Dan moved back . . . oh, a couple of years ago now, I guess."

"I didn't know." Neil frowned. "I wonder why Grace didn't tell me."

"She probably assumed you already knew."

"Yes, I suppose that's it."

"At any rate—" Bernie shut his eyes slowly, opened them, smiled—"I'm terribly glad she's back. Such a good girl. She comes often to sit with me and help out."

"I see." Neil felt hot and uncomfortable. A shiver spread across his chest, burst like a firecracker against his ribs. "How is Mary?"

"She's fine, fine. Though Dan—well . . ." Bernie paused, smiled again, only less convincingly. "All will be well, I'm sure."

There was something wrong, of course, but Neil would have to find out somewhere else. He knew better than to ask Bernard Sadler. The Saint never revealed secrets. That was part of his job. Keep the confession; tell no one.

Neil sensed a familiar bitter taste rising to his tongue. He swallowed and tried to smile. "Well, if I don't get back up tonight, I'll see you tomorrow."

Neil stood, and the two men clasped hands again.

"Go in peace," Bernie said. Half blessing, half whimsy, it was the Saint's signature farewell.

Neil smiled easily then, and acknowledging the blessing with a nod, he turned toward the stairs.

4

As Neil stepped into the narrow staircase—the descent from paradise—he wondered, *How is it that people simply disappear? Some, like Bernie, grow old and fade away, vanishing the way stars disappear when morning comes. Some, like Caroline, don't have the chance to grow old. They simply, suddenly, are no longer there. . . .*

September 16, 2002. Harrington-Glasser Day School in Manhattan. Neil returned to his office after teaching a first-period Fundamentals of Art class to a group of freshmen and found the message light flashing on his telephone.

"I'm not feeling well," Caroline said. "I'm going home to bed. I'll see you there tonight."

She rarely left work simply because she wasn't feeling well. She hated the idleness of bed rest. She pushed herself in spite of coughs, colds, and fevers to get up and go down to the agency, or at least to plug in the laptop and work at home. What in the world would send her to bed in the middle of the morning?

He reached for the handset, dialed his home number. She

picked up on the fourth ring, just before the answering machine kicked in.

"Hello?" Her voice was heavy, knocking against his ear like a rock.

"I'll come home," he said.

"No, no. It's just the flu. Nothing you can do. I have a pounding headache, and I can't think straight. I only want to rest."

"Are you sure?"

"Yes." A heavy sigh. "Yes, I'm sure."

"Maybe you should call the doctor, just to see—"

"No. Go back to work and let me sleep."

He hung up the phone uneasily, then pushed through the rest of the morning and afternoon with a sense of dread.

It was shortly after five o'clock when he finally reached Brooklyn. He got off the subway at the Bergen Street stop as usual and walked to Warren, where his and Caroline's house stood shoulder to shoulder with the row of other houses that straddled the block from Court to Smith. Normally he loved this path over the buckled treelined sidewalk, past the stoops of elegant old houses, aging like fine wine. This was where an artist should live, of course. It was part of the image that Neil had tossed easily about his shoulders when he'd first arrived in New York as a youth, green and destitute, talented and determined. *"I am no longer a small-town boy,"* he'd said to himself. *"I am a New York artist."* And he'd slipped into the image like a man shrugging into a down jacket, and it fit him comfortably and at once.

But none of that mattered now, today, when Caroline was sick. Neil hurried up the steps to his front door and unlocked it. When he pushed open the door and stepped inside, he was greeted by an ominous silence and the stench of sickness. Upstairs, Caroline lay semiconscious on the bed in their darkened room, strands of her long hair caked with vomit. Neil rushed to her side and touched her cheek. Her skin was hot and moist, and she moaned against the weight of his hand.

"Caroline," he whispered.

She didn't open her eyes. He reached for the phone beside the bed, and in moments the expected siren split the air and Neil met the paramedics at the door. He pointed up the stairs. Though laden with their stretcher and equipment, the paramedics lumbered up swiftly, feet pounding against the hardwood floor.

When they saw her, they remained expressionless and moved quickly. Neil, the helpless spectator, hung back and watched from the doorway. What did he know of medicine and illness and emergencies?

They lifted her gently, carried her down the stairs and out the door to the ambulance double-parked there on Warren Street. Neil followed in a dazed numbness, unaware of the neighbors, the children who paused in their game of hopscotch, the mothers who, arms crossed, stood in open doorways watching the commotion, the whirling ambulance light a beacon of foreboding on their street.

Neil rode with Caroline in the ambulance the short distance to Long Island College Hospital. LICH, it was called: the "Litch." Four blocks away and he'd never even been inside. He gazed at Caroline's ashen face beneath the oxygen mask, listened dumbly to the paramedic calling ahead to the emergency room.

In only a moment they stopped abruptly and the ambulance doors flung open. Someone was shouting, "Come on, come on! Let's move it!"

Neil, feeling awkward and peripheral, tumbled out the back doors and watched as Caroline was whisked away by white jackets and pale green uniforms.

Once inside, he hurried to keep up but was intercepted by a woman at the desk.

"Are you family?"

"I'm her husband."

Neil felt a clipboard thrust into his hands.

"Please fill these out and return them—"

He cursed, shaken. "My wife is sick, and I have to sit here filling out forms?"

"We need the information," the woman explained with a look that said, "Let the doctors do their job, and you do yours." Aloud she said, "You'll be able to join your wife shortly."

He wanted to be at Caroline's side, but after all, what could he do? He would have to entrust his wife into the care of strangers. He took a seat in one of the vinyl chairs, one of the little black row houses in the city of the waiting room. He gazed dully at the clipboard on his lap. He rubbed his eyes, forced himself to read. Caroline's name, address, birth date, age, health history, insurance number. His hand trembled as he wrote.

He looked at his watch. 5:46 PM. Before he had even finished filling out the forms, a doctor was there, hand extended, introducing himself, looking grim.

"Your wife is very ill," he said. "We suspect meningitis."

"Suspect?"

"A spinal tap will tell us for certain. The important thing right now is to relieve the pressure on her brain. We did a scan which showed significant swelling. . . ."

The doctor rambled on. Neil knew the man was talking; he could see his mouth move, knew that words were tumbling from it that made no sense at all.

". . . highly contagious, so we will begin you on a round of antibiotics. . . ."

Neil started, forced himself to become engaged in this absurd conversation. "Me?" he cried. "Forget about me! It's my wife—I want my wife to get better!"

"Of course. We're doing everything we can."

"Is she going to be all right?"

"We're doing everything we can."

Is there nothing else he can say? Neil wondered. "I want to see my wife."

"Of course. She's been moved to intensive care. I'll have a nurse show you to the room."

A walk down a long corridor of bright lights and dull colors. Then, Caroline in the ICU, a figure shrouded in white linen, intubated, monitored, her slumbering body the tiny battleground of a microscopic war. One plastic tube entered her sloping mouth and disappeared down her throat. Another tube snaked down her nose while a tangle of IV bottles dripped medications—Neil didn't know what—directly into a spot under her collarbone. She was surrounded by machines that kept tabs on the numbers, spewing out the war news: heart rate, respiratory rate, temperature, oxygen saturation, blood pressure.

Neil sank into the chair beside the bed and took Caroline's hand.

"Caroline," he whispered, "can you hear me? I'm here, sweetheart."

There was no answer, no indication at all that she was aware of his presence.

Neil stared at his wife uncomprehendingly. He had seen her walk out the door just that morning. He had seen her leave for work less than twelve hours ago. What was she doing here with all these monitors, these tubes, these substances running into her body, trying to keep it functioning when last he saw her it had been functioning just fine on its own? Only last night the two of them had been remembering their time in London, said they really ought to go back, yes, let's think about going back next summer. . . .

Neil didn't know that something like this could happen, that it was even possible. But no, that wasn't true. He knew of course, at some level. He knew such things happened; he read about them, saw them, shook his head at them. A person didn't have to live long before he knew. There was that time he caught the F train at Bergen Street, and by the time the subway stopped again, two minutes later, he'd seen the man across the car from him crumple to the floor, dead of a heart attack. Another time, that young woman crossing the street, jaywalking on Atlantic Avenue, was struck by a car, blood everywhere. And only a year ago he and Caroline had stood on the roof of their house and looked out toward Manhattan, saw the smoke rising into an empty sky where, just hours before, two towers had stood.

He knew, of course. He knew. But what man lives in the day-to-day with the expectation of disaster?

At some point a spinal tap was done. "Yes," the doctor said, "she has bacterial meningitis. Meningococcal meningitis, the most serious kind. Not necessarily fatal—"

"Not necessarily?"

"Some people do survive."

But, Neil understood him to mean, most people don't.

Their objective right now was to push the antibiotics and fluids, to keep the blood pressure stable, to avoid the collapse of the circulatory system, the shutting down of the body's systems.

Neil, left alone once more with Caroline, wondered what to do and was horrified to think there was nothing at all he could do. If she lived, it wouldn't be because of him, and if she died, it wouldn't be because of him. He had no control at all. He could only watch and wait.

Evening sank down to night, and Neil didn't move. The night grew dark, and the nurses came and went, and after an eternity a sliver of gray dawn touched the window, but still Neil didn't move. He didn't eat or sleep. He simply kept vigil, waiting and watching, his terror so deep it sometimes left him breathless.

Another shift change, a new face at the bedside. "Why don't you go home and rest awhile, Mr. Sadler?"

"No, I have to stay."

She slunk away on squeaking shoes. He didn't notice, didn't care.

"Open your eyes, Caroline."

The day wore on. Later Neil would learn that his students at Harrington-Glasser sat waiting for him, wondering why he didn't show up for class. But for now, for Neil, they didn't exist. He forgot to call the school, forgot to call the ad agency where Caroline worked. Everything that had mattered yesterday didn't matter today. He watched Caroline's face, waiting for a flicker of movement, a sign of life.

Finally his own eyes began to close; in his exhaustion he

drifted into a place of strange dream images. He fought to stay awake but nodded, reluctantly, into sleep. And for that reason, when the alarm went off on one of the monitors, it was all the more jolting, sending Neil into a panic.

A sudden rush of people spewed into the room. Someone grabbed Neil by the arm, moved him away from the bed. He swayed on his feet, watching in horror. Another dream image, or were these voices, these people, real?

"Blood pressure?"

"Ninety over fifty-eight."

A white blur of movement . . .

"Heart rate?"

"Fifteen and dropping."

"Get the line moving!"

"The fluids are—"

"We're losing her!"

"Blood pressure?"

"Eighty-two over forty."

"Stay with us, stay. . . ."

"Dropping."

"Try again!"

"I can't get a—"

"Blood pressure? Blood pressure!"

A distant murmuring, then human voices giving way to the slow and steady whine of the machine.

Flat line.

Forever Neil would remember how his own heart was beating wildly at the very moment Caroline's heart stopped.

5

Neil paused near the top of the stairs and shut his eyes against the memory. It still overwhelmed him to think of the day Caroline died. After a moment he opened his eyes only to discover, strangely, that she was there. Standing motionless at the bottom of the stairs, looking up at him, was Caroline.

For a long moment he couldn't move or speak. All he could do was gaze in stunned amazement, wondering at the shattered laws of logic that allowed his wife to be there. He wanted to go to her, put his arms around her, and draw her to him. But when the woman stepped back into the light of the hallway, he realized it wasn't Caroline at all. The woman was Mary, his cousin, on her way up to tend to Bernie.

Neil breathed again and laughed inwardly at himself. Of course it wasn't Caroline. It was Mary. He had simply never before realized the similarities between his wife and his cousin. Tall, slender, fair-skinned. Except that Mary's hair was slightly darker, her cheekbones less pronounced, her slender nose more rounded at the end.

They might have been sisters, Neil thought. How could he not have realized it before? But then, there had never been reason to compare the two. Caroline was part of one life while Mary was part of another.

Neil met his cousin at the bottom of the stairs in a haze of awkward silence. She was flush from the heat and slightly winded, as though she had rushed up the first three flights of stairs. She seemed to be waiting for Neil to speak first.

"Hello, Mary," he said at length.

"Hello, Neil."

He thought perhaps he should hug her, but she hung back, keeping her hands at her sides.

"Grace told me you were here," she said, "that you've come back for the summer."

"Yes."

"Well," she said, not unkindly, "welcome home."

He smiled clumsily. "How have you been?"

"Fine," she responded. "And you?"

He saw her press her lips into a taut line, as though she wished she could take the words back.

He nodded his assurance. "I've been all right."

She rushed to say, "I'm sorry, Neil, about . . . your wife."

Neil wondered, couldn't she remember Caroline's name? Or maybe Mary had never known his wife's name.

"Thank you, Mary."

"I'm sure she was a lovely person."

No one in Mason had met Caroline. In the fourteen years they'd been married, Neil had never brought her here.

"Yes," he agreed. "Yes, she was."

Another awkward silence. "Well," she said, "you must have been surprised by Mason—all the changes."

"I've only just arrived. I haven't had time to get into town. I didn't realize you were here—back here in Mason."

She nodded. "It was Dan's choice. The situation in Cincinnati—well, he just burned out."

"He still in law enforcement?"

She frowned, as though puzzled by the question or unsure of the answer. Finally she said yes, but that was all.

Neil remembered Bernie's words about Dan: "All will be well." Which meant that all was not well now, but neither Bernie nor Mary wanted to explain.

"And the children?" Neil asked. "They're . . . ?"

"Well, Beth isn't a child anymore. She's nineteen. She's waiting tables at a lodge in Pennsylvania this summer, between college semesters. And Leo's thirteen." She gave a brief laugh, though it sounded forced. "He doesn't need a mother anymore either, or so he says, now that he's a teenager."

Neil tried to smile. "That's typical, I guess." Another moment passed before he said quietly, "You look good, Mary. You've hardly changed at all."

"Well"—she dropped her gaze—"I'm a little older."

"We're all a little older."

"Yes, I suppose there's no getting around it."

Neil moistened his lips, shifted his weight to the other foot. "You're on your way to see Bernie?" he asked, nodding toward the staircase.

"Yes. I help him with his meals or get him ready for bed. Whatever he needs."

Still the caregiver, Neil thought. She'd certainly had plenty of practice when she was a kid. Aloud, he said, "That's good of you."

She shrugged slightly, one brief lift of her delicate shoulders. "There are lots of people who help. We take turns making sure he's got someone with him most of the time."

"Well, then, I won't keep you."

Mary reached for the banister, stepped up one step. "I'm sure I'll be seeing you around."

"Yes, I'm sure. I'll mostly be here at the house, I should think, helping with the renovations."

She nodded. "Well, then . . ."

There was so much to say; he could feel the weight of it, piled like layers of ashen sediment on his shoulders. But it was a weight with no clear words, no clear meaning, and though he knew that something important wanted to insinuate itself into this moment, Mary was already climbing the stairs.

He called her name and she turned, her face a question mark.

"When you can . . . when you have time . . . you'll have to catch me up . . . on everything. . . ." The sentence, a choppy mess left truncated by Neil's uncertainties, hung in the air between them.

Finally Mary said, "Of course. I'm sure there will be plenty of time for that."

And then she was gone. Neil heard the tower room door open and close, and then, cursing himself and naming himself a coward and a fool, he hurried toward the sanctuary of his room.

6

ON THE MORNING OF HIS second day in Ohio, Neil put 167 miles on his car driving through the countryside between Lebanon, South Lebanon, Morrow, Maineville, and Mason. He had driven these roads an untold number of times as a teenager, newly licensed behind the wheel of a car. Back then it had been the sense of speed that drew him. Speed and independence and freedom. Now it was space. He had intended only to shoot up to Lebanon and back down to Mason, but once on the road he was amazed at the wide open spaces of the land, and he felt himself drawn into that spaciousness where no tall buildings scraped the sky and the horizon was at an unreachable distance.

While Neil loved New York—that amazing city that was his adopted home—at this moment as he soared through the wideness that even years of new development couldn't check, he felt his time in the East to be a brief interlude away from the place he belonged. Now that he was back, it seemed strange that he had ever left. His roots were here, sure as the roots of a million crops burrowing deep in the soil, reaching for nutrients, sucking up life in order to give life back. His roots were here in the heartland, this place that pumped out life for the rest of the country.

Was that why his birthplace had called to him after Caroline's death?

Until then he hadn't thought of Mason or the Sadler house for years. Not really. A passing thought now and then, when something reminded him. But these places of his childhood were part of that other life, the one that had ended at the Mason city limits when he went on to New York.

When Caroline died, the first feeling Neil experienced alongside the grief was an insatiable urge to stop time, to find a place that was not so much outside of time but perhaps in between time, a resting place where he could sit and think and try to make sense of it all. One of the hardest parts of grieving, he decided, was the fact that time went on, and he had to keep moving forward, walking through the endless routine of living while his heart, like an anchor, dragged behind him. If he could just stop time and rest awhile, pull himself together, put his heart back in place, maybe then the journey forward would be easier. But where was that resting place?

It was after those first dark weeks without Caroline that the images had come. Vivid images, like a movie replayed, taking on a life of their own. His mind, he discovered, had returned to Mason, but even more specifically, to the Sadler house and to the land. He saw himself in the tower room, watching Uncle Tom's tractor cutting neat furrows in the fields, unfaltering, perfect, the dirt his uncle's canvas. He remembered working in Aunt Sarah's garden—planting seeds, pulling weeds, eating tomatoes picked from the vine. And there he was sitting on the stoop of the front porch with Jerry and any number of his cousins, eating thick slices of watermelon while the sweet pink juice ran down his arms and dripped from his elbows. And there, making straw forts in the haylofts of the barn. And there, swinging in the hammock, hands beneath his head, staring up at the sky, only half aware of the chatter of his girl cousins as they made clover-chain necklaces and halos for their hair. Such images had come to him unexpectedly during the day, and at night had invaded his dreams.

He had welcomed them and found them comforting. These memories were, in fact, the only thing that had consoled him in the nine months since Caroline's death. And while he could neither step in between time nor go back in time, he realized he could go to Mason to find out why it was calling him. When the school year ended at Harrington-Glasser, he bought a used car from a friend of a friend in White Plains and set out across the vast green stretch of Pennsylvania, deep into Ohio toward the town and the house and the farm that he had left behind twenty-six years earlier. He had moved away from Ohio in the midst of anger and confusion and sadness, but it was the good that sprang to mind when he needed it; it was the goodness of the place that had called him home again.

So here he was, driving through the Ohio countryside, looking for the places he remembered, seeing how much had changed. Large portions of farmland had given way to development, like the patch of land just north of Maineville, where his aunt Bernice used to grow soybeans and raise peacocks. The brick rambler was gone, the barn razed, the land divided up into half-acre lots and paved with streets so the wealthy could dwell in estate homes right there where the peacocks once strutted.

He drove on, noticing other housing developments, numerous strip malls, various industrial parks with huge concrete buildings and warehouse-type structures. Surety Wiring Company, Big Feat Design and Building Contractors, Buckeye

Electrical Sales, Apex Metals Incorporated. Progress had come to Ohio, and time had changed the lay of the land, yet the face of Ohio was recognizable; it was the familiar face Neil had left so many years ago. The spaces were still wide and the fields still plowed, and so much of what had once been farmland was farmland still.

It was mid-June now, and the corn that would be knee-high by the Fourth of July was only now springing up in the fields, neat rows of green stalks sprouting up from the earth. Neil smiled. *"Ohio,"* Uncle Tom had proclaimed often enough, his thumbs hooked in the pockets of his overalls, "is the buckle on the corn belt of America."

There were plenty of cash crops grown in Ohio, and even Uncle Tom grew wheat and soybeans, but corn—now that was the most valuable crop of all.

Neil remembered the spring morning—he was ten, maybe eleven—when he sat in the kitchen of the Sadler house eating a bowl of cereal. He recalled vividly that sudden realization, the connecting of the dots between the corn that his uncle Tom planted and the cornflakes in his bowl. He rose from the table and looked out the window at Uncle Tom driving his tractor over the fields, turning up the soil, opening the hands of the earth to receive the seeds. Then Neil understood. There was a purpose behind it all. *He is keeping people alive,* Neil thought. *Uncle Tom is putting food in my breakfast bowl.*

After that Neil had watched in wonder every year—as the land was plowed and planted, as the first new stalks broke through the soil, dotting the fields with nature's earliest hints of a plentiful harvest. And how fast the corn grew!

"Knee-high by the Fourth of July," the children chanted when the crops first appeared.

"Ah, but whose knee? That's the question!" teased Uncle Tom.

"Your knee! Your knee!" the children cried as they gazed up at Uncle Tom, all six foot three inches of him.

"God willing," he'd say with a nod.

Most years God was willing, because the corn shot up at a phenomenal rate, and by August the stalks were so high they were over your head. You could stand in the fields and practically hear the corn stretching upward, sometimes gaining three to five inches a day.

That was the highlight of the growing season for Neil and the other children, because they could play hide-and-seek in the fields for hours on end and never get caught. He and Jerry and his cousins would rush down the tractor lane dividing the fields, count off to choose someone to be "It," then scramble like mice into the corn. Neil distinctly remembered the thrill of rushing through the golden stalks, brushing up against plump ears that were almost ready to be harvested, their tassels like flaxen hair warmed by the sun.

It was a boys' game, Jerry told the girls, and the time Jennifer got lost and couldn't find her way out only proved his point. Her screams summoned help for almost an hour, and by the time Uncle Tom and Uncle Bernie found her, she had wandered practically to the property line that separated the Sadler farm from the McCurdys'.

"Now listen, kids," Uncle Tom admonished, "I know you want to play out here in the fields, and that's fine. But just don't get so far off the path that you can't find your way back."

Neil thought about that for a moment as he turned the car toward Mason, and he decided that his uncle's warning was probably still sound advice.

7

BACK IN THE 1930S NEIL'S great-grandfather George Sadler claimed he could pick up radio station WLW's programming in the filling of one of his lower left bicuspids. His story was confirmed when Edward Sadler, George's grown son, said he was sitting next to his father in church one morning when the elder man's jaw began playing Bach's Toccata and Fugue in D Minor. But then, it didn't take much to convince the locals that what George Sadler claimed was true. Plenty of people allowed that their dental fillings, their metal fence posts, their drain pipes, or their bedsprings were all picking up the 500,000-watt programming. After all, the signals were coming from a tower right there in a field off Tylersville Road.

The radio tower was still there, Neil noticed, and could be seen even from a distance as he drove toward Mason. The station's wattage, though, had been cut back to 50,000 and no longer rattled people's teeth. Neil wasn't sure when the wattage had been cut, but it must have been before he was born. After Grandpa Ed told them the story about George's tooth, Neil and Jerry sometimes crawled under the kitchen sink to press an ear against the plumbing, but they were never rewarded with more than an occasional gurgle or thump. Jerry did tell Neil once that he heard an entire soap opera coming out of the shower head while he was bathing, but Neil figured Jerry was making it up.

As Neil understood it now, WLW's tower continued to be the tallest structure in Warren County, and at 747 feet it even overshadowed the 331-foot faux Eiffel Tower over in Kings Mills, just east of Mason. That one was built in 1973 as the main attraction for the Kings Island Amusement Park.

The amusement park—now that was another interesting tidbit in the chronicles of the county's history, having been a matter of some controversy before it opened in 1972. There were those who argued that the Kings Mills acreage was meant to be farmland, not a playground, and that what was once serene countryside would be overrun with a continual mob of tourists. Others claimed it was those same tourists who would pump thousands of dollars into Warren County in a way corn never could and that Kings Island would put Kings Mills, Mason, Warren County—even the entire state of Ohio—firmly on the map. They'd be right up there with Anaheim and Orlando when it came to respectable places to vacation.

The moneymakers won out, and Kings Island was built and even enjoyed once or twice in a lifetime by the locals of Neil's generation. What they delighted in most was the nightly display of fireworks over the park, which could be viewed at no cost for miles around. Ten o'clock found entire families out on their porches or in their yards gazing up at the night sky, waiting for the first wailing rockets and bursts of light. Elinor Sadler, Neil's mother, was a big fan. At five minutes to ten she'd turn off the television or put down her latest dime-store novel to go outside and wait. Neil's dad, Jim, had no use for it, but

Neil liked to join his mom and watch the show. It was fifteen minutes of color and light, and on those long dog days of a small-town summer, it was something to do.

But when it came right down to it, Neil remembered he actually preferred the carnival that came through every year and set up for a week in some open fields in Union Township. He and his best friend, Frank Hume, spent as much time there as they could. Before the boys could drive, the folks used to drop them off, and Neil could still remember coming up over the hill and catching the first glimpse of the Ferris wheel rolling against the blue sky. They'd hand over their tickets at the entrance gate and enter a world of sensory overload: the swarming crowd thick with sweat and cigarette smoke. Sunlight glinting off the metal and chrome of the battered carnival rides. The cacophonous chorus of the carrousel's circus tune and the roller coaster's thundering wheels and the hawkers' cries of "Step right up and try your luck!" The stomach-stretching feast of popcorn and hot dogs and cotton candy and caramel apples. The itchy heat of a sunburned scalp and the cool of an icy soda pulled up through a straw. He remembered tossing a bucket of popcorn off the top of the Ferris wheel, watching the white kernels rain down over the crowd below. He remembered sneaking under the freak-show tent to catch a view for free and then feeling so sorry for the bearded lady that he went back out and stood in line and paid his quarter so she'd at least get something in return for having been stared at. He remembered winning a stuffed animal on the midway once, sitting helplessly strapped in beside Frank as his friend got sick on the Tilt-A-Whirl, and watching Jerry in line for the Tunnel of Love with his arm around the waist of some long-haired beauty. He remembered, too, wanting to do the same thing himself and always being on the lookout for a certain face in the crowd, and the way something thumped in his chest whenever he saw her.

But that was a long time ago. Best not to think about that now.

So what about old Frank, then, Neil wondered. Even back then, Frank had wanted to be a dentist. He was probably doing pretty well for himself these days, in private practice somewhere, living in a large house with a double garage and a Jacuzzi. He'd gone right on to Ohio State after high school, and last Neil heard he'd graduated at the top of his class and settled in Columbus. After that he'd quietly slipped off the radar screen of Neil's life, like so many others.

As he drove his circuitous route from Lebanon to Mason, Neil realized the wide open spaces in his own life, the gaps that had resulted from his break with the past. Many of the people he had grown up with—friends, cousins, classmates—were now one-dimensional memories with no present or future. They had to be out there somewhere, working, raising families, watching themselves age; some of them, no doubt, still asking the "What's it all about, Alfie?" questions they were asking back in the 1970s. What is reality? That was a big one, spat out as a joke but secretly pondered.

"Hey, dude, what's happening?"

"Yeah, I'm sitting here wondering, like, what is reality, you know?"

"A-ha-ha, yeah, right. You got a cigarette?"

And no one had an answer. No one knew.

Mason, Neil couldn't help noticing, had expanded like a middle-aged waistline, from the center outward. The outer ridge now was rimmed with malls and fast-food restaurants and clusters of freshly built homes on lots without trees.

But at the center, at the heart of Mason—that was where time had stopped.

Neil had approached the town from the south, heading north on Mason-Montgomery Road, past the high school and Rose Hill Cemetery, up to where the road intersected with Main Street. And suddenly it wasn't even the twenty-first century anymore, but it was 1970-something, and Neil was a teenager and he was home.

Because while the buildings had maybe changed hands and the houses were perhaps owned by other people, they looked the same on the outside. There to the right was the Rebecca McClung house, now a restaurant offering fine dining and a possible glimpse of Rebecca's ghost. Turning left onto Main, he passed Gilbert's Dry Goods (now a sporting goods store), the VFW Hall Post 9622 (still there), Yost's Pharmacy (still there, still owned by the Yost family), the Dinner Bell restaurant (still there, still advertising the Friday night fish fry), the Sinclair gas station (now a towing company), Gary's Barber Shop (still there, still run by Gary), the Chamber of Commerce (still there), and the Mason Lumber and Coal Company (closed, buildings left vacant).

Neil pulled into the lot in front of Mason Lumber, where his father, Jim Sadler, had spent forty-five years of his life. As Neil put the car in idle, he felt something inside of him deflate like a balloon leaking air. Who needed ghosts like Rebecca when your life was haunted by memories? The good ones had brought him back; the worst one had greeted him here, waving at him just a moment ago from the corner of Main and S. East Street.

The old building that stood there was empty now, unused. He had admired it once, that example of art deco architecture that was Mason's original municipal building. It was a square structure of sand-colored brick and long vertical windows, built in 1939. On the front, up toward the roof, was the name Mason welded in chrome, the *s* stretched out like a piece of taffy so that without the rest of the letters you wouldn't have known it was an *s*. Very avant-garde. Even a bit daring, Neil had once thought, for a small midwestern town. With an eye for the way things looked, Neil appreciated the building that housed the city manager's office, the city council chambers, the Office of Economic Development, the police station, and a couple of holding cells.

But now, on this June day in 2003, it wasn't the forlornness of a deserted building that shook him. It was the memory of a day in 1977 when Cal Syfert was taken there in handcuffs, having been arrested on charges of murder.

8

NEIL HAD LIKED CALVIN SYFERT. No, the truth was, Neil had loved him. Loved him like a father. Neil called him Uncle Cal, though he wasn't really his uncle, wasn't any real relation at all, Cal having married into the branch of the family that had come about through adoption in the first place.

Cal's wife was the former Helen Patch, who was the daughter of Edith Sadler, who'd been adopted by George of the musical tooth and his wife, Harriet Sadler, when Edith was but an infant. Edith's birth mother was an unmarried hired girl who lived and worked at the farmhouse in 1906. When she was discovered to be with child after a brief encounter with a migrant laborer who had already left for the coast, Harriet took pity on the unwed mother-to-be. The baby was born right there in the house and became the fifth and last child of George and Harriet Sadler.

When Cal Syfert wandered into Mason some fifty years later, he married Edith's daughter Helen, thereby becoming to Neil—once Neil was born—a first cousin by marriage once removed, or some such thing. But none of that mattered to Neil. Cal Syfert was Uncle Cal, and Neil loved him more than he loved his own father, because Cal was the one who believed in him.

Neil's one dream was to become an artist, a goal that drew polar responses from Jim and Cal. Jim Sadler swore up and down that no son of his was going to make a living at that sissy stuff. Jim Sadler hadn't survived the world war and spent untold years breaking his back at Mason Lumber just so his son could go to art school and paint pictures. No, sir, it was out of the question. Neil tried to tell his father that most of the great artists were men, but Jim Sadler had never even heard of Michelangelo, let alone Monet or Van Gogh or Degas. To Jim Sadler, paint on one's hands was the same as perfume behind the ears, and his son was lost, an embarrassment, one of those not-quite-right fellows who choose to live their lives in a feminine world.

Cal Syfert, on the other hand, heaped genuine praise on Neil whenever he showed up with his sketchbook. The two would sit on the front porch of the Syfert home while Cal studied the drawings slowly, lingering on one before turning the page to the next. He'd shake his head, let out a whistle, punctuate the air with words like "Fine work" and "Mighty pretty" and "Well done."

Cal was not an educated man—he worked the assembly line at Reading Manufacturing out on Reading Road—but he pretended to know what Neil was talking about whenever the conversation turned to art, which was often. Cal lighted up a cigarette while Neil ranted about the turn that art had taken in the twentieth century—the soup cans of Warhol, the squares of Rothko, the paint splatters of Pollock. And the collages of trash—literal pieces of trash—in the Museum of Modern Art in New York City, for pete's sake! What was that supposed to be? Neil didn't know, but it wasn't art. It wasn't art the way art was done before the turn of the century.

"Can't argue with you there, son," Cal would say.

And, *"I think you've got a point."*

And, *"Have to say I never quite thought of it that way."*

Neil's best guess was that Cal Syfert hadn't thought about art much at all, but at least he was willing to listen, unlike Jim Sadler. And there was that story he told about Van Gogh, the one Neil thought was the most beautiful story he'd ever heard.

"I was in the third grade," Uncle Cal related, "when our teacher, Miss Montgomery, thought she'd instill some culture in us. She showed us a picture in a book of that Van Gogh fellow's *Starry Night.* That picture stuck in my head like a fly in honey, and I never forgot it. For a long time after that, I thought stars could do somersaults the way they were somersaulting through the night sky in Van Gogh's picture."

Neil told Cal he wanted to go to New York and become a great painter like Vincent Van Gogh. "But I don't know, Uncle Cal. Dad's dead set against it. Should I go to New York?"

Neil watched intently as Uncle Cal took a long pull on his cigarette. He appeared to be deep in thought. Finally he said, "If you don't, I'll hunt you down and kick your backside all the way from here to there. You got to be true to yourself, Neil, no matter what. You got a gift, son. It just wouldn't be right if you didn't use it."

Neil Sadler loved Cal Syfert, and even in the later years when Neil came around to the house to see Cal's daughter, Mary, Cal himself was still a draw. Many nights, long after Mary had settled her mother and herself into bed, Neil and Cal sat up talking on the porch or watching late-night television in the den.

Neil had to feel a little sorry for Cal, his wife being practically an invalid. It couldn't be easy being married to Helen. Helen the Hypochondriac, they'd called her for years. Always something wrong with her, some strange ache or pain.

"Come on bowling with us, Helen."

"Can't tonight. I'm too tired."

Or, *"Aunt Sarah's putting on a barbecue up at the house. Come on up."*

"I'll try, but I've got this headache I can't get rid of."

Or, *"Come on for a walk with us, Helen. It's too nice a night to be sitting around."*

"My legs are tingling like there's a thousand needles in them, and I can't even feel my feet! How do you expect me to get up from this chair?"

"Sure, sure," everyone would say while they rolled their eyes and shook their heads and shrugged at Helen the incorrigible hypochondriac. And then people couldn't help noticing that she started falling down a lot, and sometimes she couldn't keep her fingers wrapped around a pen, and other times she refused to even get out of bed, and after about five or six years of going to different doctors and seeing different specialists, she was finally diagnosed with multiple sclerosis.

"I told you so," the look on her face said. The look became permanent, brushed on with a bitter paint. "I told you there was something wrong, and you all just laughed."

Cal Syfert didn't laugh, though. That was one thing Neil noticed for sure, even if nobody else did. Cal Syfert had never laughed at Helen in the first place, but after she was diagnosed, he didn't laugh at much of anything anymore. He watched his wife's health wax and wane and take an overall downhill slide over the years until she finally seldom left the house, just stayed at home in bed or in a chair. It was her legs and her eyes that were affected most, so she used a walker to get around the house. She couldn't see well enough to watch television or to read a book. Her world became very small.

Neil eventually became aware that Cal and Helen Syfert slept in separate beds in separate rooms, and being a young man, he wondered what kind of marriage that was. Uncle Bernie had wed them. It was Uncle Bernie who had said she was Cal's to have and to hold from this day forth, and now Cal had Helen without being able to hold her, and it seemed like Cal had been shortchanged in some fundamental way when it came to marriage.

She had to be a burden, Neil thought, but Cal never complained. He just quietly took care of her, with Mary's help. Day and night they cared for Helen, and though she was the one who complained and she was the one who was often angry, Cal and Mary did their duty like a couple of well-trained soldiers.

Neil admired them both and liked them both, and in ways he didn't want to admit, not even to himself, he loved them both. For a time they were the most important people in his life.

And then one day in 1977 Neil was working at Mason Lumber, saving up his money for New York, when he heard Cal Syfert had been arrested for the murder of his wife, an unbelievable charge to which Cal would later plead guilty.

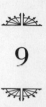

9

NEIL LOOKED AT HIS WATCH; it was just past noon. In an attempt to push Cal Syfert to the back of his mind, he said aloud, "So where can a guy get something decent to eat in this town?" He wondered whether the Main Street Roadhouse was still open for business. He turned around in the empty lot of Mason Lumber, swung left onto Main, crossed Mason-Montgomery, and found the place he was looking for. Must have changed hands—probably a dozen times over—because now it was called McNulty's.

Inside, the place was dimly lighted, windowless, a womb away from the world. Smoke hovered like fog near the ceiling, and the pungent aroma of tobacco mingled with the odor of overcooked grease, Clorox bleach, and unwashed flesh. Thin strains of music hung in the room like an afterthought, piped in no doubt from a stereo system back in the manager's office. Neil recognized Carly Simon singing "You're So Vain." Great Scot, it *was* 1977 here in Mason, Ohio. Neil remembered he had sneaked into this place a couple of times with Frank, back when it was the Roadhouse, but they'd been kicked out for being underage. It was hard to get away with anything in a small town.

He sat down at the bar and looked around. The other stools lining the bar were empty. A few men, loners mostly, were scattered about the tables, eating, drinking, smoking. A middle-aged woman sat by herself in a booth, her eyes shut, both hands clutching a glass; she appeared to be asleep. In the booth beyond her, in the corner, two men sat hunched over their drinks. No one laughed. No one seemed even to be talking. Not yet happy hour, Neil thought. Just the regulars nursing their wounds.

"What can I get—"

Neil looked up at the bartender, who seemed to have appeared out of nowhere. The man's mouth was open, his eyes two circles of surprise. "Neil? Neil Sadler! I don't believe what I'm seeing. Is that you?"

Neil watched the man's mouth break into a toothy grin and tried to place him, tried to remember who all those teeth belonged to.

"Don't you know me, Neil?" the man asked, laughing and flinging his arms wide. "Vincent. Vincent McNulty." Neil was pumping the man's outstretched hand before he knew what was happening. He studied the round-faced man with the double chin and receding hairline until he finally saw the lanky and long-haired teenager the man had been.

"Sure, Vince. Of course I remember you."

"Well, what on earth you doing in Mason?"

Neil reclaimed his hand and said, "First things first, Vince. What are *you* doing on that side of the bar? What are you doing *in* a bar?"

Vince laughed loudly, drowning out Carly Simon, startling the sleeping woman who snorted, sipped her drink, closed her eyes again.

"What am I doing in a bar, he asks? Listen, Neil, I own the place. Been here fourteen years."

"Come again?"

"I said I own this place. I bought it back in eighty-nine. Best investment I ever made."

Neil laughed while he shook his head. "Since when do priests own bars?"

"Oh, that! Yeah, that's good! Priests owning bars. Yeah." Vincent McNulty slapped the counter top. "Listen, I gave up all that stuff a long time ago. I never took the vows."

"Uh-huh," Neil said. He grinned. "Yeah, well, you always said you'd have trouble with the celibacy part."

"Yeah, that and everything else," Vince said loudly, punctuating his sentence with another slap on the counter, another booming laugh.

"And here I thought you were looking forward to listening to people's sins."

"Hey." Vince laid both hands flat on the bar. "You want sins? Boy, have I got sins. *This* is my confessional. You wouldn't believe the things I hear. Guys come in, have a couple of drinks, spill their guts. I pat them on the back, tell them it's all right, send them on their way." He threw his hands up in the air. "Abracadabra, they're absolved!" He leaned forward then, resting his beefy arms on the counter. "I feel like I'm filling a need, you know. Doing a service. Anyway, they keep coming back for more."

Neil chuckled. "No doubt."

"I found my calling."

"I'll buy that."

"Say, listen, you remember Teresa Bigelow, pretty little

thing with dark hair, about this tall?" He held up a hand to his shoulder.

Neil frowned, thought a moment. "A year behind us?"

"That's the one."

"Sister Teresa?"

Vince shook his head. "Sister Mary Catherine."

"Oh? So she made it in? Took the vows?"

A laugh, a slap on the counter, a finger pointing at Neil. "Get this! She's Mrs. McNulty now!"

Neil eyed Vincent McNulty with some suspicion. "You married a nun?"

"*Was* a nun, Neil. Not anymore. I talked her out of it."

"You persuaded her to leave the order?"

"Yeah." A flash of teeth.

"She thought you were a better deal than God?"

Vincent flung his arms wide, struck a pose of mock surprise. "You have to ask? Aha-ha-ha!"

Neil laughed too, shook his head. "Unbelievable."

"Believe it. She's right here, back in the kitchen. Hey, honey!" Vince hollered through the window behind the bar. "Look who's here, will ya?"

A woman appeared at the window, her face without color, her head crowned with a hairnet.

"You remember Neil Sadler, don't you, hon? Class of seventy-six, same as me."

The wan face took on a look of vague recognition. "Well, I'll be—yeah, sure, I remember. How you doing, Neil?"

"I'm good, Teresa. Yourself?"

"Good, good. Can't complain. Listen, the phone—"

She disappeared; Vince turned back toward Neil. "Hey, you came in for a drink. What can I get you? It's on the house."

"You don't have to—"

"Just name it. Whatever you like."

"All right then, how about a beer?"

"Bottle or tap?"

"Tap."

"Comin' up."

Vince drew the beer, his back to Neil. He hollered into the kitchen again, "Hon, bring out a roast beef, will ya?" He turned again toward Neil and set the mug down. "Hungry? We got the best roast beef in town. You like horseradish?"

"Yeah. That sounds good."

Neil Diamond was singing now. Must be a CD, *Greatest Hits of the Seventies,* something like that. *"I am, I said to no one there, and no one heard at all, not even the chair. . . ."* Neil sniffed and thought, *We listened to this stuff?*

In a moment the sandwich was on the counter in front of him. "Thanks, Vince."

"Sure thing, Neil." Vince shrugged, waved a hand. He leaned on the counter again. "Listen, how long's it been?"

"Since we graduated? Or since I last saw you?"

"I don't know. Have I seen you since we graduated?"

Neil took a bite of the sandwich and chewed thoughtfully. "Well, you know, I worked here at Mason Lumber for a year after graduation, before I left for New York."

"New York? You in New York now?"

"Yeah. Didn't you know?"

"Guess I lost track. What are you doing there?"

"Teaching art at a private school."

Vincent McNulty let out a long low whistle. "Small-town boy makes it into the big time, eh?"

Neil smiled. "Not exactly. But I like what I do."

73

"So let me ask you again, what are you doing *here*?"

Neil shrugged, looked beyond Vince's shoulder to the lighted neon Pabst sign on the wall. "I don't really know."

Vince belched out another amused laugh. "Can you beat it! Sheesh, you musta missed us or something."

"Something, yeah."

"What about the family? You got a wife, kids?"

Neil had known this would come. He'd known long before he ever came back to Mason that he would have to explain. He had laid out the script. He had thought he was prepared. Now he was embarrassed by the tremble in his voice. "No kids. My wife died last year. Meningitis."

Vincent McNulty's shoulders sagged visibly as his friendly enthusiasm slid off his back. He stood motionless a moment before swearing softly, then saying, "Hey, I'm sorry, Neil. I didn't know."

"Of course not, Vince. How could you?" Neil raised his eyes to Vince's face, where he saw genuine concern.

"Listen," Vince said, "you doing all right?"

"Yeah." Neil nodded. "Yeah, I'm doing all right."

Vince shook his head slowly, was still shaking his head when one of the men in the back corner booth stood up and approached the bar. Neil was surprised to see he wore the uniform of a cop.

The man raised a hand toward Vince. "Take it easy, bud."

"Hey, you too, Chief."

"Oh, and don't forget to tell Teresa about the tickets to the fund-raiser."

"Will do. You know we'll be there."

The cop turned to Neil, nodded a combined greeting and farewell, and left the bar.

"Chief Harris," Vince said by way of explanation. "Great guy. Best chief this town ever had."

"Yeah? He come here often?"

"Not often enough, far as I'm concerned. But his friend there—" Vince nodded toward the back of the bar—"he keeps me in business."

Neil glanced over his shoulder, then back at Vince. "Do I know him?"

"You should." Vince leaned forward, lowered his voice. "Dan Beeken."

Neil felt something roll through his stomach and knock up against his ribs. "Mary's husband?"

"You got it." He straightened up, arched his back as though it ached. "Chief hates to see one of his men go down. Not that he's ever seen one go down before. Dan's the first."

"What do you mean, go down?"

"Haven't you heard?"

Neil shook his head.

"Shot and killed a guy, couple of weeks ago. Says it was self-defense, in the line of duty and all that, but now he's on administrative leave while they do an investigation, the whole nine yards." Vince paused, clicked his tongue. "Huge waste, if you ask me. No one's asking me, of course, but listen, far as I'm concerned, Beeken deserves a commendation for offing that thug. The guy was worse than a loser. I mean, he was bad news six ways to Sunday. He'd come in here, pick fights, tear the place up. I got tired of calling the cops, so I permanently banned him from the property. Turned him into a human yo-yo; soon as he tried to come in the front door, he'd find himself bouncing right back out. Uh-huh," Vince shook his head, "I wasn't gonna put up with it anymore. I'll tell ya, Beeken did me a favor. And now he's going down for it."

Neil looked back down at his beer and asked quietly, "So what happened?"

Vince lifted his shoulders. "I can only tell you what I read in the papers. So who really knows, you know? I mean, the guy Dan shot was asking for it."

"And?"

"Okay, so here's what the papers say. Beeken's pulling the night shift as usual, cruising around his district about two AM when he pulls into this apartment complex right up here." Vince pointed toward the door. "The Millwood Garden Apartments. You remember the place?"

Neil nodded. Souped-up cars, broken tricycles, sheets instead of curtains in half of the windows. Even when the place was built more than thirty years ago, a person's mood could drop by ten degrees just by driving into the lot. Mason's microscopic Cabrini-Green, except that here all the residents were white.

"So, just as he pulls into the lot," Vince went on, "a girl comes running outta one of the apartments, screaming bloody murder. Begs him to help. Her dad's beating up her mom again, and he's really gonna kill her this time. So Beeken rushes outta the squad car, doesn't even call for backup, just hoofs it after this girl to the apartment. He knows exactly who he's gonna see there too. All the cops know Ralph Traylor, call him 'Traylor Trash' behind his back. Weak, but hey, it fits. How many times they been called to 4C on a domestic? Traylor Trash beating up the old lady again."

Vince paused and looked over at the corner booth. Neil followed his gaze. Teresa was there picking up Dan Beeken's glass. "Ten to one, he finished that drink so fast the ice hasn't even melted," Vince said with a shrug. "And now he'll ask for another. It's the same every day, at least since the shooting."

"He know when to stop?" Neil asked quietly.

"Yeah. When he can't remember no more."

Neil nodded. "So, go on. What happened at the Millwood?"

"Okay, so Dan follows the girl inside and finds Traylor beating his wife with a table leg. She's on the floor; there's blood everywhere. There's a little kid sitting on the floor, bawling his eyes out. Dan yells, 'Police!' and goes for his gun. He tells Traylor to put down his weapon and put his hands up. Traylor jumps back, freezes a minute. Dan can smell the alcohol on his breath across the room. Dan tells the girl to take her kid brother and get him outta there, get him away into the bedroom or someplace. She does, and it's Dan and Traylor and the lady half dead on the floor, and that's when it gets tricky. Dan says Traylor grabbed a knife off the top of the TV and lunged at him, so Dan shot him."

Neil waited, but Vince seemed to be finished. "Well, that's probably what happened, isn't it?" Neil finally asked.

Vince shrugged. "Sure. 'Cept Traylor's old lady says it ain't so. Says old Ralph there was a good sport. So according to *Mrs.* Traylor, Ralph put down the table leg and was just waiting for the handcuffs when Dan pumped a bullet into his chest, just for the heck of it."

Neil sniffed. "That's ridiculous."

"Sure it is. But there's a guy dead and two different stories. A cop kills someone, and they gotta pull in all sorts of people to investigate what happened."

"They find a knife?"

"Sure they did. With Ralph Traylor's fingerprints and

Rhonda Traylor's blood all over the handle. And Rhonda Traylor's saying it was already on the floor when Beeken came in."

"She's lying."

Vince nodded.

"She wants to protect the man who was beating her?"

"People are crazy, Neil. On top of that, Beeken made a fundamental mistake for a cop. Tried to do it himself. Didn't call for backup. No one knows why."

Neil lifted the mug of beer to his lips, discovered it was empty.

Vince shook his head, saying quietly, "You gotta feel sorry for Mary."

Neil was silent. Jim Croce was singing about saving time in a bottle. A trio of construction workers came in the front door, letting in a shaft of light. Then it was dark again.

Vince leaned in closer. "I mean, you remember about her folks, don't you? How the old lady died, and then Cal Syfert dropping dead himself in the slammer? You remember all that?"

Neil raised his eyes from the mug to look squarely at the other man's face. "How could I ever forget, Vince?"

Vince glanced once more at Dan Beeken, then back at Neil. "I mean, Mary don't deserve . . ." He left the sentence unfinished while he shook his head. "Life's funny, huh?"

"Yeah." Neil's voice was flat. "Yeah, I'm cracking up."

Vince turned to the tap and pulled Neil another beer.

10

A COUPLE OF BLOCKS EAST on Main Street, where Kings Mills Road branches off to the right, a white clapboard house, in its latest permutation as a florist shop, advertised a sale on patriotic floral arrangements for Flag Day. Rose Henry, owner of the Rosebud, always appreciated the boost in sales that any holiday brought, even an unofficial one like Flag Day. Last year she had discovered flag-studded wreaths to be a hit with those who had family members, especially veterans, lying beneath the shady lawns of Rose Hill Cemetery, so this year she had doubled her inventory of such wreaths. Then, too, this weekend was a double whammy, as the next day was Father's Day. Not the money-maker among florists that Mother's Day was, but still, there were generally elevated sales in boutonnieres, as some fathers wore them on their lapels to church.

Mary Beeken found herself questioning her decision to work part time at the Rosebud whenever any holiday rolled around. There were the extra preparations, the altered calculations, the proportionately higher volume of customer complaints. It was all a source of stress that Mary could do without. But she needed the job to supplement her husband's income while they put their daughter through college.

Beth had two more years to go at Denison in Granville. Then, of course, not long after Beth finished, Leo would be ready to enter college and they'd be starting the whole financial juggling act all over again. Working, scraping, sacrificing. Mary only hoped Leo would be more appreciative than Beth, who seemed to take for granted everything her parents did for her. Just a couple of weeks before, she'd gone off to Pennsylvania for the summer to wait tables at a union workers' lodge, more with the idea of having fun than of making money. The folks could pick up the slack when it was time to go back to school. Her father, though, had warned Beth that she'd better come home with a certain percentage of every paycheck in the bank. Beth had laughed and shrugged her shoulders and said she didn't necessarily have to spend money to have fun, and Mary had worried as she watched her daughter drive away toward the Ohio-Pennsylvania border. She had lost Beth, she was sure. She had most likely lost her long ago, when the child was thirteen or fourteen and decided her mother was a bore, her mother didn't understand anything, her mother was the greatest barrier between herself and the good life.

"That's how adolescent girls are," Dan had said. "Don't you remember what it's like?"

Mary tried to remember, but all she could recall was her mother sick in bed, self-absorbed, yelling for Mary to help her with this or that. Mary and Helen Syfert had had no real mother-daughter relationship. They had never laughed together, never even enjoyed each other's company. Mary certainly hadn't confided in Helen the way other girls might talk to their mothers about the joys and struggles of growing up. She had considered her mother to be an empty well into which anything tossed was lost and irretrievable. That's why Mary swore that when she had a daughter, things would be different. Things would be as they should be. They'd have a good relationship. They'd be friends.

And Beth had driven off to Pennsylvania saying, "See you in August," and she didn't even know that every turn of the car's wheels was pulling her mother's heart right out of her chest.

When the shop's bell jingled over the door for the umpteenth time that afternoon, Mary was relieved to see twelve-year-old Amy Wagner enter the shop. Such a sweet child. She often came in with her allowance to buy a few flowers to hang up to dry. She'd been making dried floral arrangements for all sorts of occasions since her mother had taught her how a year before. Nancy Wagner, known around Mason as the Craft Lady, owned a craft shop in one of the strip malls on the south edge of town. Amy spent much of her time there, working alongside her mother, helping out simply because she enjoyed it.

"Hello, Amy," Mary greeted the child.

"Hi, Mrs. Beeken." Amy smiled, and her brown eyes shone. "I've got four dollars, but I don't know what I want. I'm just going to look around."

"You go ahead; take your time." Mary often wanted to take Amy home. Nancy Wagner probably didn't even know what she had in that child. That was the crazy thing, Mary thought. Mostly, you only knew what you didn't have, not what you did have.

The shop bell jingled again, and Peg Riley blew through the door like a small tornado. Mary and Peg had been friends since first grade, when they were Mary Syfert and Peggy Wirth.

They had done everything together all the way through high school—joining the choir, the girls' basketball team, the yearbook staff, the booster club. They'd had sleepovers at each other's homes, learned to dance watching *Soul Train,* waited tables at the Dinner Bell, where every Friday night they'd come away smelling like fish and cigarette smoke. They'd seen each other through puberty, dreamed about the future, and joined their local chapter of Future Homemakers of America. "We are the Future Homemakers of America. We face the future with warm courage and high hope!"

Yes, they had been filled with hope, most of it vested in the opposite sex. Even in the years of liberation when women began in droves to break out of the bonds of homemaking, Mary and Peg wanted nothing other than to be wives and mothers. That was dream number one. Dream number two— or more accurately, the backup plan—was a career. For Mary, teaching grade school. For Peggy, becoming a nurse. Peggy surprised herself by actually finishing nursing school, but only as a means of passing the time while she waited to marry Mike Schwankl.

Mary and Peg had never been interested in the same boy, which Mary considered fortunate, as it might have put a strain on their friendship. Peg had her eye on Mike Schwankl all the way through high school, which as it turned out, was not so fortunate, because she married him, and a dozen years later he ran off, not with his secretary but with his secretary's nineteen-year-old daughter. Peg claimed that if he'd stayed, she would have divorced him anyway, as their relationship just wasn't working. Irreconcilable differences described it nicely.

Peg was now married to J. Martin Riley, president of the First National Bank in Lebanon. They owned a rather grand house, furnished with antiques, on a couple of acres just off Route 42 on the way into town. Though they didn't need the income, Peg still worked part time as a nurse, mostly to have an excuse to get away from her three children and two stepchildren. All in all, though, she was happy this time around and was, in fact, a vocal advocate of second marriages.

"What do we know when we're eighteen, nineteen years old?" she was often known to say. "The first husband is bound to be a mistake."

Even all the years after high school when Mary lived in Cincinnati and Peg in Mason and Lebanon, they stayed in touch, making every effort to see each other on regular occasions.

Now Mary smiled at Peg as she entered the shop. But Peg wasn't smiling.

"What's up?" Mary asked.

Peg gripped her leather handbag with both hands at the clasp. She moved to where Mary stood at the cash register, parked her bag on the counter, and stared coldly, though Mary thought Peg's eyes spoke more of hurt than anger.

"Why didn't you tell me?" she snapped.

Mary frowned and shook her head. "Tell you what?"

Peg threw up her hands dramatically. "We've been best friends for—" She rolled her eyes toward the ceiling as she appeared to calculate the years, then said instead, "I can't believe you didn't tell me about Neil's coming back."

"Oh, that."

"Oh, that!" Peg mocked. "Mary, what's the matter with you? I have to find out from your second cousin once removed or whatever she is—Heidi Sadler—when she's coming off night shift this morning—"

"She told you Neil's back in town?"

"She was telling *every*one Neil's back in town."

"But Heidi doesn't even know Neil. She wasn't even born until after he left Mason."

"Well, she knows him now. She was over at the Weatherstons' last night visiting with Grace, and there he was, but—" she grunted her disgust—"the thing is, Neil's in town and I didn't hear it from you."

"Well, all right. So?"

"So? Wha—!" Hands flying, eyes wide, mouth a crimson O.

Peg, the drama queen, Mary thought. She should have got the lead in *South Pacific* back in senior year. She would have done much better than Marianne Willard, who though beautiful, didn't have a lick of talent.

Peg sighed heavily.

Mary did likewise. "Peg," Mary said, "what's your point?"

"What's my point?" Peg fairly shouted.

Amy Wagner turned, startled. Mary tried to smile at the child, who smiled in return and went back to browsing.

Peg said more quietly, "The point, Mary, is this: Neil's back. This is your chance."

"My chance for what?"

"To pick up where you left off!"

"With Neil?"

"And who else!"

"Oh, Peg, get real. Look at me, will you? What do you see?"

Peg leaned in and narrowed her eyes. "I see a woman who needs to get a life before it's too late."

Mary sniffed and shook her head. "That's just it, Peg. It's too late. Tuesday, I'll be forty-three. *Forty-three.* Get it? You know, that was then; this is now."

"Oh, Mary, it's not too late yet—"

"Peg, forget it. Let it lie. The last thing I need is someone digging up the past."

"Listen, Mare, you don't know what you need."

"Yeah, and what's that supposed to mean?"

Mary realized that Amy Wagner had turned again and was staring at her, wide-eyed. "Have you decided what you want, Amy?" she asked pleasantly.

"No." The child shook her head. "I think I'll come back later." She scurried across the shop and out the door, the bell jingling behind her as she left.

"Oh, great," Mary said, "we've scared her away."

"Forget the kid, Mare," Peg said, dismissing the child with a wave of her hand. "Do you know who's on transitional now?" Peg worked in a nursing home on the transitional care unit. It was a halfway stop of sorts for patients who were too well for the hospital and not quite well enough to go home.

"And how can I possibly know that?"

Peg paused a moment to make sure she had Mary's attention. "Rhonda Traylor. She was admitted yesterday."

Mary started at the name of the woman whom Dan had made a widow.

Peg went on, "Her loving husband beats the living daylights out of her, puts her in the hospital with a concussion, four broken bones, and sixty-eight stitches, and you know what Mrs. Traylor is saying now?"

Mary stared at Peg, unwilling to answer.

"She's gonna sue, Mary. Everyone within a mile radius of the nursing home knows Rhonda Traylor's going to sue Dan Beeken for killing her husband."

"She wouldn't—"

"She is, Mary."

"No one's going to believe it wasn't self-defense."

"Is that what you believe? That it was self-defense?"

"Of course!"

"And how do you know what happened?"

"Dan told me—"

"Sure, Dan told you. But were you *there*?"

"What do you mean?"

"Were you there in the apartment when Traylor was killed?"

"Well, no, but—"

"So how are you so sure what happened?"

Mary was silent.

Peg went on, "Listen, maybe Dan was down at that Mc-Nulty's place before he went on duty—"

"You're saying he was drunk?"

"Not necessarily. But he might have had a drink or two before he went on duty."

"No way, Peg. They're not allowed—"

"Not allowed! Oh, Mare, you're so naïve! So what's Dan going to do? Arrest himself for breaking rule number one in the police officers' handbook? 'Boy, howdy, I've been drinking. Better put my badge on and take myself in.'"

"He wasn't drinking, Peg."

"He drinks all the time. Or haven't you noticed?"

Mary had noticed. "So what are you saying?"

"I'm saying no one knows what went on in that apartment when Traylor died except Rhonda Traylor and Dan. Maybe it was self-defense, maybe not. But I can tell you this: Rhonda Traylor smells money, and she's got herself a lawyer who's sniffing it too."

Mary raised a hand to her mouth. Quietly, she said, "Now what will we do?"

"I don't know, but I'll tell you what you ought to do. You ought to get out."

"What do you mean?"

"You know very well what I mean. You and Dan haven't been married for a long time. Not really."

"You're saying I should leave Dan?"

"I've *been* saying it for years, Mare, only you don't want to hear it."

"Because it's crazy."

"It's not crazy. You're not happy. You haven't been for a long time. I should know; I'm your best friend."

"I can't just leave him."

"Why not? You love him or something?"

Mary didn't answer. Instead she said, "You're thinking I should leave Dan and run off with Neil, aren't you?"

"I just want to see you happy."

"Now I know you're crazy."

"I could say the same for you, Mare."

The bell jingled. Ira Lehmann came in, smiled, turned to examine the potted marigolds.

"Listen, Peg, Neil was married. He had a wife."

"She's dead, Mare."

"Don't be flippant."

"I'm just stating the facts."

"Neil didn't come back here because I'm here."

"How do you know?"

"Because he thought I was still living in Cincinnati."

Peg fell silent. Mary figured she had trumped this time.

Then Peg whispered, "You can't tell me Neil Sadler's coming back to Mason doesn't mean anything to you."

Mary wasn't going to let Peg have the satisfaction. She stood unflinching, poker faced. Taking a deep breath, she said evenly, "Neil Sadler's coming back to Mason doesn't mean anything to me."

It was fortunate that at that same moment Ira Lehmann dropped a potted marigold, sending plant, dirt, and shards of pottery flying across the floor. Ira's clumsiness prevented Peg from looking into Mary's eyes and calling her a liar.

11

In 1917 LULA SADLER HAD a footbridge built over the Little Muddy Creek so she would have easier access to her husband, who lay in the family plot in Rose Hill Cemetery. Frank and Lula Sadler had no children, and when Frank died of a staph infection at the age of forty-seven, Lula wasn't about to give in to the loneliness of widowhood as easily as all that. Her house on Short Street backed up to the cemetery, though because of the creek she'd have a far trek through town just to reach Frank if it weren't for the bridge. She made the visit daily, in all kinds of weather, seating herself on Frank's headstone and settling in to tell him the news. Lula rather enjoyed having Frank in the position of captive audience. He had never been a very good listener when he was alive. He always seemed to interrupt right at the important parts. Not so much with words as with the wall of newspaper he erected in front of his face or by the way his head fell back when he nodded off. But now, for the first time in their married life, Frank listened, and Lula could talk to her heart's content.

Mary Beeken was indebted to her distant relative Lula Sadler for having built the Widow's Bridge. Lula was long dead by

the time Mary was born, but Mary couldn't remember a time
when she didn't know the story of the footbridge. The bridge
itself was right there at the end of the street where Mary had
lived as a child, where S. East Street curved around to Short
Street. If you walked straight ahead instead of following the
road, you'd come to the steps leading down the hill to the
bridge.

Young Mary Syfert knew those twenty-one cement steps as
well as Lula Sadler ever had. One short, one long, one short,
one long until you reached the wooden footpath over the
creek—narrow planks sided by two elaborate metal railings
painted green.

While the bridge was Lula's route to her dead husband,
Mary thought of it as her bridge to the future. At least that's
how she thought of it when she happened to be feeling poetic.
She came to the bridge all through her growing-up years just
to sit and dream, the bubbling of the creek her background
music, the light streaming through the trees her romantic
muse. She was a small-town girl, and she wasn't asking for
much out of life. No more than the basics. Just the opportunity
to love and be loved, to make a home, to raise children.

Mary knew, though—even as she faithfully repeated the
creed of the Future Homemakers of America—that the role of
housewife had declined of late in popularity. And that was putting it mildly. In truth, no girl in her right mind in 1970s
America wanted to be "just a housewife" anymore. Girls were
scrambling fast to be a part of the first generation to disdain
hearth and home. They were willing even to hold their own
mothers in contempt for having done nothing other than get
married and produce children.

Yes, life for women was all changed now, pressed down and

rearranged by the swift and powerful juggernaut known as Women's Liberation. The message was clear: Women are free! A girl can dream big, can hitch her wagon to a star! So help yourself to a career! Anything endorsed by *Ms. Magazine* will do nicely. The more masculine the job, the more appealing. Anything a man can do, a woman can do better. Women don't need men to support them anymore, and as for children—well, there are plenty of those in the world without adding any more. After all, the average woman produces 2.5 children, far too many for our overpopulated, undernourished, and vastly polluted earth to sustain.

Sometimes Mary wished she'd been born fifty years earlier, even twenty-five, when getting married and raising a family had been a given for women. She could understand the feminist movement, the desire women had to be seen as equal to men. They *were* equal. That should go without saying. The fact that it had ever been thought otherwise was the whole problem. Women just wanted to be recognized for what they already were, but apparently men weren't willing to go along with that. So women decided they had to put on hard hats, combat boots, sheriff's badges just to get some respect! But, Mary wondered, couldn't women keep the aprons and still be thought just as good, just as important?

Mary supposed not. That simply wasn't how it was. What society says, goes. You buy into it or get left behind. Even the girls of Mason High wanted to *do something* with their lives. Become doctors, write Pulitzer Prize–winning news stories, travel to the moon. And why not? They should have the chance to do those things if they really wanted to.

Mary Syfert didn't. Mary didn't want a career, except for maybe a few years of teaching elementary school. That would be fun, for a while. But what she really wanted was a husband, a home, a houseful of children.

She wanted everything her own mother didn't have. Helen Syfert was married, lived in a house, and had a daughter, but it wasn't real. Not in the way Mary thought it should be. She couldn't imagine that her parents were in love. She couldn't imagine that they had *ever* been in love, that they had ever wanted to be together, that they had dreamed of each other the way she dreamed of . . .

Mary Beeken stood on the footbridge over Little Muddy Creek on a June day in 2003, looking back along the arch of her life, wondering what she would have done all those years ago if she could have seen into the present. She had never expected her bridge to the future to bring her here. She had asked for such a small and fundamental thing, and look what life had given her.

Maybe the feminists had been right after all. You find yourself in yourself, not in a man.

"You and Dan haven't been married for a long time," Peg had said.

Twenty-three years.

But how many of those years had they not really been married?

Who could say? Who can know when a marriage ends and you just keep moving forward together out of habit, and even though there's someone right there beside you, you feel like you're completely alone?

Funny, Mary thought. She didn't even know who Dan was anymore, and that's what was odd. She had always thought people started out as strangers and then got to know each other. But it hadn't been that way with Dan. At first they'd been kindred spirits, and now they were strangers.

"I wonder," she said aloud, "how that happens."

How did anything happen in this strange and unpredictable experience called life?

You think you know someone and you don't; and you think someone else has completely fallen out of your life, and suddenly he's back.

So Neil Sadler was back. But like she'd said to Peg, "So what?" That was all a long time ago. She'd been a kid, and kids were always envisioning dreams that didn't have a snowball's chance of seeing spring.

Face it, Mary, she thought, her hands gripping the chipped green railing, the creek below spinning its worn-out tune. *None of it matters now.*

Somewhere along the way, Mary's star had gone out, and there was nothing left to hitch her wagon to.

12

NEIL FOUND BERNIE SITTING in the overstuffed chair reading the Sunday paper. He was deep into the sports page, the other sections strewn about the floor at his feet.

"Hey, Uncle," Neil said.

Bernie dropped the paper to his lap and blinked against the waves of sunlight that streamed in through the tower room's tall windows and rebounded off his glasses. "Hey, yourself, young man," Bernie said cheerfully. "To what do I owe the pleasure?"

Neil shrugged. "Just thought I'd come see what you're up to."

Bernie laughed out loud. "Don't want to disappoint you, Neil, but this isn't the place where things are happening."

"Yeah, well, you're looking pretty sharp there, Uncle Bernie. Like you were expecting company."

The old man wore a light blue short-sleeve dress shirt, buttoned up to the collar, and a pair of tan trousers, neatly creased. His hair—what was left of it—was slicked down with water, the flyaway pieces pressed firmly, if temporarily, against his scalp. On his feet were the brand-new pair of Nikes, double knotted, that Neil had noticed when he first came across Bernie sleeping. Rather a waste, Neil laughed to himself, for all the action those shoes would see.

Bernie glanced down at his clothes with a grin. "No. No plans for company. I'm just being the atheist in his coffin today—all dressed up and no place to go."

Neil stepped across the room and started gathering up the newspapers on the floor. "That's where you're wrong, old man. You're coming with me."

"I am? Coming where?"

"Outside." Neil nodded toward the door. "Grace is throwing a big shindig, and everyone's coming. That includes you."

"Oh, that. Hate to disappoint you, Neil, but I've already given Grace my regrets. I can't possibly get down those stairs." He put one hand on the walker beside the chair, as though to emphasize his point. "Though come to think of it, maybe that's why Grace insisted on a clean shirt today. No doubt some of the family will pop up to see the old man. That'll be nice, won't it?"

"Listen, Bern, how long have you been in this room?"

Bernie frowned in thought. "A month, a year. I don't know, Neil. You get to be as old as I am, and time doesn't have much meaning anymore."

"Well, it's time for you to get out for a while."

"But—"

"Listen, I know what you're thinking."

"Oh?"

"Don't worry, Uncle Bernie. Trust me. If you start to see the chariot swinging low, just holler. I'll bring you back up here. I won't let your Maker pick you up at the wrong stop."

Bernie laughed merrily once again. "Well, that wasn't

exactly what I was thinking. But, no, the problem is, I simply can't make it down those stairs. I'm stuck here for the duration."

"No one's asking you to walk down any stairs, Uncle Bernie," Neil said. He turned around, looked over his shoulder, and pointed with a thumb toward his back. "Your elevator awaits."

Bernie looked incredulous. "You're going to carry me down?"

"You got a better idea?"

"Yes. You go on and have a good time." He picked up the sports page and snapped it open. "I'll stay up here."

"Uh-uh, Uncle," Neil said, gently taking the paper from the old man's hands. "Nothing doing."

"You'll kill yourself and me with you."

"You can't weigh more than a hundred pounds."

Bernie shrugged.

Neil nodded toward the door again. "Come on. The gang will be showing up soon."

Bernie took a deep breath, let it out, smiled. "It would be nice to see everyone."

"Better than that, wait till you see the food. What I just saw in the kitchen is a feast fit for the gods. And there's more to come. It's potluck. All the ladies will be bringing a dish or two of their best home cooking."

Bernie sat quietly a moment, his eyes glazing over in thought. Then he pushed himself up from the chair. When he reached his full height, he tapped Neil's shoulder. "All right, so where's the down button on this contraption?"

Neil smiled and positioned Bernie's walker in front of him. Then he moved over to the staircase, descended two steps, and stopped. "Can those Nikes get you this far?"

"Of course!" the old man snapped, feigning offense. "I can walk perfectly well along a flat surface."

"Then start walking."

Bernie moved slowly to the stairs. At the doorway he put his walker aside and fell with a grunt onto Neil's back. Neil hitched the old man up, told him to hold on, and started down.

He stepped gingerly through the cluttered third-floor hall, then paused on the landing long enough to catch his breath. He hitched Bernie up higher once more, then descended the next staircase. On the second-floor landing he began to question the sanity of his offer.

On the first-floor landing Neil said, "Listen, old man, on second thought, if your Maker comes, you might just have to meet Him down here. I'm not sure this elevator's going to make it back up!"

Bernie was laughing too loudly to respond.

Neil carried him through the long hallway and out to the back porch. In the yard, Grace, Dennis, and their son and daughter-in-law were setting up the last of the folding tables and chairs while Mike and Valerie's three children chased each other over the grass.

When Neil stepped off the porch with Bernie clinging to his neck, Grace cried, "Sakes alive, Neil! I didn't think you'd really—Oh, my stars! Careful there. Put him down gently. . . ."

"Don't worry, Grace. I've got him."

"Bernie, what on earth—Are you two crazy?"

"Oh yes, and it's wonderful!" cried the old man gleefully.

"You could have both fallen and broken your necks!"

"Not likely, Grace. Bernie's got mine locked firmly in a half nelson."

"Uncle Neil!" Lila hollered, running toward him from across the yard, "will you give *me* a piggyback ride?"

"Me too!" cried Lacey, her twin.

"Not just yet, girls," said Neil, trying hard not to look winded. "Let the piggy catch his breath, will you?"

"Girls!" Valerie called, "don't pull on Uncle Neil's shorts. Just wait a minute till he puts Uncle Bernie down."

"Lila! Lacey! You heard your mother," Mike added. "Just cool your jets a minute."

The twins let go of Neil's belt loops and ran off to giggle together under one of the tables. Neil carried his load to the shade of the maple tree, where he had readied a lawn chair for Bernie. Slowly he sank down onto the cushion and sighed. "Ground floor, old man." He pulled his shirt up and used the hem to wipe the sweat from his forehead. Then he stood and allowed Bernie to stretch out on the chair.

"Oh my," said Bernie. "Oh my, but that was some ride!" He lifted his glasses with one hand while wiping away tears of laughter with the other.

"Scot," Grace ordered, "run up to the tower room and get Uncle Bernie's walker, will you?"

"Sure, Grandma!"

"As long as you're down here, Bernie, you might as well take a walk, get a little exercise."

Dennis laughed. He pointed to the "Kiss the Cook" apron he was wearing. "Long as you're down here, Bern, you can flip the burgers if you want. We got some sweet young things coming today. Might be some fringe benefits in it for you."

Bernie grinned while shaking his head from side to side.

"No thanks, Dennis. I wouldn't mind working the grill, but the fringe benefits would probably kill me. I'll let you do the honors. I'm fine right here."

"Mike and I will take a little walk with you later, Uncle Bernie," Valerie offered. "I've always thought you should get out and get some fresh air."

"That'll be fine, dear," Bernie agreed. "Whenever you're ready, you know where to find me."

Neil, his breath returned, tucked his shirt back into his shorts and straightened his belt. "How are you feeling, Uncle Bernie?" he asked quietly.

Bernie leaned his head back and looked up at the sheltering arms of the tree. "I feel very . . ." He paused a moment, breathed deeply, nodded. "I feel very alive. Thank you, Neil."

Neil gave a small smile. "You're welcome, old man."

13

WHAT NEIL DIDN'T TELL Bernie was that he'd brought him outside just as much for his own sake as for the old man's.

Neil was nervous, and he wanted Bernie seated right there under the maple tree, where he could see him. Uncle Bernie was for Neil an unwitting source of moral support. Grace was throwing this get-together for Neil so that everyone could welcome him back, could shake the hand of the long-lost relative who had finally come home.

But Neil was only too keenly aware of a sense of having abandoned these people, and he wondered whether they would be genuinely happy to see him. After all, he had left Mason on the heels of the tragedy that had sent them all reeling, and except for a couple of obligatory visits early on, he hadn't bothered to come back. Some of them, like Uncle Gene, had supported him financially in his first years in New York, while Neil had done little in return. He had thanked them with a few hastily written letters, and that was all. Once he was graduated from school, he had more or less successfully disappeared, cutting himself off from the folks who had not only given him life but had started him on his new life in New York when his own father refused to pay for his education. If they were angry now, or hurt or bewildered, it would be only too understandable. If they asked why he had stayed away, he would have no words to explain. If they asked why he had come back, he would have no words to explain that either.

And so he was afraid to see them, to look into their faces and read the questions there. For a moment, and for the thousandth time, he almost wished he hadn't come back.

Neil stood beneath the shade of the maple and looked around at the familiar scene—the house behind him, the weathered barn ahead, the aluminum silos, the rows of young corn twining over the land like braids on a young girl's head, stretching out toward the line of trees that once separated the Sadlers' farm from the McCurdys'. He breathed it all in, trying to draw strength from it. But he had only a moment to gather his thoughts before he heard the crunch of tires over gravel, the signal that the first cars were coming up the long drive toward the house.

After a reassuring glace at Bernie, Neil turned to see his uncle Gene coming around the corner of the house, his long legs scissoring across the grass. Neil watched him come until at last the older man had reached him and caught him up in a hug that squeezed the breath out of him.

"Let me look at you, son," Gene Sadler said as he stepped back. He stood at arm's length, one beefy hand on each of Neil's shoulders.

Neil wanted to say something, but the words were stuck somewhere in his throat. His uncle's eyes were clear and shiny, and in them Neil saw only joy.

"Lillian!" Gene called over his shoulder. "Get on over here and get yourself a good look at this boy. Doesn't he look just like Jim about a hundred years ago? Honest, Neil, you're the spitting image of the old man."

"Land sakes, Neil!" Aunt Lillian cried as she hurried over. "I just can't believe you're home. Let me give you a hug!"

The tiny woman stood on tiptoe and threw her arms around Neil's neck. Neil returned her embrace and kissed her cheek.

When he pulled back and looked at his aunt and uncle, he felt renewed, like a fever had broken. All the apprehension that had been churning inside of him was gone. In its place, a rush of love and joy and thankfulness.

Uncle Gene slapped Neil's shoulder again and said, "Welcome home, son. It's just so good to have you back."

"It's good to be back, Uncle Gene."

And it was true, more true than he could have imagined five minutes ago. He wanted to say more, but there was another crunch of gravel and the slamming of car doors, and then Neil was surrounded by familiar faces—aunts, uncles, cousins, in-laws, and new faces too—folks who had married into the family, children he had never seen. They were all talking at him at once, reaching out to hug him, take his hand, slap his back. He felt like a celebrity at a film debut. But it was better than that. Because they weren't his fans, they were his family, and they were glad he was home.

"Great to see you! How you been, Neil?"

"Neil! Just look at you!"

"What's big city life done to you? You're actually looking *good*!"

"Neil Sadler! Is it really you?"

"Come here, child, and give your aunt Agatha a hug."

"I'll be a monkey's uncle, Neil. I swear you look just like your father did at that age."

"That's just what I said not a minute ago, Ben. Jim Sadler all over again."

"Come to the country for a little vacation, didja?"

"Yeah, he better enjoy it today. Vacation's over tomorrow. Then he goes to work."

"Yeah, what about the Gothic Horror, huh? Gonna be pretty swanky when she's done with it."

"Hey, Neil, want to introduce you to my wife. She's been hankering to meet a real live New York artist."

"Listen, people, start eating before everything spoils!"

As the initial greetings subsided and people began to eat and mingle, Neil floated among them, talking, listening, simply taking it all in. It was an odd sensation being there among them, the folks who formed the very foundation of his existence. He felt as though his life were a train that had been derailed, then hoisted back on track, except that a quarter-century stretch of rail had been excised out. The year 1977 had been connected right up to 2003, and the patch was seamless.

At the same time the surety that time had passed was in the men and women themselves; they carried the lost years in their flesh. All the familiar faces, the youthful forms, aging now or old. Neil saw them as they were, but he saw them too as they had been, the former juxtaposed over the present, the young over the aging, back and forth like changing holograms.

Mary came, looking cool in a white linen sundress, white sandals, her hair swept up off her neck in a twist at the back of her head. She had her hand on a boy's shoulder as he walked beside her. Sandy-haired, freckled, lanky—that must be Leo.

He was a Beeken, but there was no arguing that he was a Sadler too.

Neil watched the boy as he and his mother approached the crowd and was startled at the thought that dropped suddenly into his mind: *He might have been my son.* He wondered where the thought had come from, but then he remembered it was Father's Day. Yes, that must be it. One naturally thought of children on Father's Day, even the ones you never had.

Neil moved through the crowd toward Mary. He saw her shake her head, heard her say to Lillian Sadler, "No, Dan's not feeling well. He sends his apologies. He's very sorry he couldn't make it."

"Oh, such a shame. But we understand."

A grandmotherly pat; Mary's embarrassed smile. Yes, Neil was sure everyone understood why Dan Beeken wasn't there.

"Hello, Mary," he said, reaching her.

"Hello, Neil." She smiled, squeezed the young boy's shoulder. "I want you to meet my son, Leo."

Neil held out his hand, circled the young boy's uncertain grip. "Very glad to know you, Leo."

The boy smiled awkwardly. "Yeah. Hello," he mumbled. "Mom, I'm going to eat."

"Go ahead." Mary waved him off. She said to Neil, "He's always hungry."

"Well, there should be plenty here to fill him up. We've got quite a spread going."

Mary laughed lightly. "And what else could you expect? It's a Sadler picnic."

"Yes," Neil shrugged, smiled. "I remember." He pointed a palm toward the tables of food. "Shall we?"

Two hours later, sated with food and conversation, Neil stepped inside for a moment's quiet in the kitchen. He'd enjoyed only half a moment, though, when Gene Sadler stepped up to the porch and came in through the kitchen door. "Neil," he said. "I saw you come in. Hope you don't mind."

"Of course not, Uncle Gene. Get you something from the fridge?"

"No." Gene Sadler patted his stomach. "I've had enough to last me well into next week."

Neil smiled and nodded. He wondered what it was his uncle had come to say.

"Listen, son." Gene winced, as though it hurt to speak. "You've been through a tough time lately. I just wanted to see how you are. I mean, you doing okay?"

"Yeah, I'm doing okay. Thanks for asking."

The older man nodded, looked at the floor. Neil had always wondered how Jim and Eugene Sadler could be brothers. They weren't alike at all, not on the outside, not on the inside.

"Well, we're all of us real sorry about Caroline. Just as sorry as we can be. I wanted you to know that."

"Thanks, Uncle Gene. I was just thinking, I should have brought her here." She had asked to come, had asked numerous times in the first years of their marriage. She wanted to see where he was from. But every time she asked, Neil told her there was no reason to go back; there was nothing there, nothing worth seeing in Mason, Ohio. "I should have brought her out to meet all of you and to see this place. She would have liked it here. I don't know why . . ." Neil's sentence hung in the air, unfinished.

"We would have liked to have known her. But it's all right, Neil. You can't beat yourself up about it now."

"Still, I was wrong not to bring her. I was just plain wrong to stay away so long."

Gene Sadler shifted his ample weight from one foot to the other. "Listen, son, it was a bad time for all of us, that summer you left Mason. Given half a chance, most of us would have left too and not come back, just to put it all behind us."

Neil was quiet a moment. Then he said, "Thanks, Uncle Gene. I appreciate that. I don't think I could have made it in New York without your help. I don't think I've ever properly thanked you for that."

"Don't have to thank me, Neil. I wanted to do it."

"You're a good man, Uncle Gene."

"Better run that one by your aunt Lillian. She might not agree."

Neil smiled. "I think she would."

Gene returned the smile, then asked, "So what do you hear from the old man? Anything?"

"Not much."

"Uh-huh. Me neither. Jim never was very good at keeping in touch, I guess."

"I guess not."

"You suppose he and Elinor are doing okay?"

"Sure. They're fine. I called Mom last month. Mother's Day. They're enjoying the good life out in California, enjoying Jerry's kids. Yeah, everything's fine."

"Good, good." Gene nodded slightly.

"You and Lillian been doing all right?"

"Can't complain. Would like to, but I can't. Too much to be thankful for. Well, speaking of Lillian, guess I'll go hunt down that bride of mine, see what she's up to."

"I'll be back out in a minute, Uncle Gene."

"Sure, Neil. And listen, son, if there's anything we can do to help, I mean, you ever want to just talk or anything, you let me know."

"I will. Thanks."

The older man nodded, then turned to leave. Neil watched through the open kitchen window as Gene Sadler rejoined the noisy, undulating crowd outside. Neil's family. Uncle Gene had already done more than he could know, simply by being the good father who ran with open arms to greet the prodigal son.

14

NEIL POURED HIMSELF SOME ice water from the refrigerator and drank it down. The day was hot and he was sweating. He went into the bathroom and splashed his face and neck with cold water before heading back outside. A moment later when he stepped off the back porch, he saw an older woman seated in a lawn chair beside Bernie. She was a latecomer to the picnic, and Neil wasn't certain who she was.

Bernie and the woman were conversing animatedly, as though they hadn't seen each other in a long while. And they probably hadn't, Neil thought, with Bernie sequestered up in the tower room.

He strode toward the maple tree and smiled when he recognized Aunt Vivian. Though her hair was startlingly white now and her hands bore signs of arthritis, her cheeks were two smooth patches beneath still-bright eyes, and her smiling mouth was full and youthful. When Neil reached her he bent down and kissed one soft cheek. "Hello, Aunt Vivian," he said.

"Neil," she replied softly, and her blue eyes filled.

He knelt in the grass beside her.

She took his hand. "I thought I'd never see you again."

Vivian Zwirn was Helen Syfert's sister and Mary's aunt, though only a distant cousin to Neil. But Neil had always been fond of Vivian, and she of him. They had often run into each other at the Syfert house when Neil was there visiting Cal and Vivian was there visiting her invalid sister.

"I'm so glad you came back," Vivian said.

"So am I," he answered. "I only wish I'd come back sooner."

Vivian patted his hand. She gave him a look that said she understood, that she knew why he hadn't come back sooner. After all, few people understood the loss better than she did.

Mary had lived with Vivian after Helen died and Cal went to prison. Vivian and Henry had taken Mary in for that last year of high school and the two years after, before she married Dan Beeken. Vivian knew her sister Helen would have wanted it that way. They had loved Mary just as much as they loved their own five children.

"We're late to this lovely gathering, Neil, and I'm sorry. Henry's peptic ulcer always acts up at the worst times—"

Neil waved away her excuse. "It doesn't matter. I'm just glad you're here. Did Henry make it?"

"Oh yes. He's around here somewhere. Eating all the wrong foods, I'm sure."

They exchanged a smile. Neil said, "So, how have you been, Aunt Viv?"

"A few aches and pains, but I can't complain," she said mildly. "Henry's enjoying retirement, and it's nice having him around the house. We're in the same house over on Hanover Drive. You know the one."

Neil nodded. He knew it well.

"I'll come by and see you. I'll be here all summer."

Another squeeze of the hand. "I do so hope you will, Neil. Come by anytime."

Their conversation was interrupted when a young woman, a baby on her hip, approached them and said, "Grandma, would you mind watching the baby while I get the boys something to eat?"

Vivian reached out her arms. "Of course I don't mind. You just leave that precious bundle right here with me."

The young woman handed the baby over, saying, "Thanks, Grandma. I won't be long."

"Take your time. By the way, this is Neil."

The young woman smiled at Neil and stuck out a hand. "Glad to meet you, Neil. I'm Donna Simms."

"She's Ross's daughter, my granddaughter."

Neil shook Donna's hand, said hello, and marveled that Vivian had a granddaughter who was herself a mother.

When she was gone, Neil looked quizzically at the child in Vivian's lap. "She doesn't look a thing like Donna, does she?" Vivian said with a chuckle. "And no, not like Donna's husband either. They just brought her home a month ago from China!"

Neil moved his gaze from the child's face to Vivian's and back again. "A little Chinese girl in Mason?"

The child, squirming and cooing on Vivian's lap, seemed to smile at Neil. She offered four perfect baby teeth and one string of saliva that wormed its way down her chin.

"Oh, she's not alone!" Vivian said happily. "Several families in the area have adopted baby girls from China. Isn't it wonderful?"

At that moment Mary wandered over carrying a tray of

plastic cups filled with ice water. "Anyone want water?" she asked.

"Look, Mary," Neil exclaimed, an amused smile on his face. "Uncle Denton was right after all. The Chinese *have* invaded Mason, Ohio!"

Mary felt her jaw tighten. Uncle Denton had been dead more than twenty years, but just the mention of his name sent a tremor of anger through her that shook her to the core.

Back when he was alive and working at the Sinclair station on the corner of Main and S. East, the folks of Mason had a running joke about Denton Patch. "He's not completely cracked," they'd quip, "but he's more than a little dented." Even some of his own kinfolk called him "Dented Patch" behind his back.

Speculation abounded as to how much of his "not being quite right" was brought on by the war. Some said he was strange even before he went overseas, pointing to his propensity for daydreaming in school, his shunning of sports to spend time tinkering with his 1939 Ford standard coupe, his preference for solitude over the usual social activities of young people. Then there were those who argued that other than being shy, he was more or less like anyone else until he came home from battle.

He'd graduated near the bottom of his class in 1949, but not for any particular lack of intelligence, his teacher explained. On the contrary, he was quite bright and imaginative. He simply wasn't interested in school. After graduation he went on to work at a variety of low-paying jobs until his number came up and he was drafted into the Army.

As soon as he finished boot camp, Denton Patch was assigned to the 23rd Infantry Regiment of the 2nd Infantry Division. A little scuffle was going on over in Asia, a place called Korea, and the 23rd was filling up its ranks in preparation for going over. Seems the divided country was having a civil spat, with the government of the north attempting to share the wonders of Communism with the people of the south, and the United Nations thought it might be prudent to nip the attempt in the bud. Nothing to worry about, of course. Scuttlebutt had it that after firing a few warning shots, the U.S. Army would slide smoothly into occupation duty, all in all a piece of cake. Nothing to it. *"Those North Korean soldiers—they can't even shoot straight. They don't know how to handle ammunition. And they're afraid of the dark!"* That was the rumor making the rounds on the troop ships. Even Denton Patch laughed.

The laughter didn't last long, though, once they arrived and the bullets starting flying and the soldiers started falling along the banks of the Naktong River. The unexpected brutality of fighting the Korean People's Army of North Korea was bad enough, but no one, not even General Douglas MacArthur, commander of all United Nations forces in Korea, foresaw the invasion of the fierce Chinese Communist Forces from the north.

It happened in October of 1950. The CCF moved over the border of Manchuria to join the Korean forces in a huge offensive push, with a little help too from the Russian-built MIG-15 jet planes. With the entrance of the CCF, the whole color of the war took on a darker hue.

Though General MacArthur promised that the American troops would "be home by Christmas," the holidays came and went, and that winter of 1951 the troops of the 23rd moved up into hills that looked like mountains to a boy from the plains. Mountains usually have names, but these hills had numbers, military style: Hill 453, Hill 248, Hill 345—more hills than a boy at the bottom of his class cared to keep track of. All Denton Patch cared about really was reaching the end of another twenty-four hours and finding himself still alive.

Up in the hills the American troops joined the French forces to do battle against Communism and an unexpected second enemy, the cold. Both enemies took their share of casualties. When the temperature dropped to twenty degrees below zero and the wind chill was sixty degrees lower than that, there was just nowhere to go to get away from the penetrating cold. The men's limbs ached and their bodies went into spasms of shivering, and the icy tongue of the wind licked plenty of flesh with frostbite. With inadequate clothing and no shelter, the soldiers curled up in their foxholes and chipped away at their frozen C rations with the tips of their bayonets while praying to God they would live long enough to know what it was to be warm again. Plenty of soldiers didn't.

And so the men of the 23rd, alongside the French, pushed forward through those brutal months of fighting and freezing, freezing and fighting. In February alone they took part in the Battle of the Twin Tunnels and the Battle of Chipyong-ni, two of the deadliest battles of the war.

There Denton was, thousands of miles from the heartland, hunched over in an icy foxhole with a .50-caliber machine gun in his hands. One day he's bent under the hood of his car and the next he's up on a mountain half a world away trying to pump bullets into Chinese flesh. It's dark and it's cold, he's tired and hungry, and the Chinese are blowing horns and whistles and bugles like there's a party going on. There are aircraft flying overhead dropping flares that light up the battlefield with an eerie yellow glow, making everything look like the outer edges of hell. Mortar flies and men scream and soldiers fall onto the frozen earth and never get up again. And Denton Patch feels the fear in his belly and the death at his back, and he says to himself over and over again, "O God, my God, why have you forsaken me?" He doesn't even know where the words are from; they just float up to the top of his mind from somewhere deep inside, and they seem somehow appropriate to this place and time that not even God would care to visit. Then, at long last, one more night passes, and a quiet falls, and the sun rises on a mountainside littered with bodies and watered with blood. And another day starts in Korea.

Somehow—by miracle, fluke, or just dumb luck—Denton Patch survived. He was wounded sometime that summer and sent home by way of a MASH unit, a mobile army surgical unit where he was sliced open, sewn back together, and readied for shipping Stateside.

When he arrived back in Mason, Ohio, just before Thanksgiving of 1951, he was missing six toes, the calf muscle of his left leg, and an intangible slice of his mind. The toes, three on each foot, were a casualty of frostbite. The calf had been blown away in a barrage of Chinese artillery. His mind had fallen victim to what he had seen, though no one in Mason knew what that was. No one would ever know, because Denton didn't have the words to tell them and wouldn't have said even if he could.

There was no question that Denton Patch would not be taking advantage of the GI Bill and going on to college. He would have to go to work. His future brother-in-law, Henry

Zwirn, owner of the Sinclair station, gave him a job pumping gas and fixing cars. A few years later, after they were married, Henry and Vivian had an extra room added on to the back of the house for the slightly dented brother who would never be able to live on his own. Denton Patch never married. Never dated. Never really had any friends, for that matter.

He made only two allusions to his experiences overseas, both of which became fodder for the joke mill. Everyone had seen Denton Patch on a day that was hotter than blazes, rubbing his hands together and muttering, "No matter what I do, I just can't get the cold of Korea out of my bones." He'd walk down Main Street at the height of summer in a zipped-up jacket, a brace on his gimpy leg, rubbing and blowing on his hands as he moved along. It wasn't unusual to see a string of children limping along behind him, rubbing their hands and stifling laughter.

Then there were the strange utterances about the Chinese. Most of the locals had been on the receiving end of his warnings at one time or another. Denton often gave out these warnings as he handed over a person's change for a gallon of gas: "Have a nice day, and if you see any Chinese, you let me know. They're a tough lot, but I can take care of 'em." It was the people from outside Mason who drove away scratching their heads. That area was white bread. Unusual enough to see a Negro this far north of Cincinnati. No one could remember ever seeing any Chinese.

"Denton," Henry would admonish, "stop bothering folks about the Chinese. It's bad for business. You talk like that too much, you'll spook folks and they'll end up getting their gas elsewhere. 'Sides, this is Ohio. Only thing Chinese you're gonna see around here is a game of Chinese checkers."

But Denton Patch wasn't so sure. The Chinese were wily. He should know. They showed up when you least expected, and they were ruthless. He'd killed a bunch of them, and he wasn't afraid of killing some more. He would too, if it meant protecting Mason, Ohio. He wasn't about to let the Communist forces blow away his own family the way they'd blown away the American troops over in Korea.

And he was vigilant about it. He spent a good portion of most nights out on reconnaissance. He said the CCF made few daylight attacks. Their usual strategy was to start shooting sometime between midnight and 0300 hours. Henry and Vivian, and even Helen and Cal, knew about his nighttime wanderings, but they were helpless to know how to keep Denton Patch from scouting out Chinese battalions in the cornfields of Ohio. So they let him go. He didn't do any real harm, anyway, except maybe to alarm a farmer now and again until the farmer realized who was leading point through his crops. Everyone knew Denton Patch.

Denton's nieces and nephews, Henry and Vivian's kids, took the ribbing they got in stride, even joined in when it came to jokes about Dented Patch. But his one niece on Helen's side, Mary Syfert, was mortified by her relationship to the man. In fact, she saw herself as the recipient of a double insult: first her mother was Helen the Hypochondriac, and then her mother's brother was the town buffoon. It was an adolescent's nightmare.

But what could you do? Everyone shrugged his shoulders and chuckled a bit and simply allowed Denton Patch the freedom to scout out his Chinese enemies. He was faithful to his charge for thirty years, right up until he passed away in 1981. He met his death unexpectedly one night when he fell through a walking bridge over the Little Miami River and drowned.

Rumor had it that he fell to his death cursing the Chinese, but that was probably only an urban legend of sorts, since no one was with him when he died.

15

MARY STOOD AT THE EDGE of the lawn, gazing down the tractor path between the fields of corn. She wished she could walk down that path and keep on walking. She didn't even care where she ended up, as long as it wasn't where she was now.

The sun was sinking behind the line of trees, and the crowd of family members dwindled as people gathered up their children and their belongings and left for home. Wayne Sadler, a former defensive lineman at Mason High, was even now carrying Uncle Bernie back up to the tower room, with Neil spotting them. A handful of women were cleaning up the kitchen with Grace, and Mary knew she should be there too, helping out. She should be. She would turn and go inside in just a minute. But right now she was collecting the splintered pieces of a memory that had burst open, like an exploding light bulb, when Neil mentioned Uncle Denton. All those broken pieces had to be stuffed back inside, where the painful recollections were supposed to lay hidden.

It wasn't Neil's fault, of course. He didn't know. He had never known what Denton revealed to her after she had gone to live with Aunt Vivian and Uncle Henry. . . .

"Your dad was a bad man. He deserved what he got."

"You're crazy."

"He killed my sister, my helpless sister."

"Get out of my way. Just leave me alone!"

"You think I don't know?"

"You don't know anything."

"See this?"

"I don't care what it is."

"I think you should. See here? See these initials?"

"You want to walk?"

Mary was suddenly aware of Neil standing at her elbow. She turned to him, and suddenly she wanted to laugh. *Yes, I want to walk. I want to walk and walk and keep on walking....*

"I should help Grace in the kitchen."

"I just checked. There's too many hands in there as it is."

Mary nodded slightly, then turned her attention back to the tractor path.

"Come on," Neil urged. "It's a nice evening."

"Have you seen Leo?"

"Inside playing video games with the other kids."

From the corner of her eye, Mary saw Neil restlessly shift his weight from one foot to the other. "You know we don't own the land anymore," she said. "We haven't owned it in twenty years, if you can believe that."

"Bill McCurdy owns it, right?"

"Yes."

"He won't mind. And if he comes out and gives us a hard time, I'll just rough him up a bit, show him who the land really belongs to."

Mary did smile then, sadly. It should still be Sadler land. It should never have been lost. "And he'll remind you that he bought it fair and square to the tune of seven grand an acre. Of course that's nothing compared to what it'd be worth today."

Neil whistled. "Still, seven grand. Okay, so it's his. But I'll still rough him up if he tries to kick us off."

He started forward and Mary followed, falling into step at his side.

How many times had they walked this strip of earth, their sneakers following the tire treads made by Uncle Tom's tractor? Neil, Mary, Jerry, any number of their cousins.

"Hey," Neil said, "you remember how we used to play hide-and-seek out here in the fields?"

"Sure. Every year, soon as the corn was high enough."

"Jerry's 'It' this time."

"Okay, everybody, just remember, don't get too far off the path!"

"Hide your eyes, Jerry. And no fair peeking like you usually do."

"Yeah, no fair!"

"One, two, three, four—"

"Yahoo!"

"Run!"

"Eight, nine, ten. Ready or not, here I come!"

"So," Neil said, "It's been . . ." His voice trailed off.

Mary waited.

"It's been—I don't know—quite a day, I guess," he fumbled awkwardly. "I mean, it was good to see everyone after so many years."

They walked for a moment in silence. Then Mary asked

softly, "Why did you come back, Neil?"

He strode along with his hands clasped at the small of his back, like someone deep in thought. He looked up at the sky, at the corn, at Mary. He seemed to be searching for an answer. "I don't really know, Mary," he finally admitted. "I just felt compelled after Caroline died—" He stopped.

Mary nodded to let him know she understood, though she didn't really. Why should he come back because Caroline died? What was he looking for here, in this place he once couldn't wait to escape?

He went on, saying gently, "I could ask the same of you, you know. I never thought you'd return to Mason."

"Neither did I," she said. "For a long time, I couldn't imagine moving back here."

"So, if you don't mind my asking, why did you?"

She shrugged. "It was the best thing for Dan. He'd spent his whole career with the Cincinnati police force. Eighteen years. It was just too much. I mean . . ." She paused, shook her head. "What you see as a cop, you can't imagine."

"No," Neil conceded, "no, I suppose I can't."

"The very worst of the worst," Mary went on. "Every sordid thing that people can dish out, day after day."

In the beginning, fresh out of the Academy and a rookie on the streets, Dan would come home after working the night shift and tell her what he had seen, all that had been happening while she slept. Unbelievable things. Stories she didn't *want* to believe, of shootings and stabbings and bodies found tied up in dumpsters, floating in rivers, buried in backyards. Stories of wife beatings, strung-out prostitutes, gang wars, drug houses, senseless vandalism, crimes of whites against blacks and blacks against whites. And worst of all, the abused children, battered and bruised by the very people they wanted most to trust. Dan saw on their small round faces, in their young eyes, the same question over and again, "What kind of world is this anyway?"

Dan would cry when he came home at the end of the night shift, a quiet, controlled weeping as he related what he had seen. Another typical day on the job.

Mary didn't say these things out loud to Neil. Only, "I think all those years with the force wore him out."

Or tied him up. Or hardened him. Yes, that was it—he had eventually hardened just to survive. Another cop's wife—Nick's wife—had said to Mary once, "They build walls around themselves; they have to, in a job like this. How else are they going to keep on doing what they do?"

Walls, yes. After all, what was the alcoholism rate among cops? The divorce rate? The suicide rate? Sky high. But, Mary thought, if you built a wall around yourself, it was to protect who you were. It was an attempt to keep your essential self intact and untouched. Dan, then, hadn't built a wall. He had become the wall. He was hardened like stone. After too many years on the Cincinnati police force, Dan Beeken simply wasn't Dan Beeken anymore.

Neil said, "I've been acquainted with a couple of cops in Brooklyn. I don't know much, but I do know it's a tough job."

An understatement, Mary thought. "One of the worst things, I think, was when Dan's partner was shot. Dan had a partner named Oliver Ribnick; everyone called him Nick. They were really close, Dan and Nick. Like brothers." Mary paused long enough to laugh briefly. "Except that Dan's white and Nick was black. Not that that matters. But about three years ago when they were called to a robbery at a convenience store, Nick was shot. Dan blamed himself."

"Nick die?"

"No, thank God. But he was left paralyzed from a bullet to the spine. There's nothing left from the waist down. Of course, he'll never work again."

"So why does Dan blame himself?"

Mary thought a moment. "Because . . . I don't know. Most cops would blame themselves, I think. Especially someone like Dan. He's always thinking, If only I'd done this, or if only I'd done that. But there wasn't anything he could have done differently. Even an investigation into the shooting showed that."

Neil didn't press for details, saying simply, "I'm sorry to hear about that."

Mary sighed. She never thought she'd be telling Neil Sadler her husband's stories. Now that she'd started, she couldn't seem to stop. "And then there were the riots back in '01. Just a year after Nick was shot. You remember that big episode of rioting in Cincinnati?"

Neil nodded. "I remember reading about it in the paper."

On April 7, 2001, a black man ran from police as they pursued him through the dark, blighted streets of Over-the-Rhine. It was two in the morning, and he'd gone out to buy a pack of cigarettes. But before he could get back home again, Timothy Thomas was recognized by officers as someone who was wanted on more than a dozen outstanding warrants. Misdemeanor charges, all of them—traffic violations, driving without a license, failing to show up for court dates.

Five officers chased Thomas through the streets, over fences, in and out of alleys, until one finally shot him in the chest and killed him.

"The gun went off by accident," explained Officer Stephen Roach, a white man. That was his story, at least for a while. On further reflection, he said, "He reached toward his waistband, and I thought he had a gun." There, that sounded better. But no, wait. "I had my revolver out, and when Thomas came around the corner, he startled me and the gun went off."

Didn't matter, really. Whatever the story was, nineteen-year-old Timothy Thomas was just as dead. He'd been unarmed. It was just him, his waistband, and his pack of cigarettes up against a nine-millimeter semiautomatic in an unlit alley.

African Americans all over Cincinnati rose up and cried foul. Fifteenth killing of a black man by white police in six years. Something's wrong here. Police brutality. Trigger-happy cops. And—all too obvious—racial profiling.

The shooting death of Timothy Thomas brought about the worst racial violence in Cincinnati since the assassination of Martin Luther King Jr. in 1968. The week leading up to Easter Sunday 2001 saw three nights of rioting, looting, and vandalism. Dozens of protesters were injured and eight hundred arrested before the rioting stopped and an uneasy calm settled over Cincinnati.

Then in September, in spite of his varying accounts of the incident, Officer Roach was acquitted in the killing. And all the white cops took the fall, became the bad guys wearing badges, committing murder and getting away with it.

"That was the final straw," Mary said. "So one day Dan tells me that back in Mason the house next to his mom's is up for sale and he wants to buy it. He says to me, 'Back in Mason if you're a cop, all you have to do is hand out parking tickets and check on barking dogs and help old ladies who've locked their keys in their car.' And then he says, 'Mason doesn't even have one murder a year, you know.'" Mary paused, making a taut line of her mouth. "And I told him, 'Yes, I know.'" She looked at Neil.

He returned her gaze briefly before turning away. "So you bought the house and moved back."

"Yes, to get away from it all. To return to a quieter life. And in the beginning it was all right. I mean, there's lots of memories that are really hard, but there are people who have helped me out just by being kind. Like Grace, Uncle Bernie, Uncle Gene. They made it easier for me to come back. Do you know what I mean?"

"Yes. I know exactly what you mean."

"So for a while I thought things were going to be better for us than they were in Cincy. But now . . ."

Her voice trailed off. Her silence pulled Neil's eyes back to hers.

"And now," he finished for her, "someone has been killed in Mason, and it was Dan who shot him."

"Yeah." She shrugged helplessly. "Can you believe it?"

"But it was self-defense."

"That's what Dan claims."

"Don't you believe him?"

"I want to," she responded. "Of course there's a huge investigation going on. Dan's on administrative leave while everyone, including the BCI&I, try to figure out exactly what happened."

When Neil lifted his brows, she explained, "The Bureau of Criminal Identification and Investigation. To make things even messier, even though Dan's claiming self-defense, the wife of the man is saying it wasn't. She's saying Dan killed an unarmed man, and I hear she's planning a lawsuit."

Neil sighed heavily and shook his head. "How long will the investigation take?"

Mary shrugged. "I don't know. They say it could take weeks."

"And then what?"

"Depends on what they find out. There's not a separate set of rules for cops. If they kill someone and a jury says it's murder, they go to prison."

They had reached the line of trees at the end of the tractor path. They stopped and faced each other awkwardly. Neil stuck his hands in the pockets of his shorts.

"You'll have to trust the people doing the investigation," he said gently. "They'll find out what happened."

Mary remembered the mother of Timothy Thomas on the evening news after Officer Roach was acquitted. She had stood there on the courthouse steps, her face a mask of pain as she cried out to reporters, *"But I still don't know what the truth is."*

Mary lifted somber eyes to Neil. "Maybe. And maybe not."

She turned and started walking back toward the house. Neil strode beside her. "There's only one thing I know for sure," she said, stopping suddenly again and looking up once more at Neil. "Our lives are in a shambles when we don't know what the truth is."

They walked all the way back to the house in silence.

16

CALVIN SYFERT SWORE UP AND DOWN that he didn't kill his wife that summer day in 1977.

The evidence, however circumstantial, said that he did.

Even Cal's defense attorney, Earl Hoback, said he was hard put to plant reasonable doubt in the minds of a jury. Technically speaking, Calvin Syfert might be considered innocent until proven guilty, but it looked as though Joshua Bain, lead prosecutor on the case, was going to have smooth sailing toward a guilty verdict.

All this from something that, at first glance, appeared to be simply an accident. Neil should know. The first glance had been his.

It was the last weekend in June. The carnival had just opened over in Union Township. Neil spent all of Saturday there with his buddy Frank Hume. Mary was there too, with her friend Peggy Wirth. Sort of. Neil couldn't help noticing that Peg was intertwined with Mike Schwankl, the two of them walking everywhere with an arm around the other's waist, while Mary more or less stood off to the side, the third one out. Well, Neil was going to take care of that. He couldn't pair up with

Mary while Frank was there, making Frank the fifth wheel. But today, Sunday, he planned to go back to the carnival as soon as church was over, and he was going alone. No offense to Frank, who was heading out of town on a camping trip anyway.

Neil knew Mary was spending the night at Peg's and that he'd see the girls back at the carnival, most likely with Schwankl. Neil figured he could just happen to run into them and offer to make it a foursome. A double date of sorts. After all, Mary had just turned seventeen the week before, and Neil was nineteen, not a kid at all but a young man ready to strike out on his own. He'd be leaving for New York in the fall. Time to start making some decisions. Time to start thinking about whether he and Mary ought to be more than distant cousins by adoption and more than just friends.

Neil's dad had asked him to cut the lawn and trim the hedges around the house sometime before the weekend wound down. Neil elected to do it Sunday morning before church, to get it done so he'd be free to go to the carnival in the early afternoon. The trouble with Jim Sadler was that, though he worked with power tools on the job at Mason Lumber, he couldn't see his way to upgrading his lawn equipment at home. Neil still mowed the lawn with a hand mower, the kind with the long handle attached to the cutting cylinder. Sure, it was quiet and you didn't have to pay for gas, but they had to be the last family in Mason that didn't have a gasoline-powered mower. And to trim the hedges, the best Jim Sadler could offer was a pair of slightly rusted shears. Took forever to trim the hedges with those, and when you were done your arms were so tired, you could hardly lift them for an hour afterward.

Neil had an open invitation from Cal Syfert to come over anytime and borrow his lawn mower or his gas-powered hedge trimmer. Well, this being early Sunday morning and his not wanting to break the quiet, Neil cut the grass with the hand mower. But when he was ready to tackle the hedges, Neil drew the line. He was going to use Cal's hedge trimmer and save some time and energy. It might be noisy, but it was time for folks to wake up and start getting ready for church anyway.

Neil headed down Church Street, turning right onto N. East Street toward Main. The streets were hushed, the light a soft mist rising in the yet unbroken morning. Neil saw no one until he came to the Sinclair station. The station was closed, but Denton Patch was there, leaning up against a pump. He stood casually, his bad leg crossed over the good one, his arms at his sides. He was flexing his fingers, opening and closing his fists in a lethargic rhythm. He often did this, he said, to ward off the cold. His eyes, peering out from beneath a Cincinnati Reds cap, moved back and forth in the same slow rhythm, sweeping the street.

"Hey, Uncle Denton, what's up?" Neil called with a wave.

"Not much, Neil." Denton shrugged.

"Nothing happening?"

"Nothing to speak of. But you never know."

Neil chuckled to himself. Nothing ever happened in Mason. True, Rita Sadler had died earlier in the year, throwing everyone for a loop, especially Bernard Sadler. But even that would be considered part of the ordinary flow of life. Denton Patch, though, was in a whole other world, waiting to be ambushed by phantom soldiers that existed nowhere but in his own head.

"Yeah, well, see you in church, huh?" Neil called.

Denton nodded, shrugged his jacket up higher over his

shoulders, peered uneasily down the western side of Main Street.

Neil crossed Main, becoming aware of the birdsong and the newly blooming flower beds along the street. It was a day of gentle beauty, and that appealed to Neil. If he had time, he would have stopped, maybe sat on the front steps of the Syferts' house for a while, drinking it all in before the day opened up and the heat arrived and he lost this sense of quiet charm to the noisy excitement of the carnival. But he was in a hurry now. He couldn't stop and sit. He had to trim the hedges before church started in an hour.

Neil turned up the Syferts' drive and went around to the back of the house. The back door was always unlocked, but Neil knocked anyway. He thought Uncle Cal might be up by now, and he didn't want to simply walk in unannounced.

When there wasn't an answer, he knocked again softly so as not to disturb Helen. She would still be asleep. She never got up for church. She never got up for anything. She rarely left the house.

Neil cupped his face with his hands and pressed his forehead against the door's Plexiglas window. He didn't see any movement inside, no shadows in the kitchen to indicate that Uncle Cal was up fixing breakfast. Well, he would just slip in quietly, tiptoe down to the basement, and get the hedge trimmer. He knew exactly where it was. He could be in and out without waking up Uncle Cal or Aunt Helen. Mary, of course, was over at Peg's, probably just waking up herself and giggling with Peg about whatever it was girls giggled about together. Neil smiled a moment and felt anxious for the afternoon to arrive.

The back door opened noiselessly when Neil turned the

knob. He went in, shut the door behind him, then stepped lightly through the den and toward the basement door. That was the squeaky one. Uncle Cal was always talking about oiling the hinges, but he never did. Neil pulled the door open slowly, releasing the squeal as a low drawn-out moan, and stopped when the opening was wide enough for him to slip through. He felt along the wall at the top of the stairs for the light switch. The light in the basement popped on, and Neil started down.

But just as suddenly, he stopped, his right foot suspended over the second step, his right hand clutching the handrail, his left pressed flat against the opposite wall. He froze. He didn't breathe. There was a split second of confusion as his mind tried to make sense of what he saw. And then he felt something rising up in him that he had never known, not in all the years that his brother had talked of murder and Rebecca's ghost and the haunting of the Sadler house. That something was horror. Genuine horror.

She was lying on her back at the bottom of the stairs, her bare feet propped up on the bottom steps, her arms askew. Her head was at an odd angle, her neck bowed so that her ear almost lay against the right shoulder of her summery cotton nightgown. Her eyes were open, staring lifelessly up at the bare bulb overhead. Her walker lay on its side on the floor, several feet from her outstretched hand.

Neil thought, *Oh, but she's alive, of course. She must be. She's fallen and hurt herself.*

He moved down the steps, picking up speed as he went.

"Aunt Helen?" He didn't recognize his own voice, a quivering noise in the air.

He slowed down and stepped gingerly around her feet, then

133

kneeled on the cold cement beside her. "Helen?"

Her jaw was slack and her mouth hung open, as though she were trying to speak. But there were no words. Her skin and even her lips were white. And those eyes—two bloodshot orbs—stared right at him, unseeing.

Neil forced himself to touch her face, trembling fingers tentatively pressed against cold flesh. He jerked his hand away and wiped it, open palmed, against his jeans, trying to wipe away the icy feel of death. Because he knew that she was dead. He was seeing death in its barren state, without the undertaker's cosmetic touch. This was death, unadorned, and it was ugly.

"Uncle Cal!"

Neil stumbled up the steps, two at a time, and rushed into the bedroom where Cal Syfert slept.

"Uncle Cal, wake up! Helen's fallen down the stairs!"

The slumbering figure rolled over, murmured, "Neil? What is it?"

"Aunt Helen! She's at the bottom of the basement stairs. I think she's—"

Neil couldn't say the word, but Cal was already up, the sheet flung back on the bed as he rushed from the room. Neil followed him, watching as he raced down the stairs, his feet barely touching the steps. Neil stayed in the doorway, watching from above, as Cal, naked except for a pair of shorts, leaned over the body of his wife. Neil didn't know what he expected Cal to do—search for a pulse? Try to revive her? Run for the telephone extension by his workbench in the basement?

He did none of those things. Cal Syfert kneeled beside his dead wife and tenderly scooped her into his arms until her head rested in his lap. For a moment he stroked her hair. "Helen?" he whispered. He embraced her then, her body limp, unresponsive, moving in Cal's arms as he cradled her. "Helen. Oh, Helen."

And Neil thought, *Didn't you hear her fall in the night? How could you not have heard? Maybe if you'd come and helped her right away, you could have saved her.*

When Cal turned and looked up at Neil, his moist cheeks glistened under the glare of the light bulb. Neil noticed then the three red marks on his left cheek, three fresh scratches slicing through the small stubble of beard. Must have been the neighbors' cat again, Neil thought briefly, then realized how odd it was to wonder about three scratches on a man's cheek when a woman was dead.

Quietly, Cal said, "Neil, call the operator and ask for help."

Two police officers arrived first, heavy in their starched uniforms, stiff in their embodiment of the law. They crashed in on the scene, ignoring Neil, wearing their authority like expensive cologne, eager to get at the body.

One of the officers, after circling the scene, sniffing it out, went to call the coroner. The other officer squatted on the heel of one shiny black shoe, shook his head over the dead body, raised questioning eyes at the distraught husband. Sergeant Stu Hamilton had known Cal Syfert for a long time, had even worked with him briefly at Reading Manufacturing before changing directions and going into law enforcement. He liked Cal. But he'd been with the Mason police longer than he'd been on the assembly line. And his instincts told him now that there was something fishy about a crippled woman falling down the stairs in the middle of the night and her husband not even knowing about it.

He pulled a small notebook out of his back pocket and flipped it open. "I think you maybe better start telling us what happened, Cal." He clicked open a ballpoint pen and scratched the nib against the paper to get the ink flowing.

Then Stu Hamilton looked up at Cal and waited. Neil, at the top of the stairs, waited. Cal's mouth fell open, but no words came out. Slowly he shook his head. And that was the story that he stuck with right up to the end of his life.

17

MARY KNEW SOMETHING WAS WRONG that same Sunday morning when her aunt Vivian and uncle Henry, dressed for church, appeared instead at the front door of the Wirths' house and asked if they might speak with her alone. Mrs. Wirth, looking concerned, relayed the message to Mary, saying she wondered whether it had anything to do with the sirens they'd heard going off at the fire station not a half hour ago. The first thought that came to Mary's mind was something must have happened to Uncle Denton last night while he was out roaming through the cornfields in the dark.

She was still in her robe and slippers, her lips sticky sweet with the syrup she'd poured over a stack of blueberry pancakes. She left Peggy at the breakfast table with the casual promise that she'd be right back.

Stepping out onto the porch, she hugged her bathrobe more tightly around her, as though she were cold. Uncle Henry stood with his head bowed and his lower lip stuck out while Aunt Vivian dabbed at mascara-darkened tears.

"What is it, Aunt Viv?" she asked, trying to sound calm.

"There's been an accident, Mary," her aunt replied in a

faltering voice. "Your mother fell down the basement stairs in the night and—" she took a deep shuddering breath—"Mary, she's dead."

Mary cocked her head as she tried to take it in, and even before she fully understood, she felt something heavy, a long-time burden, tumble off her back and land with a thud at her heels.

"What was she doing walking around at night?" she asked. "She's never done that before."

Aunt Vivian shook her head while dabbing at her face with a crumpled tissue. "We don't know all the details yet, dear. Oh, Mary, I'm so sorry." She opened her arms, and Mary stepped into the offered embrace.

She knew she should cry. She knew she should be weeping on her aunt's perfumed shoulder. That's what daughters did when their mothers died. They wept bitterly at the loss. But Mary's eyes were dry, and there didn't seem to be any tears behind them. Instead, she marveled at the feeling of having come to the end of a long and tedious task. Yes, that was it. Her work was done. There would be no more nursing duties, no more medicine bottles, doctor appointments, trays of picked-over food, soiled sheets. No more rushing home to take care of her mother when she wanted to be with her friends. And perhaps best of all, no more walking into the sickroom, where the air was heavy and rank with her mother's anger and bitterness and self-pity. No more of any of that. Ever again.

She closed her eyes to imagine it, to take it all in. She knew she should be ashamed. Yes, of course, she was ashamed—her mother was dead, and the emotion that rushed in to fill her was relief. What kind of daughter was that? And yet, the freedom . . .

"Where's Dad, Aunt Viv?" she asked, pulling back from her aunt.

"At the house."

"Is he all right?"

"Shaken. He wants you to come home."

Mary wondered whether her father felt the same underlying relief that she was feeling. Maybe even the sense that he could start a new life now, one in which he wasn't tied down to an invalid. After all, an illness doesn't affect just one person, doesn't confine its crippling influence to just one soul. An illness can invade and weaken entire relationships, can't it? Cal Syfert had married an energetic young woman and ended up with an invalid, and somewhere in that slow deterioration, the marriage stops being a marriage, doesn't it?

Her father was lonely, had been lonely for years. That much Mary knew. She could see it in the way he sat at the kitchen table in the early morning, his eyes downcast while he sipped a cup of coffee before going to work. She could see it in the look on his face when he sat on the porch at night after a long day on the assembly line and an evening of taking care of Helen. He'd stare out at the street, quietly taking drags on a cigarette, seemingly watching for something that he knew would never come. Where was his satisfaction? Certainly not in his work. Certainly not in his marriage. And what else was there in life?

The thought of her father brought tears to her eyes. And she was glad that she was crying. She ought to be crying for someone.

"Let's go home, then," she said.

———

139

Some days later Mary stood beside her mother's open casket at the funeral home. The service would be starting shortly, and she was supposed to be saying good-bye. But instead, she was remembering an evening, only a couple weeks or so ago, when her mother had said, "Sit down a minute, Mary."

"What do you need, Mom?"

"Nothing. Just to talk."

Talk?

Mary sat on the edge of her mother's bed. Helen was propped up on pillows, looking tired and bland in the same faded cotton gown she'd worn on summer nights for years. Mary sighed inwardly and asked, "What's the matter, Mom?"

Helen smiled wanly. "You've turned into a lovely young woman, Mary."

Mary shrugged, feeling uncomfortable. What was her mother getting at? Was this some attempt at explaining the birds and the bees, the requisite mother-daughter facts-of-life lecture? It was too late for that. Mary knew all about sex, had got the details from Peg, who had got them from her older sister. Or maybe Helen Syfert was simply taking a stab at having a real conversation, a genuine heart-to-heart with her daughter.

Well, it was too late for that too.

Mary waited.

"I so want to see you grow up and get married," Helen said. "I want to see my grandchildren."

Oh, that was it. Another pity party. Helen Syfert feeling sorry for herself and inviting her daughter to join in. Well, no thanks. Mary wasn't interested.

"Don't worry, Mom," she said flatly. "You'll be around for all that."

She started to rise, but Helen grabbed her hand. Mary was surprised to see her mother's eyes fill with tears. "You don't understand," Helen said in a voice thick with emotion. "Your father doesn't want me here. I'm just a burden." She shut her eyes and moaned softly. "Mary, I'm so afraid. He'd just as soon see me dead."

Mary was shocked and at once defensive. "Mom, how can you say that about Dad?"

"It's true—"

"It *isn't* true. That's ridiculous. He's never once said anything like that."

Helen let go of Mary's hand. She sighed and settled herself down among the pillows. "I'm going to sleep now."

Mary rose, her gaze fixed on her mother's face. *Crazy old woman,* she thought. *Crazy, pitiful old woman.*

Helen Syfert looked better in her coffin than she had in her sickbed. She wore a cream-colored dress of eyelet material. Her hair, freshly washed and curled, framed her face like a dark halo. Lipstick, powder, blush, and eye shadow brought life, oddly enough, to her face. Her favorite pearl earrings were clipped to her ears, the matching pearl necklace circled her neck. She almost looked pretty again, and as though, if she were to wake up, she wouldn't be sick anymore.

The only thing missing, Mary noticed, were her wedding rings. It hadn't been a marriage in the end, but still, a woman ought to be buried with her diamond and her gold band.

"Dad?"

"Yes, Mary?"

"Where's—"

"Excuse me, Mr. Syfert. Can I see you a moment before the service begins?"

Her father went off with the funeral director, and Mary, frowning, turned back to her mother. Oh well. Helen wouldn't know one way or the other, and besides, she'd hardly worn the rings in years. Just kept them tucked away in her jewelry box, as though they meant little to her. They might as well belong to Mary now, though what she'd do with them she couldn't imagine.

Mary looked over her shoulder. People had begun arriving. The folding chairs were beginning to fill up. Around the room pockets of so-called mourners spoke among themselves in hushed and solemn tones, clicked their tongues, and shook their heads. They expected a large crowd today, not because the deceased was Helen Syfert, but because the deceased had been murdered.

"Coroner Rules Death a Homicide," the headline had read. The death was no accident, the coroner decided. Helen Syfert had not died of injuries resulting from a fall. The petechial hemorrhages in her eyes, her face, her lungs—these told a different story. Her oxygen had been cut off, and she was dead before she ever reached the bottom of the stairs. The probable scenario was that she'd been smothered with a pillow, then her body carried to the stairs and tossed down.

I just can't believe it, Mary thought while gazing at her mother's face. *Who in the world would want to kill Helen Syfert?*

That's what the police were asking, of course. The police were all riled up like a swarm of angry bees, and they were buzzing all over town, searching for clues and questioning people. They'd interviewed her father a half dozen times already.

"Let's go over this one more time, Mr. Syfert. Tell us in your own words what happened the night your wife died."

"But I already told you, I don't know what happened. I just don't know what happened."

They had even asked the question of Mary.

"Do you have any idea—any idea at all—of who might want to see your mother dead?"

"No, I have no idea. I can't believe anyone *would want her dead."*

"Did your mother have any enemies?"

"No, of course not!"

It was crazy! Her mother had fallen down the stairs and broken her neck, and now the police had made their home a crime scene and they were searching for a nonexistent killer. Mary knew there was no killer. It was the coroner who was wrong, the guy who did the autopsy. He was just as wrong as all the doctors who couldn't figure out for years what was ailing her mother. They'd gone through half a dozen doctors and half a dozen diagnoses before they learned that she had multiple sclerosis. So even in death her mother had a way of confusing the doctors. Someday they'd get the story straightened out, and then maybe she and her dad could live in peace.

Mary heard Uncle Bernie's voice coming from somewhere, and suddenly organ music wafted up from a speaker on the floor, half hidden by a floral arrangement. The service was starting. It was time now to say good-bye to her mother.

"I wish everything could have been different for you, Mom," she whispered. "And I want you to know that I really did . . ." She paused, pursed her lips. "I really did want to love you."

She felt her father's hand come to rest on her shoulder. She was looking forward to getting all this over with and going home.

18

Two more hours, Mary thought. Two more hours before she could clock out at the florist shop and go home. She wondered what was in the refrigerator that she could turn into supper for herself and Leo. Dan would most likely be going down to Cincinnati tonight to hang out with Nick and some of the other cops he used to work with, just as he did every Tuesday night. And sometimes Thursday night. And sometimes several nights a week. It didn't matter that today was her birthday. She didn't want to think about that anyway.

She was watering the potted marigolds when the front door opened abruptly, startling the bell overhead. Mary was startled too to see Dan enter the shop. He was carrying a bag; not a brown paper shopping bag but one of those colorful gift bags that they sold down at Yost's for a couple of dollars.

"Mary, listen," Dan said quickly, striding toward her. "You probably thought I forgot . . ."

His voice tapered off. He stood face-to-face with Mary, the bag and the watering can suspended in the air between them.

"Here," he said lamely. "It isn't much but . . ."

"That's all right, Dan." She smiled gently, accepting the gift.

"I should have said something earlier, happy birthday or something—I don't know. I've had a lot on my mind."

"It's okay, really. It doesn't matter." She looked at the gift bag in her hand, lifted it up slightly. "Thanks," she said.

"Like I said, it isn't much. But listen, there's a card. . . ."

Mary waited. But Dan was disinclined to finish his sentences at the moment. She set both the bag and the watering can down on the counter and pulled the card out of the unsealed envelope. On the front was a smiling young couple—younger than she and Dan—and words in a flowing typeface, *Happy Birthday, to the best wife in the world.*

Mary raised her eyes to Dan, to that all-familiar face. She knew every inch of that face, every crease and line, every expression—the pained frown, the questioning furrowed brow, the small intense mouth. And the eyes: two blue disks emblazoned with yellow flecks like shards of sunlight in two circles of sky. In the beginning she couldn't look at that face without recalling a phrase she'd stumbled upon once: a historian had described the brotherhood among battle-weary soldiers as a fierce male tenderness. It was a phrase Mary had understood at once. In Dan she saw the savage strength and the gentle tenderness that both rest easily in a good man's soul.

Mary opened the card and read the Hallmark poem inside.

You're the very best, hon,
You're tops in every way.
That's why you deserve
The very best today.
Happy Birthday!

He had signed it, *Love, Dan.*

Mary slipped the card back into the envelope. She smiled

at Dan. "It's beautiful. Thank you."

When he had first told her, all those years ago, what he wanted to do with his life, he hadn't used the word cop or policeman. What he had said was peace officer.

"I want to be a peace officer." Because that's what it was all about for him—keeping the peace. Making life better for people. Keeping people safe, helping them out. "You can do a lot of good when you're a peace officer."

Dan's uncle, a twenty-year veteran on the Cincy force, tried to tell Dan it was tough, warned him not to glamorize it. "We're not out there playing Starsky and Hutch, you know. You're gonna see the worst of the worst. You're gonna see even worse than the worst."

Dan only laughed. "Yeah, well, I hope so," he answered confidently. "Those are the people I want to help."

How she had loved him once! She tried now to find in that face the Dan Beeken she had loved, the Dan he had been when they were eighteen, nineteen, twenty years old, the Dan that had embodied the fierce, protective male tenderness that she adored. But it was gone, the tenderness. Squeezed out by the relentless hardening required for survival.

"There's something in the bag," Dan said. "Just some chocolates."

"Oh!" Mary carefully tore the wrapping off the box, a Whitman's Sampler. "Well, thanks."

"Listen, about tonight—"

"You going to Nick's?"

"Yeah, I'm heading out right now. Ace is going to be there too. I haven't seen him in a while."

"Sure. Tell him I said hi."

"I'll make it up to you, Mary. Friday—dinner maybe?"

"Don't worry about it. You know I'm not big on birthdays."

"Well, we'll do something," he promised.

"Sure. Whatever. Have a good time."

"I'll be home late."

"Okay. I won't wait up." She tried to laugh a little but failed.

He took one step back, but for a moment he seemed frozen between saying good-bye and leaving.

She waited.

"Listen, Mary," he offered quietly. "I'm sorry . . ."

Another unfinished sentence. Mary shook her head, smiled solemnly. "It's all right, Dan. Really. I don't feel much like celebrating anyway."

"Well, I don't mean about your birthday. I just mean . . . everything." He took a deep breath, then sighed heavily. "Everything."

Like how his being a peace officer had sucked all the peace right out of their own lives. Mary knew. He didn't have to say the words.

"It's all right, Dan," she said again. "Tell Trish I'll call her soon."

"Yeah. Yeah, maybe on Friday we can go to Cincy together, see Nick and Trish at their place."

"Sure. Yeah, maybe. That'd be fine."

He stepped forward awkwardly and planted a kiss on her cheek, then left the shop.

Mary looked down at the box of chocolates in her hand. She felt as though she could weep. It was silly, of course, such a small thing, and yet, after twenty-three years of marriage it seemed a husband ought to know that the woman he was married to didn't like chocolates.

19

NEIL KNOCKED ON THE plate-glass window of the florist shop and waved as Mary looked up. When she smiled at him, he couldn't help but laugh out loud. He felt oddly happy.

Earlier that afternoon he had stopped scraping away at old wallpaper long enough to go downstairs and pour himself a glass of iced tea. Wandering into the ballroom, he found ten-year-old Scot playing the piano while his sisters, Lila and Lacey, danced freestyle to the music in their pink leotards and ballet slippers. Scot, with one year of lessons behind him, was attempting to play a tune that Neil didn't recognize. It was a hit-or-miss performance, painstakingly slow, with Scot's eyes bouncing like twin Ping-Pong balls between the sheet music and the keyboard. The girls, their dance as choppy as the tune, laughed their way through a series of twirls, leaps, kicks, pirouettes, and grand pliés.

The scene captivated Neil as he watched the children in their simple and spontaneous joy. For the first time since Caroline's death, he felt that he had stepped into a small space where he himself, like the children, was completely satisfied. Their childish glee gave him a sudden and unexpected taste of goodness, a reminder of something he had once known.

For as long as Neil could remember, the ballroom had been a place of celebration. During the drawn-out winters of his youth, when the farm lay frozen and the landscape was bleak, Uncle Tom and Aunt Sarah held lavish parties here for the extended families. All the women, working together, put on a spread with something for everyone and more besides. Tables were piled high with steaming casseroles, platters of fried chicken, corn on the cob, mashed potatoes, scalloped potatoes, homemade breads and jams, corn muffins, cranberry sauce, salads of all kinds, jars of pickles made from the cucumbers of a dozen gardens. And the desserts! Apple, cherry, pumpkin, lemon meringue pies, cakes and cookies and cupcakes and homemade fudge and ice cream.

Uncles, aunts, grandparents, in-laws, cousins—anyone connected in any way to the Sadler family and even a few people who weren't—came from as many as four counties to enjoy these gatherings. Even Uncle Denton called a truce with the Chinese long enough to come and join in the festivities. They all ate until they were full, and then they ate some more—just one more bite of this or that while explaining with a laugh, "It's all too good to pass up."

Some of the men then moved over to the library to smoke cigars and play checkers or poker while the rest of the family stayed in the ballroom to chat and laugh and dance and maybe have even one more bite. Uncle Tom piled up albums on the spindle shaft of his record player so that when one record finished the next one started right up. He played mostly Big Band music like Glenn Miller and Tommy Dorsey and Duke Ellington, but sometimes he gave in to the younger folks and put on Jim Croce and Elton John and Creedence Clearwater Revival.

And John Denver, since even the older folks enjoyed "Thank God I'm a Country Boy." Other times Uncle Alvin Primrose, husband of Susannah Sadler, brought his fiddle along and played with amazing energy far into the night. That got the family going like mountain folk at an old-fashioned hoe-down—clapping, stomping, do-si-doing till they were exhausted from the dancing and the belly laughs both. And for Neil, nothing mattered then, not one single thing beyond the delight of the present moment.

He remembered a certain Christmas party, must have been 1973. Everyone was all decked out in suits and dresses. At fifteen he felt a little awkward in his starched white shirt and carefully creased pants. He wore his hair long then, below the ears, but unlike some of the guys in his class, at least he kept it clean.

"Why don't you get a haircut?" his dad chided. "Long hair is for sissies."

"All the guys have long hair these days, Dad." In case you hadn't noticed.

"Jerry doesn't. And you shouldn't either."

Yeah, well, Jerry was Jerry and Neil was Neil, and he was going to be who he was, no matter what his dad thought. Besides, Uncle Cal liked his hair. He'd said so.

Uncle Alvin was there, standing by the fireplace with its snapping flames, playing Christmas carols on his fiddle. Neil's sense of awkwardness melted away as soon as Uncle Alvin smiled at him. He grabbed a plate and headed for the food, and that was when Mary entered the room with Uncle Cal and Aunt Helen. And when Neil saw her, he paused with his hand over a wicker basket of hot biscuits and thought, *Balls of fire! She looks like a girl!*

Mary wore a green velvet dress with a black sash around the waist that was tied into a huge bow in back. Her long legs, covered in black fishnet stockings, ended in a pair of shiny patent leather shoes—with heels! Her soft brown curls were held back from her face by a black headband that matched the sash of her dress. Even from across the room Neil could see that she'd painted her fingernails and colored her lips with a peculiar shade of red that looked amazingly appealing on her young and newly blooming face.

And Neil, used to a rough-and-tumble kid who could swing on a rope out of the hayloft with the best of them, thought, *She'd even look kind of pretty if you didn't know she was Mary.*

Thirteen-year-old Mary stepped into the ballroom and noticed Neil there with his outstretched hand not quite touching a biscuit, and she smiled at him. Shyly. And he smiled back.

And that was the point during his reminiscing that something bubbled up in his conscious mind and told him that Mary's birthday was in June, and if he was remembering right, he had just missed it.

"Mary!" he said now as he entered the florist shop and moved swiftly toward her.

"Well, hi, Neil," she replied in genuine surprise. She gave him a quick up-and-down look, laughed, and said, "Grace really has put you to work, hasn't she?"

His T-shirt and workman's overalls were sticky with solvent and freckled with bits of wallpaper. After glancing at himself, he looked up sheepishly and said, "Yeah, I guess I didn't take time to clean up. I wanted to catch you. I called your house, and Leo said you were here."

"Yeah." She waved a hand at an open box of chocolates by the cash register. "They're for the customers. Help yourself."

"Hey, thanks." He pulled a dark cream from its wrapper and popped it into his mouth. "Listen," he said, "I missed your birthday yesterday, so I just wanted to say happy birthday."

"Oh!" Mary smiled. "Thanks, but actually you didn't miss it. It's today."

Neil's eyebrows peaked. "Even better, then." He grinned. "I'm not such a schlep as I thought. Though"—he turned his hands palm out at his side—"I didn't even bring you a card or anything."

"Well, good grief, Neil, I didn't expect you to remember at all. I don't think I—"

He jumped in, not noticing her unfinished sentence. "Well, if *today's* your birthday, I'm glad I drove over and caught you before you go out tonight."

She shook her head and laughed indifferently. "Oh no," she said, "no big plans for tonight."

"You're not going to celebrate?"

"No, not really." She shrugged. "In fact, I was just thinking about what to make Leo for dinner."

"You can't cook on your birthday."

"And why not?" She laughed again, loudly this time.

"Because it's your *birthday*," he repeated.

"Yeah, well, that's hardly an excuse for not feeding your family."

Neil reached for another chocolate to give himself a moment to think. It wasn't often that he felt something like happiness, and he wanted to prolong the moment. He wanted to go on feeling happy, and he wanted Mary to be happy too. "Listen, instead of you cooking, how about you and me and Leo having dinner out? My treat," he suggested suddenly. "I

remember a really good place up on Broadway in Lebanon—"
Neil stopped.

Mary was actually smiling. "The Village Ice Cream Parlor,"
she finished for him. "I haven't been there in ages."

He chuckled. "Actually, I was thinking of the Golden
Lamb. You know, the place where presidents dine. But, hey, if
you want ice cream, that's fine. That's probably what Leo
would prefer too."

"Yes." Mary stopped, her eyes darting to the side. "But I
just remembered." She looked back at Neil. "Leo's got a game
of basketball lined up with some of his friends later this evening."

"So can he get out of it?"

She shook her head. "He'd rather die than get out of a
game. But, hey, thanks anyway. I appreciate the offer."

"Well." He knew he should let it drop. What business did
he have taking a married woman out on her birthday, even if
she was his cousin? That was her husband's place. But then
again, where was the guy? Where was Dan Beeken on his wife's
birthday? Stewing in his juices as usual over at McNulty's so
that his wife had to spend her special day alone? Yeah, well
then, "Listen, it's a Sadler tradition to celebrate birthdays. You
can't break tradition now. When Leo goes to his game, let's you
and I run up to the Village and grab a bite, okay?"

Mary's smile evaporated then, and she looked uncertain.
Neil knew he had said the wrong thing. He wished he could
take the words back, wished he had left well enough alone. He
thought quickly. He could offer her some sort of escape hatch,
some way to politely decline—again—and then they could
both simply go on and pretend that he'd never made such an
offer.

Before he could get the words off his tongue, though, Mary brightened and said, "Tell you what. I'll have Leo's grandmother give him some dinner. She won't mind. And then you and I can just go on to the Village."

"Um," Neil hedged. He was surprised, caught off guard by her response. "Okay, great." Wondering what he had done, he knew it was too late to back out. He glanced down at his clothes again. "Well, I'll have to clean up. What if I pick you up at seven?"

He watched Mary draw in a deep breath, then smile again. "Yeah. Seven," she said, exhaling a sigh that sounded oddly satisfied. "That sounds fine."

"Good. Okay." He started backing up toward the door. "Sure you wouldn't prefer the Golden Lamb?"

"No." She smiled. "I'm in the mood for a burger and a sundae."

"I just hope their burgers are as good as they used to be," he said with a laugh.

"Guess we'll find out," she called to him as he opened the door and waved.

Neil exited the shop, amused and perplexed by the turn of events. He'd come to offer Mary belated birthday wishes, and now he was taking her to the Village Ice Cream Parlor for something to eat. It wasn't a date of course, but still, he marveled that his forty-five-year-old body suddenly felt fifteen again.

20

"ARE YOU CRAZY OR JUST STUPID?" Mary asked herself as she climbed the steps to her mother-in-law's front door. Or maybe it was something else.

"People get lonely, Mare. Men, women—we get lonely. Makes a person do funny things."

Mary paused midstep and shut her eyes a moment. She hadn't heard her father's words, her father's voice, in . . . she didn't know how long. And she didn't want to think of him now. Not right now.

The front door was open to let in a breeze, and the storm door, Mary knew, would be unlocked. A person could still do that in Mason, Ohio. "Mom?" Mary called through the screen.

"In the kitchen, dear."

Letting herself in, she walked through the living room to the kitchen, where her mother-in-law stood at the table arranging fresh daffodils in a vase.

Sylvia Beeken looked up and smiled. "Well, you caught me in the act, Mary. These are for you, straight from my garden. Happy birthday."

Mary returned the smile. "Thanks, Mom. They're beautiful."

"It's the least I can do for my favorite daughter-in-law." It was a running joke between them, one of endearment. Mary was Sylvia's only daughter-in-law. Sylvia had two daughters, both married, who lived out of state.

"And this too." Sylvia reached for a small package on the kitchen counter. Mary opened it to find a hardcover book by a British novelist, Mary's favorite. "It's her newest," Sylvia went on. "I hope you don't have it already."

"I don't, but I've been meaning to buy it. Thanks so much!" At least the mother knew what Mary liked, even if the son didn't. She gave Sylvia a hug and kissed her cheek. It had taken her years to get used to such intimacy, as she had touched her own mother only to help her bathe or to rub her numb feet. But Sylvia was a hugger, and Mary had been folded into those matronly arms right from the beginning.

"I was just about to carry these over to your house," Sylvia said. "I figured you'd be off work by now. Are you looking for Leo?"

"No, he's home, I think. But the reason I stopped by was to ask if you'd mind feeding him tonight while I go out for a couple hours."

"Mind? Of course not, dear. You know I'd be glad to. I'd have that boy move right in with me if I could just persuade you to let him go." She laughed unconvincingly, and Mary knew what was coming next. She had heard her mother-in-law say it a thousand times in that singsong way of hers. "I'm just an old mother hen in an empty nest with no one to take under my wing, you know!"

Mary smiled but with little empathy. Sylvia Beeken knew what it was to be alone by herself, but she didn't know what it was to be alone in a marriage. And that, as far as Mary was concerned, was a far deeper loneliness.

"You know, Mom," she said, trying to sound lighthearted, "he'd probably move over here in a heartbeat if he thought it meant eating your cooking every day instead of mine."

Sylvia nodded, her eyes twinkling.

She *was* a good cook, and Mary knew how she appreciated the occasional compliment.

"Tell Leo to come on over," Sylvia said. "Where are you and Dan going?"

Mary wavered for a moment, wondering how it would sound to her mother-in-law. But then, it wasn't her fault, was it, that she wasn't celebrating her birthday with Dan? She would have, if he'd offered to take her somewhere.

"Dan's on his way down to Cincy—to see Nick. It's Tuesday, you know, and some of the guys . . ."

Sylvia frowned visibly and leaned her head to one side. "He's going to see Nick on your birthday?"

Mary waved a hand. "Listen, Mom, don't worry about it. I told him to go and have a good time. I don't mind."

"But you're not going out by yourself, are you?"

"Oh no. I'm just going to grab a burger with Neil." She could tell from the look on Sylvia's face that this wasn't going well. "Neil Sadler. My cousin. Neil's my cousin. He lives in New York, but he's in town for a while."

Then, to Mary's relief, the older woman's face brightened with recognition. "Oh yes, I remember. You've mentioned him. That artist fellow who's come back for the summer to help with the bed-and-breakfast."

"Yes, that's him. We thought we'd run up to the Village and grab a burger and ice cream."

"That sounds like fun, dear." Sylvia was tying an apron

around her ample waist. She bent into a cupboard and pulled out some pans. "I just can't imagine Dan . . . but then—" She stood and looked Mary in the eye. "He hasn't really been himself lately, has he?"

Mary took a breath, let it out. "It's been tough, Mom. This whole thing with Traylor—"

"I know. I know." Sylvia waved a hand. "God knows for years I've worried about Dan getting shot. I never bothered to think much about the other side of the coin. I don't know why he couldn't have followed his father and hired on at Reading. I know he had bigger dreams, but, well, at least people aren't shooting at each other when all you're doing is working the line." Again she tried to smile, but the corners of her mouth trembled and her eyes had glazed over.

"Mom," Mary said, laying a hand on Sylvia's arm, "it's going to be all right. They're going to discover it happened just the way Dan says it did. It was self-defense, and that's all there is to it."

"You and I and Dan know that, but he told me what that Traylor woman is up to. That's all we need now—a lawsuit to deal with. As if things aren't bad enough without it."

"I know, but just remember, the suit hasn't been filed yet. It's just talk at this point."

"Well, dear, talk is deadly in a small town like this. Talk can have you tried and convicted before you ever set foot in a courtroom."

"I know, Mom. I really do."

The two women stood in silence for a moment. Mary knew Sylvia was thinking of Dan, but it was her father that Mary was remembering. Her father, who had been tried and convicted before . . . well, probably before he was even arrested.

Finally Sylvia said, "You think Leo would like spaghetti?"

"He'd love spaghetti, Mom."

"I'd better set the water to boil, then."

Mary kissed her mother-in-law's cheek, gathered her gifts, then went next door to her own house to get ready for Neil. My cousin Neil, she said to herself. My distant cousin, by adoption. That was all.

"People get lonely, Mare. . . . Makes a person do funny things."

21

In the first days after his arrest, Cal Syfert felt his stomach drop whenever he was summoned from his cell to meet with his attorney. He knew he was in trouble the first time the guard punctuated his announcement of the lawyer's arrival with a snicker. It seemed Cal's public defender was a source of amusement for the employees of the Warren County Jail.

Earl Hoback was a matchstick of a man—small of stature, slight of build, short of fuse. It might have been his lack of size that contributed to his explosive temper, or he might have simply been naturally inclined to burst into flame at the slightest friction, but either way, Earl Hoback was famous for being small and fiery.

By 1977 Hoback had twelve years in the public defender's office under his tooled-leather belt. He was a man with no sense of fashion, which meant that his clothes really did define him. He took advantage of the current fashion trend of platform shoes to add a couple of inches to his height, but it was an attempt that worked to his disadvantage. According to the joke making the rounds among the jailhouse guards, the platform shoes made Earl Hoback look like a monkey on stilts. On top of that, his neckties were in constant disagreement with his suits. His shirts often had screaming matches with his ties. He wore narrow ties with suits with wide lapels, wide ties with polyester leisure suits, and no ties with wide-collared short-sleeved shirts that he left unbuttoned down to his hairless breastbone. His '50s flattop was directly at odds with his '70s sideburns. His diamond pinkie ring clashed with his cheap Timex watch. His horn-rimmed glasses, a holdover from the '60s, were in direct dispute with the entire present decade, and the peace symbol medallion he sometimes wore seemed blatantly out of step with his advancing middle age. All in all, Earl Hoback appeared outwardly as a man engaged in an ongoing battle with himself.

He was not the kind of public defender Cal Syfert would have chosen for himself. He was certainly not the polished and pragmatic-looking defense attorney Cal would have hired had he the money to hire one. But Cal, not one to complain, had accepted the decision of the court and placed his fate into the hands of the unfashionable and uninspiring but otherwise self-assured Earl Hoback.

"It doesn't look pretty," Hoback said at the start of his initial meeting with Cal, and it actually took Cal a moment to realize that Hoback wasn't talking about himself but about the case.

Hoback snapped open his briefcase and pulled out a file folder. Pushing the briefcase aside, he opened the folder on the stark table in the stark meeting room of the Warren County Jail. He paused a moment—a bit dramatically, Cal thought—before saying, "Here's what we've got." He peered at Cal over the rim of his glasses, then looked back down.

"Listen," Cal interrupted, "before you get into all that, let me ask you something, okay?"

"Sure. Fire away."

"What are my chances of being found not guilty by a jury of—how do they put it—a jury of my peers?"

Cal was immediately put off by Hoback's frown.

"That depends on you, Cal," the lawyer explained. "On how much you're willing to cooperate with me."

Nodding slightly as though in agreement, Cal said, "But I'm not sure it has anything at all to do with me at this point, Mr. Hoback."

"What do you mean?"

"I mean . . ." He paused. He couldn't help sniffing out a small sarcastic laugh. "I'm a celebrity now, you know? I'm the talk of the town. Everybody's talking about Cal Syfert."

Hoback shrugged. "That's to be expected."

"Yeah, well, the thing is, I've already been tried and found guilty."

When Hoback didn't respond, Cal went on, "You read the papers, Mr. Hoback?"

"Of course."

"Then you've seen the editorials, the letters to the editor. They're saying it's an open-and-shut case. I ought to just confess and save the taxpayers the cost of a trial."

"I'd suggest you avoid the papers for a while."

"Doesn't matter if I do. They're still going to be saying the same thing."

"Listen, Cal, forget it. Someone's murdered, people talk. That's the way it is. Let's build your case."

"Mr. Hoback?"

"Yes?" Impatient sigh.

"You think I murdered my wife?"

Hoback made a V with his hands and tapped at his bottom lip. "What I think is irrelevant," he finally replied.

"It is?" Cal didn't try to hide his surprise.

"I'm your defense attorney. I'm here to get you off the hook."

"Okay. But . . ." Cal gazed at Earl Hoback, trying to read his expression. He decided whatever was there was indecipherable. "I don't know, Mr. Hoback, but I think I'd feel better if I knew you believed me."

His lawyer sighed again, dropped the V, and began sifting through the papers on the table. Something about his manner didn't sit right with Cal.

"I'd like to take a polygraph." Cal had wanted to sound stern, but he knew he failed. He knew he sounded just the way he felt—afraid.

Hoback looked up. "Sure, you can do that. But it won't help your case."

"Why not?"

"Polygraphs aren't admitted as evidence in a trial."

"Why not?"

"They're not reliable."

"Then what good are they?"

Hoback stopped shuffling papers, leaned forward, settled his small dark eyes on Cal. It made Cal shudder. "Listen, with all due respect, I'm not here to tutor you in the American justice system. I'm here to defend you. You're in deep trouble, friend."

"That much I've grasped on my own, Mr. Hoback."

"What you don't know yet is that the district attorney's office is going after a first-degree-murder indictment. They're taking it to the grand jury in a couple of days."

"First degree?"

"Yeah."

"Right now I'm facing second, right?"

"That's right. But chances are good the prosecutor's going to come away with what he wants."

"And that's first degree?"

"Yes."

Cal was quiet a moment. Then he said, "We got the death penalty back in this state now?"

He watched his lawyer nod curtly. "Yeah, we do."

Cal paused, then said, "Okay. So what's that mean for me?"

Hoback exhaled until Cal thought he might deflate completely.

"To get death in Ohio," he said at length, "the indictment would have to include a specification of aggravating circumstances."

"Okay. So?"

"In your case, that's not likely."

"But it's possible?"

"To tell you the truth, I wouldn't put anything past Joshua Bain. He happens to like the death penalty. He probably missed it when it was off the books. But, listen, even if he goes for death, that doesn't mean he'll get it."

"But he might try."

A lift of the shoulders. "He might."

Cal Syfert fell silent.

"I didn't kill my wife," he said at length.

"Okay, Cal."

"I want you to believe that."

"Like I said, what I believe or don't believe has no bearing on this case. I'm here to defend you. That's my job."

"Yeah, well, I'd feel a whole lot better if I knew you believed me."

Hoback impatiently jabbed at his glasses with one index finger, pushing them farther up his narrow nose. "Listen, we're going to get you out of this mess, but you've got to work with me. Let me tell you how it's looking right now."

"All right."

Hoback picked up the papers and read silently to himself. Watching his lawyer, Cal felt as though the molecules of his body were breaking apart and that in the next moment he might explode, or he might simply disintegrate, pieces of himself settling like dust over the room.

He tried to concentrate as Hoback said, "The coroner has determined conclusively that your wife was murdered."

"Uh-huh." He felt the molecules drifting farther apart.

"She was smothered and was already dead by the time she was tossed down the basement stairs."

Cal winced. "Uh-huh." *Keep it together, Syfert.*

"Near as the coroner can determine, the time of her death was approximately ten o'clock on the night of June 25."

Cal nodded. He took a deep breath.

"Now, what you don't know yet is that the results just came back this morning from the lab, and I'm afraid it's the most solid evidence against you that Joshua Bain has to date."

"You mean the blood and skin under her nails?"

"Yes. The ethnicity of the skin was determined to be that of a Caucasian—" he glanced up—"that is, a white person—"

"I know what Caucasian means, Mr. Hoback."

"And the blood type—AB negative. That matches yours,

Cal. Chances of having AB negative blood are about one in fifty thousand."

"So you're saying the skin and blood under Helen's fingernails are mine."

"That's what the lab says."

Cal laughed out loud. The lab report was as good as a joke, and that gave him a temporary reprieve in his coming apart. "Well, they could have saved the taxpayers some money right there. They didn't have to be sending those samples off to the lab. Of course that skin was mine. I told you that before. She went crazy on me, Hoback. I'm putting her to bed, getting her settled down for the night, and next thing I know she's screaming and hollering and clawing at me. Scratched my face so it bled. I don't know what got into her, but that's what happened."

Earl Hoback remained expressionless. "When we come to trial, that's not how the prosecutor is going to portray it."

"But that's how it was."

"Joshua Bain's going to say otherwise. He'll say your wife was trying to defend herself—"

"Against me?"

"Yes, against you. He'll say she was fighting for her life while you were suffocating her."

"All I was doing was putting her to bed, same as always, when she blew up on me."

"And why would she do that?"

"It was sheer craziness. She was angry at me, angry at the world. She was sick, Mr. Hoback."

It might have been the light, but to Cal, Earl Hoback appeared to be turning red. Finally Hoback said, "When someone is murdered, Cal, the prosecutor gets busy looking for a motive."

"So you're saying I have a motive for killing my wife?"

"Not me. Bain. He says you have a motive."

"And what's that?"

Hoback shrugged. "Your wife's an invalid, a burden. It'd be nice to be free of her."

"That's no reason to kill a person."

Hoback shrugged again. "Some might argue otherwise."

"Well, I didn't kill Helen because she was a burden! I'm telling you, my wife is dead because someone killed her, but that someone isn't me. They got the wrong man here, Mr. Hoback. Whoever killed her is still out there."

"There are no signs that an intruder entered your house on the night of your wife's death."

"And?"

"No signs of a break-in—"

"We usually leave the back door unlocked."

"No fingerprints other than those you'd expect to find—"

"So maybe he was wearing gloves."

"No tracks in the yard."

"There must have been footprints, shoe prints, something."

"Nothing unaccounted for."

Cal didn't like the way his lawyer was staring at him, like he was waiting for something.

When Cal didn't respond, Hoback added, "Nothing appears to have been stolen."

"Wait a minute," Cal said, suddenly remembering. "My daughter says she can't find Helen's wedding rings."

"Yeah, and Mary told *me* her mother rarely wore the rings and that the two of you don't necessarily know where she might have kept them. They may be in the house somewhere, and you don't know where. Is that right?"

Cal nodded reluctantly. "We thought sure they'd be in the jewelry box, but they weren't."

"Does that mean you're positive she didn't put them somewhere else?"

"No."

"No what?"

"She might have put them somewhere else."

"Okay, so say she put them somewhere else, and you just don't know where they are. With nothing else missing, we can assume robbery wasn't a motive," Hoback concluded. "And the neighbors don't report any suspicious comings or goings on the night of the twenty-fifth."

"No one saw anyone enter the house?"

"No."

"Didn't see anyone leave?"

"No."

"Yeah, so all that means was no one was looking out their windows. People have better things to do than stare at the street. Anyway, I left, and no one saw me, right?"

"What time did you leave?"

"Around nine o'clock, like I already told you. Right after I put Helen to bed. Guess no one noticed, huh?"

Hoback leaned forward, laced his fingers into a pile of white-knuckled flesh on the tabletop. "Where'd you go, Cal? That's what you haven't told me."

"I went out."

"That's it?"

"I left the house at nine o'clock and returned home around three in the morning. I thought Helen was in her room asleep.

I didn't check on her. I just went on to bed."

Hoback waited.

"That's the God's truth, Mr. Hoback."

"Can anyone verify that?"

"What do you mean?"

"I mean, did anyone see you during that time? Do you have an alibi?"

Cal stiffened. His mouth was a taut line. "Yes," he said. "Someone saw me."

Hoback's brows perked up, ever so slightly. "You were with somebody?"

"Yes."

"Did that person see you before ten o'clock?"

"Or right around ten o'clock, I'd say."

Hoback leaned forward. "And who exactly is this person we're talking about, Cal?"

He shifted his weight in his seat uneasily. "I can't tell you that, Mr. Hoback."

Hoback peered sharply at Cal from behind the horn-rimmed glasses. Then he put an index finger in his right ear and turned it, as though to remove a piece of wax blocking the ear canal. "You can't give me the name of your alibi?"

"No, sir, I can't."

Hoback remained motionless for so long that Cal began to wonder whether he'd been locked up in a sort of seizure. When at last he spoke, it was in slow, measured syllables. "Are you quite sure you know what you are doing?"

Cal nodded once, a slight lift of the chin. "I'm sure."

It wasn't the light. Earl Hoback's face was definitely glowing red. The color, Cal noticed, matched the crimson stripes on

Hoback's tie and the little red threads that snaked through his lapel.

"Now listen here, Syfert," the lawyer said slowly, "don't tell me your alibi is a broad and you're willing to cut your own throat to protect her."

"Don't worry, Mr. Hoback. I'm not going to tell you anything like that."

Judging from the look on his lawyer's face, Cal could only surmise that his efforts to keep himself together for the past thirty minutes had been wasted. Earl Hoback was ready to blow sky-high, taking Cal, the snickering guard, and the whole of Warren County Jail right along with him.

22

AFTER HE SAW MARY AT the florist shop, Neil went back to the house and showered and shaved and put on a fresh shirt and a clean pair of slacks. It was while he was walking across the backyard toward his car that he realized he was letting go of Caroline. Not fully; his fingers were still curled around her memory, but he held her more loosely now. He wasn't sure he liked that. But at the same time, he was keenly aware of the lowering sun caressing the cornfields beyond the barn, and he felt the cool air that touched his skin like a soothing hand, and from somewhere the words came to him, *People do go on, you know.*

Neil paused, his grip on the door handle of the car. . . .

"Not the living, but the dead," Caroline said. *"The dead go on living, you know."*

Neil shook his head. *"I'm not sure I believe in all that."*

"Oh, but it's true. There's something eternal after all, Neil. It's the only thing that makes sense."

She had said that after she started attending that Episcopal church on Carroll Street.

He wondered, was she alive then, somewhere? He wished he could believe that she was.

He didn't know, but for the moment he would let the question go. For the moment he would step away from all that and simply be here, in the car, driving to Mary's house. It felt good to be going to Mary's, to be anticipating her company, to be looking forward to an evening away from everything his life had been.

A burger and an ice-cream sundae at the Village. Imagine that. Just like old times. Just like the summer evenings when he and Mary ran up to Lebanon for something to eat, a couple of teens full of the stuff of life, full of untarnished dreams.

Youth, Neil reflected, was like a print by Currier and Ives—lovely and chaste and idealistic. Age was a canvas by Picasso or De Kooning or Pollock—all jagged lines and clashing colors and nothing that anyone could really make sense of, and for that reason, far closer to the center of what was real.

Oh, Mary, Neil thought, *I shouldn't be here. I shouldn't be coming to your home, knocking on your door, waiting for you.*

When she opened the door, he smiled. She looked beautiful. Just as beautiful—no, even more so—than she had when they were kids and he had come to the Syfert home to visit Uncle Cal. And Mary. Yes, to visit her too.

"Hello, Mary."

"Hi, Neil. Come in for a minute while I grab my purse."

He wondered, self-consciously, what she was thinking and if she was glad he was there, and if he was the only one who suddenly felt shy and awkward, as though they had only just met.

He stepped inside and she turned away, and as she did so, the telephone rang. She moved toward the phone there in the living room. "Just let me see who it is," she said over her shoulder.

But she didn't pick it up. With her back to Neil, she listened as the answering machine told the caller that this was the Beeken household, please leave a message.

After the beep a small strained voice came through the machine. "Mary, this is Madylyn." Pause. "If you're there, please pick up." Pause. "Mary, I really must talk with you. Please . . ."

Neil watched quizzically as Mary reached out for the receiver, lifted it from the cradle a couple of inches, then set it back down. The answering machine turned off, its tape rewound, and the message button began to flash.

She stood with her back to him for a full thirty seconds. He wanted to call out her name, to ask her if she was all right, but he didn't dare. Finally she came to herself and picked her purse up off the couch and turned around.

Neil felt a small chill run through him when she smiled a small deliberate smile. "All right," she said evenly. "I'm ready now."

23

WHO IN THE WORLD IS MADYLYN? Neil wondered. He sat across from Mary at the small round Formica table, wanting to ask her the question that had nagged him all the way from Mason to Lebanon—the question he almost *had* asked her, more than once, before stopping himself each time. If Mary wanted him to know, she would have told him. Well, she was probably no one, this Madylyn. An elderly pest, maybe. One of those old folks who's constantly calling to ask a favor. Still, whoever she was, she was obviously someone Mary found distressing.

But now she was sitting there smiling. She had somehow managed to let the call from Madylyn roll off her back the minute they'd stepped into the Village and found this table by the window.

A young waitress arrived with a hurried smile, an asymmetrical haircut, and a couple of menus. "Get you anything to drink?"

"I'll have a vanilla Coke," Mary said.

"Same for me, thanks," Neil added.

The waitress nodded and turned on her running shoes.

Beneath her red apron, she wore shorts and a tank top that revealed a snake tattoo just above her right shoulder blade. Neil wondered briefly what had become of Eunice and Jo and Charlene in their pink uniforms and white ruffled aprons, their hair caught up into beehives or French twists with little finger curls framing their faces. They must be long retired now, or dead. Heavens, yes, Eunice had had one foot in the grave even back in 1975.

"Let's see," Neil said as he opened the menu. "You'll have a cheeseburger, no onions but plenty of mayo, fries, and coleslaw, and for dessert a butterscotch sundae, hold the nuts and make sure no chocolate gets dribbled in there by mistake or you'll send it back."

Mary sat in a stupor for a moment before laughing out loud. "Neil, how did you know!"

He shrugged. "Face it, you're completely predictable. It's what you always got when we ate here."

"But, your memory—it's amazing!" She smiled.

He shrugged again. "You're the only person I know who doesn't like chocolate. Who could forget something like that?"

For a moment Mary's smile wavered. But she found it again quickly. "Well," she said, "that's exactly what I'd like. And you?"

"I'd order the usual myself, but then, Eunice isn't here to know what the usual is, is she?"

Mary shook her head and looked out the window. "Eunice. I haven't thought of her in ages."

Their young waitress came back with their drinks, took their order, and scurried off to the kitchen, where, amid the clanking of dishes and pans, a voice was hollering, "Order up!"

Neil and Mary both sipped their drinks, eyes averted until

Mary said at length, "So, how's it going with the house?"

Neil nodded. "It's going. There's plenty to be done, but I think they'll be able to start taking guests by September."

"Seems kind of strange, doesn't it? The old house a bed-and-breakfast."

"Seems very strange," he agreed. "And kind of sad, in an odd sort of way."

Mary looked pensive, stirred her drink with the straw. "I know what you mean. The house full of strangers, coming and going all the time. It won't be the same anymore, will it?"

"No, it won't. But then, what's 'the same'? Everything's always changing. There isn't a place where things just stay the same."

She laughed. "That's for sure."

"Still, I know what you mean. We were lucky, weren't we, to have had what we had when we were kids?"

"Yeah, I think we were. Life wasn't perfect but . . ." Her voice trailed off.

The innocence—that had been the best part, Neil thought. The not knowing what lay ahead.

He tried to smile, was thankful for the interruption when their hamburgers came. They ate, chewing thoughtfully. For someone with such a sharp memory, Neil chided himself, he couldn't remember a single item on his mental list of things to talk about. He'd always done that—made lists of topics he could draw upon so as to avoid those awkward lapses in conversation. But as he sat there across from Mary, he realized that his carefully constructed list had dissolved like a lump of sugar in hot tea, leaving his mind an uncomfortable void. There was something inside, though—he could feel it kicking at his ribs—that wanted to be said. Something insistent, though Neil

ann tatlock

couldn't put together the words to explain it. It was an echo of a long-ago conversation between him and Mary, one that had been cut off and never finished. Something left unsaid when they were young.

He saw himself then, his nineteen-year-old self, pulling into Uncle Henry's driveway, his car loaded down with suitcases and all the odd-and-ends he was taking to New York.

"I've come to say good-bye, Mary."

And the look on her face asking, *"That's it? Just good-bye? You have nothing more to say than that?"*

He did. But he couldn't say it. Not then. Not now.

"So," he said, feeling awkward, inadequate.

But she was speaking too. She was saying, "Not to change the subject, but . . ."

Neil felt at once perplexed and relieved. "Were we on a subject?" he asked.

She laughed, as though of course they had been talking of something important, as though there had been no gaping wordless spaces between them. "Well, since you live in New York, I've been meaning to ask you—"

"Uh-huh?"

"What did you see, on 9/11? I mean, you were there, right? What was it like?"

"Oh. Well . . ." He looked out the window and down the sidewalk, but instead of seeing South Broadway in Lebanon, Ohio, he saw the Twin Towers in lower Manhattan, the smoke and ash, the paper raining down like confetti, the people trapped . . .

"Not that you have to tell me," Mary added quickly, "if you'd rather not."

"No, it's all right." But even as he spoke, he knew that it

182

was not all right. There were many places he didn't want to go. That was one of them.

He gazed across the table at Mary. She was waiting expectantly. He would tell her briefly, then, skimming the surface like a rock skipping over a pond. He didn't want to go too deep, didn't want to tread too far into that memory.

He looked down at his burger, a suddenly unappetizing stone, and took a deep breath.

24

"I WAS HAVING BREAKFAST with an art dealer, an acquaintance of mine, in the financial district," Neil began. "Normally, on a Tuesday morning, I would have been at school, but I was arranging for this dealer to come and speak to one of my classes. He asked me to meet him for breakfast at a coffee shop on Broadway."

"Was it close to the World Trade Center?" Mary interrupted.

"Yes, very close. We were in the Equitable Building. Do you know where that is?"

She shook her head. "I've never been to New York."

"Oh yes. Well, it's just blocks from where the towers were. Norm and I had finished eating; we were just sitting there drinking coffee and talking about the class when the first plane hit." He took a sip of Coke, frowning as he tugged on the straw. "It was like an explosion, like a bomb going off somewhere nearby, but of course we didn't know what it was. I remember Norm and I just looking at each other, not quite sure what to make of it, when someone ran in yelling that a plane had just crashed into one of the towers. Of course my first thought was that it was a small plane and it had hit the tower by accident.

"People started pouring out of the building and into the street to see what was going on. So Norm and I followed, and we were standing there on the sidewalk, part of this crowd looking up at the tower that had just been hit. It had a huge hole ripped in the side and smoke was pouring out, and I just kept thinking, *There are people in there!* I couldn't move, but inside my head I kept yelling, *Get out, get out!* There were sirens going off everywhere. People were screaming. Norm just stood there swearing over and over, cursing someone or something, I don't know what.

"And then the second plane appeared. I mean, it just seemed to come out of nowhere. When it hit the other tower, we felt the explosion like waves coming down the street, and all around me people were screaming and running and—I remember there was a woman crying, just standing there on the sidewalk with her face in her hands. When the second plane hit, we knew it wasn't an accident, that this was some sort of attack. We didn't know what was going to happen next. There was this sense then that we were all completely vulnerable. I mean, how many planes would there be and how many people would be dead before the day was over?

"Norm turned to me then and said, 'Get out of Manhattan, Neil. Get home somehow.' But what I wanted was to find Caroline, or at least to know where she was. Norm left, but I went back in the building and found a phone booth. I owned a cell phone, but I always seemed to forget it at the worst times." He smiled sadly. "I managed to leave it home that morning. So I went to a phone booth and found that of course the phones were out and I couldn't get through to Caroline's office. I figured she was okay at that point, since her office was farther north in Manhattan. So really it was what *might* happen that worried me.

"When I got back out on the street, that's when people started talking about terrorists. That's when I first heard the word. People assumed there was more to come—more attacks—and that we ought to get out of Manhattan. People were already moving in droves, headed for the bridges. I knew Caroline was probably heading back to Brooklyn, so I started to make my way to the Brooklyn Bridge."

Not right away, though. He wouldn't tell Mary how long he stood on the sidewalk outside the Equitable Building looking up at the burning towers, at a clear blue sky closing over with smoke. He wanted to get home to Caroline, but he simply couldn't move. He knew people who worked in the World Trade Center. Not family, not close friends, but acquaintances. He knew their names. And he wondered where they were now, if they were making the descent down the endless stairways, if they had reached the ground. Or if they would never leave the towers at all, having already perished. To his horror, as he stood there looking up, he realized there were undulating lines at some of the highest windows and that those lines had moving appendages—arms and legs—because those tiny lines were people, corporal exclamation points dangling between two deaths, caught between fire and air.

"My God," Neil whispered, and even as the words left his mouth, he knew there was no god that was his, that there was no god at all.

His gaze settled on one lone stick figure on the side of one of the towers. He couldn't be sure, but he thought it was a man. Neil wanted to reach up and let that man step into the palm of his hand. He wanted to lift him from the burning building and set him on solid ground, to offer him a way out, to save him. It's what anyone would have done if they could. It's what God should have done but chose not to. His open hand was not invisible. It simply wasn't there.

"No!" Neil had cried aloud, and yet in the next moment, the man leaped.

But Neil wouldn't tell Mary about that.

"It was crazy," he went on, "this huge mass exodus out of the city. Like we were a bunch of war refugees or something. People seemed . . . shell-shocked, I guess. Stunned. Scared. If the terrorists wanted to terrify us, they'd pretty much succeeded. As I moved along in this huge crowd, it was like we all just wanted to get across the Brooklyn Bridge before it blew up on us, or before a plane flew into it. I don't really know how to describe it all."

When he paused, Mary said, "But you got across the bridge okay?"

He nodded. "Yeah, I did. But before I even got as far as the bridge, the south tower collapsed, and when that happened it was like a tidal wave washed over Lower Manhattan, only it wasn't water. It was ash and debris. After that there were tons of paper everywhere, falling out of the sky like confetti." He stopped for a moment, recalling the scene. "It was like the terrorists were celebrating with ticker tape, and we had to march in their parade." Yes, that was it, confetti, sirens, whistles, screams, ash-covered clowns marching in a macabre parade. "Paper blew into our own backyard over in Brooklyn for days," he went on. "I mean, memos, documents, photos, all sorts of stuff from the towers ended up all the way across the river in our yard. Caroline collected it all and saved it in a box."

They were quiet a moment. Neil looked down at their food, largely untouched. Neither had bothered to eat while Neil spoke.

"So," Mary said, "you found Caroline at home when you got there?"

"No." He shook his head. "But she had farther to walk. I didn't expect her to arrive until later. She got home a couple of hours after I did."

Up until that point, the longest couple of hours of Neil's life. She came through the front door and fell into Neil's arms, exhausted, stunned, weeping. She had abandoned her heels somewhere and trekked home in a new pair of tennis shoes she had bought along the way. The city was being attacked, and Caroline, ever practical, had stopped somewhere to buy the shoes she needed to get herself home.

He held her there in the front hall, kissing her lips, her cheeks, her brow. Across the river a war had started, but at the moment this was what mattered to Neil, that Caroline had made it home safely.

He raised his eyes to look at Mary. "After Caroline got there, we went up to the roof. It's flat. You reach it by climbing a ladder in a third-floor closet. We'd go up there sometimes, when the weather was nice, to view the skyline of Lower Manhattan. And on the Fourth of July we'd sit up there and watch the fireworks over New York Harbor.

"But that day Manhattan looked like a war zone. I guess it was, in a way, because we knew this would be the start of a war, kind of like Pearl Harbor, except we didn't know who the enemy was. Terrorists, sure, but I mean, who were they and where had they come from? That's what was so odd. We didn't even know who the enemy was. Well, I guess you know what I mean."

Neil paused again, took a breath, exhaled. "So anyway, where the towers used to be, there were just these huge billows of smoke. It went on for days, that smoke. And when it finally cleared, there was nothing. I mean, it was incredible. It was the largest gaping hole . . . it was the largest nothing I'd ever seen. Just nothing left where those two huge towers had been, and that was it."

Except for one thing. One indelible thing. The image of the man, his outstretched arms a pair of failed wings, his soaring a surrender. Where the towers had stood, there was for Neil now the unforgettable image of a man caught in an eternal free fall, his death leap tacked up against the wide open spaces of an indifferent sky.

25

"IT MADE ME REALIZE," Neil said, "that I have a problem with endings."

When he finished, he settled his eyes on Mary's face and saw that she looked pained, and puzzled, as though she understood in part but not completely. It was death, Neil wanted to say. The death of strangers, of acquaintances, of Caroline. All the senselessness of coming finally back around to nothing. What was the use of anything, when everything simply ceased to be?

Mary said quietly, "There should be only happy endings."

"No." He shook his head. "There should be no endings. That's the thing. There should just be no endings at all."

He picked up his burger and finally took a bite. It had grown cold. When he finished chewing, he said, "Well, I certainly didn't mean to talk about all that when we're here to celebrate your birthday."

Mary laughed. "I'm the one who asked."

"So you did." A lift of the shoulders.

"And I probably shouldn't have."

"It's all right."

"It's just so awful, Neil. You probably lost people you knew."

"Yes. Acquaintances from Brooklyn, Cobble Hill, the fire company on DeGraw Street, all those firefighters . . ." He shook his head. "Some of my students lost mothers or fathers—or both."

"So awful," Mary whispered.

Neil said nothing.

They ate then, quietly. Someone popped a quarter in the jukebox, and a thumping noise rattled the room. Neil almost made a comment about the music, but Mary looked deep in thought.

At length she said, "The funny thing about what you said, about endings . . ."

"Hmm? What's that?"

"Well . . . do you remember? You probably don't—"

"Try me."

A small smile. "Okay, then. Well, we were in grade school. I think I must have been in first grade. Oh yes, I was, because Miss Hoppe was my teacher. You remember Nina Hoppe?"

"How could I forget? Half the boys in grade school had a wild crush on her, till she married that fellow—what was his name?"

"George Mullarky."

"That was it! What a name. Till she married old George Mullarky and broke all our hearts. But anyway . . ." He waved a hand to tell her to go on.

Mary hooked a stray bit of hair behind her ear, then said, "Anyway, some sort of musical trio came to the school that year to play for us during assembly. Or, I don't know, there must have been more instruments than that because they were playing *Peter and the Wolf.* How many instruments would that take?"

"I have no idea."

"Me either. So anyway, there we were, sitting on those folding chairs in the cafeteria, listening to these people playing *Peter and the Wolf,* and I was sitting next to Miss Hoppe, and about—I don't know—maybe twenty minutes into it, I leaned over and whispered, 'Miss Hoppe, when's the show going to start?' Well, the look she gave me! Like I'd just asked the dumbest question in the world." Mary gave a short laugh that trailed off into a sigh. "And then she says to me, 'But Mary, this is it!'"

Mary stopped then and smiled wistfully. Neil waited for her to go on.

"You see," she said after a long moment, "I was waiting for something else. I didn't know what. *Peter and the Wolf* was. I thought there was going to be a play, a real play, with a boy and a wolf and maybe—I don't know—all sorts of animals, and words, of course. I thought there would be words to tell us what was going on. I thought it was going to be fun and exciting, like other plays I'd seen. But it was just this bunch of people up there doing nothing but playing their instruments, and all of us kids bored silly out in the audience. I thought the music was leading up to something, but it wasn't. And . . . I guess I was disappointed."

She looked at Neil then, placidly, with shining eyes.

He said, "I do remember that. You're right. I could hardly sit still. I thought it would never end." He realized, after a moment, the irony in his words. "Well! See there, some things should end, I suppose. Bad concerts. Bad dreams. Bad days. All right, I change my mind. There should be endings."

"But there should be beginnings too," Mary shot back,

"and that's what bothers me. Do you know what I mean?"

He thought a moment, smiled apologetically. "No, I guess I don't."

She frowned then, two distinct lines forming between her eyes. "How to put this? During the concert I sat there the whole time waiting for it to begin. And I'm right there still. Even right now. Even if I live to be eighty, more than half my life is already over, and I'm still just waiting for it to begin. I've been in this waiting mode since day one, and I can't quite seem to grasp the fact that this is it."

The last three words were a whisper.

This is it.

A weighty silence settled between them. Neil swallowed the question that rose to his tongue: *But aren't you happy, Mary?* Of course she wasn't happy, not with the mess Dan was in. Maybe after all that was settled, maybe . . .

She said, "I guess I should do what Uncle Bernie always says. You know, count your blessings and all that. I'm better off than most, I suppose. I shouldn't complain."

"You're not complaining."

She shrugged.

"What would it take," Neil asked, "to make you feel as though life had started?"

Another long moment passed before she said, "A purpose, I suppose."

Neil ran his fingers up and down the sweaty exterior of his glass. "You always said you wanted to be a wife and mother, and you are."

"Yes," she agreed. "Yes, and I have two great kids. It's just . . . you expect life to be a certain way, and then you eventually realize it isn't going to be that way. That it's all hugely

194

different from what you had hoped for. You're still waiting for the original scenario to kick in, and finally one day you realize . . . Well, never mind, Neil. I'm not sure this is making any sense."

"Oh yes." He leaned back in his chair. "It's making sense. I do know what you mean. A kid has dreams, and he's absolutely sure he's not going to end up like the old man, discontented and disappointed. His life's going to be different. He's going to make his dreams come true, and he's going to be happy. Then he grows up, and he ends up like the old man, discontented and disappointed. So life goes."

Mary sighed deeply. "For you too, Neil?"

"In some ways, yes. Of course. I suppose it's like that for everyone, isn't it?"

"Then we accept the disappointment as the way life is."

He wasn't sure whether Mary was asking a question or making a statement. If it was a question, he didn't know the answer. If a statement, he wasn't sure he wanted to agree. He pushed his plate aside, folded his hands on the table, leaned forward. "All right, my turn to see if you remember something."

"Okay. And what's that?"

"The Maypole."

"The Maypole?"

"Back to grade school again. You know, the Maypole dance you girls did every May Day."

"Oh yes. Sure, I remember."

"And every year two girls were chosen from every class."

"There was a drawing. Two names from each class. We all prayed like mad that our name would be drawn so we could dance around the Maypole." She laughed, remembering.

"And one year your name was picked."

"I was in third grade," she said, nodding. "I was so excited. Mom actually bought me a new white dress and a pair of white gloves."

"And then there was that freak snowstorm. Not much of a storm, really, but hey—it was snowing."

"I remember! May first, and we're out there dancing in the snow. I was freezing."

Neil shook his head. "You were laughing, Mary."

"Was I?" She smiled, looked beyond Neil's shoulder and into the past. "I guess I was. Oh yes, I remember now. Mrs. Lemming was shaking her head at us, trying to get us to stop laughing. She had told us to smile, but I don't think she counted on us cracking up hysterically. But I mean, there we were, celebrating spring while the snow was falling. It was hilarious."

"Not to Mrs. Lemming."

Mary chuckled. "No, not to her. But she was the only one who didn't crack a smile. Well, you know, she'd worked so hard putting it all together, and here it was snowing, and we girls were all but howling. I guess we ruined it for her."

"Maybe, but not for anyone else. You know, Uncle Bernie was there, and afterward I heard him say to someone, 'That was just about the best picture of hope I ever saw.' And if you think about it, you have to agree."

Mary thought about it, and a small smile crept across her face. "I suppose he had a point."

"And it seems they'd almost called it off, right before all the festivities started."

"I think that's right. I'm glad they didn't. Freezing or not, I'm glad we danced anyway."

"Come to think of it, that's really the only May Day I

remember. Must have made an impression on me, you and the other girls dancing in the snow."

Neil gazed at Mary's profile as she turned toward the window. He had kept that picture with him all these years; the little girl Mary dressed in white cotton, holding a pink ribbon, weaving in and out with the other girls as they wrapped the pole. The air was still and the sun was shining, but from somewhere the snow fell, the silent flakes like frozen blossoms whirling toward earth and joining in the dance. And above it all, Mary's laughter, a sound that rippled through the circle of girls, rising like a song so that the moment was drenched in cheer.

He touched Mary's arm and raised his sweaty glass of soda.

"Happy birthday, Mary." He gave the glass a gentle lift.

She raised her own, acknowledging the toast. "Thank you, Neil."

"May you always be able to dance in the snow."

She nodded. "Okay, I'll drink to that."

They touched glasses and downed the remainder of their drinks.

26

To Neil, NOTHING HAD EVER seemed quite right about this particular painting. The scene was the ballroom at Christmastime, 1920-something. Maybe 1930, judging from the way the people were dressed. They were dancing, some of them. Others were mingling, laughing. In one corner a three-piece band. Stockings hung on the mantel; a fire roared in the hearth. Boughs of holly strung along the walls, a sprig of mistletoe in the doorway. And an enormous decorated tree. It might have been pleasant enough had it been done right. But that was the problem. The people were disproportionate—legs too long, torsos too short, heads too large or too small. The features were indistinct, as though these revelers' faces were balls of wax. And that one musician's foot—not a foot at all but a sloppy splash of paint! The room itself seemed tilted, making it a wonder that those painted people didn't roll from one side of the canvas to the other. And the way the tree was lighted . . . now there was the most vexing question. What was the source of light? Evelyn Sadler had provided no apparent source of light, and yet the tree glowed like a house on fire.

"You look perplexed, Neil," Bernie said. "What's the matter?"

Neil turned from the painting, newly hung on the wall of the tower room, and offered his uncle a smile. "Nothing really, Uncle Bernie," he said. "It's just that of all Evelyn's paintings, I never cared for this one."

"Oh?" Bernie's eyes narrowed behind the lenses of his glasses as he squinted. "What's wrong with it?"

"Well . . ." Neil stopped. Where to begin? "Your mother was an illustrator, not an interpreter. She did wonderful still lifes and landscapes. But in this painting"—Neil shook his head—"she must have been wanting to try her hand at Impressionism. I don't know, maybe she was feeling particularly inspired by Mary Cassatt or Monet or someone like that. But it just didn't work. At least this painting was her only detour from illustration, which is probably a good thing."

Bernie leaned back in the overstuffed chair and took a long swallow of his iced tea. "I don't know, Neil," he said, "but I've always rather liked this one. In fact, it's one of my favorites. It's always made me feel . . . well . . . cheerful, I suppose. It's such a happy picture. That's why I asked Grace to hang it up here when she came across it in the basement yesterday. It used to hang in the ballroom, you know."

"Oh yes, I remember. How many hours of my boyhood were devoted to gazing at Evelyn Sadler's paintings?"

Bernie waved a hand toward the gray windows. "Come back tomorrow and look at it when it's sunny. It might look different then."

Neil chuckled lightly. "I've studied this painting in every kind of weather, every kind of light, but still, it makes no sense to me. But if you like it . . ." He shrugged and offered Bernie another apologetic smile.

"Well, Neil, you might just as well take off your art critic's hat and sit down and enjoy your tea. You can't change Mother's painting, after all."

"No, that I can't."

Bernie nodded toward the rocking chair by the bed. "Drag that rocker over here closer to me and rest a bit. You've been working hard all morning."

"You can say that again," Neil said. "Dennis, Mike, and I have been scraping wallpaper in the larger back bedroom down on the second floor. The room suddenly seems a whole lot bigger when you've got to remove every inch of several layers of paper from the walls. Even with a steamer, it's a lot of work."

"I can well imagine. Thought I felt the house shake a time or two this morning."

"Well, I don't think that was us. More likely the contractor they've hired. He's doing a pretty good job of ripping things up down there."

"Oh? What's he doing?"

"Adding a bath to each room. You know the original bathroom on that floor? Yeah, well, now there's a doorway between my room and that bathroom. But Grace doesn't want the guests to share a bath, so every room is getting one. They won't be huge, but they'll be private."

"Grace is really going to town, isn't she? It'll be something when it's finished."

Neil nodded. "You know, I think it will. I wasn't so sure about this bed-and-breakfast thing at first, but Grace knows what she's doing all right." He paused at the bedside table and picked up a prescription bottle from among the clutter. "Good grief, Bernie, you've got a regular pharmacy going here."

Bernie nodded. "That's what happens when the body gets tired. Just wait; you'll see."

"But—" Neil read the label on the bottle aloud, then said, "What exactly is ailing you? I mean, is it your heart? Blood pressure?"

Bernie rested his head against the back of the chair. He shut his eyes and smiled. "Nothing that a little dying won't take care of, Neil."

"Ah." Neil sniffed out a laugh, returned the bottle to the table, and dragged the rocking chair closer to Bernie. He then retrieved his glass of iced tea from the bookcase, where he had left it.

When Neil was settled, Bernie asked, "So tell me, how are you, Neil?"

"I'm fine." He paused, sighed. "I'm better. I'm confused. I'm happy and I'm sad. Honestly, Bernie, I don't know how I am. I miss Caroline."

"Of course you do." Bernie gave him a knowing nod. "I miss Rita. But I will be seeing her soon."

"Yes." As though Rita were waiting for him somewhere in the next county, and all Bernie had to do was pass through the valley of the shadow of death and come out on the other side to join her. Neil tried not to show his skepticism.

"We will both be reunited with our loved ones, Neil."

"Hmm." A conveniently timed sip of iced tea. Put a little cold drink into the hollow where there were no words.

"But you," Bernie went on, "will have to wait a little longer than I, I'm afraid."

Neil nodded. Best to agree and let the old man have his comfort. Once dead, he wouldn't know the difference anyway.

"Not that I'm willing to go quite yet, mind you."

"Oh?"

"I've got a bit of unfinished business."

"You do?" Neil couldn't imagine what.

"Oh my, yes. I'm Jacob wrestling with one last angel."

"You are?"

"I won't let go until he blesses me."

The two men sat in silence for a moment. Bernie looked satisfied. Neil felt puzzled. "Can I ask what your bit of unfinished business is?"

"You can ask," Bernie said, "but I can't answer you."

"No, I didn't think so."

Sealed-lipped Sadler, they'd called him once. Whatever you told the Padre stayed with the Padre. You could count on that.

"Think God will let you hang around till it's done?" Neil asked. "Whatever it is?"

"That's my final prayer."

"Then I hope He grants it."

"He will, one way or the other."

It must be nice, Neil thought, to be so sure about everything. In a way, he envied Uncle Bernie.

"You saw Mary last night?" Bernie asked.

"Yes. We had a bite to eat at the Village."

"Delightful!" The old man's eyes shone. "Goodness, I haven't been there in years. Rita used to enjoy their triple fudge sundae."

"That's a good one. I went for the butterscotch last night myself."

"Ah yes." Bernie closed his eyes, smiled, looked as though he could taste the butterscotch even now. "I must remember to wish Mary a happy birthday. I'm afraid I forgot."

Neil shrugged. "There are lots of people to keep track of around here."

"Yes, aren't there! And there are more little Sadlers around every year, it seems. Isn't it wonderful?"

"Uh-huh." Neil pushed with his foot against the floor to set the rocking chair in motion.

"We both would have made good fathers, Neil, but it wasn't God's will."

"No, I guess it wasn't." First, the deceased wives. Now, the nonexistent children. *There must be more pleasant topics of conversation,* Neil thought.

"But we are blessed in other ways."

What could Neil do but agree? He nodded, said yes, went on rocking.

"I'm glad you could be with Mary on her birthday."

"So am I."

"She doing all right?"

"Seems to be doing as well as can be expected."

"The investigation still going on?"

"Yes. It probably will be for some time."

Bernie moved his head from side to side. "You wonder what makes these things so complicated."

"Oh." Neil stopped rocking, hitched his left ankle up onto his right thigh. "Sometimes it's hard to figure out exactly what happened, I guess. They've got two different stories going, and they don't know which one's true."

"People always make the truth so complicated, don't they? It should be so simple."

Neil shrugged. "I suppose so."

"Mary's a tough girl, but I pray for her."

"That's all we can do." Though as he said it, Neil realized it wasn't anything he did at all. He dropped his foot and started rocking again. He thought a moment, then said idly, "Strangest thing . . ."

"What's that?"

"Last night when I picked Mary up, someone called her. Someone named Madylyn."

"Madylyn?"

The old man's eyes widened and his face went so white that Neil was startled. He stopped rocking and leaned forward in the chair. "You okay, Uncle Bernie?"

Bernie ignored his question and asked insistently, "Madylyn who? What's the last name?"

"I have no idea."

"Well, what did she say?"

"That she wanted to talk to Mary."

"And did she?"

"Talk with Mary?"

"Yes. Did they talk?"

"No. Mary wouldn't pick up. Madylyn was talking to the answering machine. That's how I could hear what she said. Uncle Bernie, are you sure you're all right?"

He didn't seem well at all. His hands were trembling. "Tell Mary she must speak to Madylyn," he said firmly.

"But why?"

"Tell her I said she must."

"But Uncle Bernie, why is it so important? And who is Madylyn anyway?"

As the two men looked at each other, the color slowly rose again to Bernie's face, and he seemed to compose himself.

After a long moment, Neil said, "You're not going to tell me anything, are you?"

"I would if I could, Neil."

"Maybe I need to know."

"If you're supposed to know, you'll find out."

A wave of frustration passed through Neil's throat and exited as a sigh. Bernie Sadler's closed-lips policy could be a positive, as when the teenaged Neil confessed to a solitary episode of drunkenness, and the story, safely deposited with the Padre, never got back to Jim and Elinor Sadler. Uncle Bernie had bestowed the sought-after assurance of forgiveness upon the contrite Neil Sadler and sent him away with the warning not to do it again. But now that same closed-lips policy was simply annoying.

Neil knew, though, that he was defeated. "All right," he said, raising his free hand in surrender. "I'll tell Mary to talk to Madylyn, whoever she is. But I don't think Mary's going to like it."

"Tell her it's important that she does."

"If you say so. But maybe it's not even the Madylyn you're thinking of."

"I believe it is."

"How do you know?"

"I just know. Promise me you'll speak with Mary."

Another sigh. "All right. I'll speak with Mary."

"And do me another favor, Neil?"

"As long as it has nothing to do with mysterious old women, then sure."

"Run down and tell Grace I'd be eternally grateful for a bowl of her homemade chicken soup."

Neil rose and pulled the rocking chair back into place beside the bed. "That I can do." He took Bernie's empty glass and headed for the door.

"And Neil?"

"Yes, Uncle Bernie?"

"Go in peace."

Neil laughed out loud. "Sure thing, old man. You're driving me crazy one minute and telling me to go in peace the next."

"You can handle it, Neil."

"I have no choice, do I?"

"I'm afraid not."

"Then I'll do my best."

"I've always known I could count on you. Now have Grace send up that bowl of soup before I starve to death."

27

"Neil? Is that you?" The voice at the other end of the line sounded thin and reedy. That bothered Neil. It made him feel as though he were talking with someone who was fading away.

"Yes, Mom. How are you?" Neil spoke loudly. His mother wore hearing aids, but she often forgot to turn them on.

"I've been wondering when you might call. How long have you been in Mason now anyway?"

"Less than a week." Though to Neil it seemed weeks, months even. "I got here only last Friday."

"I thought you might call before this."

"Sorry, Mom. I should have. Guess I've been busy."

"Well, that's okay. But I'm anxious to know how everyone is. Have you seen Gene and Lillian? And Vivian Zwirn? How's Vivian and Henry? And Cousin Don and Midge—have you seen them?"

"Yes, yes. Everyone's great. Grace had a big get-together here at the house last Sunday. Invited everyone. Wish you could have been here."

"Yes. Well, me too. Why your father ever dragged me out here to California is beyond me. Twenty years and I still don't feel at home. I mean, I look out the window and I see palm trees, and you know I never liked palm trees."

"I know, Mom, and I'm—"

"And the cost of living here, Neil. *Un*believable. We could be living pretty high on the hog back there in Mason for what we're spending on this apartment here, and I don't even have a washer/dryer. And I have to haul the garbage clear across the complex just to dump it, which is no picnic, let me tell you, when it rains."

"I know, Mom, but—"

"I don't know how you feel about New York, Neil—"

"Well, like I've always said, I really enjoy—"

"But I think we should have all stayed right there where we belong. You hear that, Jim Sadler?" The last sentence was hollered away from the phone. Then she came back to Neil. "Your father's sawing logs again, and it's only six o'clock here. I'll tell you, Neil, it's like he's getting that sleeping sickness . . . what's it called? Necromancy?"

"Um, no. I think you're thinking of narcolepsy. But Dad doesn't have that. He's just getting old."

"Tell me about it. And here he is wanting to pretend we're a couple of twenty-something sun-seekers."

"Well, just remember, Mom, you went out there to be closer to Jerry and the grandkids."

"Oh yes. Well, that was fine, wasn't it, until the kids became teenagers. Soon as they hit puberty, all three of them, they didn't want anything to do with their parents, let alone Poppa and Nana. Won't be caught dead in public with any of us. So now I'm stuck out here in Pomona with the palm trees and the weirdos, people all dressed up like I don't know what, and all the liberals up in arms about this and that."

"Do you ever think about coming back here, Mom? I know it's a big move, but—"

"Every day, Neil. Every day I think I got to get back there where I was born. Now you know I'm going to get back there one way or the other, since your dad and I, we've got our burial plot right there in Rose Hill. You know where the Sadlers are, don't you, son? But I got to ask myself, now what's the use of coming back dead? What good is *that* going to do?"

"I can see your point."

"But your dad, uh-uh, there's no persuading him. He loves it here, which I guess only makes sense since he fits right in."

Neil wasn't sure what she meant by that, but he didn't ask her to explain.

"I'm sorry about that, Mom, but listen, you should at least come back for a visit. You should see what we're doing with the house. You know Grace and Dennis are planning to open it as a bed-and-breakfast this fall, right?"

"So I heard."

"At first I wasn't so sure I liked the idea, but now, I think it's the right thing. I like Grace's plans. It's going to be pretty nice when it's done."

"That house has always been nice. I've always loved it, no matter what your father said. Gothic Horror, ha! Grace was right when she said Jim was just jealous. He never said so, but I know he always wanted that house."

"Yeah, well, it's a good thing it fell to Grace, because she knows what she's doing. You and Dad are going to have to come back and see it, Mom."

"We will, sure. Maybe I'll even just buy myself a one-way ticket and stay there. Your dad can come on back here. He won't even miss me. All he does is sleep anyway. You hear that,

Jim Sadler? Maybe I'll just go on back home and stay there. Aw, doesn't bother him any. Wouldn't bother him even if he was awake to hear me."

"Yeah, well, how are you and Dad anyway? You staying healthy?"

"Sure, we're not doing too bad. Except I can't seem to keep your father awake these days. And when he *is* awake, he's always complaining about something or other. His blood pressure or his feet or his arthritic hips. Listen, Neil, if you know what's good for you, don't bother growing old."

"Hmm, I'm not sure I like the alternative either."

Elinor Sadler laughed lightly. "Listen, dear, you doing okay? I worry about you."

"I'm fine, Mom. Really. It's good to be here. I'm glad I came."

"Yes, I can imagine. You can't go wrong by going home."

"No, I guess you can't."

"People ought to just choose a place and stay put."

"You might be right about that, Mom. Oh, before I forget, Bernie said to be sure to tell you hello."

"Bernie! How is he? Last I heard, he was ailing."

"Well, he's getting old."

"Aren't we all."

"But otherwise he's fine."

"You give him my love. Tell him I miss him. He still in the house over on Elmlinger?"

"No, he hasn't been there in a while. He's here, living up in the tower room."

"Land sakes! What's he doing up there?"

"Waiting to meet his Maker, or so he tells me."

"His Maker wouldn't meet him on the ground floor?"

Neil laughed out loud. "I asked him the same thing."

"Whatever suits his fancy, I guess. Seems I did hear something about him living up there, now you mention it. I'm getting forgetful these days."

"That's okay, Mom."

"Just a part of growing old."

A wave of silence washed over the telephone line. After a moment, Neil said, "Hey, Mom, let me ask you something."

"Sure. What is it?"

"You know anyone named Madylyn?"

"Marilyn?"

"No. Madylyn."

"Madylyn who?"

"That's what I'm asking you. Do you know anyone by that name?"

"Let me think a minute. Well, now, the lady in the apartment upstairs has a granddaughter—"

"No. I mean here. In Mason."

"In Mason?"

"Yeah."

"Do I know any Madylyns in Mason? Is that what you're asking?"

"Yes, Mom. That's it."

"Well, it would help if I knew her last name. Do you know her last name?"

"As I said, that's what I don't know. That's what I'm asking you."

"Oh."

Another silence. Neil could hear his mother breathing on the other end, lightly, as though deep in thought. Finally she said, "I hope you're not talking about that awful woman,

Madylyn Fricke. Goodness, I haven't thought about her in years. Makes my stomach turn just thinking about her now. Wicked thing. She and I never ran in the same circles, thank heavens. Is that who you're talking about, Neil?"

"Well, I don't know, Mom. Who is she?"

"Don't you remember? She was the one that had herself an affair with Cal Syfert. And poor Helen, practically bedridden and all, and here her husband—"

"Cal Syfert had an affair?"

"He sure did. Don't you remember?"

"I don't think so."

"You might've already been in New York by the time all that came out. Come to think of it, not many people knew of it. Just a few of us, seems like."

"So how'd you find out?"

She thought a moment, then said, "I don't even remember now, Neil. It's been so long. Someone or other found out about it and told a few of us. It was all kept in the family, though. We kept our mouths shut. It was bad enough that one of our own *killed* somebody, even if he wasn't a blood relation. But to throw in an affair on top of that—uh-uh. We didn't want that part getting around town."

"So it never did?"

"Never did what?"

"Got around Mason?"

"I don't think so."

"That's amazing."

"Well, who knows, Neil? Maybe everyone knew about it eventually. But the Frickes went on living in Mason, happy as you please, like nothing ever happened. That makes me think it wasn't common knowledge. Certainly Bill Fricke never found out about the affair, I can tell you that."

"How do you know?"

"Why, he'd-a killed Madylyn! At least he'd-a divorced her. He'd never have stood for his wife having an affair. Not the Bill Fricke I knew. Whew—what a temper! But they never got divorced, at least not that I know of anyway."

"Okay. So you're saying that part of the reason Cal murdered Helen is because he was in love with Madylyn Fricke?"

"Sure. Makes sense, doesn't it?"

"I guess so."

"Listen, dear, I know you liked Cal, and I know how disappointed you were when all this happened. He was like a second dad to you; I know that, dear. And sure, he had his good points like everyone else. I had to feel sorry for him for years, his being tied down and all, the way he was. But like I said then, and I'll say it now, he should have just got himself a divorce, not killed the poor woman. But anyway, Neil, just forget it. Let sleeping dogs lie. That was a long time ago, and the less we think about it, the better. Why in the world would you ask about Madylyn anyway?"

"I just heard the name, is all. I was wondering who she was."

"Well, take my advice, dear. Stay away from that woman."

"Why's that, Mom?"

"Why, she's a tramp, of course! Having an affair and all. No good can come from befriending a woman like Madylyn Fricke."

"I'm not planning on befriending her. I was just wondering who she is. Besides, she's pretty old now."

"Oh? Yes, I guess she would be. I still picture her as that

young floozy. Who knows but maybe she's not even alive any-more."

"I think she is."

"Well, if she's alive, she's not in Mason like you're think-ing."

"Oh?"

"Seems to me she and Bill eventually left Mason and moved down to Cincy. Not that it matters. Listen, you want to talk to your dad? I can wake him up—"

"No. Let him sleep. Just tell him I said hi."

"Sure, I'll tell him."

"And tell him to think about making a trip back this way."

"I'm coming, with or without him. Maybe I can even get there before you head back to New York. How long has it been since I last saw you? Oh yes, last fall."

"Yes."

His parents had flown out to New York for Caroline's funeral in her hometown of Poughkeepsie. When his father flew back to Pomona afterward, his mother had returned with Neil to Brooklyn. She'd stayed for a month, cooking and clean-ing and ironing and crying. Mostly crying. She spent a great deal of time alternately lamenting the plight of humankind and proclaiming the sovereignty of God. By the time she left, Neil was certain that if he had to hear one more time that the Lord giveth and the Lord taketh away, he would go quietly and irre-versibly insane. He loved his mother and appreciated her attempts at support and consolation, but when she left, it was something of a relief for Neil. He could at last begin to grieve in solitude.

"Well, dear," she said now, "I'll see what I can do about getting there."

"That'd be good, Mom. It'd be good to see you. Well, you take care."

"You too, son." She was quiet for a moment. She seemed reluctant to say good-bye. "Neil?"

"Yes, Mom?"

"It doesn't have anything to do with Madylyn's daughter, does it?"

"Madylyn's daughter?"

"Yes. I mean, you're not thinking of taking up with Madylyn's daughter, are you?"

Neil laughed lightly. "Heavens, no, Mom. I didn't even know she had a daughter."

"That's good, dear. Listen, I know it's hard to be alone. . . ."

"I'm all right, Mom—"

"And I know someday you'll think about marrying again . . ."

"Probably not for a long time."

"But I don't want to see you hooking up with any loose women."

"You don't have anything to worry about there."

"Good. You're a good boy, Neil. You were always my best son."

"Just don't tell Jerry."

"Not on your life."

"Good-bye, Mom. I love you."

"I love you too, dear."

When Neil hung up, he stood at the bedroom window that overlooked the cornfields and the highway winding up toward

Lebanon. Bernie wrestling an angel. Madylyn calling Mary. A part of aging, he knew now, maybe even a part of the preparation for death, was this ritual, somehow inborn, of tending to unfinished business.

28

IT WAS A HOT SUMMER NIGHT in 1977. Dusk was still an hour off when Mary ran out of the house on Hanover Drive, away from Aunt Vivian's sighs and Uncle Henry's clumsy stabs at lightheartedness and Denton Patch's craziness. She fled in search of solitude, a place to escape this thing that had become her life. There had to be some small place, she reasoned, where she could forget for a moment her mother's death, which she had come to accept as a homicide, and her father's arrest.

As she ambled down Cox-Smith Road, she breathed deeply of the warm night air, taking in the earthy scent of things in bloom and the pungent fragrance of freshly mown grass. Maybe the breath of night would clear her mind in a way nothing else could.

But the quiet was broken when somebody cried, "Mary, wait! Please wait! I need to talk with you."

She turned to see Madylyn Fricke hurrying toward her, scurrying from her house in a sleeveless dress and high-heeled pumps, as though she were ready to go out for the evening. Mary's heart sank. Another word of condolence. Another "I'm so sorry about your loss; your mother was a wonderful

woman." Lies, all lies. No one had thought Helen Syfert was a
wonderful woman, and nobody really cared about Mary's loss.
They were, more than anything, morbidly curious about her
death. A murder in Mason! A man has killed his wife—isn't it
dreadfully exciting! Finally something to set tongues wagging at
a furious speed, something to break the monotony of small-
town life.

Mary took one deep breath to fortify herself. "Hello, Mrs.
Fricke," she said flatly. She stood impatiently on the sidewalk,
hands stuffed deep in the pockets of her cutoff jeans, waiting
for the woman to reach her.

Bill and Madylyn Fricke had often played bridge and gone
bowling with her parents, years ago, before Helen got too sick
to go out anymore. Bill Fricke worked over at Reading Manufacturing, where Cal Syfert worked, though in a different area.
Mary hadn't seen much of Bill and Madylyn Fricke in quite
some time, which she thought just as well, as she considered
Mr. Fricke a beer-guzzling grouch. Helen herself had called him
a brute, a Saturday-night drunk who became loud and vulgar
after too much elbow bending. His verbal assaults were famous
all over Warren County, and once he punched Lloyd Dingle in
the nose simply for bowling a perfect three hundred game. Bill
Fricke spent a night in jail for that one but was released the
next morning because Lloyd decided not to press charges. For
his own protection, though, Lloyd Dingle never bowled again
when Bill Fricke was at the lanes. He said with Bill around, a
man could get killed just for having a winning streak.

Madylyn, on the other hand, was well liked. Wherever help
was needed, Madylyn was there. She'd been a homeroom
mother in her three children's classrooms since the oldest one
started first grade in 1969. She was a tireless member of the

Mason Booster Club, served as president three years running for the Four Seasons Garden Club, and actively participated in the annual fund-raisers for the Mason Art Club. She was also a dependable presence at the meetings of the Loyal Sisters down at the Methodist Church. On top of that she was a pretty woman, with shiny dark hair and rich brown eyes and skin like polished marble. Quite young looking for her age, Mary thought. You had to feel sorry for her, being married to a jerk.

"I must talk with you, Mary," Madylyn said breathlessly when she finally caught up with her.

Mary lifted her brows. "All right." *Say your piece and get it over with.*

"Keep walking," the older woman urged quietly.

"Sure, okay." Mary shrugged and started down the sidewalk.

For a moment Madylyn Fricke didn't say anything. Mary resented the intrusion and was just about to tell Mrs. Fricke that she really needed to be alone right now when the woman blurted, "You have to know that your father didn't kill your mother."

Mary was so startled she abruptly stopped short. But Mrs. Fricke kept walking, and after a moment Mary scurried to catch up. "What?" she asked.

Madylyn Fricke had picked up speed in spite of her heels. The two strode furiously side-by-side for a while, as though they were in a hurry to get somewhere. Mrs. Fricke seemed reluctant to speak, but after looking over her shoulder, as though to see if they were being followed, she suddenly confessed, "He was with me that night."

Mary gasped, and her already rapidly beating heart started pounding. Her mind was scrambling madly to understand the meaning behind the words. "What do you mean? Where were you?"

A distinct shade of crimson crept up the older woman's neck and fanned out against the marble-smooth cheek. "It doesn't matter where we were. What matters is that we were together."

"But, I mean . . ." Her head was suddenly spinning. She lifted both hands to her forehead and started rubbing at her temples. "Why were you with Dad? What were you guys doing?"

Madylyn looked heavenward, sighing deeply. "Oh, Mary," she said quietly. "Don't you understand?"

Understand what? The only thing her father had told her was that he was "out with friends." He had a circle of buddies from work he sometimes socialized with. Not close friends, just a group of guys who sometimes went bowling or down to the American Legion Hall or to the Main Street Roadhouse for a couple of beers.

"But who were you with, Dad?" Mary had asked.

"Don't worry about it, Mare."

"But Dad, they're the ones who can get you off. If they testify that you were with them, then of course you weren't home when Mom was killed. Any jury would—"

"Listen, you let me and Hoback worry about all of this."

"But, Dad . . ."

"You have too many other things to worry about."

"Like what!"

"Well, school and . . . your whole life, Mary. You have your whole life ahead of you."

"But Dad!"

"It's all right, Mary. It's all right."

"I guess I don't understand, Mrs. Fricke," Mary said peevishly. "Dad told me he was out with some friends. So who else was with you and Dad?"

Another deep sigh. "No one else was with us. That's the thing. We were alone."

Mary stopped. So did Madylyn. They turned to face each other slowly. In the falling darkness, Mary's eyes shone with sudden understanding. Her father had not been bowling with the guys. He hadn't been blowing the head off a beer down at the Roadhouse. It was something other than that.

"Your father and I were having an affair," Madylyn said quietly.

"No you weren't," Mary shot back.

"I'm sorry, Mary. I know it's hard, it's one more thing—"

"You and Dad?"

"Yes, Mary. Yes."

Mary started to cry. Madylyn lifted a hand and briefly touched her shoulder, but Mary pulled away. She turned and started walking.

"How could you do that?" Mary asked angrily. She pulled hard at her cheeks with the palms of her hands, embarrassed to be wiping at tears.

"Listen to me," Madylyn said firmly. "The important thing is this—your father was with me, and I can testify to that."

"Why are you telling me this?"

"Because, don't you see, I'm your father's alibi."

"How long were you having an affair? How long was all this going on?"

The woman shook her head, her dark hair brushing her shoulders. "Not long. A few months is all."

"Are you in love or something?"

"Listen, Mary—"

"I can't believe Dad . . . I just can't believe it. . . ."

"Whether you believe it or not, it's true. It's the truth. He was with me. Don't you see? The Saturday your mother . . . died . . . Bill went out of town that afternoon. Went hunting for a few days with his brother down in Kentucky. I'd shipped the kids off to my sister's in Springboro for the weekend, saying I needed time alone. Everyone was gone. I knew I could stay out all night if I wanted. And so your father and I made plans to meet."

No wonder Dad wouldn't tell me who he was with!

Mary stopped again, suddenly. A car drove by, windows down, full of teens tossing out laughter. An elderly man walked a dog on a leash on the other side of the street. Here and there children played, while men and women sat on their porches, waiting for the cool of the night to settle in. Mary felt distanced from the lovely ordinariness around her and wondered how— and if—she would ever find her way back.

Madylyn Fricke was her father's only alibi. It just might be that his fate hinged on the testimony of this woman.

Great. Even Mary could see how that would look to the prosecutor, to the jury, to the whole town of Mason. She could see the headline in the *Pulse Journal* even now: "Man Accused of Killing Wife Was Having Affair."

"Mrs. Fricke?" Mary said quietly, so quietly her voice was almost a whisper. "What are you going to do?"

"I want to admit that your father was with me."

"And Dad doesn't want you to testify for him?"

"No. He won't even tell the truth to his own lawyer. I told him he had to; how else can Hoback build a case? Cal said he had the right to remain silent, and I said, 'With your own counsel?' and he said yes, no one had to know about us. Only him and me. And now you."

"So you've talked to Dad, then?"

"Just once. I didn't dare go to see him more than once." She sniffed out a small laugh. "I told them there at the jail that I was representing the Loyal Sisters of the Church, and I had come to extend our condolences and see if the church could do anything to help."

When Mary didn't respond, Madylyn went on, "Your father is trying to protect me. I can't let him. I know the cost. I know what it all means. I get up there and admit I was having an affair with Cal, it can only be ugly. My marriage ends—not that that matters—but I'd have to leave Mason, start over somewhere else. How could I stay here after that?"

"You'd go somewhere with Dad?"

Madylyn touched her forehead. "Good heavens, Mary, I can't think that far ahead."

"So what do you want me to do?"

"I want you to talk with your father, try to convince him to let me testify."

"But he's already made up his mind he doesn't want you to."

"Yes. Well, he claims it would not only ruin my life, but only make things worse for him. I mean, I'm the other woman in this whole sordid story. He says that's all he needs—one more reason for the jury to think he wanted to get rid of his wife."

Mary was silent for a moment. Then she said, "Dad probably has a point. It can't look good, the two of you being together on the night Mom died. I mean, it's not a very good alibi, is it?"

"No. But there's more, according to your father. He says the prosecutor will argue that he killed Helen and then met me."

Mary stopped cold. She hadn't thought of that. She shifted her gaze to Madylyn's face and saw that the older woman was staring at her expectantly. "Mrs. Fricke?"

"Yes?"

"How do you know that didn't happen? I mean, how do you know Dad didn't kill my mom and then go on and meet you?"

Sorrow clouded Madylyn's eyes like a shade pulled down against a window. "Oh, Mary . . ."

Mary's heart swung wildly, a fleshy bell clapper in her chest. "How do you *know?*" she repeated, wiping at tears.

"I know," Madylyn said quietly, "because I know your father. He would never hurt anyone. You know that too, Mary."

Mary took a deep breath, shuddered as she let it out. "Yeah," she said. "Yeah, I know."

The two exchanged a sad smile. They were at odds, and yet they were on the same side too. They both believed in Cal Syfert's innocence.

"I don't want your father to save me," Madylyn said. "I want to try to save *him.* We have to tell the jury what happened that night. We have to lay it all out the way it happened and hope people recognize the truth when they hear it."

"But you know, we don't really know what happened. That's the problem. We don't know who killed Mom."

"Oh dear," Madylyn sighed. "You sound just like Cal. The important thing, he says, isn't to try to prove he didn't do it, but to try to find who *did* kill Helen. Well, the police aren't even looking. They think they've got the killer. So who else is supposed to go out there and find out who did it?"

They stood at the corner of Cox-Smith and Kings Mills Road, Madylyn clenching her jaw and staring off at the darkening sky. The moon was out, and Venus, and a smattering of stars.

"Mrs. Fricke?" Mary asked. She had stopped crying, but she struggled to catch her breath as the night closed in around her like an airless tent.

"Yes, Mary?"

"Who do *you* suppose killed my mother? I mean, who in the world would have any reason to kill her?"

Madylyn closed her eyes. "God alone knows."

But even as she said it, both she and Mary knew at once that she was wrong. Someone besides God—some person out there—knew the name of Helen Syfert's killer. And surely that someone was never going to tell.

29

HER FATHER'S FACE HUNG HEAVY with fatigue, but his eyes were bright with anger. He gripped the phone with both hands and leaned toward the glass that separated them in the visiting room of the Warren County Jail. When he spoke, his lips barely moved, as though he didn't want to let the words slip into the open, where they might take on a life of their own. Once they started moving about, there would be no gathering them back, and if they landed in the wrong place, they could wreak havoc.

"Yes, I was with Madylyn Fricke, but she shouldn't have told you, Mary," he whispered hoarsely. "I wish she'd kept her mouth shut."

"It wasn't my fault, Dad—"

"I'm not saying it was. I'm just saying she shouldn't have told you. It was between me and her and no one else. No one else knows, and that's the way it's going to stay. You understand me, Mare?"

"Yes, Dad."

"You, me, and Madylyn, we're the only people who ever have to know. You promise me, Mare, all right?"

She had never seen him so frantic, and it alarmed her. Her

eyes settled on a blue vein that throbbed out his heartbeat on his forehead. She had the sense that it was ticking out the seconds until he exploded. She rushed to say, "Don't worry, Dad. I promise. I won't tell anybody."

He took a deep breath; he seemed to be breathing in her words. In the next moment the fire in his eyes died down. His skin went pallid against the orange backdrop of his prison jumpsuit. "Good," he said. "All right. I'm holding you to it."

She should let it drop, she knew. She should let it go and move on. But how to so easily give up on her father's best chance to be vindicated? Quietly, hesitantly, she said, "But, Dad, you do know that she *wants* to testify, right?"

In his eyes there was a brief rekindling of the hot light. "And I told her already that I won't allow it."

They were quiet for a moment, bobbing in a murky sadness.

"You're not even going to tell Mr. Hoback where you were?"

Cal shook his head.

"Think you're doing the right thing?"

"Yeah, I do. Listen, Mare, I may be going down, but I'm not taking Madylyn with me."

She couldn't stop herself from pointing out the obvious, what they both already knew. "But she's your only alibi."

Her father surprised her by laughing a small sardonic laugh. "Some alibi. Joshua Bain would have a heyday with that one. Don't you see, Mary? Having a lover gives me one more reason to get rid of my wife. All Bain would have to do is point out to the jury that we don't really know what time Helen died. Could have been ten o'clock, could have been nine o'clock. So say it's nine o'clock and Madylyn testifies that I met her at ten o'clock. That's plenty of time to kill the wife and go meet the lover. So there you go; open-and-shut case. Simple as that."

Mary nodded slightly, lifting her brows. "Yeah," she said. She'd heard it all from Madylyn. "If you put it that way, it doesn't look good."

Cal reached into the front pocket of his jumpsuit and pulled out a pack of cigarettes. He pressed the phone between his right ear and shoulder to free up his hands to strike a match. He inhaled deeply as he lighted the cigarette, put out the match with a flick of his wrist, and squinted through the smoke at Mary.

"No," he agreed flatly. "It doesn't look good."

"But still, the truth is that you didn't kill Mom and you weren't even home when she died because you were with Mrs. Fricke."

His eyes sank to a deeper shade of sorrow. He shifted his position, leaned close to the glass again. "Listen, Mary, in a court of law, the truth is whatever the prosecutor wants it to be. Joshua Bain says I killed your mother, and he's got the circumstantial evidence to prove it."

Mary chewed at her lower lip and blinked against the tears that stung her eyes. Quietly, she said, "So what's Mr. Hoback going to do?"

Cal shrugged, took a deep drag of the cigarette. "Don't know yet. We got some time still to come up with some sort of defense. But the thing is, we don't know what happened, do we?"

She shook her head reluctantly. "Dad?"

"Yeah?"

"Who do *you* think killed Mom? I mean, who do you think would do it?"

A brief sad smile. "Honey, I'd give a million bucks just to have an idea. I've been wracking my brain day and night trying to think who'd want to hurt your mom. Mare, I have no idea. None."

But Mary had an idea, and a small thrill ran through her as she thought she might be able to offer the defense that would save her father. It was a defense that neither her dad nor Earl Hoback would ever have thought of. The idea had come to her early one morning just as she awoke, and she knew she would share it with her father soon, when the time was right. Now was the time. "Listen, Dad," she said quietly, her eyes darting toward the guard. "I've been thinking. I've been thinking about it a lot."

"Yeah?" He languidly crushed out the cigarette in the ashtray below the wall phone.

"Yeah. That was the week the carnival was here, you know."

"So?"

"There were strangers in town, lots of them, and the creeps that work the midway. . . ." She could see him as he looked that day as clearly as she could see her father sitting across from her now. The hawker at the ring-toss game. There was something wrong with the guy. Something evil. And it wasn't the greasy ponytail, the pockmarked face, the cigarette dangling from cracked lips. It wasn't even the twisted pictures inked into his flesh beneath the forest of hair on his forearms nor the dotted line tattooed across his throat with the words *Cut here* above it—as odd and telling as that was. Rather, it was his eyes. It was something in those Charles Manson eyes that said this guy's mind was tripping in a place that his body wasn't. He was high as a kite on something, and though she didn't know what, she could well imagine it was coke or ludes or PCP or one of those street drugs that was outside the circle of her own experience. When his eyes met hers, she shivered. Shivered visibly, with the fear poking tiny mountain peaks down her arms and legs. He held up three colored rings, beckoned her over. She shook her head. She wasn't about to play that game. Not on her life.

Mary drifted back to meet her father's gaze. She had his attention, but she couldn't read what was in his eyes.

"You think one of the carnies killed your mother?" he asked.

"Yeah, I do, Dad. I mean, who else? It's a possibility, isn't it?"

Cal reached for another cigarette, changed his mind, let his hand drop to the table. "Why would some guy from the carnival kill your mother?"

So why did Charles Manson's druggie entourage kill a pregnant Sharon Tate and four of her friends a few years before? That bunch of barefoot hippies broke into that Beverly Hills mansion and stabbed and strangled and snuffed out the lives of six people, one unborn, just for the sport of it. Because their drug-altered minds told them it was the thing to do.

"But that's the whole point, isn't it? Why would anyone kill her? There's really no reason. I think it was random. I think that carnival worker just came upon our house and found Mom alone—"

"Well, just what carnival worker are you talking about, Mary? You have somebody in mind?"

"Yeah, I can see him, Dad. I can see him plain as day. He was tripping on something, some kind of drug. And he was weird. I mean, he looked really bad, like Charles Manson, you know? People like that just kill people for no reason. If the police can track down the carnival and arrest him—"

"Slow down, Mare. You can't arrest someone for looking like Charles Manson. That doesn't mean he killed someone. Some guy with the carnival's got no reason to kill your mother."

"But like I said, Dad, he doesn't have to have a reason—"

It was her father's expression, or lack of one, that stopped her.

Suddenly, her hope plummeted. "Don't you even think it's a possibility, Dad?"

Cal shrugged. "Mary, there was no sign of a break-in—"

"But there wasn't a break-in. You told me yourself you'd left the back door unlocked. Whoever it was just walked right in."

"Yeah. Yeah."

"There *had* to be someone in the house. Mom didn't smother herself and then throw herself down the stairs when she was already dead! *Someone* had to do it!"

He nodded wearily. "Sure, someone had to do it. But they've got no evidence of any strangers in the house. No fingerprints. Nothing."

"The police are just overlooking it. They think they've got the killer, and they're not even going to bother looking for any clues that might point to anybody else. Listen, Dad, won't you mention it to Mr. Hoback? Just say maybe it's a possibility that Mom's killer was with the carnival, and that he's moved on and that's why they can't find him."

Cal smiled wanly. He nodded. "Yeah, all right. I'll mention it to Hoback, see if he wants to do anything with it. Maybe he'll think it's worth pursuing."

"And you know, Dad, maybe there was a reason. Maybe the guy was looking for money or valuables. Maybe it was a robbery."

"If you're talking about her rings, they're there somewhere. We just don't know where Helen might have put them."

"Maybe I can look around again. Maybe—"

She stopped when she realized her father was no longer listening. His eyes were shut, and he was rubbing circles into his forehead with the hand that didn't hold the phone.

"Dad?"

His mouth drew up into nothing. He opened his eyes and looked straight at her. His bottom eyelids quivered, tiny seas tossed by a wet wind.

"Mary," he whispered.

"What is it, Dad?"

"Sometimes I think . . ." More circles, fingertips kneading the furrows of his brow. "Sometimes I think maybe I blacked out. Maybe I didn't know what I was doing—didn't know then and can't remember now."

Her breath stopped. She felt the room tilt. "No, Dad. No. Don't start thinking that way. You didn't do it."

"Sometimes I don't know. There's just no explanation, nothing I can make sense of."

"Dad. Dad." She spoke the word into the phone until he looked at her. She locked onto his gaze, held his eyes with the strength of her own fledgling determination. "You didn't black out. Don't ever say that."

"I don't know, Mare—"

"Please, Dad. Please."

He dropped his hand. His brow was a field of red. He sighed. "I lie awake nights, wondering, Do I even know myself, what I'm capable of?"

Mary started to cry. "We're going to find out what happened, and when we do, you can come home. I just want you to come home."

"Yeah." He pulled a hand down over his eyes, shutting the shades against the tears. "I want that too, sweetheart."

An awkward silence ensued. At length Cal said, "Hey, Mare, about Madylyn—I want to explain."

"You don't have to say anything."

"No, I want to. I mean, I don't want you to think—"

"It's okay, Dad."

"Grown-ups," he began again, then stopped. He rocked forward on his elbows. "I did the best by your mother that I could, for a long time."

"I know."

"It isn't that I didn't love her—"

"Yeah." The word was a sigh. Mary looked beyond her father's shoulder as he spoke.

"I did the best I could," he repeated.

"But do you love *her*, Dad?" Mary glanced at him briefly, then looked away again.

"Madylyn?"

"Yeah."

He exhaled heavily. "People get lonely, Mare. Men, women—we get lonely. Makes a person do funny things."

"Yeah." But it didn't seem much of an answer.

"She's not a bad woman, sweetheart. You've got to believe that."

"I didn't say she was a bad woman."

"No, but I know what you're thinking."

Mary didn't respond. Cal looked helpless, pressed a hand to the glass, let it drop.

She chewed her lip, then asked, "You going to marry her?"

"Marry Madylyn? Naw. I'm not going to marry her. If I get out of here, you and I, we're going to go somewhere, start a new life."

She took a deep trembling breath. "I'm scared, Dad."

"I am too, sweetheart."

"Why'd all this have to happen?"

"I don't know. But we'll get beyond it, somehow."

"What'll I do if you don't get out?"

He looked at her a long while, his eyes tender. "You're going to go on and live your life. And you're going to make me proud."

"I don't think I can live without you."

"You can, Mare. If you have to."

Another awkward silence. Then Cal said, "How's it going over at Uncle Henry's?"

"All right. Except I have to see Uncle Denton all the time."

He gave her an understanding nod. "You getting enough to eat?"

"Yeah." She laughed a little, sadly. "Aunt Vivian's a good cook."

"That's good. Wish I could say the same for the jailhouse cook."

They shared a smile.

Cal glanced at a clock that hung on the wall behind Mary. "I'm going to have to go now."

"Okay."

"Listen." He leaned forward on both elbows and looked at her intently. "No matter what happens, sweetheart, I love you. You're my best girl. You know that, don't you?"

"Yeah." She nodded.

"See you tomorrow?"

She nodded again, smiled. She had stopped crying, but her sadness had settled in her throat like dregs in the bottom of a cup, and she couldn't speak. She wanted to tell her father that she loved him too, and that no matter what happened, she would always believe in his innocence. And she wanted to tell him too that she would even try to forgive Madylyn Fricke for giving him a reason not to be home when her mother was murdered, even though between the two of them, she and her father always made sure Helen Syfert was never left alone at night.

But before she could get rid of the lump in her throat, her father had hung up the phone and called for the guard and disappeared again behind the impenetrable brick walls of the Warren County Jail.

30

MARY WAS ON HER HANDS and knees digging dandelions out of the front yard when Neil showed up at her house on Church Street. She rocked back on her heels, tossed a weed on the pile, and squinted up at him against the early afternoon sun. She lifted a gloved hand to shade her eyes, and when she did, she understood something that she had not understood for twenty-six years.

"People get lonely, Mare. Men, women—we get lonely."

She was Madylyn Fricke looking up at Cal Syfert, and she knew then that when your heart was free-floating and wanting to be grounded, it might settle anywhere, even where it didn't belong.

Neil smiled at her. Beyond that smile, inside that head somewhere, buried in the storehouse of that mind, was the answer to the one question she wanted to ask of him. *Was I completely wrong, or did you love me once?*

It might be a simple yes or no. It might be, *I don't know, we were so young, but I know I felt something.* Any answer, any explanation would do. Anything at all.

But when he spoke, the words were splashes of gray on an

already dull canvas. "It might be easier," he said, "just to spray some sort of weed killer on those dandelions."

Oh yes, of course. Weeds, the moist earth, the smooth-handled dandelion digger in her hand. This was life. This was her life.

"I like to dig them out by hand," she said, rising. "It's relaxing."

He shrugged. "To each her own."

Mary clapped away the dirt and tattered leaves that clung to her gloves, then slipped them off and let them fall to the ground. She hadn't seen Neil since her birthday. That was a week ago now. She wondered whether, in that time, he had purposely avoided her, just as she had avoided going to the Sadler house. She wanted to help take care of Uncle Bernie, but she wasn't sure she wanted to see Neil. No, that wasn't true. She did want to see Neil. But she didn't want to feel what she felt when she saw him.

"So what brings you out this way?" she asked.

Pushing his hands into the pockets of his painter's overalls, he said, "Actually, I have a message for you from Bernie."

"Oh?"

"Yeah." He paused.

He seemed a reluctant messenger.

"He says you should talk with Madylyn."

Mary gasped, feeling suddenly exposed, and angry. "What?" She shook her head. "How does he know about Madylyn?"

Neil shrugged again, this time sheepishly. "Hope you don't mind, Mary. I happened to mention her while Bernie and I were talking. I shouldn't have, I guess."

"But, how do *you* know about Madylyn?"

He frowned visibly, as though she had asked a silly question. "Well, the night we went to the Village, she called, remember? You didn't pick up. I heard her voice over the answering machine."

Mary exhaled heavily and turned aside. She reached for a rake leaning up against a wheelbarrow and began dragging together the various small piles of dandelions languishing on the grass.

Neil took a step toward her. "I'm sorry if this upsets you, Mary."

She stopped and stared at him, her face a smooth stone. If she spoke, she might say something she regretted. She might cry, and that would be worse. She needed just a minute to hold her breath a certain way, to cut off the tears. She jabbed again at the dandelions on the grass, buying a moment of time.

Neil went on, "I told Bernie I didn't think you wanted to have anything to do with Madylyn, but he seems to think she has something to tell you."

Mary stopped again, abruptly, and clutched the rake handle. "Do you know who she is?"

"No." He shook his head. Then he added weakly, "I'm not sure. . . ."

"What can she tell me that I don't already know?" She didn't want to sound angry, but she couldn't help it.

Neil went on shaking his head. "I guess I can't answer that."

Mary gave a vexed laugh. "She doesn't have anything to tell me. She wants me to tell *her* something. What she wants is for me to forgive her. She wants to ask . . ." Her voice drifted off as her mind followed the trail of a thought. Only a moment ago she had stepped inside Madylyn Fricke and had felt that floating heart. Madylyn Fricke had been lonely, yes. That Mary could understand. Still, if she hadn't agreed to rendezvous with

Cal Syfert that week the carnival was in town . . .

"Mary." Neil's voice was gentle. "Does this have anything to do with your dad?"

She met his gaze and answered bluntly, "Dad should have been home the night Mom died."

Neil fell silent. His face told Mary he wasn't following her.

"He was with Madylyn Fricke, you know."

After a long moment Neil said, "Okay." As though he had decided to agree.

"He wasn't home when he should have been. He left Mom alone at night, and he left the back door unlocked, and someone just walked right into the house and killed Mom. I've always known that."

"But who? Do you know who it was?"

Mary could see him still. The ponytail, the tattooed line across his throat, the glassy eyes. "It doesn't matter anymore."

"I don't understand. Cal admitted to the crime. He pleaded guilty."

Mary could feel the anger bubbling up again and bouncing through her veins. "No. He didn't. Not really."

"No? I was gone by then, but I heard there wasn't a trial because he admitted he did it. I mean, Mom sent me the news clippings. She sent me everything."

Mary shook her head slowly as Neil spoke. "He always maintained his innocence. Not many people believed him, but I did, and Madylyn did."

But Neil didn't, Mary knew that. Even before the guilty plea, Neil had left Mason believing that Cal Syfert had murdered his wife. He'd told her so once, not in so many words, but he'd made his doubts clear the day they met by accident on the Widow's Bridge. He was leaving for New York soon, and she wanted to tell him, straight out, before he left that her father was innocent. What he'd said in reply was, "That's for the jury to decide, isn't it?" And Mary knew that if Neil had been on the jury, he'd have voted in favor of Cal Syfert's guilt.

"If Madylyn believed in your dad's innocence," Neil said now, "maybe you should talk with her. Maybe she has something to tell you."

She suddenly wanted Neil to leave. And yet, too, she wanted him to stay. She wanted him to understand, to talk, to listen. All the ill-defined longings bound her like rope so that she was unable to respond when he said again, "Maybe you should talk with her."

The screen door opened and banged shut, and suddenly Dan was on the porch, looking down at Mary and Neil. He didn't smile.

Mary knew she had to speak. She worked to reach inside herself to pull out the expected introduction. "Dan, you remember my cousin Neil, don't you? Neil Sadler."

Dan looked at Neil for an unusually long minute, as though trying to make him out through a fog. "Sure," he said. "I remember."

"Neil, this is Dan. My husband."

She wondered whether Dan appeared to Neil the way he appeared to her—someone tired, hung-over, worn out, with a day's worth of beard on his jaw and a night's worth of alcohol still traveling through his veins.

When Mary looked back over at Neil, she was surprised to see him smiling. It may have simply been his upbringing to be polite, and yet Mary felt a sudden gratitude toward him.

"You were on the debate team," Neil said to Dan. "You came in first in '76 when the topic was women in the military."

Dan looked at once both puzzled and pleased. He offered a vague smile in return. "You have a good memory."

Neil stepped forward, held out a hand. Dan accepted it. They shook.

"You in Mason for a while?" Dan asked.

"For the summer. Helping family renovate an old farmhouse. They're making it into a bed-and-breakfast."

"Oh yeah." Dan squinted again. "Mary mentioned that."

"Speaking of which—" Neil looked down at his work clothes—"I've got to get back. I promised Dennis I wouldn't be gone more than thirty minutes, and I'm past that now already."

"Sure," Dan said. "Take it easy."

"Right. See you later. Good-bye, Mary."

"Bye, Neil. Listen, tell Bernie I'll talk to him about it."

"Sure. Okay, I'll do that."

When Neil's car turned off Church Street and disappeared, Mary turned to find Dan looking at her questioningly. *He wants to ask me about Neil,* she thought.

Instead, he asked, "What do you have to talk to Bernie about?" Neil was, apparently, only her cousin after all.

She hadn't told Dan about Madylyn's trying to contact her, hadn't intended to tell anyone. It was only by accident that Neil knew, and now Bernie. Dan might as well know too.

Mary took a deep breath. "Madylyn Fricke has tried to get in touch with me a few times. It's no big deal. I just don't want to talk with her, is all."

"She's called?" Dan knew who she was, of course. He hadn't heard her name in years, but there was no forgetting it. Still, if he was surprised by Mary's admission, he didn't show it.

"Called and written both. A couple of times."

"I didn't even know she was still alive."

"Yes. She's in a nursing home down in Cincy."

Dan shook his head, a slow movement from side to side. "What do you suppose she wants?"

She shrugged. "I don't know."

"Aren't you the least bit curious?"

Mary's eyes drifted down Church Street to where Neil's car had been a moment ago. "Like I told Neil, my guess is that she wants me to forgive her before she dies."

Dan shifted uneasily. "And you can't?"

"I just don't want to live it all again. If I talk to her, it's 1977 all over again. You know what I mean? I just don't think I have the strength. . . ."

They stood in silence a long while, avoiding each other's eyes.

Finally Dan said, "Okay. Do what you think is best. I'll be back in a little while. I've got to go meet Stan." Stan Sawtell, his lawyer.

"What about?"

Dan lifted tired shoulders, let them drop. "Same old, same old. The investigation. The Traylor woman. He talks, I listen."

And drink, Mary thought. "Be back for supper?" she asked.

"Oh sure. I'll be back long before then."

Depending on how much he drank.

"Leo's been wanting to make a day of it out at King's Island."

"Oh yeah."

"Think we can all go soon?"

"Sure. Why not?"

"Maybe later this week?"

"Sure. Let me think about it." He looked at his watch. "Listen, I gotta run."

245

And then he was gone. But it didn't matter. He was gone even when he was home. The boy who had saved her once—the young man who had single-handedly carried her through the greatest crisis of her life—now needed saving himself. Sadly, she wasn't sure she had the means within herself to return the favor.

31

THOUGH SHE HAD KEPT MOSTLY to herself, a kind of voluntary solitary confinement in her uncle's house on Hanover Drive, Mary somehow managed to meet Dan Beeken the summer her mother died. She wasn't looking for love. She wasn't looking for anything other than a patch of steady ground, a place to lay her feet that wouldn't suddenly shift beneath her. She'd been sent reeling by her mother's death and her father's arrest, and she hadn't even begun to stand upright again when she was dealt another blow. The grand jury came back with an indictment of first-degree murder.

"So what's that mean for you, Dad?" she asked when he told her the news.

"I don't know for sure yet, Mary. But you've got to understand, you've got to know that Joshua Bain is going for the death penalty."

A stunned silence, followed by pieces of her life falling to the jailhouse floor, shattered like glass. Did anyone else hear the crash? Or was she the only one?

"I thought we didn't have the death penalty anymore."

"It's on the books again. Ohio hasn't used it yet, but it's on the books."

She was too dazed to cry. "But it's not for sure that Bain's going to do that?"

"Hoback tells me that's what Bain intends to do. Doesn't mean it'll end up that way. Hoback says in my case it's more likely I'd get life. There aren't the aggravating circumstances you usually have when a person gets death. That doesn't stop Bain from trying, though."

Who was this Joshua Bain that he should want to see her father dead?

"Listen, Mare, Hoback's arranging for me to take a polygraph. It'll show I didn't do it. Mark my word. I'll pass this polygraph and we'll see what Bain says then, all right?"

"Sure, Dad. Sure."

———————

And three days later she's supposed to tie up the laces on a pair of battered skates and go out on the rink to do the hokey-pokey?

She almost hung up on her best friend when Peg called to invite her. "I can't go skating with you, Peg. Don't you get it?" Hers wasn't a private grief. It was a public spectacle. *She* was a public spectacle, a two-ring circus, daughter of the slain and daughter of the alleged slayer all in one. The name Syfert was the biggest money-maker the local paper had seen in a long time. "Everywhere I go, people stare at me. I'm a freak. I can't stand it, Peg."

"Yeah, but listen, Mare, I know you're going crazy staying inside that house all the time. Stay too long and you're going to end up as screwy as your uncle Dented. You have to get out, just to take a breather from that guy, if nothing else."

Peg had a point, Mary thought. Bad enough that Uncle

Denton spent most nights searching for Chinese battalions in the Ohio countryside, but lately he'd started giving Mary looks that left her unnerved. Sometimes, as he stood watching her, his lower jaw fell open, and he seemed to be trying unsuccessfully to shake a few words off his tongue. Giving up, he'd move his head from side to side and walk away, his hound-dog eyes blinking slowly. After a few weeks of that, Mary decided she was probably already a little crazy.

"Besides," Peg promised, "I'll be with you."

And so they went. And Peg was skating a couples skate with Mike Schwankl when Mary, sitting at a table trying to look busy with a cherry Coke, saw Dan Beeken approach her, rolling awkwardly over the carpeted portion of the roller rink's snack bar area. Mary dropped her eyes, hoping he'd pass by. She recognized him from school. He was a year ahead and had just graduated last month. He'd been a bigwig on the debate team, had lettered in track, was branded forever by the yearbook staff as "Most likely to get out of Mason." For whatever that was worth. Ninety percent of the kids were going to try to get out of Mason, and probably fifty percent of those were going to succeed, settling in Cincinnati and Columbus and maybe even venturing across the state line.

Mary and Dan had never spoken, not that she could remember. He was all right, though; a nice kid, and certainly not bad looking. But she wasn't interested in couples skates. Unless it was with Neil, and he wasn't there.

She set her cup on the table, the heel of her hand settling against the sticky remnants of earlier drinks. She thought, *As soon as I finish this Coke, I'm leaving.* She'd driven Uncle Henry's car instead of having Peg pick her up; that way, she could leave when she wanted. And she wanted to leave now. An hour into the evening and she had already felt the heat of too many stares, had seen too many curious eyes dart away as soon as she looked up. No thanks. She was better off at home with Denton Patch and his Don Quixote quest for Chinese windmills.

Soon as I finish this Coke, she thought, but the thought was interrupted when she realized Dan Beeken was no longer approaching her. He had dropped none too gracefully onto the empty chair beside her and swung his size-twelve skates beneath the table. So there he was, insinuating himself right into her solitude with his lanky presence. She set her mouth, determined to discourage him.

"Hey," he said, "I'm Dan." He had to speak loudly over the background noise of music, voices, laughter, wheels against wood.

She looked at him, nodding slightly. "I know." She braced herself against the expected invitation to skate.

But when he spoke again, it wasn't to invite her to skate. "I want you to know I believe your dad is innocent."

Mary felt the heat run up her neck and seep into her cheeks. Was this a joke, some sort of cruel come-on?

"I'm serious," he said, reading her face.

"I don't even know you. And you don't know me."

"Then maybe we ought to get to know each other." He said it matter-of-factly, without smiling. "My uncle—he's with the force down in Cincy. He did the polygraph on your dad today."

Mary gasped, an inaudible intake of air. "And?"

"He passed."

She didn't move for a moment, for fear that Dan would start to laugh, admit it was a joke. But he didn't laugh. Finally she said, "Are you sure?"

"Of course I'm sure. I spoke with my uncle not two hours ago."

"He called you about my dad's test?"

"Yeah. He knows I'm interested—" he cocked his head— "in the case."

"You are?"

"Yeah."

Of course he was. Wasn't everyone in Mason?

"And my dad passed the test?"

"Are you surprised or something?"

Oh no, not surprised. Not surprised at all. More like elated. Ecstatic. Filled for the first time with a hope that actually had some meat on its bones, something she could hold on to.

She raised both hands to her lips. "What did your uncle say?"

"That your dad passed the polygraph. That as far as he's concerned, your dad's an innocent man."

"Oh, dear God," she breathed.

"What's that?"

But she couldn't say it again. She had to shut her eyes a moment against the tears.

"You all right?"

She opened her eyes, dropped her hands, and smiled. "They'll let him go now, right?"

Dan Beeken still didn't smile. "Not right away, I guess."

"What do you mean?"

"I mean, I don't suppose the prosecutor's going to let go of the case as easy as all that."

"Well, what's next then?"

"Your dad's lawyer—what's his name?"

"Earl Hoback."

"Hoback, yeah. He'll take the polygraph results to the district attorney, show him that according to the test your dad isn't lying when he says he didn't kill your mom."

"Yeah?"

"So then probably the D.A. will want to have another polygraph done with a different tester, one he chooses himself."

"Okay." Cautiously. "So, Dad will pass again."

Dan nodded. "My uncle—he's one of the best in Cincy. He's got—I don't know—a certain instinct about all this stuff. He says he knows almost as soon as he straps a guy up to the machine whether he's going to be lying or not."

"Yeah?"

"Yeah."

"And he believes my dad is telling the truth."

"Yeah."

She was seventeen years old again. And the ground felt firm beneath her feet. And it made perfect sense to be at a roller rink on a Friday night.

After Cal Syfert passed one more polygraph test, he could come home.

"Good thing my uncle's a pro," Dan was saying. "Those polygraphs—they're tricky things. I mean, my uncle tells me about some pretty weird cases. Like the time this one guy was a suspect in a murder case, and the police brought him in and gave him the test, and he failed. I mean, according to the polygraph, this guy was lying up and down when he said he didn't do the shooting. Turns out, he didn't. Some other guy confessed. First guy almost went to trial for a murder he didn't commit."

"Oh yeah?"

"Yeah. And some of these criminals—man!" A slow shake

of the head. "They try to do what's called 'beating the machine.' They're good at it too, some of them. They pass the polygraph when they're guilty as sin." Dan finally gave a small laugh, shook his head once more. "But my uncle's good. He isn't wrong very often. Can't remember the last time he was wrong."

Mary nodded. She wanted Dan Beeken's uncle to be right. Wanted it desperately.

"So you know a lot about police stuff," she said. It was meant to be a compliment. He took it that way.

"Sure." He nodded confidently. "I'm going to be a peace officer myself someday."

She liked the way he said that. Not cop. Not policeman. Peace officer. Put the job in a whole new light.

"But I can't get into the Police Academy until I'm twenty-one. So I'm biding my time."

Mary lifted the Coke to her lips, pulled on the straw. Her heart was pounding. Her dad had passed the polygraph, just like he said he would. And of course he did. He was innocent! He was still behind bars, but he must be smiling now. He must be high on hope, knowing he had passed, knowing he had the truth on his side. Soon everyone else would know too that Cal Syfert had nothing to do with his wife's death. The police could get back to the business of finding the real killer, and her dad could come home. Home, wherever that might be now. Not the house on S. East Street. They'd never live there again. They'd leave Mason, like her dad had said. They'd leave, start over somewhere, some place brand-new to both of them, where no one knew them. . . .

"My mom's not big on the idea," Dan was saying, "you know, about my joining the force. She says it's too dangerous, especially in a place like Cincy. But it's what I want to do. I don't want to end up like my dad, you know?"

"Your dad?"

Dan shrugged. "He's on the line at Reading."

"Oh." Reading Manufacturing, where Mary's dad worked. Used to work.

"I mean, it brings home a paycheck and all," Dan went on, "but it's not really doing anything. Nothing good for people, anyway. My dad says he's just an arm of the machine. That's it. Just a part of the machine, and some days he thinks he's going to go crazy with boredom."

"Yeah, I understand." Her dad said the same thing. Not in words, but she could read it in his face when he left for work in the morning and when he came home. Dissatisfaction. Boredom. Well, he wouldn't have to do it anymore. They'd settle somewhere else and he could get another job, something better.

"My dad said he could get me a job there, something temporary, to pass the time till I can get into the Academy. I said no thanks."

"Oh." She laughed. She was feeling good. Everything was going to be all right now. "So what are you doing?"

He smiled proudly, a smile that said he'd been hoping she would ask. "I'm a dispatcher with the Mason police."

"Yeah?" Her eyes were wide. "That's cool."

"It's just part time, but I'm learning a lot. And I like it. It's good experience until I can get started down in Cincy."

"You want to join the police force down there instead of here?"

He nodded. "Yeah, you know, that's where the action is."

"I guess so."

Well, the action certainly wasn't here in Mason. You know

a town is pretty quiet when a homicide is the news of the decade. Of the century, even. Helen Syfert and Rebecca McClung. They'd both go down in Mason history.

"I'm working here too," Dan added.

"Here?"

"Yeah, here at the rink. My cousin owns the place."

"Oh, I didn't know that."

"It's a paycheck. Something to do."

"Until you can get into the Academy."

"Right." He smiled. "You got one more year, huh, before you graduate?"

Mary nodded.

"Then what?"

She shrugged, smiled softly. "I don't know." She didn't even know where she'd be a month from now when Cal Syfert was out of jail and they were headed to their new home.

She looked out over the rink. The place pulsated to the beat of "You Should Be Dancing" by the Bee Gees. Strobe lights flashed, breaking up the movements of the skaters into a staccato series of freeze-frames. Lithe young bodies on the verge of adulthood rolling with the beat, dancing on skates, tumbling into the excitement of what they were sure life owed them now that they'd made it this far.

Dan followed Mary's gaze, then turned back to her. "So, you wanna skate?"

Yeah, she wanted to skate. She wanted to dance. She rose and took Dan's hand, and together they eased into the wild flow, into the whirlpool of young kids blindly enjoying the moment before being irredeemably sucked down into the rest of their lives.

32

"IF I HAD KNOWN HOW IT was all going to turn out," Peg said, "I never would have insisted you come to the roller rink that night."

"What night?"

"The night you hooked up with Dan."

"Oh yeah." Mary stirred cream into her coffee. She looked at Peg sitting in the booth across from her. It was just after four o'clock, too early for the dinner crowd that would start trickling into the Dinner Bell around five. At the moment, Mary and Peg were the restaurant's only customers. "So now you're blaming yourself for my marital problems, is that it?"

"Gracious, no." Peg shook her head. "I'm just saying, if I *could* have known—"

"Yeah?"

"Well, I would have just stayed out of it, that's all."

Mary knew the story. She knew how Dan, who was a friend of Peg's older brother, had called Peg every day for a week, trying to convince her to convince Mary to go to the rink. He wanted to meet her.

Peg had put him off. *"Listen, just call her yourself."*

"I can't do that."

"Why not?"

"She might say no."

"And?"

"If we just happen to meet at the rink, she can't say no. She'll have to talk to me."

"Come on, Dan, you're asking me to set you up with my best friend. I don't like playing Cupid."

"You're not playing Cupid. I'm just asking you to help me out here. Get her to the rink. I'll do the rest."

And he had done the rest. And the rest was history now, played out and unchangeable.

"Listen, Peg," Mary said. "I'm not so sure it was the wrong thing."

Peg's eyebrows arched like a pair of frightened cats. "What do you mean?"

"Meeting Dan. Marrying him. Maybe it wasn't the wrong thing."

"Good *night*, Mare, how can you say that? Look at him! He's a drunken cop who might end up doing time for killing some poor slob—"

"Peg! Don't talk like that!"

Peg stopped. She took a sip of coffee, then said, "If the shoe fits . . ."

"Well, it doesn't."

"Oh? So are you and I talking about the same Dan Beeken?"

"Probably not."

"Listen, honey," Peg said, "I'm not trying to upset you. I just want you to look at the facts before it's too late."

"Too late for what?"

"As if you don't know! And the fact is this: you married Dan Beeken on the rebound."

"What?"

"Admit it, Mare. Neil split, so you took the next one to come along."

"I did no such thing!"

"You were in love with Neil for years."

"I was a kid, Peg. Having a crush hardly counts as being in love. Besides, I married Dan three years after Neil left. I don't call that on the rebound."

Peg shrugged. "And, you know, there was another reason you married Dan too."

"Oh? Care to clue me in?"

"I'm about to. You married him because he believed your dad was innocent. Even after he failed that second lie detector test, Dan still believed he was innocent. He turned into your big hero, and you married him for that."

Mary sat shaking her head from side to side. She had long ago learned how to let Peg's blunt and irregular remarks fall away from her without penetrating the skin. Her shield was the thought *That's just Peg*. Crazy and eccentric Peg, who was, above all else, a devoted friend.

"Listen, Peg," Mary said, "I can see where you're coming from. But you're wrong. I married Dan because I loved him."

Her friend gave a small harrumph.

"The problem is," Mary went on, "you just never liked Dan."

"I've always liked him just fine! That doesn't mean you should have married him, though."

"Well, I don't remember you objecting to the marriage when you were my maid of honor."

"Yeah, and I also didn't object to myself marrying Mike Schwankl, and look how that turned out." She raised a hand and flagged down the waitress. "I'm dying for a banana split," she said. "Want one?"

"I thought you were on a diet."

"I am."

"Well?"

"This time it's that Atkins thingy. It's great, Mare. I can eat anything I want, as long as it's not fruit or vegetables."

Mary gave a look that said she didn't understand. "Well, you don't need to lose weight anyway. And no, I don't want one."

The waitress came and Peg ordered. When she left, Mary said, "Funny you should mention that night at the rink. I was thinking about it just the other day. Yesterday, maybe. I don't know, I lose track of time."

"Yeah? So why were you thinking about it?"

Mary gazed out the window before answering. "I don't know, Peg. It's like, Neil comes back, and 1977 starts playing itself out in my mind. And it's not because I feel anything for him anymore." As she said the words, something inside her head screamed, *Liar!* She looked at Peg to gauge whether the voice could be heard beyond the dome of her own skull. Peg sat placidly, her face expressionless, as she waited for Mary to go on. "It's just that Neil comes back, and so it follows that 1977 comes back. It's the last thing I want to think about, but there it is. I have no choice but to let it play out."

"Uh-huh." Before Peg could say more, the waitress returned with the banana split. Peg scooped out a large bite, popped it into her mouth, then waved the spoon for emphasis. "People have a way of triggering memories, don't they?"

Mary frowned in thought. "But it's not just Neil. It's Madylyn too. They've both come back."

"Madylyn?"

"Madylyn Fricke."

"Okay." Peg took another large bite. A crescent of whipped cream clung to each corner of her mouth. "Refresh my memory."

Mary sniffed and turned her face aside. "You know, the woman Dad was seeing when Mom died—"

She was interrupted by the crash of Peg's spoon as it landed heavily against the speckled Formica tabletop. "Good *night*, Mare! *That* Madylyn? What do you mean she's come back? And why haven't you told me before this?"

"Well, it's just that—"

"You mean she's still alive?"

"Apparently so."

"What does she want?"

"I—"

"Good *night*!" Peg cried again. "I'm hurt, Mare. I mean, are we best friends or not?"

"Of course." Mary tried to smile apologetically at the waitress, who was staring at them from the kitchen doorway.

"So fill me in," Peg said anxiously. "What's the scoop here?"

Mary took a deep breath, let it out. "I don't know what she wants. And I haven't told anybody about it, not directly, anyway. It's just . . . well, never mind. It's complicated."

"Never mind? This woman pops up after twenty-five years as good as dead, and you say never mind! Listen, something's going on, and I'd like to know what it is."

"If I knew what it was, I'd tell you."

"What do you mean? Have you seen her? What'd she say?"

"I haven't seen her, and she hasn't said anything. She's tried to contact me, but I'm not interested in being in touch."

"So you're not going to talk with her?"

"I doubt it."

"But what does she *want?*"

I shouldn't have brought it up, Mary thought. *What's the use of talking about any of this?* She stared across the table at the banana split, at the tiny avalanches of whipped cream sliding down the vanilla mountains.

"There must be something left undone," she said finally.

"Like *what?*"

Mary shook her head. "I don't know."

"Don't you *want* to know?"

"No. Not really."

"Are you crazy?" Peg stared at Mary for a long moment before her face softened and the sticky corners of her mouth turned up in a small smile. She picked up the spoon and jabbed at the ice cream. "All right," she said. "I talked you into going to the rink all those years ago. I'm keeping my nose out of it this time."

"Okay."

"But I think you're crazy."

"I'll make a note of that."

Peg ate half of the banana split before saying, "Listen, have some ice cream or something. Better yet, have a drink."

"Oh, Peg, you know I don't drink."

"It's not too late to start."

Mary laughed.

Peg smiled. "All right, listen. Whatever you decide to do about Madylyn, just keep me posted, all right?"

"All right."

"Promise?"

"Yes."

"No more secrets."

"I haven't been keeping secrets."

"Well, personally, I think you ought to talk to her."

"I thought you were keeping your nose out of it."

"I'm just offering my opinion."

"I think I *will* have that drink."

She called the waitress over and asked for a refill. "Decaf, please."

"Going straight for the hard stuff as usual, I see," Peg said.

"Yeah. You know me."

Peg scraped at the bottom of the glass bowl, scooping up the last soupy spoonful of ice cream. "That was good," she commented. "I love this diet."

"Life is sweet."

"Can be. If you work at it."

The waitress arrived with the coffeepot. She poured another cup for Mary, then turned to Peg and asked, "Heat yours up?"

Peg slid her cup over. "Sure, why not? And you can take this ice-cream dish; I'm finished."

When the waitress left, Peg said, "You want to know what I think, Mare?"

"Do I have a choice?"

"Not about Madylyn. About Neil, I mean."

"Oh, boy."

"Yeah, I've been thinking about it. I think he came back to Mason to reconnect with you."

"With me?"

"Of course. I mean, look, his wife's dead and—"

"Peg, like I told you before, he didn't even know I was here.

263

He thought I was still living down in Cincy."

"Oh?"

Mary nodded.

"Still, I don't think he ever forgot you, Mare."

"Oh, Peg." Mary sighed, but even as she sighed, she laughed. "You're incorrigible."

"Well, I hope so."

"There's nothing going on between me and Neil."

"Then there should be."

Mary shook her head, sipped her coffee. "The last thing I need is to have an affair."

"I'm not talking about an affair. I'm talking about a new life. And that's what I mean about not waiting until it's too late. You've got to act before Neil goes back to New York."

"Give it up, Peg."

"Not a chance. I want you to be happy."

"Neil Sadler isn't my ticket to happiness."

"And Dan Beeken is?"

He had been, once. A long time ago. "You know," Mary said, "it was Dan who got me through . . . the whole thing . . . when Mom died, and then Dad. He was the one who got me through it all. I have to wonder what would have become of me if Dan hadn't been there."

Peg sipped her coffee, settled the cup in the saucer. "You'd have gotten through it one way or the other. You've always been tougher than you look."

Mary laughed lightly. "Well, thanks. I guess."

"The one thing Dan was good for was getting you out of Mason. But then, you could have done that on your own."

"I'm not so sure," she said. "Don't you see? My senior year—that awful year—Dan was always there for me."

"Hey, I was there too, don't forget. You had plenty of friends."

"Yeah. Yeah, I know, but . . ." She stopped. None of those friends had really believed in her father's innocence. Not even Peg. Sure, Peg *said* she believed, but she didn't mean it. Not really. At best Peg simply wasn't sure. She wasn't convinced, not the way Dan was.

That had been Mary's one sure sphere, her place of safety. Dan's arms, his words, his love. Maybe Peg was right when she said Dan had become her hero. But she hadn't married him only because he believed in Cal Syfert's innocence. She was sure of that. She had loved him once. She had been in love with him. She could almost remember what it was like.

"You want some more coffee, Mare?"

Mary looked at her watch and shook her head. "No. I've got to get home and start dinner. I promised Leo I'd make lasagna. Then I'm going over to the Sadler house tonight to help put Uncle Bernie to bed."

"Oh, hey, how's the old guy doing?"

"Great. He's doing great. He's the Energizer Bunny; he just keeps going."

Peg laughed. "Yeah, well, that's good. Oh, by the way, did you hear Rhonda Traylor was released? Yeah, the doctors sent her home."

Mary was quiet a moment. "Good for her, I guess."

"We were all pretty glad to be rid of her down on transitional. She was one of those patients who thinks the staff is there to personally wait on her hand and foot."

"I can imagine."

The two women stood and leaned toward each other for a

hug. "Listen, honey," Peg said, "you take care. And *call* me if anything happens."

"Sure. I will."

The shadows were starting to lengthen on Main Street. Peg fished around in her handbag and finally pulled out a pair of sunglasses she didn't need. A second dunk reeled in a tube of lipstick. "Oh, and don't forget," she said. She made an O of her mouth, ran the stick of color over her lips, then snapped the cover back on. "Martin and I are going to be in the Bahamas next week. *Sans children,* of course. Thank *heavens* for the in-laws. Normally I can't stand Martin's folks, but at least they're good for watching the kids."

"Well, have a great time. Send me a postcard."

"Oh, honey!" A wave of the hand. "Martin and I haven't had a real vacation in two years. I'll be too *busy* for writing postcards."

Peg walked away laughing. Mary watched her go. She tried to imagine vacationing in the Bahamas with Dan. She decided there would probably be plenty of time for writing postcards.

33

THIS SURELY WAS THE VERY best hour of the day, Bernie thought. This moment of sinking down into the cradling arms of the bed, tucked like a child between clean fragrant sheets, resting one cheek against the soft pillow. Sleep was only a few sighs away, several unbroken hours of slumber, that most restful of places.

Bernie chuckled. Wonderful thing about being old. You could be a child again, with someone there to take care of you, to turn out the light, to say good-night. And when Mary was there, sweet Mary, she never left without first kissing him on the cheek, just as his mother had done.

"Good night, Uncle Bernie."

"Good night, my dear."

"Are you comfortable?"

"Oh yes. Very."

"Well, then . . ."

Soft footfalls moved toward the tower room door. The moon was a lamp beyond the tall windows, filling the room with a tender light. He could see her figure, an impervious shadow, pause at the door, turn to him, turn away again.

"What is it, Mary?" he asked quietly.

"I'm afraid," she replied.

"You needn't be."

"You sound as though you know exactly what she wants to tell me."

"I have no idea what she wants to tell you."

"Well, then?"

"You might as well let her tell you, whatever it is. Even if you don't, you will still find out in the end . . . what it was she wanted to say."

"And why do you think that?"

"Because there is a God in heaven who reveals secrets."

Silence a moment. "I suppose that's in the Bible somewhere."

"Daniel two, twenty-eight."

"Ah."

She opened the door but didn't leave. "You really think it's important—what she has to say?"

"Yes, I think so."

"Maybe it's nothing at all."

"And maybe it's everything."

A sigh. "You've almost convinced me."

"You'll do what's right. I have no doubt of that."

Another silence. Then, "You do know what today is, don't you, Uncle Bernie?"

"Yes, Mary, I do."

"Twenty-six years since Mom died. I've never liked June 25, not since then."

"I'm rather glad myself when the day is over."

"Good night, Uncle Bernie."

"Good night, my dear."

He drew the sheet up to his chin, was conscious of his limbs—each muscle and bone—at rest. The room darkened, then lightened as a cloud passed over the moon. Even here, in the tower, he could hear the night songs rising up out of the fields, lulling him to sleep.

This was the sweetest hour of the day, when he surrendered to his dreams. They amused him, those whimsical and vaporous images. All manner of people and events emerged from the unconscious depths of his mind—solely, it seemed, to entertain him, to soothe him, to refresh him. Sometimes he woke up laughing. Sometimes he woke up floating. Sometimes he woke up feeling absolved and as new as the day itself.

The best dreams were of Rita, of course. When he dreamed of his wife, she was there, really there, for a moment, and that comforted him. Sometimes he dreamed of the farm, acres of corn, wheat, soy, perfect rows of provision sprouting up from the earth. He dreamed of this room, in which he was born, this house, in which he had grown up, his mother, his father, his brother and sister. Security embraced him, and he knew that his life had been good, very good.

And it was finished now. He knew that too. He was ready to go, except for one thing.

"I won't let go until you bless me," he whispered into the dark. "You see, there's still a bit of fight left in the old man."

His thoughts turned then toward a memory he didn't like very much, but it was keeping him alive. Maybe he didn't like it *because* it was keeping him alive, a wall between him and paradise. But there it was: the man sitting across from him in his church office, that Anglican confessional, that dome of confidentiality. The man's head hung low as he spoke, and his face was hidden by the brim of his cap, so that all that he was, all that Bernie could see, was a weeping plaid shirt and a trembling Reading Manufacturing cap.

It was an image that haunted him by day. Only by day. He was glad that it hadn't yet, blessedly, entered his sleeping mind. He didn't want to lose the joy of going to sleep, the one place he knew he wouldn't be bothered by the man in the cap.

"I won't let go until you bless me," he repeated.

That done, he turned his mind toward the dreams that were already pulling him down into sleep.

34

WHEN HE AWOKE, NEIL WONDERED where he was. Where were the Brooklyn sounds, the early morning echoes of traffic, the voices calling, footfalls tapping out a hurried beat on the jutted concrete sidewalk outside the window? Where was Caroline?

And then he remembered. Of course. This was Ohio, and he lay in a room in the Sadler house, and Caroline was dead.

He turned over on his side and tucked an arm beneath his head. From where he lay he could study the picture of the house that he had painted as a child, the Gothic Horror suspended in space between heaven and earth. One green strip of grass, one blue strip of sky, the house a ship sailing through an open chasm of white space.

Gazing at the picture, Neil couldn't help but smile for the rush of memories it brought back. He smiled in spite of the longing that hung in his gut like a too heavy meal, weighty and undigested. A longing for Caroline. And more than that, a longing for the long ago, the life that had been his when he painted that picture as a kid, because life then was . . . what? As it should be, he supposed. Full of hope.

Everything was different now. He had stood on the lawn of a house on Church Street and shaken Dan Beeken's hand, and he knew in that moment that everything was wrong. Nothing had turned out as he had once hoped, and as it should have been.

He had loved Caroline, had loved her deeply beginning the day they met at an exhibition of fifteenth-century Dutch paintings at the Metropolitan. But even his love for Caroline couldn't free him from the burden he carried because of Mary.

He was like a laborer balancing across his shoulders a pole with buckets on either end. One bucket was filled with guilt, the other regret. The burden was heavy, especially at first, but he carried it around like an act of penance. Even after Mary was Mrs. Dan Beeken and Caroline was Mrs. Neil Sadler, he still became aware sometimes of the rub of that pole against his skin. He could never quite set it down, because he had left Mason with one fundamental thing left undone.

It wasn't that he had never told her he loved her, though he hadn't done that either. But the greater wrong was that he'd never told her why he couldn't love her anymore. The breaking apart had been unexplained, and that was what had wounded them both. Words were the balm that he had withheld when he drove away in silence.

But we were kids, and isn't that what kids do? Go around breaking one another's hearts simply because they don't know how not to? It happens and you shrug it off and get over it.

He couldn't accept that though, no matter how much the argument hammered against his brain. Even a kid can speak, for crying out loud. Even a kid can offer some sort of explanation, however bumbling or weak. So long as there is the effort at offering words, there might be some chance at healing.

But a closemouthed nineteen-year-old Neil Sadler went off to New York, more angry than in love, more angry than sorry, more angry than he had ever been in his life. Too angry for words.

Even now Neil liked to blame Cal Syfert for what happened between him and Mary. Sure, Neil was at fault for running from her, but why not go back even further than that? Why not go right back to the root of the problem?

If Neil could change anything, he'd change the day Calvin Syfert wandered into Mason, Ohio, looking for a job. He'd rewrite the trek that brought Cal from the coal mines of Pennsylvania to the small Ohio town where the manufacturers were looking for men to work the lines. How many times had Neil heard the story from Uncle Cal? How many times when they were passing an evening together did his uncle talk about the coal mines of his hometown, the life that he had come from and had gladly left behind? Neil knew it all by heart.

Cal's father and his father's father had breathed in enough coal dust to paint the linings of their lungs black, and after his grandfather had successfully hacked himself to death, Cal Syfert had said, "No thanks, I'll do something else. Anything. Anything but go down into those shafts with a light in my hardhat and a death warrant on my head."

And so he'd drifted west to Mason, Ohio, willing to work the lines, willing to endure the boredom of the lines if it meant keeping his lungs free of coal dust.

Sure, that's fine. Who could blame the man? But then Cal Syfert settled down and married Helen Patch, and he insinuated himself into the close-knit Sadler family like a parasite clinging to its host. But who suspected? Certainly not Neil.

They'd welcomed Cal, with no idea that he came to town

carrying evil in his pocket like a pack of cigarettes. They'd figured, "Fine, he's a nice young man and an honest worker, and
he'll take good care of Helen," and they figured as much right
up to the day he killed her.

Of course when Cal arrived in 1955, Neil Sadler wasn't
even born and couldn't do a single thing about it. And if Cal
Syfert hadn't come in the first place, Mary Syfert would never
have been born, so where do you draw the line? How far back
do you go to change the event that changes everything?

But then, that's the thing, isn't it? You can't go back at all.
You can only go forward. So Neil had moved angrily forward
into the maze of New York City, while the man who had been
a father to him sat in the Warren County Jail and the young
woman who might have been his wife was left the damsel in
distress that he would never save.

Neil sat up and swung his feet over the side of the bed. It
was a drab morning, overcast and cool. He and Mike Weatherston were going up to Lebanon first thing after breakfast for
more supplies. More paint and wallpaper. More turpentine,
wallpaper paste, sandpaper, nails. They were making great progress. The Gothic Horror would be the Sadler House Bed-and-
Breakfast by September at this rate. No problem. The old
homestead completely new and transformed. "A Country Getaway for City Folk."

Neil stood and looked out the window at the gray dawn.
Something about the morning reminded him of Dan Beeken,
of how Dan had looked the day before when Neil stepped forward to shake his hand. Neil had thought, *So this is what he
looks like by the light of the sun, away from the eternal twilight of
McNulty's.* In the light he appeared even more shadowy, even
more vague. The eyes that had met Neil's were vacant.

"Nobody's home," they said. "He was here once, but he's gone away." Gone and left Mary a widow, just as solitary as Neil.

What should he say to Mary now, and was it too late for words? Can people loop around when they miss a turn and start over again?

He'd like to start over with Mary. Not go back and start over from the beginning, which no one could do, but start fresh from here. He wanted to smooth out the frayed parts and paint over the mistakes and make everything fresh. What exactly that might mean, Neil didn't know. He wasn't even sure what he wanted it to mean. He only knew that he wasn't going to leave her the way he did last time. Before heading back to New York at summer's end, he was going to know the right words to say.

And more than that, he was going to say them.

35

"WHAT ARE YOU GOING to do, Dad?"

Mary tried to take a deep breath, but the air in the jail's visiting room seemed more stifling than usual. She could hear the blood pumping in her ears, echoing the mad race of her heart. The phone's handset slipped in her sweaty palm; she clutched it more tightly so she wouldn't drop it.

Her father had failed the second polygraph test, the one arranged by the prosecutor. This test was stipulated; the results of this test, unlike the first, were admissible in court. And they pointed to his guilt.

Before her dad could respond to her question, Mary said, "They're the ones who are lying, Dad. Joshua Bain and this guy he got to do the test. I mean, they're lying when they say you failed. You can't have failed."

A fly circled her father's head and landed on the streaked window that separated them, showing Mary its dark underbelly. Cal Syfert waved a hand and the fly shot off toward the ceiling, toward the fan that whirled lazily overhead.

"Listen, sweetheart." He leaned forward, both elbows on the table so that his face was very close to the glass.

Mary was alarmed at the dark circles under his eyes, the gray in his hair. He had aged by years in only a very few days.

"Like Hoback said, we were taking our chances messing with these tests. He warned me it might just backfire on us."

Mary remembered Dan telling her about the guy who failed the polygraph when he was actually telling the truth. That's what had happened to her dad. Of course it was. So what good were the tests? How was anyone who had to make life-and-death decisions ever supposed to know what the truth was?

"So what are you going to do now, Dad?" she asked again. The words trembled across the phone line in a strained whisper.

He nodded. He tapped nervously at the table with the tips of his fingers. "Hoback asked me . . . he said, did I ever hear of a guy named Alford? I said no, I never heard of him. So he tells me about this Alford guy who a few years back was accused of murder and up against the death penalty. Of course he was afraid if he went to trial he'd get death. So he pleaded guilty and got thirty years instead, but the thing is, he kept saying he was innocent even when he pleaded guilty. I mean, when he pleaded he actually made a statement, on the record and all, that he was innocent. So now there's this plea called the Alford plea. Hoback thinks it's my best shot."

He stopped and looked at Mary for a long time. The fly returned and buzzed around his ear; he absently waved it away again. He took out a cigarette, lighted it, blew out the match. "Do you understand, Mary?"

"You're going to plead guilty?"

He took a deep pull on the cigarette and let the smoke out slowly. "I'm facing the possibility of death, Mare. He may not get it, but Bain's asking for it."

Silence. The fly landed abruptly on the window. Cal swatted at it with the back of his hand. Mary saw it there, a dark spot between glass and flesh, suspended a moment before it fell lifeless to the table. Cal brushed it away, never taking his eyes off Mary.

"You're going to plead guilty."

"I'm going to enter an Alford plea, Mare. I'm going to make a statement on the record that I'm innocent."

"But, Dad, this way you'll go to prison for sure. If you go to trial, you could get off."

"Sweetheart, if I go to trial, I could get the chair."

She wanted to call Dan. He'd know what to do. Just yesterday afternoon they'd spent hours talking about the law, trial cases, and Rebecca McClung. They'd even wandered over to Rose Hill Cemetery by way of the Widow's Bridge to see Rebecca's tombstone, which was the largest monument on the property. Her final resting place was right beside the man who'd been arrested and tried in her murder.

"You think he did it?" Mary had asked.

Dan nodded, shrugged. *"Yeah. Seems pretty obvious."*

"Dad," Mary said, "don't you remember about Rebecca?"

"Rebecca?"

"Rebecca McClung."

Cal Syfert looked weary. "What about her?"

"You know, her husband. I mean, it was so obvious he was guilty." After all, the trail of bloody footprints that began at Rebecca's body led directly to John McClung. He was found wandering around outside the house in bloodstained clothes and was subsequently arrested as the prime suspect in his wife's murder.

Still, on July 11, 1901, after a trial that Mr. McClung practically slept through—press reports had him leaning back in his chair with his eyes closed throughout the entire ordeal—-he was acquitted by the jury and released. Imagine! He killed his wife, enjoyed a nice nap, and moseyed on home.

"Well, Mary, that was a long time ago—"

"But still, he went to trial and they found him innocent. The same thing could happen to you."

"That was a long time ago," Cal repeated. "Things were different then."

"But Dad . . ." She couldn't believe it. She couldn't believe her father was just going to give up. How could he do that to her? "You've got to at least *try*. If John McClung could be acquitted, so can you. I mean, he was *guilty* and he got off. You're *innocent*."

"How do you know he was guilty?"

She sighed, almost rolled her eyes. "It was so obvious, Dad."

"Yeah, and that's what people are saying about me."

"It doesn't matter what people are saying—"

"Doesn't it?"

Mary was quiet a moment. Then she said, "What matters is that you *are* innocent. You can go in there and tell the jury the truth, and they can acquit you just like John McClung. What have you got to lose?"

Cal Syfert snuffed out his cigarette in the ashtray before answering. He leaned forward, and holding Mary's gaze, he tried unsuccessfully to smile. "Everything, Mary. Don't you understand, sweetheart? I have everything to lose."

He took out another cigarette and lighted it. His hand trembled. Another fly appeared and buzzed around his head. He didn't notice. Apparently his mind was on other things.

36

NEIL PEERED OUT ONE of the tower room windows and watched the gathering storm with fascination. He'd been back in Ohio for several weeks now, but today was his first chance to witness a real midwestern storm. He hadn't seen one like this in years, a huge assault rolling in over open countryside as a fleet of clouds stole the sun, pounded the earth with watery fists, drew swords of lightning that cut the sky. Sometimes, during such storms as this, there was the extra fury of funnel clouds that made matchsticks of entire city streets. No telling what damage nature might do before passing on or petering out.

"We're under a tornado watch, you know, Uncle Bernie," he said.

"I'm not surprised." Bernie sat in the overstuffed chair reading the newspaper. He didn't look up when he spoke.

"I'd be glad to take you down to the basement if you'd like."

"Don't bother." He turned the page and took a moment to glance at the headlines. "It would be a long hike down there for nothing."

"And what if there's a tornado, and it happens to hit this very room?"

Bernie lifted his shoulders in a shrug. "I'll consider it a jumpstart on my journey to heaven."

Neil smiled, then looked back at the clouds, dark churning whirlpools in the sky.

"But," Bernie went on, "you go on down. Don't let me stop you."

Neil shook his head. "No, I think I'll stay here. I've always wanted to see a tornado. Maybe I'll get lucky."

He had stood right here in 1974 when the storm that would later be called the Super Outbreak spawned 148 tornadoes in two days all across the Upper Midwest. Two of them hit Warren County. One of those traveled straight down Main Street in Mason as if it were following a road map, damaging businesses all along the way, leaving the Dream Theater a pile of rubble and jumping across the street to peel the roof off the McClung house.

Neil didn't see the actual tornado itself. Thirty minutes into the storm, Uncle Tom came up and dragged him down to the basement, where his cousins and his brother, Jerry, were huddling in the dark. The electricity had gone out, and the house was being pelted with rain and hail and even bits of Mason itself that the storm had carried eastward. Neil was disappointed afterward that he'd missed the best part of the show.

"You remember that tornado that hit Mason in '74?" Neil asked.

"How could I forget?"

"Where were you when it hit?"

"On my knees in the church basement with Miss Abernathy and Charlie Bitner."

Neil tried to imagine Bernie, the church secretary, and the janitor praying away the tornado. Maybe their prayers had actually done something. Who could say? The tornado had come within yards of the church but hadn't hit it directly.

"So you didn't actually see the twister?"

Bernie let the newspaper drop to his lap. "I heard it and felt it, and that was enough. I'm not a huge fan of tornadoes myself."

Neil nodded and gave a small laugh. "They said it was Rebecca blowing through. They said she tore the roof off the old McClung house because she was angry that her husband got away with murder. Remember that?"

"Uh-huh. Though I can't say I believe it."

"No, but it used to scare the pants off some of the younger cousins when Jerry told that story late at night."

"I can well imagine. I wonder how such rumors get started."

Neil laughed out loud. "I wouldn't be surprised if Jerry made that one up himself."

Bernie folded the local section of the newspaper and tossed it onto the rocking chair, where Neil had been sitting a few moments before. "Well, when you're done watching the storm, here's the newspaper."

Neil stood at the window awhile longer, until the worst of the storm passed and all that was left was a tentative rain spitting at the windows.

He looked at his watch and said, "Guess I still have a few minutes before I head down to supper."

"What's Grace cooking up tonight, do you know?"

"I haven't the foggiest notion."

"Well, whatever it is, tell her to give me a generous portion, will you?"

"Sure thing."

The two men sat in silence for a moment before Bernie said, "Oh, by the way, do you remember Bill Mahoney?"

"Bill Mahoney," Neil repeated, frowning in thought. "I knew a Bill Mahoney in school. His dad was school superintendent or something."

"That's the one."

"I didn't know him well, but I remember him. What about him?"

"He died."

"He died?"

"I just saw the notice in the obits."

"But he was my age."

"Cancer." Bernie nodded. "Leaves behind a wife and three children. It's a shame. Bill was quite active in the church while I was still pastor there. After I retired too, far as I know. He was a good man."

Neil found the obituary page while Bernie spoke. There was the notice. "William Alan Mahoney, age forty-five, stepped into heaven on July 8 after a short but courageous battle with cancer. He will be sorely missed by his wife. . . ."

Neil stopped reading. He had never been one to read the death notices, though Caroline had. He could still see her sitting at breakfast, two pages of obituaries spread out on the table before her.

"What on earth are you reading the obits for?" he'd asked once.

She'd looked up, perplexed. *"They're here to be read, aren't they? What else am I supposed to do with them?"*

"But it's depressing, reading those notices."

She shook her head. *"I don't think so. I like to see what people have to say about their loved ones after they're gone. It's sweet, in an odd sort of way."*

It wasn't sweet, Neil thought. It was sickeningly sentimental. The survivor's grief made people say such silly things. So-and-so hadn't died; he had fallen into the waiting arms of Jesus. So-and-so hadn't passed away; she had been carried by the angels to her heavenly mansion. And what was that one that took the prize? Something about, "He heard the Lord call in his heart, 'Come home,' and he gladly responded, 'Lord, I come.'"

Like Neil's students would say, *Yeah, right. Get real.* These people had died, and they'd probably been none too happy about it either. Neil couldn't imagine anyone using his last breath to cry, "I'm coming home!" And there was no way he was going to believe in angels providing transportation for dead souls in need of a ride to glory, even though the beloved old man in the overstuffed chair was waiting for just such a lift.

Neil dropped the paper and moved to the window again. The rain had stopped. A light mist rose from the damp earth.

Maybe there was something after death. Maybe Caroline was somewhere. There might even be a heaven.

But the thing that made it so unacceptable was all the foolishness. If he was going to believe in something, he wanted it to be wrapped in dignity, not in the puerile trappings that too many people were so fond of.

Without looking at Bernie, Neil said, "Why do you suppose God makes himself so vulnerable? It's like He's this powerful creator who leaves himself wide open to ridicule." Neil turned and frowned at the old man. "Why do you suppose that is, Uncle Bernie?"

Bernie seemed to know exactly what Neil meant, because

he asked for no clarification. He simply lifted his chin and said, "He does it to confound the academicians, I should think." Then he snapped open the newspaper again and went back to reading.

37

VINCENT MCNULTY ALWAYS MADE Neil feel welcome, greeting him with an enthusiastic handshake and the words, "Neil! Good to see you! How goes it?" And then he waited for an answer. Neil liked that. Vince was a good man.

Neil dropped in often at McNulty's, two or three times a week, to have a beer at the end of the day. After six or seven or eight hours of working on the house, a beer tasted good. And it was relaxing, coming in and swapping stories with Vince. Sometimes, if the place wasn't too busy, Teresa would come around from the kitchen and join them. They'd kick around the latest news: the killer heat wave in Europe, the war in Iraq, on-going bloodbath in Liberia. They'd talk about Mason, the people they knew, the local news in the *Pulse Journal,* all of which seemed so wonderfully benign and insignificant in the light of world events.

And they'd laugh. That was the best thing. Neil knew he could go to McNulty's and enjoy not just a beer but a laugh. It was the laughter that revived him. The beer was all right, but the laughter kept him going.

The evening after the storm Neil found himself at this now-familiar haunt, listening to Vince as he went on about the time capsule. This was the first Neil had heard about it; he was only vaguely aware that Warren County was celebrating its bicentennial that year. For one of the special events, according to Vince, some of the local bigwigs were planning to bury a time capsule under the Warren County Administration Building in Lebanon in October. After fifty years the capsule would be dug up, by whoever happened to be around in 2053, for the entertainment and inspiration of whoever cared to see it.

"So get this," Vince said. He threw a dish towel over his shoulder and leaned his hairy arms on the counter. "Anyone who wants to can put something into the time capsule. Mostly messages is what they're looking for, I think. Yeah, they got a Web site for the Warren County Bicentennial. You click on there, and they got this information about the capsule. And they're asking, 'Anyone out there want to send a message to the future?' and I'm saying, 'Yeah, I want to send a message to the future.'"

Neil took a swallow of his beer. "So what's your message?"

"I don't know for sure yet, but something like this: 'Vincent McNulty may be dead, but you can still go to McNulty's on Main in Mason and get the best roast beef sandwich in Warren County.'"

Neil waited a moment before saying, "That's it?"

"Sure. What else?"

"You have a chance to send a message to the future, and you want to tell them to eat a roast beef sandwich?"

Vince shrugged, a swift lifting of his large shoulders. "Eat, drink, and be merry, right?" He laughed, then excused himself to wait on a customer. When he came back, he said, "Yeah, so what would you say?"

After thinking a long while, Neil said, "I don't have the slightest idea."

"You don't have anything important to say?"

"I suppose I should."

"And you're complaining about my roast beef sandwich?"

Neil nodded. "You're right. Maybe roast beef *is* the most important thing. Not to a vegetarian, though. Maybe I should say something about vegetables. Or sweet potatoes. Yeah, maybe sweet potatoes."

Vince laughed loudly, waved a hand toward Neil, and slapped the counter like he was swatting a mosquito.

Neil went on, "Seems like there must be something to say that's a little more . . . I don't know . . . philosophical or something. I'll think about it."

"Maybe another beer would help."

"I doubt it."

"Well, you're not a Warren County resident anymore, so you can't say anything anyway."

"It's probably just as well."

"Speaking of philosophical, they got a motto for this time capsule. . . . How's it go? Hey, Teresa, what was it they said about that time capsule?"

A voice from the kitchen said, "What are you talking about, Vinny?"

"That motto we got a kick out of. The time capsule. You remember, honey, don't you?"

"Don't bother me now, Vinny. I'm cutting onions."

Vince turned back to Neil, undeterred. "Oh, hey, I remember. Yeah, it says, 'Today will be . . .' Let me think now. . . . 'Today will be yesterday, come tomorrow!' Yeah, that's it. Get it? 'Today will be yesterday, come tomorrow!'" he repeated.

"Now that's saying something, isn't it."

Neil nodded. "Yeah, that's deep."

Vince pulled the towel off his shoulder, wiped at a spill, waved at a middle-aged couple who walked through the door. "Jack, Sheila. Long time no see. Where you been hiding on me?"

"Can it, Vince," the woman said. "We were here yesterday, remember?"

"So what took you so long to come back?"

Vince told Neil he'd be right back; he was just going to take care of Jack and Sheila.

Neil sat nursing his drink and thinking about the time capsule. What would he say to anyone who cared to listen fifty years from now? *Keep on dancing, even in the snow?* Or just, *Keep on dancing?* But what did it matter anyway? Fifty years from now he'd be dead, and it wouldn't really matter what he'd done. The people who dug up the time capsule fifty years from now would be dead one day too. That was the problem with death; it brought you right back to the same place you'd started. Nowhere. And you'd end up there whether you'd danced or not.

"So what do you say, Neil? Another beer?"

"Sure, Vince. Thanks. I could use it."

Vince pulled another beer and set it on the counter in front of Neil.

"So, Vince, you never told me how you ended up here, owning a bar."

"Simple." He shrugged. "The place was up for sale, so I jumped on it."

"No." Neil shook his head. "I mean, how come you didn't become a priest?"

"Oh, that. That's simple too. I finally just started thinking for myself, you know? I sat myself down and asked myself, 'McNulty, you really believe all this stuff? I mean, a virgin with one in the oven, Jesus Christ coming back from the dead, people burning in hell forever just because they don't believe in him or maybe never even *heard* of him?'" Vince shook his head, laid an open palm on the counter. "And I realized, uh-uh, nope, count me out. I don't believe any of that mess. I mean, you start to think about it, how *can* you believe it? Makes no sense. And anyway, there's no proof for any of it. I say, if God was there and wanted us to know about it, he could have told us loud and clear. So far, he's told us diddly." Another shrug of the shoulders and a large smile.

Neil stared at the mug clasped in both of his hands. "So," he said, "you stopped believing."

"Yeah, thank God."

Neil lifted his brows, let them drop again. He wasn't sure whether Vince was joking or not. "Well, are you sorry about it? I mean, losing your faith and all?"

"Sorry?" Vince looked surprised. "Listen, Neil. Best thing ever happened to me was to give up all that stuff. The day I knew I didn't believe anymore, it was like a huge boulder dropped off my back. That's all it was, religion. Just this giant boulder I was carrying around for years. Now I can do anything, and it doesn't matter. Now I'm free!" He spread his arms and smiled brightly, ready to soar on autonomous wings.

For a second Neil almost envied him. Nodding, he said, "So now at least you don't have to worry about going to hell."

Vince waved a hand. "Sheesh, Neil, I don't know how anyone can believe that stuff. But listen, whatever. I'm not here to judge. Someone wants to believe in heaven, hell, purgatory, nirvana, I'm not going to try to change their minds. Someone wants to believe they're coming back as a cockroach or a cow or the king of Jordan, that's all right too. Makes no difference to me. Whatever anyone wants to believe, if it helps them, I'm all for it."

Neil was quiet for a long time. Vince didn't interrupt his thoughts. Neil appreciated that about Vince. He was used to listening and to waiting. This was his confessional. Finally Neil said, "But there must be a lot of people out there believing a lot of stuff that isn't true."

Vince nodded, his lower lip protruding. "People are funny, you know. Most people seem to find it helpful to believe in something, even if they can't see it. Even if they can't prove it. So like I said, whatever works. Doesn't really matter what it is."

"Even if it's a lie?"

"So who can know what's true? I mean, really, you know? Best we can do is decide what's true for us and just stick to it."

"So if I'm hearing you right, there's no such thing as absolute truth."

Vince laughed. "Neil, my friend, there's no such thing as an absolute anything. One thing I know is that there are no absolutes."

"You absolutely sure about that, Vince?"

He knocked on the counter with his knuckles. "Absolutely."

Neil looked up from his beer to see if Vince was smiling. He wasn't.

38

NEIL WAS WORKING BY HIMSELF, painting trim in the back bedroom on the second floor, when Mary suddenly appeared.

She didn't bother to greet him but simply blurted, "Will you drive me down to Cincinnati?"

"Umm," Neil glanced at the paintbrush, at his hands covered with paint, at his paint-splattered overalls. "Sure." Flustered, he looked around, trying to decide what to do with the brush.

"You don't mind, do you? Because if you do . . ." She shook her head. "I just don't think I can get there by myself."

Where was Dan? Neil wondered. But then, of course, he was probably at McNulty's already. Or in bed with a hangover. Either way, he no doubt wasn't up for a drive, or Mary would have called on him.

"Of course I don't mind," Neil answered. "Let me just— Is everything all right?"

"I'm ready to see Madylyn."

"Oh! All right." He dropped the brush into a pan of turpentine, picked up a rag, and started rubbing his fingers. "Does she know you're coming?"

"No." She looked agitated and in a hurry.

"Don't you think you'd better call, let her know you're coming?"

"If I hear her voice, I might change my mind."

"Okay."

"I just have to do it now, before I lose my nerve."

"Okay. Can I just clean up a bit? Maybe wash my hands?"

"Yes. But do it quickly."

Twenty minutes later they were on I-75 headed south toward Cincinnati.

Neil, in clean clothes and still smelling of turpentine, said tentatively, "I guess I should ask if you know where we're going."

Mary turned to him wide-eyed, as though he had just made a terrible pronouncement. She hadn't smiled once since she'd shown up at the Sadler house. She appeared frightfully stoic or perhaps simply frightened. Neil wasn't sure which. Either way, she was obviously doing something she didn't want to do.

"Oh yes. I've got the address right here." She picked her purse up off the floor and began to rifle through it. "And I got a map off the Internet. It's here somewhere."

When she found the directions, she gave Neil the address. He nodded. After a moment, he said, "I don't suppose you'd want to tell me what changed your mind?" He glanced over at her, then back at the road. "About seeing Madylyn?"

"I don't know what changed my mind," she answered quietly. "But whatever it was, I don't like it."

He suppressed a smile. "Fair enough." A couple miles later, he added, "I think you're doing the right thing."

She looked at him but didn't respond.

Neither spoke the rest of the way to the nursing home, but

Neil was keenly aware of her presence. He wanted to comfort her on this journey she was making, but he didn't know what to say. Why was it that words were always so hard for him? It was as though he didn't think in words but in colors, that if he could he would bathe her in colors, offer them as a gift. *Blue to soothe you, Mary, and yellow to keep you warm. Green for rest, and gold to give you hope. These are what I would give you if I could.*

If he could. And yet—even if he could bathe her in colors, he would not, because she was Mary Beeken, not Mary Syfert. He instinctively wanted to comfort and protect her, but he knew he had to keep the distance that he himself had willingly placed between them years ago.

When they arrived and he'd parked the car, he broke the silence by asking simply, "Are you all right?"

She nodded. They got out of the car. Next to the parking lot was a strip of grass and a bench where an elderly gentleman sat methodically peeling a banana. Neil gave the man a nod before walking with Mary through the heavy July heat into the cool air-conditioned lobby of the nursing home—a large room made harsh by fluorescent lighting and dark-paneled walls. It seemed to Neil a warehouse for the decrepit. They were every-where—draped across couches, poured into padded rockers, strapped into wheelchairs. Only the eyes moved, offering a minimal assurance that these bodies were still alive and still functioning—at least to some extent. Neil wondered whether one of them might be Madylyn Fricke.

Mary looked pale now, and small, like a panicked child. He wanted to take her hand but didn't. "Do you know which room she's in?" he asked.

She shook her head. "We'll have to ask."

"I'll ask."

A receptionist sat at the front desk squinting at a computer screen. She frowned when Neil and Mary approached, as though she didn't want to be bothered with a question at the moment. Reluctantly she said, "Can I help you?"

"Yes," Neil replied. "Can you tell us which room Madylyn Fricke is in?"

The woman took off her half-framed glasses and cocked her head. "You family?"

Neil looked at Mary, back at the receptionist. "Friends," he said.

"Then I guess you haven't heard."

Neil waited a moment. When she didn't continue, he frowned, said no, shook his head.

The woman put her glasses aside and laced her fingers together on top of the desk. "Mrs. Fricke passed away," she explained. "Two days ago." Then, as though remembering it was part of her job description, she added, "I'm sorry."

It took Neil a moment to say, "I see." He started to ask the woman if she was sure but changed his mind. Of course she was sure.

To his surprise he felt Mary clutch his right arm at the elbow. *So she has come to me, then,* he thought. He lifted his left hand slowly and laid it over her fingers. Her skin was oddly cold. *But it's nothing, her reaching out for me,* he told himself. *It's only because of the shock of Madylyn's death.*

He guided her away from the desk and back out to the parking lot. When they reached the car, Neil noticed that the man on the bench had had just enough time to peel the banana and was only now lowering his head to take the first bite. Just enough time to learn that Mary's timing had been bad. Neil thought of a phrase they had laughed at in high school, as though it were the most hilarious joke in the world: *"You're just in time to be too late!"*

Somehow it didn't seem at all funny now.

Neil helped Mary into the car, and except for the muffled sounds of her weeping, they drove all the way back to the farmhouse in silence.

39

WHEN THEY ARRIVED AT THE Sadler house, Neil invited Mary to come in, but she declined, saying she had to get home. He watched her yellow Honda Accord bounce over the gravel drive, then turn left onto Route 42 toward Mason. He stood there for some time after her car disappeared, trying to unravel his twisted emotions. He wanted to comfort her, but he wasn't able. And he knew now suddenly, at this odd moment, that he wanted to love her too, to love her fully, but he wasn't able to do that either. Not so long as she belonged to somebody else.

Neil climbed the front porch steps and kept on climbing until he reached the tower room. He knocked once but didn't wait for Bernie to respond. He opened the door and stepped out of the dark stairway into a room full of midafternoon light.

Bernie was stretched out on the bed, lounging on top of the covers and propped up by half a dozen pillows. In spite of the heat he wore a brown cardigan over his blue button-down shirt. His bony legs were lost inside a pair of baggy corduroy pants, and the space between pant cuffs and slippers revealed a pair of fancy argyle socks. The lower half of his face was hidden behind a hard-cover copy of Tolstoy's *Anna Karenina,* which he clutched in both hands. Neil could see that he hadn't got far in the story. Only a chapter. Maybe two.

How strange, Neil thought. *Why bother starting something like that when you may not live long enough to finish it?*

But then he thought it strange, and morbid, that he should think such a thing in the first place, and he tried to smile when Bernie looked up from the book.

"Well, hello, Neil!" Bernie said cheerfully. "Didn't hear you come up the stairs. What a nice surprise. Did you knock off work early today?"

Neil sat down on the edge of the rocking chair and exhaled heavily. He rested his elbows on the arms of the chair and laced his fingers together. "You won't believe what just happened, Uncle Bernie."

Bernie let the book drop to his lap while gazing at Neil expectantly.

"Mary and I just got back from Cincinnati," he began.

Bernie nodded, though he hadn't known that they had gone.

"We went down to see Madylyn Fricke."

"Oh?" A lifting of the brows and a widening of the eyes. An explosion of sunlight bounced off his glasses like an old-fashioned flashbulb. "And?"

"She's dead, Bernie. She died a couple of days ago."

The old man was quiet a long while. Then he said, "I see. Where's Mary now?"

"She went home."

"How is she?"

"She cried most of the way back. I think she's mad at herself for not going down sooner."

Bernie nodded again. "How terribly disappointing."

"Rotten luck," Neil added. "So that's it. We'll never know what Madylyn wanted. Whatever it was she had to say to Mary, she's taken it to the grave with her."

The older man turned his face away from Neil and looked straight ahead toward the tall windows on the far side of the room. "Oh, dear God," he said quietly, "what are you going to do now?"

Neil sat with his shoulders hunched, his eyes on the floor. He shook his head. "I don't know, Uncle Bernie," he replied. His voice hung heavy with weariness. "I don't guess there's anything *to* do."

Bernie looked back at Neil. In the next moment his face opened up into an amused smile. He reached out and patted the younger man's hand. "You're as fine a person as they come, Neil," he said, "but with all due respect, I wasn't talking to you."

40

WHEN CAL SYFERT DIED IN 1977, the Lebanon Correctional Institute turned over his effects to Mary. There wasn't much; all of it fit into a small paper bag, the kind a kid might use to carry his lunch to school. Inside were Cal's watch, reading glasses, wedding ring. A small New Testament. He hadn't had that going in. Someone must have given it to him—the prison chaplain, most likely. His wallet, which contained two dollars, a driver's license, and a dry cleaning receipt for shirts that were never picked up. Mary's letters, an even dozen of them, one for every week he was in prison.

Though he had been sentenced to more than thirty years, the full length of his stay at the Lebanon Correctional Institute was a little more than three months. He was forty-four years old when he fell to the floor of his cell clutching his heart. For three days afterward he clung to the tenuous thread connecting him to life. On the fourth day he let go. Mary didn't know about the heart attack until after he was already dead, as no one at the prison took it upon himself to notify the next of kin.

One more item in the bag was Mary's photograph, the one that had been taken on school picture day when she was twelve.

There were more recent photos of Mary, of course, but this one had always been Cal's favorite. In one of his letters to Mary, he told her how he had taped it to the underside of the top bunk in his cell. The upper bunk had already been claimed by his cell mate, a young guy doing time for armed robbery, when Cal moved in. Cal preferred the lower bunk anyway. He lay there at night before the lights were turned out, his hands beneath his head, staring up into the laughing eyes of his daughter.

"If looking at your picture could wear it out," he'd written, "I guess your picture would just about be all worn out by now."

It *was* worn out, at least the edges where he had handled it for years between the day the picture was taken and the day he finally taped it to the bottom of the bunk.

Now Mary cradled the photo in the palm of her hand. In her other hand she held her father's letter, the final one of the thirty-two he had written her from prison. She hadn't pulled these items out of the closet in years, but she thought this might be the time to do it. She had been too late, and Madylyn was dead, and suddenly she needed to feel close to her father.

She looked at the photo and smiled plaintively. The photo smiled back. It showed a gangly adolescent, her hair an odd array of curls framing an unadorned face. She hadn't bloomed yet, wouldn't begin to reach her beauty for another year, but the preteen in the photo looked happy and slightly mischievous and completely hopeful. The eternal optimism of youth! "We are the Future Homemakers of America. We face the future with warm courage and high hope!"

Things weren't perfect, of course, mostly because there was a mother at home with a strange and as yet unexplained illness. But Mary knew life wouldn't always be that way. Kids don't have much say about things, but adults can set their own agenda, can make life what they want it to be. Mary Syfert was going to grow up to be beautiful, and she would fall in love and get married and have children. She was going to have a daughter for herself and a son for her husband, and she was going to give her father grandchildren who would make him proud and happy. It was so simple, and it was all ahead of her, as certain as the road that's already been surveyed, cleared, and paved. All she had to do was walk forward.

She was feeling especially good the morning of picture day because her hair had turned out the way she wanted. She never would have thought it possible the night before.

Long straight hair was in style. All the popular girls had long straight hair, parted in the middle, hanging down their backs. They'd brush it in class, those soft and shiny waterfalls of hair that no boy dared reach out and touch, however tempting.

But Mary's hair was wavy. And unruly. Her mother made her wear it shorter than Mary wanted because Helen didn't have the energy to fool with it. Peggy had shown Mary several times how to curl it so that at least it would curl in the direction she wanted it to go. But Peggy was good at those things; Mary wasn't.

The night before school pictures, she lined up her mother's sponge curlers on the bathroom counter. Helen was too tired to help; in fact, though it was only seven o'clock, she had already fallen exhausted into bed. More and more that was becoming the norm. Now Mary would have to try to curl her hair by herself.

Thirty minutes later her father appeared at the open door. "Mary?" he asked softly.

She turned to him. Huge tears rolled down her cheeks. "I

305

can't get the curlers to stay in right."

"Oh." He joined her at the sink, picked up a curler, turned it over tentatively. He seemed to be studying it. "You going to sleep with these things?"

"Yeah. That's why they're sponge."

"Can't be comfortable. Why don't you forget it?"

Her eyes widened suddenly, and her chin trembled. "Tomorrow's picture day."

"Oh. Well, then . . ." He unclipped one of the curlers, clipped it again. "I've never done this," he confessed with a brief smile, "but I guess I can try."

She sniffed and combed out a strand of hair with a wet comb. "You have to roll it tight enough that it'll stay."

He nodded, positioned his hands awkwardly above her head. His hands were accustomed to metal, machinery, bolts, and nuts. "Kind of like this?"

He pressed the ends of her damp hair against the pink sponge and slowly, cautiously, started to roll. In the next moment she took over, finished rolling until the curler was flat against her head. He fastened it. They let go, fingers dangling in space, ready to catch the curler should it fall. It stayed in place.

"Like that?" he asked again.

"Yeah," she said. "That's good."

"Okay."

She glanced at him in the mirror. His eyes were lowered, focusing intently on the curler successfully positioned on top of her head. His expression was deadly serious, as though he was doing something important.

"Where do you want the next one?" he asked.

In the morning when she removed the curlers and brushed

out her hair, she coyly presented herself to her father with a blush of pride. "What do you think?" she asked.

"I think we make a mighty good team!"

She kissed him. "Thanks, Dad. You're the best."

Years later she would realize that she didn't look half as good as she thought. The curls were uneven, lopsided, too tight on one side, not tight enough on the other. But on that morning when she sat on the photographer's stool, half blinded by the single studio light, she felt pretty. She felt hopeful. She thought of her dad and how much she loved him and how one day she was going to make him proud and happy.

She smiled brightly, and the photographer snapped the picture.

The prison chaplain, in a condolence call, told Mary he had found the photo clutched in Cal Syfert's hand when he was called in to pray for him as he lay dying. No, he didn't know how it had gotten there. But there it was. After Cal Syfert died, they had to pry his fingers open to remove the photo from his grasp. They almost let him take it to his grave, but they decided Mary might like to have her picture back.

41

MARY COULDN'T SLEEP. Cal Syfert was fresh in his grave, and Mary was fresh in her grief, and at night the whole waking nightmare came crashing in and drove her from her bed. To sleep, Mary discovered, a person needs either a certain amount of peace or a great deal of exhaustion. The former was elusive; the latter gained only by walking the house for hours, sometimes until just before dawn.

A week after her father's death, she found herself once again pacing the rooms, hugging herself against the chill, hurrying to outdistance the thoughts that plagued her. At length, sometime after midnight, she went to the kitchen, flipped on the overhead light, and poured herself a glass of milk.

She was standing at the counter, the glass in her hand, when she heard someone say, "Your dad was a bad man. He deserved what he got."

Mary swung around to find Denton Patch framed in the kitchen doorway. He was bundled up in his tattered and filthy coat, his worn knitted cap, his heavy winter boots. He was ready to go out on patrol, his nightly pursuit of Chinese soldiers.

Mary gripped the glass more tightly and pursed her lips in disgust. "You're crazy," she said evenly. "Look at you—dirty, smelly—coming in here and saying that, and Dad not even buried a week."

"He killed my sister, my helpless sister," Denton said. "He had to pay for that."

Mary moved toward the kitchen door, hoping her uncle would step aside. But he stood his ground. "Get out of my way, you old fool. I'm going to bed. You go on out and do whatever it is you do at night." She wanted to add that she hoped he'd never come back, but she didn't. "Just leave me alone."

He limped toward her then, coming close enough that she could smell his unwashed flesh, could see each dark whisker dotting his face in the dull light of the overhead lamp. His hands were in his coat pockets; his cap was pulled down so low that his haunted eyes had to peer out from beneath the frayed cuff. "You think I don't know?" he asked quietly.

Mary felt her jaw tighten. She squeezed the glass of milk until she thought it might break in her hand. "You don't know anything," she said. "Just get out of my way."

Denton Patch didn't move. With his eyes fixed on Mary, he pulled a clenched fist out of his coat pocket.

For a moment Mary felt panicked. She could scream, she thought. She could scream and wake up Uncle Henry and Aunt Vivian. That was it; she had to cry out for help.

But before she could open her mouth, Denton slowly uncurled his fist. "See this?" he asked.

Reluctantly Mary dropped her gaze to his calloused palm. There was something silver there, a piece of jewelry maybe; she couldn't quite make it out. She didn't dare step any closer. She looked up at him questioningly but didn't speak.

"Don't know what it is, do you?" he asked.

"I don't care what it is," she replied stiffly.

"I think you should." He smiled briefly, triumphantly. He took a couple more small steps toward her. "See here? It's a brooch, one of them pins ladies wear when they want to look fancy. See these initials?" He pulled his other hand out of his pocket and pointed with a thick grease-stained finger to each letter: *M F K.*

Mary suddenly felt cold. "So?" she whispered.

"I don't know what the *K* stands for, but I do know what the *M* and the *F* stand for." Denton smiled again.

Mary stared at a broken plastic button on his coat, halfway between the collar and the waist. She didn't want to look at his face. Every one of his smiles fueled her anger. "Just say your piece and hurry up. I don't have time for your games."

"*M, F,*" he said. "Madylyn Fricke."

Mary stiffened. She hoped her sick surprise wasn't evident on her face. She swallowed, said nothing.

"Your dad and Madylyn," he went on, "they had a thing, you know. They were lovers."

The button, Mary thought. Concentrate on the button. "How do you know that?" she demanded evenly. No one was supposed to know other than the three of them: her father, Madylyn, and herself. That's what they all said. That's what they all believed. Only the three of them knew. Earl Hoback knew about the affair, but not the name. Never the name.

"I seen them myself," Denton explained smugly. "There's an old abandoned farmhouse a few miles from town. No one's lived there in I don't know how long. That's where they'd meet nights. I seen them there with my own eyes. Seen them one night through the window when I was out scouting. It was a clear night, full moon, moonbeams shining right down on that house like they was telling me I had to go there. Sure enough. Someone was there. I thought maybe I'd come on the enemy. Thought maybe soldiers had found themselves a place to camp. But there they were, the two of them, your dad and Mrs. Fricke. . . ." His voice trailed off. Mary felt his grin. She refused to lift her eyes. "I got her brooch, see. A couple weeks after I first seen them I went back and found she'd left her sweater there with this on it. So I took it. Left the sweater, though. In case she come back for it."

Mary couldn't breathe. She moistened her dry lips with her tongue. When she spoke, the words came out in a choked whisper. "Did you tell Mom?"

He laughed quietly. " 'Course I did. What do you think? I had to tell her. Told her right off, first time I seen them."

"What'd she say?" The button. The cracked button straining to hold the jacket together.

"She wanted proof. I went back to hunt some down. Lucky thing Mrs. Fricke forgot her sweater." He laughed again.

"So you showed Mom the brooch."

"Yup." He sounded proud.

"What'd she say?" Mary asked again.

"She said she was sure now that Cal was planning to kill her."

The floor beneath her feet seemed uncertain; her knees threatened to buckle. Her father, Madylyn, and herself. And Denton Patch. And her mother.

Mary backed up until she was leaning against the kitchen counter. She slowly lifted her eyes to Denton's. "Who else did you tell about this?"

"No one. Till right now. I'm telling you."

She pursed her lips. "So, why didn't you ever tell anyone?"

He shrugged and pushed the cap up higher on his brow. "Didn't have to. Your father dug his own grave just fine on his own. Helen told me he'd get his in the end. She said, 'Denton, you just watch. He'll get what's coming to him.' So I just watched, and she was right. He got what was coming."

Mary shook her head. It made no sense. None of it made any sense. "I don't understand," she whispered. "Are you telling me Mom believed Dad was going to kill her?"

Denton shrugged. "And she was right, wasn't she?"

Years later Mary could still hear her own scream of rage, could still feel the glass of milk flying from her hand and hitting Denton Patch full in the face. She could hear his cry of surprise, her own hurried footsteps as she ran from the room, weeping uncontrollably. She could still see Uncle Henry's startled sleepy face and feel Aunt Vivian's arms around her, rocking her as they sat together on the couch.

That night Denton felt compelled to tell his sister Vivian and her husband, Henry, what he knew about the affair. They didn't want to believe him, but Mary confirmed it, telling them that she'd known for some time, that Madylyn herself had told her. The next day, in a state of shock and dismay, Henry and Vivian told her cousin Jim Sadler and his wife, Elinor, when they came for dinner. Jim and Elinor in turn told Jim's brother Gene and his wife, Lillian, who took it to her pastor, who also happened to be her husband's cousin, Bernard Sadler. Bernie gathered everyone who knew, calling them to meet in his office at the church, and together they decided to draw a circle around themselves and keep the story there. No use letting it get around town, Bernie urged. Helen Syfert was dead and Cal Syfert was dead, "God rest their souls," and Mary Syfert, their own dear Mary—Bernie put a gentle hand on Mary's shoulder—had to somehow go on living in spite of everything. Leave Madylyn Fricke to God, Bernie said. Walk on the other side of the street when she passes by if you have to, but otherwise, let it lie. God will dole out justice.

Mary remembered that now, on the day she learned that Madylyn Fricke was dead. Uncle Bernie had sounded so sure, so confident, when he said, "God will dole out justice."

So where was the justice? Mary wondered. If God was in His heaven, as Uncle Bernie was so fond of saying, where on earth was the justice now that Madylyn was dead?

42

"YOU SEE THE PAPER THIS MORNING?" Vince asked.

Neil raised his brows in a question mark, even though he knew what Vince was talking about.

"The Traylor dame. She filed the civil suit. Against Dan Beeken. You see it?"

Neil nodded, dropped his eyes to the mug of beer he was clenching in both hands. "Yeah, I did." He'd called Mary after he read the article over breakfast. It was the first time they'd talked in several days, since their trip to Cincinnati. The conversation was brief and stilted, and though he'd called out of concern for Mary, Neil felt relieved when they'd hung up.

"Dan and Chief Harris were here last night," Vince went on. "I think they were talking about it. They talked a long time."

"Yeah?"

"Dan stayed after the chief left. In fact, he closed the place."

"I'm not surprised."

"So I gave him a lift home. He was a mess, Neil. He wouldn't have made it home if he'd tried to walk."

"Good of you to give him a lift."

Vince shrugged. "It was my juice that got him drunk in the first place. I gotta start drawing the line with him."

"You probably should."

"I just feel sorry for the guy." Vince clicked his tongue. "I feel worse for Mary, though. It's just one more thing."

"It's too much."

"Yeah, you're right. Some people get dumped on more than their share. Sweet girl like Mary—she ought to have it better."

Neil nodded, took a sip of beer. "That's what I say."

"She don't deserve this."

"No, she doesn't."

"I'd like to wring that Traylor dame's neck. All she's thinking about is the money. She and her lawyer, both cranking out the lies just so they can be rolling in the dough. She doesn't care that she's bringing a lot of pain down on someone who don't deserve it."

"You got that right."

"Teresa—she whipped up a casserole and a batch of cupcakes and took them over to Mary's this afternoon. She told Mary to call us anytime she needs anything. Anytime at all."

"You're good people, Vince."

"It's not much, but you want to do something, you know?"

"Yeah, I know." Neil wanted to pick Mary up out of this life and carry her to a whole new place. He'd like to erase her memory the way Superman erased Lois Lane's memory with a kiss, blasting it all right out of her brain with his superhuman powers. Just get rid of it, like it never happened. He'd like to get rid of all the years between today and the day he found Helen Syfert dead, so as not to be starting over but starting for the first time. He wanted it so bad he could taste it, bitter like the beer.

"You think she's doing all right?" Vince asked.

Neil thought about Mary's voice over the phone that morning. Quiet but firm. Distant. Very distant. "She's tough," he said. "Tougher than you'd think."

"Yeah, but is she okay?"

He sniffed. "Who can really know, Vince? I hope so."

"Well, I'd like to wring that Traylor dame's neck," Vince muttered again.

Neil grunted. "So get in line," he said.

43

NEIL MEASURED TIME BY THE height of the corn growing in the fields behind the Sadler house. It had indeed been knee-high by the Fourth of July, and in the weeks since it had ceaselessly sprung up, gaining height daily. He could imagine Bill McCurdy standing at the far edge of the field, fists hanging loosely in the pockets of his overalls, gazing with pride over the work of his hands. He remembered his own uncle Tom doing just that when the fields were his. Often at twilight, after a long hot day, Tom Sadler would pause for a moment to look out at the rolling land, to breathe in the earthy scent of the fields, to eye with satisfaction the lengthening stalks of corn. Neil used to watch him sometimes, experiencing vicariously the satisfaction his uncle felt in those few minutes. It was good for a man to look at his work and feel satisfied.

Neil wondered whether he would ever know that kind of satisfaction again. He had once, when he finished a painting and knew that it was good, when he taught a class and saw inspiration in the eyes of his students. But his satisfaction with those things had ended with Caroline's death. It was her dying that made him realize the finality of death, the irredeemable closing of a life. Perhaps one's work remains for a time, but what of the one who did the work? Is the painting worth more than the painter?

Neil knew now that it wasn't his work that he wanted to be immortal; he wanted to be immortal himself. It seemed that only in eternal life did life have any meaning at all. *"There should be no endings,"* he had said to Mary. Yes, that was it. Because one's meaning ended with one's life; it didn't go on independent of the soul. And even if one were lucky enough to be remembered by the next generation and the one after that, ultimately, when the sun had burned itself out and the universe had wound down, there would be only the void that had been there at the beginning. Everything would come back around to nothing. And, for Neil, that wasn't enough.

If only he could say along with Vincent McNulty: *Nothing matters! Now I'm free!*

But he didn't feel free. He just felt heavy, weighed down by the enormous vacuum of nonexistence.

At the end of another long day of work, Neil dragged himself up the stairs to the tower room. It seemed like years since he had climbed these stairs and discovered Bernie living up there. He had felt reasonably young then, only a couple months ago. But he didn't feel young now.

"I must be getting old, Uncle Bernie," he said. "I'm tired and I ache all over."

Bernie laughed. He sat in his overstuffed chair, one finger a bookmark in *Anna Karenina*. "That doesn't mean you're old, Neil. I believe that means you've been working too hard."

Neil pulled the rocking chair closer to Bernie and sat down. "Well, if I were a young man, I wouldn't be this tired, even after a full day of work. Face it, Bernie, I've passed the peak, and I'm on the downward slide."

"Ah well, then," Bernie said cheerfully, "if you're determined to join our ranks, let me be the first to welcome you to the golden years. I think you'll find it's not so bad as you might fear. It's really rather enjoyable, in fact."

Neil gave Bernie a doubtful look.

The old man laughed again, heartily. "Oh, I know, I know! The ailments, the aches and pains, the pills. So many pills! It's not entirely easy when the flesh begins to give out. But then again, and I don't expect you to understand, but—well, think about it, Neil. Remember all the anxiety that came with being young? All the questions: What should I do with my life? Will I make wrong choices? Will I succeed or fail? Well, you see, for a person in my position, all that's behind me now. And I'm just as glad to be done with it. The way I see it, it's good to have memories instead of question marks, and it's good to have accomplishments instead of dreams. Dreams are nice of course; don't get me wrong. But seeing one's dreams fulfilled is even better."

Neil said nothing for a moment. Then he asked, "Did you see your dreams fulfilled, Uncle Bernie?"

"Most of them, yes. Not all of them, of course, but then, you come to terms with that. That's another thing about old age. You can begin to look back and say, 'Ah yes, perhaps it's best just as it was.' There's a kind of . . . surrender, I suppose, that young people are unwilling to experience. Or perhaps unable. I'm not sure which. At any rate, at this stage of the game you can finally begin to live without all the uncertainties. What's done is done. You've finished the course, and now you can rest."

"But there's the trade-off, isn't it, Bernie? By the time you get rid of the uncertainties, or you surrender, or however you want to put it, you've come down to the end of the road. You've run out of time."

"Yes," he agreed. He shut his eyes and smiled. "When you run out of time, it's then your mind and spirit begin to lean toward eternity."

Neil waited for Bernie to open his eyes, hoping in the meantime to think of something to say. But even when Bernie opened his eyes, Neil was unsure how to respond, and so he went on waiting.

Bernie cocked his head. "I gather," he said quietly, "that the thought of eternity doesn't do much for you."

Neil sighed, lifted his eyes to the windows beyond Bernie's head. "That's the greatest uncertainty of all, isn't it?"

"Is it, Neil?"

"Well, yes. I mean, it's all this business of heaven that bothers me, Uncle Bernie. Really, as though such a place could exist. It seems too fantastic, or too fanciful maybe, ever to think we'd be there."

"Frankly, Neil, I find it pretty amazing that we're *here*. Why should it be any different, any more amazing, when we find ourselves there?"

Neil gave a frustrated shrug. "Not many people really believe in that kind of thing anymore, Bernie."

"I wouldn't say that—"

"Well, at least not in the circles I travel. I mean, some believe in a sort of afterlife, I suppose. Others believe in reincarnation. Many, I think, don't believe in anything. Who knows, though, really? It's not as though we all sit around talking about death and dying and what happens after. Most people are just living for the here and now, you know? Because that's all that makes sense. It's all we can be sure of."

"Is it, Neil?" Bernie asked again.

"Yes, I think so."

"So you believe, then, that this is it?"

Neil shrugged. What did he believe? He saw the whole of life as a series of colors, colors and shades of light, brilliant hues and shadowy tones and then, suddenly, a fading to black. With death there was no more color. No more anything. "I don't know what to think," he confessed. "I wish I did. There are so many ideas out there, and of course they all conflict, and everyone thinks that whatever he believes is right and everyone else is wrong. It's confusing. And that's the problem. It's too confusing to sort it all out. There's no way of knowing what's right and what's wrong."

He stood up suddenly and walked to the window. "You know, Bernie, the problem is God's silence. His being invisible. His leaving us alone so we just have to guess about everything. I think, if there's a God out there, He could at least put in an appearance and tell us what the truth is."

He turned and saw Bernie staring up at him with startled eyes. Bernie frowned, shook his head, gave a small confused laugh.

"But, Neil, don't you know? That's what God did. That's exactly what he did. He wrapped himself in skin and gave himself a tongue to tell us what the truth is. Don't you know that, Neil?" he repeated.

"So you told me when I was a child."

"So I tell you now. Nothing's changed."

"I've changed, I'm afraid, Uncle Bernie."

"That may be so, but don't be afraid. God hasn't changed. You'll see."

"Will I?"

"Of course."

"How do you know?"

"Because I know *Him*. That first coming was only the opening act. He's been relentless in His pursuit of us ever since. He's on your heels right now."

Neil sat in silence for a moment. Finally he said, "In that case, I'd better get back to work before he chews me out for being lazy."

Bernie smiled. "Well, then, go in peace," he said. "And Neil?"

"Yes, Uncle Bernie?"

"Don't bother trying to outrun what you know you can't outrun."

Neil nodded. "I'll consider that fair warning." He rose and, giving Bernie one more nod, turned and left the room.

44

MARY WAS AT THE KITCHEN SINK washing the supper dishes when Leo came in holding a basketball.

Mary smiled at her son. "You done shooting hoops? Want something to drink?"

Leo shook his head. He frowned and licked his lips before he spoke. "It's Dad," he said. "I think there's something wrong with him."

Mary's heart quickened and she felt her breath catch in her throat. She turned off the water and dried her hands on a dish towel. "What is it, Leo? What happened?"

The boy shrugged and shook his head again. "Nothing happened. I mean, I was just out there shooting baskets when I saw Dad in the backyard. I don't know, Mom, I think he's . . . crying or something."

"Stay here." Mary dropped the towel on the counter and headed for the back door.

"Should I call somebody?"

"Not yet."

She stepped out into the still summer evening and saw her husband on one knee in the grass, his head hung low. He must have suddenly gotten sick. The stress of the civil suit had curbed his appetite lately, but tonight Mary had made beef stroganoff, his favorite. He had put in a sullen appearance at the supper table, but he had eaten. He had had two helpings after too many days of too little to eat. It had no doubt upset his stomach. She would help him inside and make him a little broth or a cup of hot tea.

But when she knelt on the grass beside him, she discovered that he wasn't sick. Rather, he was sighing over something cradled in the palms of his hands.

"Dan?" she asked quietly.

Through the cracks of his fingers Mary could make out the feathers of a small bird, a very young sparrow. As he made a nest of his palms, the bird fluttered its wings. One wing stretched out perfectly, its feathers smooth and sleek. The other wing bent back on itself, the feathers tangled and displaced. The bird squawked and tried to move, managing only to teeter against the sides of the fleshy nest.

Mary lifted her gaze to Dan's face. His cheeks were wet with tears.

"Dan?"

Without looking at her, he whispered, "I won't be able to fix it, Mary."

She put her arm around his shoulder. "It's okay, Dan. Maybe we can take it to a vet."

"No." He moved his head slowly, side to side. "It's too bad off. I should be able to help it, but I can't."

"It's all right," she said again. "We'll let the vet take care of it, okay? He'll know what to do."

She had thought him made of stone. She had thought for years that he had built himself into a wall. But she knew now,

quite suddenly, that she was wrong. He hadn't allowed himself
to be hardened. It was something else entirely.

"Mom?"

Mary looked over her shoulder and saw Leo standing there,
confused and frightened.

"Leo, go call Chief Harris," she instructed quietly. "Tell
him to meet us here as soon as he can."

Leo nodded once, then disappeared.

Mary turned back to her husband, rested her head against
him, tightened her grip around his shoulder. "Oh, Dan," she
sighed.

He was as broken as the sparrow's wing, all bent back on
himself and unable to move without falling.

45

NEIL WALKED THE LENGTH OF the gravel drive and turned around when he reached Route 42. He stood near the edge of the road studying the house, its massive brick form, the tall arched windows, the gingerbread trim, the finials at the tip of each gable. He had stood right about here as a kid when he'd painted the picture of the house that now hung in his bedroom. No, actually, he had sat on the grass with a sketch pad in his lap, a box of dime-store paints open in front of him. Maybe it was time to paint the house again, to do it right this time. If he started soon, he could have it done before he left, framed and hung as well, a gift for Grace and Dennis. He wasn't yet sure what he had gained by being here, but it would be nice to leave something behind.

He walked slowly back up the drive, the loose gravel crunching lightly beneath his feet. Even from the lowest point of the sloping driveway, he could see the top of the corn. It wouldn't be long now before it was fully grown and ready to harvest. Neil remembered Uncle Tom's love of harvesting. *"Best time of the year,"* he'd say, *"especially when the season's been plenty bountiful."* Surely, Neil thought, this year would be "plenty bountiful," for the sun and the weather and the earth itself had been kind.

By the time the corn was harvested, Neil would be well into his routine at the Harrington-Glasser Day School. He would be back in Brooklyn, living in the house that he and Caroline had shared for more than a decade.

A pang of longing sliced through him as he sat down on the front porch steps and rested his arms on his knees. He dreaded going back to the house in Brooklyn, dreaded the emptiness of it. The thought of staying in Mason for good was sharply tempting, but he knew that he couldn't stay. There was nothing for him here, nothing for him to do once the renovation of the house was complete, no way for him to make a living. And he couldn't go on living off of Dennis and Grace indefinitely. The arrangement of free room and board in exchange for work was fine while it lasted, but it wasn't going to last much longer.

He was going to have to go back to New York. But perhaps it would help to make some changes, he thought. Maybe he'd sell the Warren Street house, move into a smaller place, a place that held no memories of Caroline.

Neil sighed. No matter where he lived, he'd be living alone. And he knew that if he could do anything he wanted, he would take Mary back to New York with him. He should have done it twenty-six years ago, but he'd been a fool and an angry coward, and even before Helen's death and Cal's arrest, he'd never had the guts to tell Mary that he loved her. Never once. He'd been a coward before he was an angry coward, and he'd let her slip away.

He wondered whether it was too late. Dan Beeken was in a rehab center down in Cincinnati, some special program set up for burned-out cops. Nice that it was around. Apparently a lot of cops needed it. Dan sure did. He'd been there for four days now, and no one knew how long he'd stay. A month, maybe more. His life after that was one huge question mark. He'd never go back to law enforcement, that much was sure. His days as a cop were over.

Not much of a future for Mary, Neil thought. Not much of a marriage, for that matter. What kind of relationship could Mary have with a man enslaved to alcohol, crushed by his job, embroiled in a civil suit, faced with an uncertain future at best, a whole bunch of ongoing trouble at worst? Mary was ripe for a new life, a better life. She *deserved* a better life. And Neil could give it to her if—

"Get a grip, Sadler," he said aloud. "You're kidding yourself if you think Mary would go to New York with you."

Even if she didn't stay with Dan, it seemed unlikely to Neil that Mary would uproot herself and her son to go to New York at this point in her life.

Best not to think about it, then. Just keep going through the motions, doing what had to be done. Neil stood, stretched, decided to go back in the house and see what Dennis and Mike were up to. But before he could turn to go inside, he saw a car turn off Route 42 and into the drive.

Mary's car—the yellow Accord.

Neil watched her pull halfway up, then stop and park right there in the middle of the drive. She had spotted Neil, raised a hand to tell him to wait. She hurriedly got out of the car, slung her purse over one shoulder, then started toward him.

Neil's heart was pumping, both because she was there and because something was wrong. He could see it in her face even before she reached him. Her eyes were wide and her skin was ashen; even her lips were drained of color. She looked like a person in shock.

She stopped when she came to within three feet of him. She looked up directly into his eyes, and even though she was so close, when she spoke he couldn't hear what she said.

He shook his head, frowning. "Mary, what's wrong? I can't understand what you're saying."

Trembling, she seemed almost ready to collapse. Her voice was still a whisper, but this time when she spoke, Neil was able to hear her. And to understand.

"I said—" she closed her eyes, opened them, two deep pools of horror—"I said, I know who killed my mother."

46

SHE'S LOST IT was Neil's first thought. *It's finally all become too much for her.* For a moment he was shaken. He didn't know what to do. His mind flew to the third floor of the house, to where he had last seen Dennis and Grace inspecting the newly installed cabinets in their private kitchen. He could call for them if need be. They'd know what to do.

He tentatively lifted a hand and laid it on Mary's shoulder. "Why don't you sit down here for a minute and tell me what's going on?" he said. He guided her gently to a couple of the padded wicker chairs on the porch. When they were both seated, he went on, "Now, what do you mean? What's happened?"

Instead of answering, Mary opened her purse and pulled out an envelope. She handed it to Neil without a word.

The letter, postmarked Cincinnati, was addressed in a handwriting unfamiliar to Neil. The top of the envelope had been slit open neatly with a letter opener. Inside was a single-page note, along with another smaller envelope. The second envelope too had been opened. "You want me to read this?" Neil asked, though he already knew the answer.

"Yes." A choked whisper.

"You get it today?"

A nod of the head.

Neil felt something like fear crawl over his skin. He pulled out the note and the smaller envelope. And then he began to read.

Dear Mrs. Beeken,

After my mother, Madylyn Fricke, died recently, I was cleaning out her things at the nursing home, and I came across this letter addressed to you. It was already sealed, but it didn't have a stamp on it. I don't know why she didn't send it; maybe she was still hoping to speak with you in person. At any rate, I didn't feel I had a right to open it, but in case you heard about my mother's passing away, I thought you might be surprised to receive a letter from her after her death. So I am sending along this accompanying note to explain the circumstances.

I know my mother tried to contact you a few times, though she never did tell me why. She was pretty sharp until right near the end, when she had a mild stroke and got confused and forgetful. She had a massive stroke just a few weeks later, and that's what caused her death. I don't know when she wrote this letter. I'm assuming it was before the mild stroke, since her right side was pretty weak after that, and I don't think she could have written anything. Maybe she dictated the enclosed letter to a nurse or someone—I don't know. Anyway, if it doesn't make much sense, please bear in mind my mother's declining health in her final days.

Sincerely,

Gwendolyn Sheppard

Neil folded the single piece of paper and looked up at

Mary. Her face had gone even whiter, if that was possible. She remained silent, her lips pressed together in a firm line. She nodded once to tell him to go on.

Neil removed the second letter from the inner envelope and unfolded it. Several pages long, it was undated. The handwriting was small and precise, though shaky in parts. It was the handwriting of an elderly woman.

Dear Mary,

You are angry with me, and I want you first of all to know that I understand. You have every right to be angry. But how I wish you would answer my calls, talk to me, let me tell you face-to-face what I know. I can't run after you in the street as I did the night I told you about your father and me. I can't go after you and make you listen to me this time. But I must hope that you will both receive and read this letter, because it is high time that somebody told you the truth, and I am the only living person who can do that.

I did not know the truth in 1977. If I had known then what really happened, I don't think I could have borne it. Even now, it is hard to bear. But I must bear it, and I must tell you what I know.

Mary, dear, I always believed that your father was not involved in Helen's death, but I wouldn't know for twenty years what really happened the night your mother died. First let me tell you that your father was *not* guilty. He was innocent, just as he claimed. He went to prison and died an innocent man, and the horror of that tragedy is only made worse when I consider who did kill Helen.

I can scarcely bring myself to write of that night, but you must know what happened. Mary, your mother planned her own death. It was, in a very real sense, a suicide. But it was more than that. She wanted her death to

335

appear to be a homicide, and she wanted your father to be implicated in her murder. For that she needed help. And that was when she called on my husband, my own husband, to do for her what she couldn't do for herself.

This is what happened. It was Denton Patch who discovered your father and me, who found us out. Cal and I never knew. We had no idea. Denton found my brooch when I left my sweater in the farmhouse where we used to meet. I remember the brooch, but I was never aware that it was missing. Denton took it to Helen to prove to her that Cal and I were having an affair.

You don't need me to tell you that your mother had been sick and tired and angry for a very long time. You know Bill and I had socialized with your parents for years, and in that time I saw the disease cripple your mother's body, but more than that, it crippled her soul. She was so bitter, Mary. In the end she was someone completely different from the Helen I first met before you were born. You would have liked that younger Helen. Really, you would. It's a shame you never knew her.

They were both a little crazy, I think—Helen and Bill. Their anger at life made them both a little crazy. So when Helen learned about Cal and me, years of anger culminated in her decision to kill herself and make it look like your father had done it. As though he had been the one to make her ill, instead of the one to care for her all those years.

Her dreadful decision to end her life—that, I can almost understand. Bill's part in it horrifies me. Helen asked Bill to help her die. She told him she wanted Cal to take the fall for her death. So why did Bill agree? Because I was the one Cal was having an affair with. And because Helen gave Bill her wedding rings as payment, as though that could compensate for a life. And because Bill had no conscience. To him, smothering Helen and destroying Cal was easy. He was furious at the thought of Cal and me together, and Helen's plan was the natural release for Bill's anger. It actually made sense to him.

I thought Bill was away on a hunting trip that weekend. He set up the trip figuring Cal and I would take advantage of his being gone, and we'd get together. He was right. I even sent the children away so that I could spend time with your father. Helen knew you would be gone too, staying with a friend because the carnival was in town. It was the perfect time to carry out Helen's plan. That night, when Cal was putting her to bed, Helen purposely scratched his face so his skin would be found under her fingernails. That was Bill's idea. He said he saw something similar on Perry Mason. While this was going on inside, Bill was waiting outside, hiding somewhere. After he saw Cal leave, he simply entered your house by way of the open back door, did the deed, and left, all the while knowing I thought he was in Kentucky. He did go to Kentucky, but not until afterward.

It was so easy to make it appear as though Cal had killed Helen. And the police helped out by refusing to consider any other possibility. They decided right away that Cal was guilty, and that was the end of it.

I went on living for twenty years with the man who killed the man I loved. The man who killed your mother, Mary, because she wanted to die.

You are wondering, I know, how I came to know all this, how I learned the truth. Bill told me himself. About two weeks before he passed away he told me he couldn't die with this on his soul. He cried and begged me to forgive him. He begged me not to tell our children.

He must have had some sort of conscience after all, or maybe a fear of death, or both. He said he knew he would probably burn in hell for what he'd done, but it might be easier to bear if he knew I'd forgiven him. I told him it wasn't me that had to forgive him, but it was you, Mary. He shook his head and told me you must never know. He made me swear I would never tell anyone.

But now, when my own death is so near, I know that it is wrong to keep this from you. You, of all people, must know the truth of what happened the night your mother died. And so I am telling you the truth.

Mary, I hope you will find some rest and comfort in the assurance that your dear father was innocent. He was a good man, the best man I ever knew. I truly did love him. I am only so sorry to think that our love for each other ruined so many lives.

I would ask you to forgive me, but I know that you cannot. I don't blame you. But please, if you can find it in your heart to do me this one thing, please don't tell my children the truth about their father. They would be devastated beyond all hope. I pray it is enough that *you* know, and that now you can live out the rest of your life in peace.

Sincerely,
Madylyn Fricke

47

NEIL DIDN'T KNOW HOW LONG they sat there on the porch saying nothing. The present didn't seem to exist any longer. It was the past that was in motion—shifting, settling, shifting again. Neil watched in disbelief as that particular piece of history rearranged itself, a mummy pushing against the confines of its stony linens, a dead man turning over in his grave. When it was finally satisfied, settling into a shape completely unrecognizable to him, Neil heard someone say, "Unbelievable," several times. The third time he recognized the voice as his own.

A dozen thoughts rolled through his mind like dark clouds, raining down a dozen feelings. Bewilderment, confusion, horror. An intense anger toward Helen Syfert and Bill Fricke. An overwhelming sadness for Cal Syfert. Regret that he, Neil Sadler, had left Mason laden with his arrogant certainty that his anger was justified, that Cal Syfert was guilty of murder, his daughter guilty by association.

And at the same time, curiously, there was a certain wonder tumbling about inside of him and a palpable relief. Cal Syfert was innocent. Cal Syfert was who he said he was. And years ago, when Neil had looked to him as a father, when he had confided to the man his dreams, when he had quietly loved the man's daughter, Neil had been right. The faith he'd had in Cal Syfert had not been misplaced. Cal had told the truth. And now Neil felt this revelation of the man's innocence the way a sick person feels the fever breaking—something falling away, a sickness exiting, a lightness rushing in to take its place.

He turned and saw Mary's liquid eyes watching him. "You always knew, didn't you, that he was innocent?" Neil asked.

"Yes." The tears fell. She lifted a trembling hand to wipe them away.

He reached out and took her hand. "Mary, I'm sorry—"

She shook her head. "How could you know?" she said quietly. "You couldn't know."

"It's—" He looked down at the letter in his lap. "It's unthinkable what they did. Bill Fricke. Your mother."

Mary pursed her lips; her jaw tightened. "How could they do it? How could they do that to Dad?" Tears coursed down both cheeks.

Neil shook his head helplessly. "It wasn't Helen that was murdered. It was Cal. And they got away with it." He followed her gaze out toward the road, then looked back at her. "What are you going to do now?"

"I don't know," she answered quietly. "The first thing I knew I had to do was show you the letter. Beyond that, I don't know."

"Don't you want to clear your father's name?"

"Yes." A tentative nod. "Oh yes." Then, after a moment, she added, "But what if—" She stopped, still focused on the road.

"What?" Neil prodded.

"What if the letter isn't true?"

Neil started to protest, but Mary stopped him. "Not the part about Dad's innocence. I'm sure about that. But I mean, what if Madylyn made it up about Bill having a part in all this? Her daughter said she'd had a stroke. Maybe she didn't know what she was saying."

"The letter is completely coherent," Neil countered. "It doesn't sound to me like she was confused. She must have written it before the stroke."

"Maybe so, but what if she made it all up on purpose? About Bill?"

"Why would she?"

"Because she wanted so badly to explain my father's innocence. We both knew Dad hadn't killed Mom, but we didn't know who did." She smiled again, sadly. "I had my theory, of course. I had myself completely convinced it was some crazy guy from the carnival. Maybe Madylyn came up with her own explanation, and that was to say Bill did it." Mary shrugged. "Bill was dead. Might as well pin it on him. Get Cal Syfert, the man she really loved, off the hook."

"And then ask you not to tell anyone?" Neil shook his head. "I don't think so. Keeping it a secret so her children don't know the truth about Bill doesn't exactly clear Cal's name."

Mary took the letter from Neil, folded it, and put it back into the envelope. "I don't know, Neil," she said. "I really don't."

"Mary, Madylyn's telling the truth. I'm sure of it." After a moment he added, "But what would you say to showing Bernie the letter, see what he thinks?"

She took a deep breath. "Yeah." She nodded and wiped her cheeks with the palms of her hands. "Yeah, Uncle Bernie will know what to do."

Neil stood and offered a hand to Mary. She took it and stood up, and they made the hike up to the tower room.

———————

They found Bernie lying on the bed, his eyes closed behind his glasses, his jaw slack, his hands laced over the open book on his chest. He was so still he didn't appear to be breathing. Neil's first thought was, *I knew he'd never finish that Tolstoy novel.* Quickly he berated himself. What kind of thought was that when an old man lay there dead? Not just an old man, but Uncle Bernie, beloved Padre, anchor of the Sadler family. Neil felt his heart skip a beat. *Bernie . . .*

In the next moment the old man's eyes fluttered open. He worked to focus them, and when he saw Neil and Mary peering down at him, he smiled broadly. "Ah," he said hoarsely, "life is sweet."

Neil sighed in quiet relief. His heart settled as he watched Mary place a bookmark in *Anna Karenina* and set it on the bedside table. "Come on, Uncle Bernie," she said gently. "Let me help you sit up." She propped him up with pillows between his back and the headboard, then offered him a sip of water from the cup on the table.

"Comfortable, Uncle Bernie?" she asked as she replaced the cup.

"Oh yes. Thank you, dear." He smiled at them. "What a pleasant surprise to wake up from my nap and find you here."

"Yes, well . . ." Neil started. He made a gesture for Mary to sit in the rocking chair while he settled himself on the edge of the bed. "I think we really do have a bit of a surprise for you, Uncle Bernie."

"Oh?" He went on smiling.

things we once held *dear*

Neil looked at Mary. Mary looked at the letter in her hand. Without a word of explanation she handed it to Bernie.

As Bernie read first Gwendolyn's note and then Madylyn's letter, Neil watched his face intently, but the old man's expression offered no clue as to what was going on inside his head. When he finished, he folded each letter carefully and put it back in its envelope. He closed his eyes a moment, opened them, smiled again, and said, "You do have an interesting way of getting things done, don't you?"

He was looking at neither of his visitors but at the window across the room. Neil, feeling a bit irritated, retorted, "I'm going to assume, Uncle Bernie, that you're not speaking to me. Nor to Mary either."

Now Bernie turned to Neil. His smile was invincible. "Forgive me, Neil," he said. "I just had to offer up that bit of thanks."

Neil expected him to go on. When he didn't, Neil asked, "Well? This letter is something like a bomb exploding, and you're sitting there as though nothing's happened. Tell us what you think."

The old man turned his placid gaze on Mary, then reached out and took her hand. "I'm so glad you know the truth. I'm just so glad the time has come for you to know the truth."

Neil and Mary shared a glance. "But, Uncle Bernie," she said, "that's the thing. Do you think Madylyn is telling the truth in this letter?"

Bernie nodded, squeezed Mary's hand. "Oh yes, my dear. I'm here to testify to that. Why else would an old man stick around?"

Mary, frowning, shook her head. "I don't understand. What are you getting at?"

"Just this, Mary—you see, Bill came to me and confessed—"

"He confessed to the murder?"

"Yes—"

"When?" Neil interjected. "How long have you known?"

Bernie thought a moment, then shrugged. "I can't remember exactly," he said. "It was shortly before Bill died. Oh, I remember now. It was the year I finally retired. What year was that? Well, at any rate, when Bill knew he was dying, he came to me at the church, seeking forgiveness. He was quite upset—"

"And you forgave him?" Neil stood abruptly and began to pace the room.

"It isn't up to me, Neil, to forgive or not forgive—"

"Forget the theology, Uncle Bernie," Neil retorted. "Are you saying you've known for years that Bill Fricke was responsible for Aunt Helen's death?"

"Bill Fricke came to me and confessed—"

"And you never told anyone what he told you? You weren't even willing to set the record straight?"

"How could I, Neil? You must understand the sanctity of the confessional. I wasn't at liberty—"

"Bill Fricke didn't even go to your church."

"That doesn't matter. My door was open to anyone. I suspect he came to me because Cal was part of our family."

"So you've kept the secret from Mary all these years?"

"Please, Neil, I had no choice—"

"But you did! You should have told Mary as soon as Bill came to you. She had a right to know."

"I begged Bill at the time to confess to the authorities, to clear Cal's name, but he refused. Beyond that, there was nothing I could do."

"You could have told Mary. You were wrong not to tell her."

"A thousand times I wanted to tell Mary the truth. But I was bound by my role of confessor to keep Bill's confession confidential."

"I don't believe that!"

"Whether or not you believe it, it's true. The deed had already been done. There was no danger to anyone. Bill wasn't even a danger to himself. He was simply a dying man looking for grace. I had no loophole, Neil. Nothing that allowed me to break confidentiality."

Neil stopped pacing. He frowned at Bernie. "And so you might have died without ever letting Mary know what the truth was?"

Bernie was quiet a long time. He continued to hold on to Mary's hand. Finally he said, "I was hoping that would not be the case. I longed to see Mary know the truth. But it was not in my hands. The truth, you see, has to come out at the right time and in the right way." With his free hand, he lifted the letter. "And so you see, it has."

He turned to Mary. "My dear, can you find it in yourself to understand?"

She nodded slowly. She was dry-eyed but seemed dazed, puzzled. "I can see your position, I think, Uncle Bernie. And now I see why you wanted me to talk to Madylyn."

"Yes. I thought perhaps that Bill had at least confessed to Madylyn, and that she in turn wanted to tell you."

Mary nodded again. "The important thing is that I finally know what really happened."

"But we still need to clear Cal's name," Neil argued. He paced the room again, then paused at the window. "I think we should take the letter to the newspaper. Or to the police. Or both, of course. Yes, to both, and right away, today."

"But," Mary countered, "Madylyn asked us not to—"

"What does it matter what Madylyn wanted?" Neil exclaimed, swinging around to face Mary. "We don't owe her anything."

"She's afraid for her children and grandchildren."

"Afraid of what? That they'll be humiliated and ostracized like you were, like we all were? That shouldn't stop us from making this public knowledge. We owe it to your father to do that. We have no business protecting Bill's family."

"And yet," Mary said hesitantly, "don't forget my mother. Bill didn't act alone. It was mother who persuaded him—"

"Dear ones," Bernie interrupted, "we have much to think about. I wouldn't act too hastily."

Neil turned his incredulous eyes on Bernie. "I can't believe it, Uncle Bernie," he cried. "Now you want *us* to keep the secret?"

"I'm not asking you to do anything but wait for a time. Think before you act. We must think and pray and talk about what we will do from here."

"But—"

"Uncle Bernie's right," Mary interjected. "I want the world to know that my father was innocent, just as he said he was. But it has to be done in the right way."

Bernie smiled again, patted Mary's hand. "It will all be made clear to us, in good time."

"Yes." Mary tried to return Bernie's smile. "I'm sure you're right."

Neil, his mouth a taut line, stared at the two of them. He disagreed. But he knew that, for the moment, he was defeated.

"Come on, Mary," he said. "Why don't we go somewhere, clear our heads, get something to eat. Maybe we can make some decisions with some food in our stomachs."

Mary rose, then leaned over and kissed Bernie on the forehead. She pulled back and smiled at him. "Thank you, Uncle Bernie."

He cocked his head. "For what, my dear?"

She gave a small laugh. "I don't really know," she confessed. "I just feel as though everything's all right now."

"It is, Mary. You'll see."

He gave her the letter, and she put it back into her purse. She turned to Neil and said, "All right, let's go."

He put a hand on her shoulder and guided her toward the door.

"And, dear ones," Bernie called out. They turned. He raised a hand, as though in blessing, and dismissed them with the words, "Go in peace."

48

IT WAS A PEACEFUL PLACE, the long drive lined with live oak trees, the building itself a hundred-year-old clapboard farmhouse. Hope Haven, they called it. Always a pot of coffee on the stove, food in the fridge, baked goods in the larder. No liquor allowed. Half a dozen beds for inpatients. A large cozy living room where any number of weary, depleted cops could gather to talk, spill their guts, cry if need be, get the support and encouragement they longed for. Peace officers, all of them, worn down, worn out, broken from a job that was anything but peaceful.

They were like enlisted soldiers in Vietnam, putting their lives on the line and derided for doing it, coming home shell-shocked, some of them physically maimed, all of them emotionally broken.

It was an occupational hazard, this breaking apart. Not that it happened to all of them, of course. Some could walk a beat for years and just keep walking, seemingly untouched. Others were pencil pushers, safely ensconced behind the lines, their territory one small desk. That helped.

Still, the casualties were far too many. More than the public knew. Those broken ones—no one outside of their circle could completely understand them. Because no one knew what they had seen or experienced or suffered. No one but themselves. They needed Hope Haven, this peaceful place, to find healing, if healing was to be found.

Mary felt overwhelmingly thankful for the place as she steered down the drive toward the small parking lot in back of the house. She knew how badly Hope Haven was needed. Through her husband, she had her own private peephole into the inner circle. She saw enough to know that it was ugly in there. She had no idea exactly how many police suicides it took to get Hope Haven underway, but she knew it was far too many. Half a dozen years ago, someone decided something should be done to help curtail the numbers, to provide an intervention of sorts. There were such programs for drug users and criminals; why not for officers? And so Hope Haven was started, a safety net for falling cops, there to catch them before they hit bottom. Funded by grants, police fund-raisers, and private donations, Hope Haven always seemed to have just enough money to keep the doors open.

Mary hadn't called ahead to let Dan know she was coming. She had, in a sense, wanted to surprise him. She was afraid if she called, she'd tell him what she knew over the phone, and she didn't want him to find out that way. Not after all this time.

Yesterday, while they were eating together at the Dinner Bell, Neil had almost convinced Mary that taking the letter public was the right thing to do. Take one copy to the police, another to the paper. Let them eat crow, reopen the case, print a retraction. After all, the police had arrested the wrong man. The paper had tried and convicted him on their editorial page. Let them know they'd been wrong, Neil said. Let Mason know they'd been wrong. Let Warren County, let Ohio—no, why stop there? Let the whole world know how wrong everyone had been! Cal Syfert was an innocent man. He'd been telling the truth.

Yes, Mary wanted that too. She wanted the world to know about her father. But even before the meal was finished and the waitress brought the check, Mary realized something she wanted even more.

She wanted to show the letter to Dan, to let him know that, in the face of so much that had been wrong, he, Dan Beeken, had been right. He had trusted his uncle's judgment about the polygraph. He had believed Cal Syfert's claim of innocence. He had held Mary up through the whole ordeal.

Mary entered the farmhouse through the back door and stopped in the small office off the kitchen. The staff member on duty greeted her, then told her to go on upstairs.

She knew the way. She knew which room was Dan's, one he shared with a cop whose twenty-three-year career had come to an abrupt close when his blood-alcohol level sent his squad car sailing through the front window of an all-night diner.

When Mary arrived in the doorway, the roommate wasn't there. Dan was alone. He stood with his back to the door, his head tilted up toward a cheap print in a cheap dime-store frame. Mary recognized *Mother and Child* by the American painter Mary Cassatt. Neil had shown it to her years ago. She had never forgotten the beauty of the woman in the long yellow gown, a golden-haired child on her lap. Now Dan seemed to be captured by the same beauty.

"Dan?" she called softly.

He turned. When he saw her standing there in the door-way, he smiled. "Mary," he said. His voice held no surprise, only a wistfulness that had long been absent. "I was just thinking about you."

She smiled in return, and in the next moment she was across the room and in his arms.

49

"ARE YOU STILL ANGRY WITH ME, Neil?" Bernie asked.

Neil shook his head and smiled. "I was never angry with you, Uncle Bernie."

The older man rested his head against the back of the chair. "Ah," he said, "then I'm happy."

"It doesn't take much to make you happy, does it?"

"No. Not much." After a moment, he added, "What about you, Neil? Are you happy?"

Neil thought a long while. Then he said, "That's not an easy question, I'm afraid."

"No, I suppose not."

"I'm glad we know the truth about Uncle Cal. But I'm frustrated that we haven't reported it to the authorities."

"All in good time."

"How much time do we need?"

"Mary wants to call a family meeting of sorts. You know that, don't you?"

"Yes. She asked me to see if Mom and Dad could come from California."

"And are they?"

"Yes." Neil shrugged. "Mom's been wanting to come back anyway. She says she's long overdue for a visit."

"Well, then, I'll be glad to see them."

"Yes. And they'll be glad, I think, about the letter, about Cal's innocence. They always thought he was guilty."

"Most everyone did, it seems."

Neil looked long and hard at Bernie. "So what did *you* believe about Cal? I mean, before Bill Fricke came to you and confessed?"

Bernie looked beyond Neil's shoulder, as though he were looking into the past. "I believed that Cal was innocent."

"Did you really?"

"Oh yes."

"But why?"

"Because I knew Cal. I knew he was incapable of doing what he was accused of doing. What I didn't know, of course, was what really happened. I thought perhaps it might have been an intruder, but there was never any concrete evidence."

"Mary thought some crazy carny guy had wandered into town."

"Yes, I remember that." Bernie breathed deeply. "I thought her theory had merit."

Neil sniffed. "It's just too bad Bill Fricke didn't leave behind some sort of calling card, something to put the police on his scent."

"Maybe he did and it was never found. The police didn't look very hard once they arrested Cal."

"No, they didn't. That's for sure." Neil shifted uneasily in his chair. "You know, Uncle Bernie," he said, "I was just as convinced as everyone else that Cal was guilty. But I knew the man as well as anyone. Maybe even better. I should have known he was innocent, the way you did."

Bernie looked kindly at Neil. "Don't beat yourself up, Neil. You were just a child."

"No." He shook his head. "I was old enough to go off to New York, to leave and not look back. I should have . . ." His voice trailed off.

"Should have what, Neil?"

"I don't know. Should have done everything differently, I guess. *Would* have done everything differently if I'd just trusted Cal enough to believe what he said."

"Listen, Neil, things were such a mess that after a while not even Cal was sure of the truth."

"What do you mean?"

"I used to visit him in jail. Shortly before he settled on the Alford plea, he told me he wondered himself whether he might have killed Helen. He said he might have blacked out or something—you know, committed the murder and then didn't remember. Some such thing as that. I told him that was nonsense. But see, things were such that even Cal questioned his own innocence. I think other people almost had him convinced that he'd done it."

"But he didn't. And he went to prison for a crime he didn't commit."

"Yes. Ironic, isn't it, how every prisoner claims he didn't do the crime he's in for. But in this case, for Cal, it was true."

"Dear God," Neil whispered. He dropped his eyes away from Bernie's gaze when he said, "You know I loved Uncle Cal."

"I know that, Neil. I was very fond of him myself."

"It's killing me to think of what he went through."

Bernie nodded his understanding. "It was a tragedy. There's no other way to describe it."

"Yes," Neil agreed. "What makes it even more tragic is that he was so alone. Abandoned, really. I mean, we should have all been speaking out for his innocence, but we just didn't believe him."

"No, not even his own lawyer believed him, from what I gathered at the time." Bernie laughed. "Your lawyer should at least pretend to believe you. Earl Hoback wasn't very good at pretending. I'm sure that was one more thing that gave Cal little confidence in his chances of winning at trial."

Neil shook his head. His whole body deflated in a sigh. "We didn't have to know the whole story to believe he was innocent, did we?"

Bernie thought a moment, then said, "I don't think so, no. As I say, Neil, I didn't know the whole story, but I did know that Cal wasn't capable of murdering his wife. Other people, apparently, thought he was. And so they decided that he did."

"But that's the thing, Uncle Bernie. We all just kind of invented our own version of what happened. No one was completely right; some were completely wrong. *I* was completely wrong. And that bothers me. Before the murder I would have said Uncle Cal could never do anything like that. After the murder I believed everything the newspapers said about him, just because that was what seemed to make the most sense. How in the world are we ever supposed to know what the truth is about anything at all?"

Bernie leaned forward in the chair and laced his fingers together. "Ah, well, you see, Neil, truth isn't invented; it's revealed." He paused and smiled briefly. "The one who knows the truth has to tell us what it is."

Neil stood and walked over to the window. The afternoon sun cast a golden glow over the rows of ripening corn. As far as Neil could see, fields of corn stretched out across the rolling hills, all the way to the horizon, where the blue of the sky bent down to touch them. There was a place where earth and heaven met.

He turned from the window. "Just one more question, Uncle Bernie."

"What's that?"

"Where can I get some good art supplies around here these days? There's a picture I need to paint before I leave for home."

50

A FEW DAYS LATER AT a little before midnight, Neil wearily entered his bedroom and turned on the light. It had been a long day, but he would have to unwind for a while before going to sleep. He kicked off his shoes, threw his socks on top of them, then lay down on his bed in his T-shirt and shorts. He put his hands beneath his head and stared up at the ceiling.

The room was filled with the faint but pungent odor of pigment from the canvas he was working on. Neil breathed deeply of it. The years had done nothing to diminish what was to him the most thrilling fragrance imaginable. Fresh paint on canvas. The scent triggered something inside of him like a burst of adrenaline in his veins.

He turned his head to look at the canvas resting on an easel in the corner. He would be finished with it in another few days and would have it framed in time for the grand opening of the bed-and-breakfast, to be held the last Saturday in August. Neil, Dennis, and Mike had worked hard and, with the help of some outside contractors, had completed the renovations a week ahead of schedule.

The Gothic Horror looked pretty good, Neil had to admit.

It would never be what it once was, the Sadler residence, home to a simple farm family, the place that Neil remembered. But it had to move forward if it was to remain standing. It had to change, becoming something it hadn't been before, in order simply to exist. But that didn't mean the past was lost, cut off like a lock of hair falling to the barbershop floor. The past remained. The history of the house was in its walls, sure as the brick and mortar that held it together. Neil would always be a part of it. Neil and Bernie and Grace and Dennis and Mary. All of them.

At the thought of Mary, Neil closed his eyes and breathed deeply before opening them again. The day he had just spent with Mary and Leo at Kings Island would leave him always with two distinct memories.

He and Leo had spent much of the afternoon riding the various roller coasters at the theme park. The Vortex, Top Gun, and Son of Beast were Leo's favorites. The last one, Son of Beast, was the tallest and fastest wooden roller coaster in the world. After just one hurtling trip over its bone-jarring track, Neil had no doubt of that. By suppertime he had never experienced so many drops, turns, vertical loops, double corkscrews, and boomerangs in his life.

But it wasn't the thrill of the rides that would stay with him. The first thing he would long remember was the thought that came to him suddenly as the three of them strolled past the faux Eiffel Tower. *So this is what it is to have a family. A wife and a son. It is just like this.*

Other guests at the park who happened to notice them would naturally assume that's what they were. A family of three out for a day of fun. Neil savored the thought. *Yes, the great American family. My wife, my son, the three of us here together like any other family.* He relished the role and thought it fit him well.

After eating supper at Bubba Gump Shrimp Shack, they took in a show of Asian dancing, shopped a bit in the souvenir shops, rode some of the gentler rides that Mary preferred, and after sundown, watched the fireworks show that burst across the sky in fiery colors.

The second moment that would always stay with Neil came as they left the park. Leo, weary but excited, exclaimed, "Man, that was great!" Mary and Neil laughed and agreed, and then Leo said, more wistfully, "I just wish Dad could have been here."

Mary, putting an arm around her son's shoulder, said, "Yes, I do too, Leo."

And Neil, offering Mary an attempt at a smile, knew that she meant it. Neil had been there, but Leo's father and Mary's husband had not been with them. Neil was the understudy playing the role that, in truth, belonged to someone else, some-one who would be coming back.

He felt jolted, felt something drop into his gut, felt it phys-ically as sure as he had experienced his stomach rising and fall-ing at every dip and turn of every roller coaster.

But by the time he arrived home and lay down on the bed, he had coasted to the end; he had come to a place of stillness. Of course. They *were* a family—Leo and Mary and Dan. And somewhere, too, Beth. *They* were the family, and that was good. It was what Mary wanted.

Neil shut his eyes, listened to the night songs beyond the open windows, breathed in the scent of color, of beauty, his life, and in another moment he was asleep.

51

A STONE-COLD SILENCE SUDDENLY descended on the otherwise airless room. The windows had been thrown wide open, but there was no breeze drifting into the sun-soaked library of the Sadler house. The people gathered there shivered anyway. A moment later someone started to weep. Neil, his back to the empty fireplace, folded up the letter he had just read aloud and looked around the room. It was his mother who wept, there in the wing chair by one of the windows. He went to her, stood beside the chair, and took her hand.

"It's just so awful," Elinor Sadler whispered. "That man went to prison, and we did nothing at all to help him."

Neil looked from her to the others in the room. Jim Sadler sat in the matching wing chair on the other side of the window. Uncle Gene Sadler and Aunt Lillian were together on one couch, while Vivian and Henry Zwirn occupied another. Grace and Dennis sat stiffly on a couple of ladder-back chairs brought in from the kitchen. Bernie was there, looking small and frail against the paisley pattern of an overstuffed chair. And Mary too, of course, in the love seat with her daughter, Beth, her son, Leo, on the floor at her feet. Beth had cut her summer short, driving home from Pennsylvania when her mother called. Mary hadn't expected Beth to come, but she did, and now mother and daughter sat side by side, their arms locked at the elbows.

Neil wanted to settle his gaze on Mary and Beth, because for the first time that summer, Mary looked serene, fully at peace. But in another moment Vivian Zwirn broke the quiet by exclaiming, "I can't believe it!" Her eyes flew to Neil and then to Mary, as she looked for confirmation. "I simply can't believe that Helen planned her own death. And that Bill Fricke helped her carry it out. How is that possible? It's as though I don't even know my own sister."

Mary replied quietly, "It's true, Aunt Vivian."

"But how can we know," Henry interjected, "that what Madylyn Fricke says in her letter is what really happened? Maybe she's making this up."

"We asked that same question, Henry," Neil offered. "I'll defer to Bernie on that one."

All eyes settled on the old man, who had so far been sitting in silence, his slippers propped up on a footstool, his fingers laced over the middle buttons of his favorite brown cardigan. Bernie smiled placidly at his audience, then said, "Bill Fricke came to me shortly before his death some years ago and told me this story himself."

Several gasps and murmured exclamations greeted Bernie's statement, and from Jim Sadler, a string of oaths. "You mean you've known for years and kept it to yourself? You didn't have the decency to tell the rest of us what you knew?"

Neil heard himself in his father's words and shuddered. "It was an act of confession on Fricke's part," Neil started, but his father cut him off.

"You had no right to keep it from us," the older Sadler

yelled. He jumped up from his seat and punctuated his sentence with another oath.

"Sit down, will you, Dad—"

"Listen, Neil, for twenty-five years we're thinking Cal killed Helen, and then for the past I don't know how many years we got Bernie here sitting on the truth when we all should have known—"

"Sit down, Jim. We don't want to hear—"

"Turn off your hearing aids, Elinor, if you don't want to listen, but I got something to say to that Bible-thumper—"

"Now listen, Jim, there's no call for being nasty—"

"You too, Gene, nobody asked you."

"Yeah? Well, I'm telling you anyway—"

"Dad, Uncle Gene, I'm trying to explain that it was told to Uncle Bernie as an act of confession—"

"And Bernie should have gone straight to the cops and had Fricke thrown in jail while he was still alive. The man should have paid. But now we find out Bill Fricke kills Helen, and then Bernie turns around and gives him absolution or whatever it is you preachers do—"

"Land sakes, Jim, I knew I should have left you sleeping back in Pomona—"

"Be quiet, Elinor—"

"I appreciate your feelings, Jim, but I wasn't at liberty to tell you what I knew. Not until now."

"That's right, Dad. There's a code of confidentiality—"

"And he's Sealed-lipped Sadler, Jim. Don't you remember? You could never get anything out of Bernie—"

"Now listen, Neil—and you too, Gene—Sealed-lipped Sadler or not, he should have told the rest of us. If Jerry were here, he'd agree with me—"

"Just a minute, Jim, I think *I* agree with you—"

"Well, *thank you,* Lillian. At least there's one sane person here—"

"I mean, I think we all should have known. . . ."

Suddenly Mary stood, stepped around Leo, and moved to the fireplace. As she looked around from one face to the next, the voices died down and the room fell quiet. Jim Sadler, who discovered he'd lost center stage, sat down. When she was certain she had everyone's attention, Mary said, "The point is, we know now. And those of us in this room are the only ones who do know. What we need to decide is where to go from here."

"Straight to the police, of course," Jim Sadler sputtered.

Lillian agreed. "We have to clear Cal's name. After all, he was part of our family."

"It may not be that simple," Neil replied.

"What do you mean?" his father retorted.

"You heard the letter. Madylyn asked—"

Another outburst of oaths. "Who gives a—"

"Jim! You need to—"

"Don't tell me what I need to do, Elinor!"

"Dad, listen."

"I *know* what I need to do. Grace, where's the phone?"

"Hold on, Jim, we need to make a decision together."

"I wasn't asking you, Dennis. You shouldn't even be in on this. You weren't there when—"

"I married a Sadler, didn't I?"

"Dad, I know how you feel. I thought the same at first—"

"I'm going to ask you again, Grace. Where's the phone?"

"Listen, Uncle Jim, this is my house, and you're not using the phone!"

"Oh yeah? Try and stop me. I'll find it myself."

When Jim Sadler stood again, Mary moved between him and the door. "Sit down, Uncle Jim," she said quietly. "We're not finished here."

He stopped short. He turned his head to look at his wife and his son.

"Sit down, Dad," Neil said. Then he added, "Please. Let Mary finish."

Jim clenched his fists once, opened them, then returned to his seat.

Mary took a deep breath. "I wanted you all to know the truth about Dad. That's why I asked you to come. That's why I asked Neil to read the letter. I know you want to clear Dad's name." She glanced at Jim Sadler. "We all want that. But you know, we're the ones who care. The people in this room—we're really the only ones who care. Ask anyone on the street out in Mason, and they won't even know who Cal Syfert was. To most of Mason it's all ancient history. To the rest of the world"—she shrugged—"it's nothing at all."

"Maybe so," Elinor Sadler agreed. "But to us it's everything."

"But only to us, Aunt Elinor," Mary said. "If we take this to the police and to the papers, more people get hurt. Madylyn's children and her grandchildren."

"So?" It was Jim.

"So they're innocent, Dad," Neil said. "They had nothing to do with any of this."

"The two people who did this thing—Mom and Bill Fricke—they're gone," Mary continued. "They're dead. We can't bring them back and punish them."

From the overstuffed chair, Bernie added, "We can only leave them to God."

Jim Sadler threw up a hand. "Oh, that's helpful. Spoken like a true man of the cloth—"

"He's right, Dad," Neil said, cutting him off. "Bernie's right."

"Somehow, there will be justice," Vivian confirmed. "But not for Helen, as I always thought." She paused and actually laughed, an expression of amazed disbelief. "I guess there will be justice for Cal."

Bernie said, "God himself exposes every lie and reveals every truth. He'll make everything right, in due time."

Jim started to say something, glanced at Neil, shut his mouth.

Mary put her fingers to her lips in thought for a moment. "On top of everything else, taking this letter to the authorities would just reopen the whole thing. We'd have to live through it all again. There'd be a police investigation and maybe even some kind of hearing or trial. And, of course, all the stories in the newspaper. I don't know about you, but I don't want to deal with all that again." Then she added quietly, "Especially not right now."

Mary reached up to the mantel above the hearth and retrieved an envelope lying there. She opened it and pulled out the letter inside. "This is Dad's last letter to me from prison. I'm not going to read you the whole thing, just a few lines." Her eyes skimmed over the pages, finally settling on the paragraph she was looking for.

"'Sweetheart,'" she read, "'that you believe so strongly in my innocence when hardly anyone else does—well, that means everything to me. That's my life, right there. I may not ever get out of here, but the one thing that matters to me right now is that you believe me and you love me. Honey, I love you too.

And I want you to do this one more thing for me, for my sake and for yours. When you have children, and they're old enough to understand, tell them about me. Tell them about their grandpa. Tell them who I was and that I love them. If you know and they know and their children know after them, then I'm satisfied.'"

She looked at her children then, her eyes shining. Beth looked expectantly at her mother, nodding encouragement. Leo's face reflected his adolescent awkwardness. "I've decided this is what I want to do," Mary went on. "Beth and Leo, this is the real story about your grandfather. He was a good man. Someday I'll tell you more about him, and then you can tell your children, and they can tell their children after that. And I think eventually, everyone who really needs to know is going to know."

Elinor Sadler was crying again. So were Grace and Vivian and even Henry Zwirn, who reached into his back pocket and blew his nose loudly on a crumpled handkerchief.

"We should have believed Cal," Elinor murmured.

"I was just so angry at him," Vivian said, "that it never occurred to me he could be telling the truth."

"It was that crazy brother of yours that caused all the trouble," Jim accused. "If he hadn't been wandering around out in the fields at night and come across that farmhouse, none of this ever would have happened."

"Now don't you be blaming Denton, Jim Sadler," Vivian said. "He *was* crazy, after the war. He just didn't know what he was doing."

"You're right, Aunt Vivian," Grace agreed. "Poor old Uncle Denton didn't know what he was doing. But *we* did. The rest of us knew what we were doing. And we as good as locked Uncle Cal up ourselves."

"We sure didn't give him the support he deserved," Gene Sadler added.

"Oh, Cal . . ." Lillian buried her face in her hands and wept.

"We should have believed him," Elinor said again.

Jim Sadler stared down at his hands in his lap. Neil put both arms around his mother's shoulder, pulling her into a comforting embrace. The room was full of weeping, sighing, the sound of shifting feet.

"You're doing the right thing, Mary," Gene Sadler said at last. "It's enough to tell your children and have them send it on down the family line."

"I agree," said Vivian.

"I do too," said Henry.

"And me too," said Grace.

The others nodded their heads at Mary. She turned to Neil then and gave him a small triumphant smile. "I think Dad would be satisfied now," she said. "Who knows, but maybe he's finally at peace."

Elinor dabbed at her eyes with a tissue. "Cal Syfert should hate me. He should hate all of us for what we did. What we didn't do. For not believing him."

Mary shook her head. "I'm sure he doesn't hate you, Aunt Elinor. He wouldn't feel that way if he were here. Dad wasn't like that."

"No, he wasn't," Elinor agreed. "He was a good man. Better than some of us here." She paused and frowned at her husband. He didn't notice. She wiped at her eyes again. "God knows, if I could, I'd ask him to forgive me."

Bernie leaned forward in his chair and peered intently at Elinor across the room. "Don't worry, Elinor," he said gently. "You'll have your chance to do that. Not everything has to be done this side of paradise, you know."

Around the room, a few blank stares, frowns of puzzlement, smiles of acquiescence, and from somewhere inside Neil, a nod of understanding and a boulder dropping off his back.

52

He took her to the Golden Lamb for something of a farewell dinner. The grand opening of the bed-and-breakfast was just a few days off, and after that he would return to New York, to his teaching job in Manhattan, to his home in Brooklyn. He didn't want to go without first apologizing to Mary, telling her how sorry he was. But it was what would come after the initial apology that he couldn't quite pin down. There was so much he regretted, so much that had once been left unsaid that needed to be said, but now as usual he was at a loss for words.

He looked at her across the table. She was beautiful. Far more beautiful than the day she had entered the ballroom in her green velvet dress and fishnet stockings and he first realized that she was a girl. She was a child then, an innocent. Now she had lived through some of life's heartbreaking cruelty. And yet, after all the years between that Christmas party at the farmhouse and this day at a restaurant in Lebanon, her face reflected a certain peace. It was in that peace that her immense loveliness lay.

Neil turned toward the window. Night was falling, and across the street the Village Ice Cream Parlor was a blur beyond the rain. It had been sprinkling two hours earlier when Neil and Mary arrived at the Golden Lamb, but since then the sky had opened and poured out a heavy shower all over the county.

Two hours. What had they been talking about for two hours? He wasn't even sure. He knew only that the words *I'm sorry* had not been spoken. He couldn't get them to move from his heart to his tongue, because once they fell from his lips, how could he explain? She would say, of course, *For what?* And then he would have to respond. *Everything. I am sorry for everything.* Would that do it? A blanket apology for every wrong against her, committed both by him and by life itself?

"The storm is getting worse, I think," he said. "Maybe I should get you home." He looked down at the table, at their empty dessert plates, their empty coffee cups. "Unless you'd like more coffee."

She held a hand over her cup. "No more for me, thanks. It was all delicious, Neil. Thank you."

"Well, then," he glanced at the window again, "shall we go?"

"I suppose we should," she agreed.

Neil paid the bill, and then they dashed together under Mary's umbrella to the car. The windshield wipers beat out a furious rhythm as they headed down Route 42 between Lebanon and Mason.

"Better check the radio," Neil said, reaching for the dial. In another moment they learned the county was under a tornado watch, though no funnel clouds had been spotted as yet.

Tree branches fought against an angry wind while leaves and raindrops danced madly together in the car's headlights. Sudden flashes of lightning broke the black sky into pieces and cleared the way for the marching drums of thunder. Neil drove slowly and cautiously, keenly aware of Mary in the passenger seat.

"Looks like Rebecca's angry at old John again," he joked nervously.

Mary frowned a moment, then smiled in recognition. "Oh yes, Rebecca. Well, if she's going to take any roofs off this time, let's hope she waits until we get home."

At length they approached the Sadler house, where a light burned in the downstairs front room and another up in the tower. Grace and Dennis were home. And Bernie, surrounded by windows, would have a grand view of the storm.

"We could stop and you could wait out the storm here," Neil suggested. "I'll drive you home after."

Mary shook her head. "I'd rather get home now if you don't mind taking me."

"Is Leo there alone?"

"He's next door at his grandmother's. Still, I think I should get back."

"And Beth's spending the night in Cincinnati, right?"

"Yes, with a friend." Earlier in the day Beth had driven Mary's car down to the city to visit her father and afterward stay with a friend from high school.

Neil nodded as he gazed intently at the foreshortened road ahead. The world suddenly seemed no larger than the sphere of the headlights as the bright windows of the Sadler house disappeared behind them. By the time they reached the outskirts of Mason, hail the size of pebbles pelted the windshield, a deafening onslaught of icy artillery. "Not a good sign," Neil mumbled, and he turned the radio up.

A tornado had touched down in Turtle Creek Township, just north of Mason, blowing apart a barn and some outbuildings before being sucked back up into the clouds. There was also word of an unconfirmed tornado sighting in Hamilton Township to the east.

They were almost to Mary's house. They just had to travel down Main Street, turn right on N. East, left on Church, clear the railroad tracks, and they'd be there.

It seemed an interminable distance. Halfway down Main the streetlights went out, businesses went dark, and Neil realized his was one of less than a half-dozen cars trying to crawl through town. A person didn't have to live in the Midwest for long to know that a car was one of the worst places to be if a tornado hit. What was a hunk of metal on wheels compared to a funnel cloud? Even a truck could be picked up, sent sailing, and overturned as easily as a kid tossing his Matchbox car across a driveway.

Neil glanced over at Mary. Even in the dim light he could see that her face was tense, but she sat in silence, looking straight ahead. Neil kept the car moving down Main Street, then turned right onto N. East. He was going to do the only thing he could do; he was going to just keep moving. He was going to get them home. Just another few blocks.

But when he turned onto Church Street, he discovered he wasn't going to make it. A tree had fallen across the road just in front of the railroad tracks. He stopped the car and looked at Mary. "We're going to have to run for it."

She turned to him and nodded. "Let's go."

She reached for her umbrella, but Neil said, "Leave it. It won't help."

At once they dashed out of the doors, and as if by some unspoken agreement, they met at the front of the car. With the wind at their backs, they felt themselves nearly lifted off the ground as they started to run, his hand on her elbow. They skirted the branches of the downed tree, leaving the sidewalk and striding across the neighbors' rain-soaked lawn. The earth sank beneath their feet like foam rubber bowing under their weight. A flash of sheet lightning illuminated the front porch steps of Mary's house, and they ran for those steps, their goal, with the intensity of long-distance runners. When they were almost there, a clap of thunder trembled up through the sidewalk and rattled their bones. In the next moment they stood on the porch, shivering in their drenched clothes, rainwater dripping from the ends of their hair, slithering down their arms, their legs, pooling in puddles on the slatted wood floor. They looked at each other and laughed. They had made it home.

Finally Neil shouted, "Well, do you have the key?"

"It's in my purse!"

"Where's that?"

"I forgot it in the car!"

"Okay. Well, do you have a spare hidden anywhere?"

"I think Dan keeps one there, under that flowerpot!"

Neil retrieved the key, slipped it into the lock, and opened the door. Mary reflexively flipped on the light switch, but the ceiling lamp didn't respond. They moved clumsily through the dark toward the back of the house. Mary grabbed a blanket off the couch and handed it to him before taking another from the recliner. She grabbed a flashlight out of the junk drawer in the kitchen and then they moved toward the basement door, following the small round beam of light down the steps to the safety of a dark and musty basement.

Mary shined the flashlight around the cluttered room. "Well," she said, "if I'd known you were coming, I would have cleaned up. I don't even have a chair for you to sit in."

"Here, hand me the light a moment." She did, and he shined it on a couple of empty crates turned on their sides. "Those will do, don't you think?"

"Better than nothing, I suppose. Well, let's have a seat."

They settled themselves on the crates. "Cold?" he asked.

"Freezing," she said as she wrapped her blanket around her shoulders. He did the same.

"That's better, isn't it?"

"Yes. I'm soaked through."

They huddled side by side, shivering still, the flashlight on the floor in front of them casting its light toward the ceiling.

"You suppose Leo's all right?" Neil asked.

Mary nodded. "Probably having the time of his life. He loves storms. I'm sure his grandmother has coaxed him down to the basement by now, though."

"Well, he got quite a show tonight anyway."

"Yes, this is a good one, even by our standards. I don't suppose you have to deal much with tornadoes in New York, do you?"

He smiled. "Not as a rule, no."

Mary hugged the blanket more tightly around her. "I've always thought I should keep a radio and extra batteries down here. Of course I've never done it, so we can't listen to any weather updates."

Neil shrugged. "Never mind," he said. "We can sneak upstairs after a bit and see what the storm is doing."

"I have a radio in the kitchen. I'm not sure it has batteries in it, though. We'll have to try it and see."

He laughed lightly. "Don't worry about it. Just stay here under the blanket and warm up for now."

She lifted a hand and pushed a wet strand of hair out of her face. "I must look a sight." She smiled apologetically.

"No," Neil said thoughtfully. "Actually you look . . . quite beautiful."

Mary laughed and shook her head against the compliment. From there they fell into an awkward silence. Neil felt the decades-old words hanging in his chest. He willed them to rise, but before he could speak, Mary said, "Well, we're giving you a fine send-off from Mason, aren't we? Rain, hail, tornadoes— just a little something to remember us by when you get back to New York."

Neil studied Mary's face, a sepia print of gleam and shadow in the indirect glow of the flashlight. He longed to raise a hand to touch that sweet face, to press his palm against her soft cheek. He let go of his blanket, began to reach out, but stopped himself. "Mary," he said quietly, "I wouldn't forget you anyway. It doesn't take a storm to make me remember."

She smiled now, solemnly but serenely. Her eyes, glistening in the light, moved across his face and caught his gaze.

"There was a time," he started, but he had to stop, shut his eyes, open them. "There was a time when I wanted to take you to New York with me."

He saw her draw in a breath, like a gasp. He watched, surprised and touched, as the glow in her eyes spilled over and ran down her cheeks.

"There was a time," she said, "when I would have gone."

He raised his hand now, touched a tear. She lifted her own hand to the back of his and rested her cheek in his palm.

"I'm so sorry, Mary."

She shook her head. "You don't have to say anything."

"I do. I can't leave without telling you how sorry I am. I

wish everything had been different, wish I had done it all differently."

She took another deep breath, let it out. "You loved me once?"

"Yes." There it was, the truth, suspended there in the air between them where they could both see it for the first time.

"Then I'm satisfied," she whispered. "I loved you too, you know."

Neil was silent for a long while. Then he said, "But it's too late, isn't it?"

She nodded her head against his palm. "Yes."

His heart sank, though he had expected nothing else. "Will you be all right?"

She nodded again.

"What will you do now?"

"We're going to leave Mason. We're going to start over. Dan says he's always wanted to live on the Oregon coast."

She smiled when she remembered her surprise. *"But I never knew you wanted to live in Oregon!"*

And Dan, sitting there under the painting by Mary Cassatt, said, *"Then we will have to get to know each other, won't we?"*

Neil said, "You believe he's innocent, don't you? That he didn't do what Rhonda Traylor is accusing him of doing?"

"I know he didn't shoot an unarmed man. I'm sure of it. I don't know exactly what happened that night, but . . ."

When her voice trailed off, Neil finished for her. "You don't have to understand something completely to know it's true, do you?"

"No," she agreed. "No, you don't."

He pulled his hand back into his own lap.

"What about you, Neil?" she asked. "Will you be all right?"

"Yes. I'll be fine."

"I . . . I wish . . . I'm just . . ." She couldn't seem to find the words.

"I know," Neil said. "You're sorry about Caroline."

"Yes. But somehow that doesn't seem like enough."

He nodded. "I loved her very much."

"I know you did. And I think it was right . . . that she was your wife . . . that you had those years with her."

"Yes, I'm sure it was."

"You wouldn't change those years."

"No."

"Then I think that everything is the way it's supposed to be."

Neil smiled "You're one incredible person, Mary Beeken."

"So that makes two of us, Neil Sadler," she replied.

Bernie Sadler's wife, Rita, had talked about finding a teapot in a tempest, that place of quiet well-being in the midst of a storm. Neil Sadler knew that he had just found his.

53

"You ready, old man? The elevator's waiting."

"I've been ready for an hour, Neil. What took you so long to get up here?"

"Well, come on then. Make your way over to the stairs, and let's go join the party."

Neil reached out a hand to help Bernie to his feet. Bernie clasped the hand firmly and made no move to rise from the chair. He fixed his gaze on Neil's face. "I shall miss you, Neil," he said quietly, "more than I can say."

Neil pressed his other hand against the old man's bony knuckles. "I'll miss you too, Uncle Bernie."

"I have finished wrestling with Jacob, you know. I'll be going home soon."

Neil nodded. Another dying. One more ending to go through.

The old man smiled. "But I suspect we'll be seeing each other again, won't we?"

Beyond Bernie's shoulder the many windows in the tower room framed a blue sky filled with light. Neil looked up a moment, then said, "Yes. But listen, old man, next time I see you, I hope I won't be having to carry you down any more stairs."

Bernie laughed heartily. "Oh no, I can promise you that. I'll be quite capable of getting around on my own, thank you."

"Good. Because these trips down to the first floor are killing me."

It was the day of the grand opening of the Sadler House Bed-and-Breakfast. Flyers had been posted around Mason and Lebanon and an invitation to the public printed in the local paper for the open house that began at noon. In the ballroom downstairs family, friends, and other folks were already gathering for appetizers. Tours of the house would begin at one o'clock and go on all afternoon.

Neil deposited Bernie on the couch nearest the bay window. Once settled, the old man was immediately surrounded by people wanting to visit with him. Bernie greeted his guests with a shining smile and a lift of his hand, as though in blessing. *Peace,* Neil thought. Wherever Bernie went, he took peace with him.

Neil looked around the room, his eyes sifting through the crowd to see who was there. A host of faces both familiar and unfamiliar—his parents, uncles, aunts, cousins, friends. People from the community. A photographer from one of the papers. And then the one he was looking for—Mary. She stood near the fireplace with Leo, who was using a toothpick to stab at appetizers on his heavily laden plate. When Mary saw Neil, she raised a hand and beckoned him over.

"Neil!" she exclaimed. "I just walked through the house. It looks fabulous! You and Mike and Dennis have done a great job."

Neil smiled and winked at Leo. "With a little help from

some professional contractors. But thanks. I think the place turned out pretty well."

"Well, that's an understatement. The old house has never looked so good." She gave a brief laugh and added, "This is where I plan to stay whenever I come back to visit."

She waved at someone beyond Neil, then turned her attention back to him.

"So you're really leaving?" he asked.

She nodded. "When I saw Dan yesterday, we decided that as soon as the civil suit is behind us, we'll put the house on the market."

"I'm going to get some punch, Mom," Leo interrupted.

"Sure, honey, go ahead."

"Then I'm going out back. Steve and Russ were talking about getting a game of hide-and-seek going out in the cornfield."

"A little old for hide-and-seek, aren't you?"

He shrugged. "I just want to scare the younger kids."

"Nice," Mary said. "Listen, don't get lost out there. Make sure the younger kids don't wander too deep into the rows. I don't want to have to send out any search parties."

"Don't worry, Mom. We're not going to let anybody get lost."

"Okay. Just be careful."

Leo shrugged again and rolled his young brown eyes before wandering away. Mary smiled as she watched her son head to the punch bowl.

"You remember that?" Neil asked.

Mary looked puzzled. "Remember what?"

"What Uncle Tom used to say when we played out in the

fields? 'Just don't get so far off the path you can't find your way back.'"

Mary thought a moment, then nodded. "I do remember that now. Didn't someone get lost once? Jennifer, wasn't it?"

"Yeah, I think so."

"Well, no wonder. When the corn's over your head, you can get all turned around in there once you lose sight of the tractor lane. I just hope Bill McCurdy doesn't mind the kids being out there."

"I'm sure he won't. I seem to remember him being a kid himself once. Besides, he won't know."

"How's that?"

"Because he's here." Neil nodded toward the archway connecting the ballroom to the front hall. Bill McCurdy had just come in with his wife, Samantha. Grace and Dennis stood just beyond the threshold, greeting their guests as they arrived.

Grace, Neil noticed, glowed with excitement. She was living the fulfillment of her dream for the Sadler house, and her joy was palpable, even contagious, warming everyone who entered the room.

Neil felt good about that. Grace *should* be happy. She had done a good thing, saving this house, preserving this place that cradled the story of their family. Neil was glad and thankful that he too had had a part in renovating the Sadler house, preparing it for future generations and keeping it in the family's hands.

He turned his attention back to Mary. "So you and Dan will be heading to Oregon?" he asked.

"That's what we're talking about anyway. We can't stay here."

"No," Neil agreed.

"His mother will come with us. We don't want to leave her here alone. So we'll be selling her house too."

"It'll be a big change for all of you. A whole new beginning."

Mary nodded, then smiled. "You know, Neil," she said, "I feel like I finally really *am* beginning. Like I can finally start to live. Do you know what I mean?"

"Yes." He lifted his chin, let it drop. "I think I do."

"You don't want to buy a house, do you?" she quipped.

"No thanks." He laughed as he shook his head. "I can't stay here either." After a moment he added, "Though I'm glad I came back."

"So am I. Think you'll ever come back here again—just to visit?"

"Sure. Grace says there will always be a room waiting for me free of charge whenever I want to come back. How can I turn down an offer like that?"

"So maybe I'll see you back here someday."

"Of course you will." He wanted to say more, wanted to tell her to stay in touch somehow, to let him know she was all right, but before he could say anything, a voice behind him blurted, "You do that, Neil?"

It was his father. Jim Sadler stood there with a cup of punch in one hand, a plate of sherried shrimp and stuffed mushrooms in the other. With his thumb he pointed toward the picture above the fireplace. Neil had hung it there himself just the day before, his painting of the Sadler house that he'd been working on for weeks.

"You paint that?" his dad repeated.

Neil felt his pride in the painting wilt under the glare of his father's frown. He took a breath and said, "Yeah, I did. I painted that."

Jim Sadler, still frowning, looked at the picture, then at Neil, then at the picture again. "It's good."

And Neil, hearing the puzzlement in his father's voice, suddenly wanted to laugh. He held his father's eye and said simply, "Thanks, Dad."

Jim Sadler shrugged, glanced once more at the painting, and said again, "Yeah, it's good."

It was the Sadler house as Neil saw it now, from the perspective of a grown man. He had painted the Gothic Horror when he was a child, had painted the house suspended in a white background, hovering between one strip of blue sky and one strip of green grass.

Now, in this new painting, he had corrected his childish mistake. He had brought the sky down to touch the grass. He had closed up the divide and brought the blue heaven down to settle upon the green earth.

Because he knew that was how it was. Heaven stretched all the way down to the world. The divine was poured out upon the flesh, the immortal upon the mortal. The Alpha is the Omega is the Alpha. The beginning is the end is the beginning.

Mary once again lifted a hand in greeting to someone across the room. Neil turned to see Vince and Teresa McNulty entering the ballroom, shaking Grace's hand, throwing out smiles to everyone.

He was a good man, Vince McNulty. And a good friend. Neil excused himself from Mary for a moment and moved across the room to shake his hand.

"Good of you to stop by, Vince."

"Wouldn't miss it, Neil. Listen, come by the place later

tonight. There's a beer with your name on it waiting for you. Don't leave town without saying good-bye."

"Wouldn't dream of it. I'll be there."

He'd miss him, this almost-priest-turned-bar-owner. Would miss his wife too, the former-nun-turned-short-order-cook. What a pair. What a crazy and wonderful pair.

Neil pointed Vince and Teresa to the spread of food at the far end of the room, and even as the two made their way to the appetizers, Neil thought that maybe in all his years of heavy religious discipline, Vincent McNulty had never once experienced the profound weightlessness of grace.

Now that would be something for the Warren County time capsule. Something for folks to know fifty years from now. Divine grace was the absence of weight. When grace surrounded you, you could pick up your feet and float.

Caroline must have known that, Neil realized. She had discovered it on the subway, had found it on a subterranean car in the form of an elderly priest whom she saw every morning on her way to work. He was on the same train heading toward the daily Eucharist in a parish that wasn't his own. *"I'm just filling in,"* he explained cheerfully, *"just until they find someone permanent or else I die, whichever comes first."* His own church was right there in Brooklyn.

The next thing Neil knew, Caroline had wanted to visit the old priest's church.

"But what on earth do the two of you talk about?" Neil had asked.

"Anything and everything," Caroline said. *"His work. My work. The New York subway system. Terrorism. The weather. He makes me laugh."*

"And now you want to go to church?"

"*Yeah. I do.*"

Neil could see her at the communion rail of that Episcopal church on Carroll Street, that huge old structure of stone and stained-glass windows. He could see her kneeling there, accepting the small round wafer into her cupped hands, lifting it to her tongue. "*The body of Christ, broken for you.*" The twinkling eyes of the aged priest as he offered the chalice of wine. "*The blood of Christ, shed for you.*"

"*But he always looks like he's ready to burst out laughing,*" Neil said.

"*He is.*"

"*Well, what's so funny?*"

Caroline thought for a long while. "*It isn't that anything's funny, really. It's more like . . . you know how you feel when you win a game or you see someone you haven't seen in a long time, or—I don't know, something good happens and you laugh just because you're happy?*"

"*Yeah. I guess so.*"

"*Well, it's like that.*"

It had made little sense at the time. But Neil thought perhaps he was beginning to understand now. He looked about the room, looked at the faces of his mother, his father, Uncle Bernie, Grace, Mary. And too, the myriad faces of other uncles, aunts, first cousins, second cousins, friends. He loved them, all of them. He loved the story that was his life, loved the larger story that was unfolding even as he stood there on an August afternoon in the third year of the twenty-first century.

He wanted to laugh. He did laugh. And it didn't matter, the looks people gave him. Someday they would understand. People laugh sometimes, not because anything's funny but simply because of something called joy.

Mason had called to him, and he'd come back. He had come back to learn to laugh again and to live. There was an empty house in Brooklyn to return to, but he would return with his pockets full of moments and images and hope, of sky and earth and birds in flight, of sunlight in windows and teapots in tempests, of little boys finding their way safely out of cornfields and little girls dancing in the snow.

⊷ ACKNOWLEDGMENTS ⊶

We all know that a book is the result of a little bit of inspiration and a whole lot of perspiration (Thomas Edison's descriptive word for plain old hard work), but I would be remiss if I didn't add a third indispensable ingredient: the help of others. Basically, these are people who know a great deal more about a subject than the author herself and are willing to sit down and graciously share their knowledge for the sake of a better story. This book combines the knowledge, expertise, and experience of many people, and to all of them I owe a debt of gratitude.

Ron Ferrell—Chief of Police, Mason, Ohio. When I traveled to Mason to research this book in October 2003, Chief Ferrell visited with me in his office at the brand-new Municipal Building on Mason-Montgomery Road. For more than an hour he patiently answered my questions about life and law enforcement in Mason. Afterward, he continued to answer my ongoing questions via e-mail correspondence. Finally, he read this book in rough draft to offer feedback and make corrections. For all his help I can only say, "Thanks, Chief!"

John Harris—If you travel north from the Municipal Building on Mason-Montgomery Road, turn left onto Main Street, and head west for several blocks, you'll come to the Chamber of Commerce—which I managed to stumble across while I walked around Mason. John Harris, president of the Chamber of Commerce, was kind enough to meet with me without an appointment and share both facts and memories of his hometown.

Janet Hamilton, Ollie Scott, and Mildred Clingner—These longtime residents of Mason (and cousins of my cousin Virginia Erbeck) kindly lunched with me at a Bob Evans restaurant outside of town. In addition to being delightful company, they were a fount of information. I wouldn't have known the story behind the Widow's Bridge without them!

Ben and Anita Todorov—Mrs. Todorov's father bought the original house and the surrounding land from my great-uncle Virgil in 1945. Ben and Anita Todorov live in the ranch house built in 1952 to replace the Gothic-style farmhouse. I called to see if I might stop by and meet them, and an hour later was warmly ushered into their living room, where we shared stories and photographs of the old house. The Todorovs still farm the land that my great-uncle once farmed. On the October day of our visit, those vast acres of corn were ready for harvest.

Trudie Smith—My dear cousin once removed. This amazing octogenarian rescued me at a gas station when I got lost trying to find her house on those winding country roads of rural Ohio. She led the way to her lovely home, one cozy bedroom of which became my base of operations while I spent a busy and yet wonderfully refreshing week researching Mason and Lebanon. I will forever remember sitting and chatting with Trudie in her den while at the same time looking out the window at the little brick schoolhouse where my grandfather learned his lessons nearly a century ago. A thousand thanks, Trudie, for your hospitality, prayers, and love.

Stephanie Smith—Trudie's daughter-in-law, whom I thoroughly enjoyed getting to know while I was in Ohio. She also treated Trudie and me to dinner at the Golden Lamb, making it possible for me to visit the famous eatery for myself. Thanks, Steph!

Outside of Mason and Lebanon, Ohio, a host of other people helped me in my research.

Robert Whitlow and James Scott Bell, both attorneys and fellow novelists, helped me with the legal aspects of this story, as did *Rahn Westby,* a former defense attorney, and *Gary Flackne,* prosecutor and former County (District) Attorney for Hennepin County, Minnesota. I also thank *Erik Peters,* attorney and magistrate, for the reams of information he provided for me on Ohio state law and the Alford plea. (Any and all legal gaffes in this story are mine.)

Janet Carlson, a friend and one-time co-worker at *Decision* magazine, shared with me her experiences as the daughter of a woman suffering from multiple sclerosis. For the record, her mother (like Janet herself) is nothing at all like Helen Syfert, but is a lovely woman of faith.

Judy Blank, my wonderful sister-in-law, lives in the house on Warren Street in Brooklyn that I "borrowed" for Neil Sadler. Thanks, Judy, for all your quick responses to my questions about Brooklyn and for your memories of 9/11. It was you who stood on the roof and looked out over the skyline of Manhattan and saw the giant hole in the sky where the towers used to be. I appreciate your letting me use that image in this story.

Debbie Bacon, nurse *extraordinaire* and cousin of my friend Linda Laiti (who introduced me to her), answered all my questions about meningitis and what might happen within the walls of a hospital once a person is admitted with this infection.

Doreen Dahl, Vincent Pinto, and Fred Butts are all accomplished artists who, either face-to-face or via e-mail, introduced me to their world of painting and helped me fashion the character of Neil Sadler.

Brad Dahl, who spent his childhood summers on various Ohio farms, revisited for my sake the sights, smells, and hard work of planting and harvesting crops. He also patiently drew diagrams and pictures of a variety of farm equipment that this city girl knew little or nothing about. He was the one who clued me in to the possibility of getting lost in a cornfield while playing hide-and-seek.

Michelle Goodspeed, owner of a fabulous old house in St. Paul, Minnesota, which she's turning into a bed-and-breakfast, gave me a tour of the place while filling me in on the work involved in such an undertaking.

And, of course, special thanks to *Virginia Erbeck* and her son *Bob Erbeck* for providing me with the photographs, floor plans, and memories of The House, all of which served as the inspiration for this book. I love you both. Cousin Virginia, if you could travel, I'd take you back to the farm at harvest time, just so you could see it all once more. And Cousin Bob, if you can get away from being a camera operator in Hollywood long enough, meet me in Mason in front of the house where you grew up. We'll wander over to Main Street to see whether anyone has turned the old McClung place into another restaurant. If so, we'll do lunch, so long as Rebecca hasn't gone and blown the roof off again.

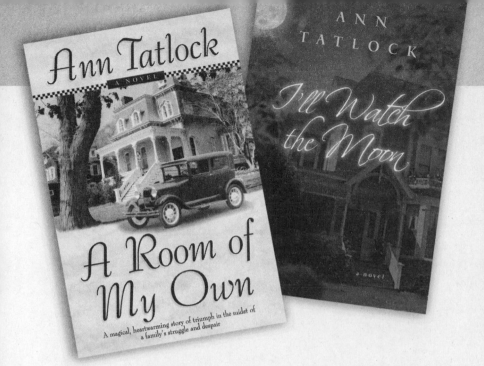

More Stories of Love & Sacrifice
FROM AWARD-WINNING NOVELIST
ANN TATLOCK

A ROOM OF MY OWN

The daughter of a prominent doctor, loyal and imaginative Virginia Eide lived in an idyllic world—a world of youthful notions of romance and hours spent daydreaming with her best friend. But Virginia's dreams are forever altered when the Depression cripples her hometown. Take a journey with Virginia as she faces hardship and sacrifice—and through it all develops a strength of character and compassion that will change the direction of her life.

I'LL WATCH THE MOON

Ann Tatlock's award-winning novel *I'll Watch the Moon* is the gracefully woven story of Nova Tierney, who desperately longs for a father. It also is the story of her mother, Catherine, angry at a God in whom she no longer believes, and Josef Karski, an Auschwitz survivor whose trusting spirit refuses to be subdued, even by his heart-wrenching past. Nova's tender reminiscence, charming and authentic, breathes life, love, and warmth into a St. Paul, Minnesota, boardinghouse where forgiveness is in short supply.

 BETHANYHOUSE